SAVAGE
Wilder

i

SAVAGE WILDER

SINNERS AND SAINTS BOOK 4

VERONICA EDEN

SAVAGE WILDER

CONTENTS

AUTHOR'S NOTE

Savage Wilder is a dark new adult high school bully romance with romantic suspense elements intended for mature readers. The Sinners and Saints series boys are all devilish bullies brought to their knees by a spitfire heroine, so if you love enemies-to-lovers type stories, you're in the right place. This mature new adult romance contains crude language, dubious situations, revenge, and intense graphic sexual/violent content that some readers might find triggering or offensive. Please proceed with caution.

If you like weak pushover heroines and nice guys this one ain't for you, but if you dig strong females and smug antiheroes, then you're in the right place! Hold onto your hearts, because these guys aren't above stealing.

Each book is part of a series but can be enjoyed as a standalone.

Sinners and Saints series:
#1 Wicked Saint

#2 Tempting Devil
#3 Ruthless Bishop
#4 Savage Wilder

Sign up for Veronica's newsletter to receive exclusive content and news about upcoming releases: bit.ly/veronicaedenmail
Follow Veronica on BookBub for new release alerts: bookbub.com/authors/veronica-eden

ABOUT THE BOOK

MAISY

THE BOY I KNEW IS GONE.
Rule follower. Straight laced. Goody-goody.

I'm as well-behaved as they get, but then the worst thing ever happened to me...I caught the interest of the bad boy. Wilder isn't the same guy I idolized when we were kids. He made that clear the day he moved back to Ridgeview.

He hunts me, stalks me, surrounds me from all sides. I'm his new favorite plaything. Again. Last year was bad enough, but as graduation looms his claws are in me once more and he refuses to let go.

And worst of all? I think I like it.

FOX

THE WILDER NAME IS A CURSE.
Pristine. Perfect. *Fake.*

Once upon a time we were friends. Then her family destroyed mine. In return, I'll destroy hers.

I'm the resident black shadow this town fears. Whispers about. Everyone remembers that a Wilder means bad news. My sweet daisy should fear me because she's the key piece in my revenge plot against her crooked parents.

I'm not her friend anymore.

I'll take them all down, starting with her.

PLAYLIST

(Spotify)

Revenge—XXXTENTACION
Killer—Valerie Broussard
Riptide—Unlike Pluto
JOLT—Unlike Pluto
I'm a Sucker for a Liar in a Red Dress—Adam Jensen
Good Girls—Elle King
Arcade—Duncan Laurence, FLETCHER
you broke me first—Tate McRae
forget me too—Machine Gun Kelly, Halsey
The Kid I Used to Know—Arrested Youth
Dreams—Fleetwood Mac
Nails—Call Me Karizma
Heart-Shaped Box—Nirvana
Riptide—grandson
Monsters—All Time Low, blackbear
Sick Thoughts—Lewis Blissett
Hate The Way—G-Eazy, blackbear

Consensual—Landon Tewers
Heart Of The Young—coldrain
body bag—Machine Gun Kelly, YUNGBLUD, The Used,
Bert McCracken
E-GIRLS ARE RUINING MY LIFE!—CORPSE, Savage
Ga$p
Gone—coldrain
Monster (Under My Bed)—Call Me Karizma
Learning to Survive—We Came As Romans
Needed Me—Rihanna
My Oh My—Paloma
Rebels—Ivy Adara
Trust—Alina Baraz
We Belong—Dove Cameron
Dandelions—Ruth B.

To complicated. Friendships, histories, the thin line between love and hate.

And to overcoming complicated to find the balance.

PROLOGUE

MAISY
10 Years Ago

"That's not fair!" I cry, chasing after my brother and our best friend. "You can't win just because you're nine, you jerk heads!"

Their laughter echoes as the three of us run down the quiet street where we all live. They're both a year older and bigger than me, meaning the boys can outrun me easily. It makes me so mad! Girls can be just as awesome at things as boys. I'll show them.

"Holden!" I yell at my brother's back as frustration bubbles up in my chest.

"Suck it up, Maisy. You lost!" Holden shoots a mean grin over his shoulder. "Maisy Daisy is a crybaby loser!"

"I am not!" I shout loud enough that a few birds startle and fly away from the towering pine trees behind the houses on the block.

Fox slows down, trailing Holden far enough that I can

catch up. Once I'm beside him, he bumps his shoulder into mine and shoots me a secretive smirk. Some of the frustration leaves me.

"I'm not a crybaby," I mumble sourly.

A huff of laughter escapes him and he gives me a sly look from the corner of his eyes. They're like the ocean, dark blue and mysterious. I really want to see the ocean again someday. Both our families went last summer and it was my favorite trip, hunting for seashells and cool rocks with Fox and Holden as the waves crashed against the beach in California. I loved it so much, I made a bracelet of the stones Fox gave me. I never take it off.

"You're not," Fox agrees. After a pause, his mouth curves into the trickster smile he gets when he wants to make trouble. It's a smile that always draws me in for his sneaky plans. "Let's get him back."

I grin. "Deal."

After high-fiving, he wraps an arm around my shoulder to tug me closer, whispering in my ear. He's warm and smells like the sweet summer grass and a little like the motor oil from his dad's garage. They must have been working on his dad's motorcycle before he came out to play. My nose scrunches at the mix, but I don't pull away.

"You distract him, and I'll find a beetle," he instructs.

I have to cover my mouth to keep my excitement from sneaking out and giving us away. It's a perfect plan. Holden stayed up late one time and saw a scary movie about an army of mutant insects that freaked him out forever. Now he's terrified of beetles because of one of the scenes.

Nodding, I try to wink at Fox, but I end up blinking twice. Lame. He grins, shaking his head and messing with his dark brown hair as he slips away to hunt through the neighbor's bushes.

My brother has stopped running, waiting for Fox and I near the end of the street.

"Holden," I sing-song, skipping to quickly close the distance between us. "If you don't stop being so mean to me, Fox says he won't trade the Flareon he caught in Pokémon last week with you." I stick my tongue out to sell my taunting distraction. "And I won't show you how to build a cool tree-house on Animal Crossing."

"What?" Holden hisses. He brushes the long ends of his floppy light brown hair from his forehead agitatedly. It's the same shade as mine. People used to think we were twins even though he's older. "You both promised. I need those for my challenges!"

Fox walks up, not giving anything away except for his hands tucked behind him. "What are we playing next? You beat us both to the finish line, so you pick."

Holden shakes his head. "Not yet." He whirls on Fox. "You swear you're going to trade your Flareon with me?"

Fox tilts his head. "Yeah, dude."

Holden relaxes and mulls over what he wants to play next.

"Hide and seek?" I suggest, unable to hold back a tiny smirk as I practically squirm with anticipation of what's to come.

"No, you lost. You don't get to pick." Holden sighs. "But hide and seek does sound good."

"Yeah?" Fox grins. "I was thinking the same thing. Can you hold this for me while we hide from your sister?"

Before Holden can finish nodding, Fox grabs his hand and shakes out a round striped beetle into Holden's palm. It's a harmless potato bug, I think. My brother looks down and his brown eyes go wide. A scream tears from his throat as he flails his hand around to get the bug off. The tiny little thing drops to the ground, wriggling in confusion for a moment before scurrying away while Holden freaks out, waving his hand around like it was poisoned.

"Got you!" I cheer, giving Fox a triumphant high five. "That's what you get for cheating."

Holden's face twists in embarrassed irritation. He swipes his hand on his jeans, over his freak out now that the bug is gone. "You guys suck!"

My delighted laughter breaks free, making me double over and hug my belly when a cramp twinges. Fox leans against me for support as we fall into hysterics at our revenge prank.

"Whatever," Holden grumbles, waving a hand to act like he's all cool. We totally got him. "I'm going home to play Xbox. This is boring."

Satisfaction fills me to the brim as I watch my brother jog across the street to our house. Holden can be such a whiny butthead sometimes, but Fox likes him anyway. I do too, because he's my brother, and he's not *always* a jerk. The three of us have grown up on this street since before I can remember. Our mom and his parents work together and they're close friends.

"Maise, come look."

Fox has wandered over to the grassy field at the end of the block. The tree the three of us challenge each other to climb every week sits in the middle. Beyond the tall grass and wild-flowers, the woods stretch up into the hills at the base of the Rocky Mountains. I walk over, automatically reaching up to catch one of the lower branches of the tree and swing back and forth like a gymnast.

"What's up?" I try to get higher, but the bark bites into my hands.

He pops up from the tall grass and reaches for me, tickling my stomach, making me shriek and wriggle until I'm forced to let go of the branch or keep suffering his attack.

Once I'm on the ground, I curl into a protective crouch so he can't mess with me. "What the heck?"

Fox snorts. "You make it too easy."

"There are rules, Fox," I point out, standing up. We have them written down and everything in a notebook with Pokémon stickers on the front. I huff importantly and recite the sacred rule: "No tickling when a climber is in the tree."

The corners of his mouth lift and his eyes are bright. "Yeah, you're right." He taps my nose. "Sorry."

"What did you want me to see?"

"I found this."

Fox holds up a wildflower he picked, his crooked smile turning proud. It's dainty with thin light purple petals, not like the white daisies we usually see. A small gasp escapes me as I take it.

"It's so pretty." I touch a soft petal carefully. "What's it for?"

"You're *my* daisy."

Fox waits until I tear my attention from the flower to look at him in surprise. He's serious, his eyebrows wrinkled as he stares at me. Reaching out, he circles his fingers around my wrist. I watch, wide-eyed as he leans down and places a kiss on the wildflower clutched in my hands.

"I'm going to marry you someday," he promises.

A feeling like butterflies fills my chest as I stare back at him.

"Okay," I whisper.

He grins and tugs on my wrist. "Come on. There's something else I want to show you. It's in my dad's garage. I wasn't supposed to find it, but I did when Dad went to answer a call and left me alone." We walk a few steps, then he stops us. "You have to promise not to tell anyone. Even Holden. Got it?"

I nod. "Promise."

Flying on the giddiness making me dizzy, I follow Fox, like I always do.

* * *

A week later my world feels crushed.

I sit outside my house with my knees tucked against my chest and my arms wrapped around my skinny legs. Holden is at the end of the block throwing a football at our favorite climbing tree over and over. Across the street, the crooked for sale sign stuck in the Wilder's front lawn mocks me.

The *someday* he promised me won't come.

Fox Wilder is gone.

ONE
MAISY

There are less than two months until graduation and Fox picks now to start messing with me again.

Well, no. He actually chose a couple weeks ago, but I slam down hard on that memory before it can assault me.

I squeeze Sam's hand tight as we descend the steps from Silver Lake High School to the student parking lot at the base of the hill where our classmates hoot and call to each other while revving the engines of their expensive cars. The warm breeze moving through the pine trees carries the seniors' rowdiness high above the school's sprawling mountainside campus.

Fox Wilder's eyes don't leave me for a second as he leans against his motorcycle with his arms crossed. Whenever his attention is on me, I know something horrible is coming. I can't decide if it was better to be ignored by my oldest friend, or to be his plaything with a target on my back.

Once he got it through my head last year that he despises me for some reason, he mostly left me alone. But that's over now. Almost every day for the last two weeks he has some new twisted way to fuck with my head.

This time I don't have my older brother or my friends to watch out for me, so I'm on my own to stand up to his bullying crap.

The leather jacket he wears stretches tight over the muscled arms I know hide beneath. He shifts his rigid posture, poised on his hunt for my pain and humiliation. Despite the warm spring weather, he's in all black from his jacket to his jeans to his boots.

Everyone else abides the preppy SLHS uniform—black blazers embroidered with the school's gold crest, slacks for the guys, and evergreen plaid skirts for the girls. There are some who bend the rules for a shorter hem, a loose tie, or more fashionable shoes, and then there's Fox, who never pays attention to the dress code, always the outlaw king of his own world.

No one can tell him what to do, not even the school faculty. They're as afraid of him as everyone else in town.

His stormy dark blue gaze is hard and angry as usual, thick brows set in a permanent scowl. It's the only way I've known my old friend since he returned to Ridgeview last year like a ghost coming back to haunt me with the heartache I've carried since he left Colorado.

At first it killed me to be reunited only to feel the impenetrable wall Fox kept around him, allowing only a select few in. Holden was one of them. But not me.

I don't know why, but it's clear he can't stand me now. I know I'm not as impulsive thanks to Mom's obsession with public image, but I'm not so different from the girl he used to know.

I brush my fingers over the bracelet I've worn forever, the braided leather soft from age. It has three stones Fox found for me on a beach in California the year before our lives changed.

Fox was my friend, too.

The bitterness that rises in the back of my throat tastes

awful and I roll my stiff shoulders. Looks like I'm in for another extended yoga routine tonight to ease the ache in my body from being wound so tightly. My heart hasn't gotten the memo, giving a hopeful flutter every time Fox is around. As if he'll suddenly get over whatever reason he's holding a grudge against me.

Lost cause, girl. Let that energy go because it ain't manifesting no matter how hard we will it.

The truth stings, but I've learned to survive with this knife hanging over my head.

Fox was ripped from my life for ten years, then blew back into this town like a violent storm, fast and without warning. I've been holding my breath for over a year waiting for the damaging force to strike once he turned those scornful eyes on me. I used to know everything he wasn't saying behind them, when he was my closest friend. But now? I don't remember what I did to make him hate me so much and he won't give me the chance to fix it.

"Are you okay?" Sam asks with a sweet, curious look, startling me out of my thoughts. He brushes his thumb over my knuckles, all shy and polite. The corner of his mouth hooks into a boyish smile that should make my heart pound, but I've got nothing. "You went all quiet on me, beautiful. Tell me more about the sights you want to see on your road trip after graduation."

This thing with Sam Blake is...new. Really new. I don't know if I'm ready to call him my official boyfriend yet, but he's been asking me to hang out since the year started and I needed a distraction from the heavy weight of Fox's stare constantly following me everywhere at school.

Rumors about me have spread like wildfire through this drama-thirsty school. Attaching myself to Sam quelled them. For now, at least.

We weren't together when Fox and I—*no*. Nope. Not thinking about that.

Sam took me out to see a movie last weekend and did the whole pick me up at my house and shake Dad's hand thing, like I'm some maiden in waiting. He's been driving me to and from school and whenever he sees me in the hall he takes my hand and carries my books without asking. Sam is...nice. The kind of guy my parents love because he's perfect on paper in every way. Good grades, good manners, good family.

I think I'm panic-dating him. Fox catches my eye again as we reach the parking lot and my body goes hot and cold all over at memories I need to forget. I really needed that distraction.

"Um, yeah, I'm great," I spit out, turning a bubbly smile on Sam.

He returns it with a wider one, the corners of his brown eyes crinkling. The color isn't as intense as Fox's dark blue gaze, which is fathomless enough to drown in when his focus is locked on me.

Crap, what did he ask? Don't read the freak out in my eyes.

"Zion," I blurt once the question registers. "Sunrise yoga in every national park I can hit."

There's more to the cross-country road trip I've been dreaming of for years, but each time I talk about it in detail Sam's eyes glaze over. My best friend Thea is the only person who cares as much as I do about my goal, and knows why I want to take the solo trip to spread my wings before I'm forced into a college my parents chose, just another part of the full life story they laid out for me as soon as I was born. The older I get, the more they try to control what I do with their expectations.

I wish I could close my eyes and go back to when I was a wild little girl who could climb trees and run free.

"Cool." Sam pulls his key fob from his pocket and unlocks the souped up blue BMW X5 parked near where Fox is watching our approach. Sam glances at me and pushes his fingers through his sandy blond hair. "Are you sure you want to take the trip by yourself? It doesn't sound safe. Maybe I can come with you. We can make it like an adventure. Just the two of us."

We're close enough now that Fox can hear our conversation. His vicious snort makes my stomach churn and my shoulders rigid.

"I'm sure. I can handle myself." I offer Sam a tight smile. "Thanks though, that's really sweet."

"Bet."

Sam is unaffected, or totally oblivious to how much inviting himself on my road trip annoyed me. Another cutting bark of amusement sounds from Fox.

Ignoring him, I get in the SUV while Sam puts both our bags in the back seat. I check my phone for messages, finding two new texts from Thea asking if I want to come by the bakery she's opening in June. Her fiancé, Connor Bishop, bought the building for her as a surprise to help her achieve her dream. They're both a year older than me, like Fox and my brother, but Fox was held back when he enrolled at Silver Lake High.

I tap out a quick reply to let her know I have volunteering and a yoga class to teach after that. Her response comes a minute later, all flowery emojis and cutesy hearts because my best friend is literal walking sunshine. My mouth curves in a fond grin at her positive energy. I smooth my fingers over the other bracelet I always wear, a brass bangle with a smooth round inlay of rose quartz. Its nurturing properties remind me of her.

Sam slides into the driver's seat and reaches across to prop his hand on my headrest, absently playing with a lock of my light brown hair from my high ponytail. "Want to come to my place?" His voice dips lower into a flirty tone. "We can do our homework, then chill in my hot tub."

The quick leer he flashes me almost has my eyebrows flying up. Wow, even the nice ones are obvious.

"Can't." I twitch my head so my hair slips through his grasp, playing it off like I'm still checking my phone. His hand drops to my leg instead, brushing my skirt up slightly and stirring another flash of irritation. "I have to be home by two so I can make it to the library on time for my volunteer shift. I don't like to let the kids down, you know? They love story time."

"Fine."

I purse my lips and dart my gaze out the window, only to meet Fox's piercing scowl a few feet away. My stomach gives another lurch of dread. He's paying too much attention to my every move, but nothing has happened yet. That can only mean—

The engine makes an awful sputtering sound as Sam presses the ignition button.

"What the—" Sam's brows pinch in confusion and he tries again.

The same thing happens and my teeth clench together. I can feel the intent press of Fox's entire presence in my periphery, but I won't give him the satisfaction of knowing he's wrecking my day. *Again.*

When Sam tries the push start button a third time with no change, I force out a sigh. "I don't think it's going to start."

"Yeah, I guess not."

Sam seems at a loss for a moment, ruffling his hair. He gets out of the SUV and eyes the front grille like it might bite him. The parking lot is emptying out fast, leaving only us and the cars of students who have after school activities.

When I hop out to see if I can help, Fox is right there, a huge wall of leather, muscle, and heat blocking my path. I stand my ground, refusing to let him intimidate me. He gives me a cool stare through the thick messy dark brown fringe hanging over his forehead. His mouth curves into a vicious smirk when he catches me staring too long at his lips.

My cheeks heat. Stupid memories. I jerk my head toward the front of the BMW so I don't have to face him or my momentary lapse into insanity. Or nostalgia? I haven't decided yet, I just know what happened at that party has brought me nothing but torment no matter how good it felt to be wild and impulsive.

"Car trouble?" Fox taunts with an edge of satisfaction in his deep voice. He doesn't spare Sam an ounce of his attention. "What a shame. Those upmarket models really aren't made to last."

Sam's head pops up from beneath the hood and he hesitates, taking in how close Fox is standing to me, almost keeping me prisoner against the side of the car. Like most of our classmates, he doesn't mess with Fox. For every new rumor about me, there have been two for him. People love to talk, everything from speculating he has a different girl every night to mob ties that bankroll him. I heard someone yesterday morning whispering that he killed a man when I was walking to my freshly vandalized locker—*thanks, Fox.*

"Yeah. It won't start."

"I can take a look," Fox offers with a merciless grin that highlights the hard-edged asshole he's become. "I know my way around cars."

My eyes narrow in suspicion. This was totally all him and he's enjoying the spectacle. Goddamn it. Why is Fox so hell-bent on torturing me?

"Thanks, man. Have at it." Sam waves his hands with a relieved breath. "I don't really know a lot about cars. My dad's dealership handles all the maintenance."

I shake my head. "It's fine. We can figure it out. Or call a tow service."

"But babe, you said you had to be home in time for your volunteering thing," Sam points out.

Is Sam crazy? Fox is the reason the car won't start, and he's just going to let him back under the hood as easy as that?

The hate-filled look Fox gives me tells me he knows he's won yet again.

He steps around to peer under the hood beside Sam, shouldering him out of the way and looking comfortable with the engine parts, like he belongs with his calloused fingers working out the mechanics. Now he has witnesses as he gets his fingerprints all over the engine, touching every single part and leaving us with no way to file a police report against him to prove he did it.

I edge closer, watching his long fingers carefully to make sure he doesn't pull any tricks. There's a scar on his knuckles, maybe from the work he does on his bike and cars, or maybe from fighting. Knowing I'm watching him, he shoots me a look through his lashes as he checks the connection of the clamps on the battery.

I huff. What if he decides to do something worse than drain the battery or steal spark plugs or whatever the fuck he pulled?

Fox's parents died in a fatal car accident when I was eight and I don't like the heartless gleam in his eyes as he works.

For the first time ever he scares me.

Does he hate me enough to really hurt me?

My heart gives a weary, aching thump. Tears sting my eyes and I touch the stones in my bracelet. I already know the answer to that.

Fox is all rough with sharp edges and an air of danger now. There's no trace of the mischievous smiling boy I used to know, the one I loved getting into trouble with.

Ever since he came back, I thought he was still in there. He has to be, or so I've believed for a year.

Maybe everyone in this town is right. Fox Wilder is a black shadow. Mysterious, terrifying, and bad news to anyone who crosses him.

And somehow, I'm the person he hates the most.

TWO

FOX

The sight of the missing spark plugs from the engine tips the corners of my mouth up in gratification.

Poor, perfect little Maisy Landry isn't going anywhere without the parts sitting in the pocket of my leather jacket. The guy she's started hanging out with doesn't have a clue what I've done.

This is nothing. I could do so much worse to her than fuck with her idiot boyfriend's car and fan the flames on the rumors about her by spray painting *EASY* on her locker. I *should* do worse.

It's what she deserves. Liars always get what's coming to them. And Maisy? The biggest liar of them all, prancing around the school like a goody-goody, fooling everyone with her act to hide what she's really capable of.

I trusted this girl once. Once upon a time she was my best friend—I thought I could tell her anything and believed a promise mattered to her. I carry the guilt of the biggest mistake of my life every day, the poisonous weight infecting my veins.

"I think we can take it from here," Maisy says tightly. "I'll just call my dad to help us out." She pushes out a breath and adds on as an afterthought, "Thanks."

The fucking fakeness slides beneath my skin like needles. Her dad is the goddamn chief of police in Ridgeview, a position he didn't earn on merit. Their lives have been so privileged after mine was torn apart. I almost release a bark of laughter at the thought of her dad helping with the car after what he's done.

Richard and Jacqueline Landry are the reason I broke every piece of myself, stamping out any ounce of goodness to become the cold, vengeful monster I am now.

"Always running to your daddy, little daisy," I sneer low enough that only she can hear me while her boyfriend is distracted with texting. "Think he can protect you from me? Try again."

Maisy stiffens. Good, I hit her where it stings. I'll always be able to get to her. There's no escape from my wrath.

She should be glad I didn't tamper with the brakes, like the fate my parents met ten years ago. As usual, thinking of them sends a sharp stab of emotion lancing through me, my throat burning with the old ache. My hands flex on the frame of the SUV and I drag in a breath through my nose. I hate Maisy and her whole family, but that would be too easy of an out for any of them.

If they're gone, they can't live with the misery like I have.

The thirst for revenge has driven my actions for the last decade as I bounced around from foster home to foster home before I found a new family of brothers just as broken as I am. Without their help, I wouldn't be here. They took in an angry, grieving punk and shaped me into the darkness I shroud myself in so I fit in with them. When the world fucks with me, now I'm adept at hitting back harder with no mercy.

Every day I think of my promise to my parents' ghosts. I

want the Landrys to know what they've done to me when I rip apart their lives and make them face the truth of their actions.

Maisy hovers at the side of the BMW, attention locked on me. Those hazel eyes haunt my thoughts more than I care to admit. She doesn't trust me anymore either, not after the things I've done to her. Well, she did beg for my fucking attention every minute since I got back to town, and now she has it.

Careful what you wish for.

"What's wrong, crybaby?" I use the old nickname her brother and I taunted her with every chance I get. I love the way it makes her lip curl, but she refuses to let anyone at this school see the real Maisy she hides beneath the shiny good girl veneer. "Is this cutting into your time to ride your boyfriend's dick before you fix your hair all prim and proper and go read to kids at the library? That's the rumor going around about you."

The one I had a hand in starting.

"How do you know I volunteer at the—" Maisy snaps her mouth shut, shock flickering on her face before she closes off her expression.

It doesn't matter, I can still read every line of her body. She barely pays attention to the cookie-cutter dude who's supposed to be her boyfriend as she squares off with me. For a second, I can't help the way my heart thuds. The fire in her expression is a small glimpse of the girl who was my entire world.

"You know what, Fox? Never mind, I don't care. You can get fucked, asshole." There's a steel in her tone that makes my pulse pick up. Was I waiting for her to fight me back? A rush of the forbidden desire I shouldn't feel shoots through me as she continues. "No matter what you do to me, I'm not going to be afraid of you."

My teeth clench. *Keep telling yourself that.*

"Whoa, beautiful." Her boyfriend isn't glued to his phone anymore. His name is something with a B, but I don't give a shit. It's unimportant to me. The wholesome vibe is condescending as fuck while he looks at Maisy in surprise for the bite in her tone. "That's not like you."

Maisy's mouth tightens and a harsh sigh rushes out when she reins herself back behind her mask. Everyone around here looks at her and expects a sweet, well-behaved girl. They have no idea who she really is, but soon they will.

"If you were paying attention instead of checking your Instagram for likes, you'd know he deserves it," she mutters with a frown.

An echo of the memory of her nails digging into my skin as she panted for more tingles my nerve endings. I left my marks all over her not that long ago. The marks can fade, but she can't erase me.

There's no way this guy knows how to touch her to drive her wild, but that's her problem. I won't touch her again. It was just another way to show her what she'll never have while covering my tracks at the party so no one caught the real reason I was there.

As I stare at her, battling the thoughts of the way she smelled pressed against me, I see another hint of the girl I thought I knew. The only one I've ever wanted, but I can't fucking have anymore because she betrayed me by breaking her promise. That girl is gone and all that's left standing in front of me is a liar. Anger thunders through me as I cut off the memory of the sounds she made.

Maisy Landry isn't my friend anymore. I'm the demon she should run from. She means nothing to me other than the weak link in her family that I'm going to break. I can't forget that.

Pushing back from the engine, I drop the pretense of helping. "Guess you're screwed. Sucks to be you."

"Wait, you seriously can't help?" Boyfriend-with-a-B-name calls as I turn my back to head for my bike. The few people left in the lot give me a wide berth, too scared to get in my way. "Babe, did you have to piss him off? He could've fixed it."

The side of my mouth kicks up and a snort escapes me. I don't hang around for her answer, swinging a leg over the motorcycle parked nearby and slipping the helmet on. The growl of the engine drowns out all the sounds around me, clearing my head.

Without looking back at the one person I never thought would hurt me, I pull out from the parking lot, the constant searing pain of my decayed broken heart keeping me going.

THREE

FOX

Driving along the road that winds through the rolling hills, I clench my jaw hard enough to feel the pressure pulse through my skull. I'm surrounded by tall pine trees, rocks jutting from the ground, and fresh mountain air whipping against me as my bike rounds the bend with a roar. None of it is familiar like it should be. All it does is make me miss the smell of the ocean and the misty cove on the coast of Maine that was my sanctuary from my nightmares.

Colorado doesn't feel like home anymore. The truth hit hard when I came back last year, but I don't want to go back to Thorne Point yet. I can't, not until I've accomplished what I'm staying in Ridgeview to do.

It's the only reason I came back—to destroy every member of the Landry family for ripping mine away from me.

The trees thin out as I near the shipping district. Dusty gravel crunches beneath the tires of the bike when I pull in to the entrance to a row of warehouses. The one on the end is mine. The whole thing.

Colt helped me out, even though I didn't ask him to. When

I got to town without a plan for where to stay, an address pinged on my phone and I followed it here to find an envelope taped to the front door of the warehouse with *To Foxy, Love Dolos* written on it. A key was inside.

The thought of my foster brother has my head shaking in wry amusement. He's always got his nose in everyone's business, from spying on their devices to charming everyone to lower their defenses before they're aware of it. It's one of the reasons Wren Thorne gained so much power in Thorne Point, with his loyal band of psychos at his side. The Crows rule every secret in the city, stretching beyond that to control the east coast.

A phantom tingle spreads across my chest where a crow wearing a crown, perched on a skull is inked into my skin, hidden in an intricate ocean design that stretches halfway down my arm.

When the DuPonts welcomed me into their home as their scuffed up project to improve their image to their other socialite friends, I had no idea it would lead me to the Crows. Colton DuPont didn't have to accept me, let alone bring me into the fold with his closest friends, but he did it with an easy grin and a protectiveness that always makes me feel guilty for being grateful for.

It's the kind of protectiveness I should've been able to provide the little sister I was supposed to have, but I never got that chance because the life I should've had was stolen from me.

I park my Harley in the garage on the first floor of the converted warehouse, next to my matte black Charger. The lower level serves as my work space when I need to clear my head by sinking into grease and metal, or whatever odds and ends I can get my hands on. Once I cut the engine, I sit for a second, resting my hand on the one scratch I couldn't bring myself to buff out of the chrome.

Tracking down my dad's bike was hell after our assets were split up and sold off, but I managed to hunt it down right before I turned eighteen last year. The DuPonts set me up with a trust fund to make up for everything lost to me with my family's death. It was a drop in the bucket to them. The money is helpful, but it's the bike that matters most.

I remember the day I accidentally dinged the gleaming metal, shortly after Dad started allowing me into the garage to teach me how the mechanics worked. He wasn't mad. I swipe my thumb over the old imperfection as his face fills my mind, the features blurred from time. At least I can still hear his booming laughter.

Riding the motorcycle, I still feel close to him, keeping the memories of us working on it together alive. It's the only piece of him I have left.

Releasing a harsh exhale, I dump the spark plugs I stole on the workbench in the corner and head upstairs to the studio apartment. I peel out of my leather jacket and toss the keys to the bike on the counter of the industrial kitchenette. I lose my t-shirt next using it to swipe at the sweat beading my tattooed chest. It's always sweltering near the summer without air conditioning.

There isn't much inside, just enough to keep me comfortable along with the odds and ends I've built myself—the reclaimed wood and steel I used to craft a coffee table and the palette platform the bed in the corner sits on. I've always been good with my hands and the tinkering empties my mind when I can't sleep.

It's an old habit I couldn't kick after so many years of growing accustomed to not having a lot in the foster system. The DuPonts indulged me, allowing me to build things from the materials I found. They'd called it art, but half the time I picked up scraps of steel at the junkyard.

I pass the leather couch in the middle of the room and brace an arm against the large window panes. The shipping district is practically a wasteland compared to the bustling heart of Ridgeview. It's far from the residential areas of town.

This place is perfect, appearing shady as hell from the outside. It allows me to come and go without worrying about neighbors to watch me. Plus, it's a welcome reprieve from the whispers that follow me everywhere in town. A muscle in my jaw jumps as I lock it.

The Wilder name has become a curse. I'm the resident black shadow this town fears. Whispers about. Everyone remembers that a Wilder means bad news.

When someone sees me—the spitting image of my parents —the same lies as the ones told about my dad in the days following the accident spill free. People called Dad a troubled, reckless, suicidal drunk who was a danger to himself and others. But it's not true. None of it. My parents were murdered and powerful people in this town covered it up.

Secrets, lies, betrayal, revenge...this town is stained in blood.

But who I am now is not the same broken, naïve kid that left this town. I have teeth now and I bite hard enough to make my enemies bleed.

The Landrys as good as pulled the trigger and I'm going to prove it. Then I'll make them pay.

Too tense to focus on anything, I change out of my jeans and head for the workout area I've pieced together at the other end of the apartment. Pushing my body until it's ready to break from punching the bag is the only other way I can shut my brain off before the constantly simmering rage boils over.

I lose track of time, only aware of the aching protest in my muscles, the sweat dripping from my body, and the rhythm of my breath as my fists strike the punching bag.

It's only when an incoming call cuts off the playlist of angry music for the third time that I finally stop, inked chest heaving when I catch the bag on the backswing to steady it. Swiping damp hair out of my face, I pick my phone up and shake my head, accepting the call.

"Colt. I'm busy."

"That's not how I taught you to talk to your big brother." Amusement laces his tone. Always the jokester. *"You've turned into such a little shit since you left Thorne Point."*

"I've always been this way." I mop the sweat from my face with a towel, slinging it around my neck as I cross to the kitchen to grab a water. "But you already knew that."

He hums in agreement. *"Not for lack of trying on my part to get you to lighten up. I swear, you and Levi are related somehow. You're both cut from the same cloth of angst-ridden edgelord."*

I scoff. Colt's friend is one of the few people who scares the shit out of me. He has no morals, no limits, and a serious obsession with knives.

"I've got a new lead for you," Colt says, turning serious.

Ice spreads across my nerve endings. I'm already moving to the laptop and files spread out on the coffee table, holding the phone between my face and shoulder. My voice is rough when I answer. "Yeah?"

"Are you by your computer? You'll get a push notification with an encrypted download package."

"On it." I drop the phone to the table, switching it to speaker phone. The file he mentioned pops up on the screen. Once it opens, I suck in a breath, reading quickly. "You're sure?"

"Yeah. When you sent the copied hard drive I was able to dig this up. It was actually hard for me to seduce it into telling me

its secrets, and that's saying something. Whoever encrypted this didn't ever want this to see the light of day. I'll send over whatever else I find."

I scan the information again. There was already someone lined up for the police chief position, preparing to transition only a week before Richard Landry was named the new chief. I suspected it—how else could I explain how Richard and Jacqueline ended up in positions of power, living in one of the most upscale neighborhoods in town without a fishy reward for their involvement—and yet seeing it in black and white makes my skin crawl. This is the biggest break I've had in my efforts to bring my parents justice.

It made it easier for them to cover up what was done to my family.

My heart pounds. Going to that party was worth it then, and not only because I found out what makes Maisy moan. She was just my cover so no one caught me sneaking around the home office.

"Thanks, Colt. I owe you."

"Pay me back later. Preferably with a sexy new waifu to beat it to." He laughs at the disgusted sound I make. I don't know how he gets off on hentai because the fake cartoon boobs do nothing for me. *"Kidding, I get the good shit on my own."*

"Whatever," I mutter.

"Later, Foxy."

He hangs up before I can tell him off for calling me by his nickname for me. "Asshole."

It doesn't carry much heat. Without him, I'd still be floundering in my hatred with no direction. It's only thanks to Colt and his friends that I now have another piece to the puzzle.

Rubbing at my jaw, I pull up the photo album on my phone. It also means I need to move forward with the next plan, the one that's formed in the last couple of weeks. I went after Holden's future first, but Maisy is the real chink in her parents' armor.

Photos of her fill my phone from when I followed her to learn her habits after the party, once I decided it was her turn to pay her pound of flesh. At first I ignored her because it was too painful to look at her, but now she's got the attention she begged me for.

It surprised me how much she stacked her extracurriculars. Volunteering at the library to read children's books, AP classes, teaching yoga, for fuck's sake. I would've guessed with how her parents were paid off, she could have her top pick of any elite college. Holden did, before I eliminated it, and as far as I could tell his only qualification to beef up his college application was playing football.

Memories from last year swirl to the surface as I look at a photo of Maisy leading a yoga class.

I'd been walking with Holden, flooded with how much I resented being around him. Just like Maisy, he turned into someone unrecognizable. It was almost hard to believe we were friends once, but nine year olds are different from douchebags at eighteen. Maisy appeared in the gymnasium doorway to stop him, wearing a crooked smile that still made my heart turn over without my permission. She ignored my scowl to ask for help setting up the stupid winter dance.

Maybe it was a moment of weakness, or maybe it was because all I could think when I saw them together was that my mom was pregnant with a little sister I'd never know the night she died, but Maisy managed to latch onto my wrist as she dragged us both behind her, reminding me of the force of nature she used to be.

Holden groaned, dropping his head back. "You're such a pain in the ass."

"Deal with it, my god," Maisy sassed back, sticking her

tongue out at her brother. "Two minutes, or I'll tell Mom where you've been going on weekends."

"Fine," Holden grumbled.

It was better to help her and be done with it than lose my bargaining chip—the secret fight rings Holden organized, raking in cash from the other hopped up, over privileged kids in Ridgeview. I'd stood frozen for a moment, glaring at the doll she was now instead of the wild little troublemaker I was familiar with, but she'd sighed and asked if I was going to help.

"It won't take long," she said, lowering her gaze. "Then you can go back to pretending I don't exist."

I had almost laughed. The one thing that was impossible was pretending she didn't exist. I tried, shit didn't work. She stayed in my goddamn head, refusing to be forgotten completely. I was about to turn around, but she wouldn't give in or get the fucking hint.

"Fox, come on." *Damn her voice. All it did was make me remember what we had a long time ago.* "You always used to—"

"No." *The furious growl cut her off.*

"No?" Maisy sighed. "Okay, it's just...if you helped, we'd get it done faster. Then I'll leave you alone."

It was too much. The docile politeness wasn't her. I hated it as much as I loathed her parents. I still didn't understand why she acted like that until I started catching the glimpses through her mask.

Where was my wildflower?

Moving at last from the rigid statue I'd become, I got in her face. "Always such a goody-goody."

When she tensed and hugged herself, I let out a cutting bark. "Yeah. That's what I thought." *I took a lock of her silky light brown hair, allowing it to slide through my fingers. The faint floral hint of her favorite shampoo had me grinding my teeth.*

"Didn't your daddy teach you to run from monsters? Get it through your fucking head."

Kicking over a bucket of paint the student committee was using to decorate with felt good, channeling the pent up fury threatening to burst free. It had skimmed across the floor in a shimmering metallic smear. The shock of pain that cracked her sweet mask drew a cruel smirk from me.

"What are you going to do about it? Cry?" My deep, biting tone mocked her. She stood her ground, but she wasn't unaffected. Tears gathered in her hazel eyes. "That's all you are. All you'll ever be. Maisy Daisy the Crybaby."

"What happened to you?" Her whisper was watery. "You were my friend, too."

"Playtime is over," I growled. "Fuck off, daisy. Stay out of my way."

I had stormed off, tearing down another decoration on my way out of the gym.

Maybe if she'd listened to me that day, I would have left her out of my plans. Now they center around her. I swipe to another photo of her smiling brightly with the redhead she's friends with.

Maisy Landry won't know what hit her. I'll attack her reputation, her spirit, and when she thinks she can't break anymore, I'll destroy her future. Liars don't get to enjoy their futures.

Another photo of her fills my screen. My mouth curves with deadly precision.

Get ready, little daisy. We're only getting started.

FOUR
MAISY

People sidestep me in the hall at school a few days later. I'm like a rock in the middle of a river, forcing everyone to go around me because I'm frozen, glaring at my locker. The words spray painted on it are a slap in the face.

LIAR.

The big bold black letters stand out against the green metal door. The worst part is it hits home in a way I don't expect. It's not the first time my locker has been vandalized in the last couple of weeks since Fox started paying attention, but this shines a light on an ugly truth: I am a liar. That's how I feel, anyway. Always obeying my parents' expectations instead of making my own choices. He sees it somehow. Knew exactly how to get under my skin.

Someone snickers, bumping into me on purpose and I shuffle on my feet to keep my balance. Their whispers have become the norm lately. All it took was one party for people to stop seeing me as the nice girl with good grades. They don't care if it's true or not when the gossip is juicy and entertaining.

Everyone lives for a good downfall story.

It doesn't matter. I repeat it in my head enough times for it to feel true. None of this matters.

Just smile through it. Play along. Ignore the whispers.

Someone laughs louder and says my name as if I'm not standing right in the middle of it all, listening to the lies grow bigger. *She's secretly a nympho and the prude thing was an act. She's sleeping with one of her teachers. She's Wilder's personal sex doll and in exchange for doing his homework he lets her suck his dick.* I'm done with this.

Turning on my heel, I head for the custodian office with my head held high. Whether I look down or not, my classmates' stares bore into me, so I might as well keep my chin up. It's just a locker.

I'm polite when I ask if a janitor could come to my locker. One of them follows me back. A crowd has formed around it, snapping selfies and laughing.

"Move aside," the janitor says.

People I've never seen or talked to before swagger away, smirking at me like I'm on display in a zoo.

"Again?" The janitor asks in a tone that makes me ball my hands into fists.

It's this side of judgmental. Just my luck I got the same janitor who spent two days last week scrubbing *EASY* off my locker the first time it was vandalized. The thing about high school is that it's not just the students who love to gossip. The staff are just as bad if not worse.

The urge to get upset and fight against these rumors is there, sitting in my chest, waiting to be unleashed. I breathe through it, feeling the bars of my cage bumping against my back. If I make a bigger scene, Mom will only bring her wrath down on me for putting a dent in our family's image. Totally more important than standing up for myself, right?

With her promotion to CEO and Dad's to police chief

came more eyes on us, which meant tempering my impulses. The words on my locker ring alarmingly true. Most days I barely feel like I know myself because of the image I've been trained to portray.

Instead of opening my mouth, I shrug and plaster on a sweet smile. That's the best I can manage right now. His gaze lingers on me for a beat too long before he turns back to examine the locker and mutter into his radio about the cleanup.

What they think they know doesn't mean anything, these people will never see the truth. It's only high school, it's not forever. I'm almost done here. Of course, rumors have a way of sticking in Ridgeview. It's a big town, but not that big. People love to talk.

* * *

On my way to meet up with Thea after school, an impulse grips me. It doesn't happen a lot, but when I'm in this part of town, I can't fight the pull to drive down the old street where we used to live. Maybe it's stronger now because of my run in with Fox in the parking lot.

If Mom or Dad knew I came here they'd kill me. When Holden and I got our licenses, they forbid us from coming back here, as if our childhood home was tainted. I never understood why, it's a nice area where we had block parties with our neighbors.

"Just to see. It's been a while," I murmur to myself, turning down the road instead of going straight.

Like always, as soon as the familiar houses pass by I'm overcome with a wave of longing. After Fox left Ridgeview, we moved to a new house because Mom got a big promotion at her pharmaceutical company. I still don't get how someone from the research department becomes CEO, but no matter how many times I've tried to wrap my head around it I can't make sense of why it happened. It was supposed to change our lives for the better—that's what Mom and Dad told us. But it didn't. The last good times we had as a family were left behind on this street.

My life has been good, but a piece of me was torn out when Fox went away. Everything changed, and the piece hasn't slotted back into place since he's returned, like the damn thing has warped, no longer fitting where it belongs.

After I pass both of our old houses, I slow the car to a stop at the end of the block by the field. It's overgrown with fresh wildflowers, dotted by a few bees and butterflies floating on the breeze above the blooms. If I close my eyes and concentrate, I can hear an echo of laughter. My throat is thick when I swallow. So many memories...

I get out of the white Audi Q7. It's really Holden's car, but he lets me use it whenever I need it, which has come in handy since he never left for college like he was supposed to. It's not fair that my brother got a car and I didn't, but there are way bigger problems in the world than not being gifted a car. Dad refuses to let me have my own and it's putting a serious damper on my road trip plans. He's not going to stop me from going on that trip, though. I've played by their rules and given them what they wanted. The road trip is my one chance to spread my wings before I go back to being a picture-perfect Landry for the college they picked out for me.

It's warm out, the late afternoon sun peeking through billowing clouds to kiss the tall grass. I brush my hands over it as I pick my way through the field to get to the tree. It doesn't look as big as it did when we were kids. I used to be so proud I could climb it. The bright green leaves rustle on the swaying branches as I press a palm to the bark.

The time Fox dared me I couldn't climb our tree flashes in

my mind. Quirking my mouth up, I picture how determined I was. I climbed higher than I ever had, almost to the top. Proving him wrong felt good, until he had to come up after me to get me down. We went branch by branch with his guidance. He kept checking if I was okay, squeezing my hand as he helped me reach the ground.

My phone vibrates in the pocket of my school blazer. I pull it out and sigh. It's a text from Mom checking in on where I am now that school is out for the day. They know my volunteer and yoga class schedule. Outside of that, I have to let them know what I'm doing, even at eighteen.

Maisy: I'm on my way to Thea's. I'll come straight home after that.

I hold my breath as three dots appear, hoping she won't decide to check my location by creeping on my phone. She doesn't do that often, but I haven't given her any reason to doubt me lately, keeping my free-spirited urges reeled in. When Dad does it, he's being overprotective like usual, but with Mom... It always feels like a collar pulled tight around my neck.

The instinctive urge I sometimes have to just *go* rushes through me. I could just get in the car and drive. The road would decide where to take me and I'd follow the wind until my heart felt free of the heaviness.

Mom and Dad would be furious, but I'd be happy.

Mom: Be home in time for dinner.

Air gusts out of my lungs in relief. While I'm typing my reply, the heavy rumble of an engine catches my attention. I put my phone away as I turn and my heart drops into my stomach when I see a matte black Charger speeding down the street, screeching to a halt right behind the Audi. It stops inches from smashing into the back bumper.

Oh shit.

It's Fox.

I've been wondering where he's been. He hasn't been around school since he messed with Sam's car. Things like his attendance record and grades don't seem to matter to him while he comes and goes as he pleases.

Fox gets out of the Charger and stalks toward me with his handsome features set in a deadly scowl. The hair on my body stands on end as he quickly eats up the distance with long, powerful strides. Before I can breathe, he's in front of me, forcing me back against the tree. The bark digs into my shoulder blades.

"What the fuck do you think you're doing here?" he growls, making my pulse thunder.

The scent of rich leather, earthy wood, and the faint hint of motor oil surrounds me.

My gaze flies around the empty field, then returns to meet his cold glare. I open my mouth, only to gasp when his fingers lock around my throat. A tremor runs down my spine while heat spikes low in my stomach, making me squirm to rub my thighs together. He doesn't miss it, a rough sound rumbling in his throat as he presses closer so the hard lines of his chest connect with mine. I struggle, testing the limits of his grip, but he's too strong for me to break away.

That's what I should want to do—get away. But...curiosity keeps me in place. This is the first time his hands have been on me since that night at Jenna's party two weeks ago and my body remembers. Vividly.

The marks he left on my skin have faded. My stomach dips when I think of him doing it all again.

Fear and desire fight for control. It's so wrong that Fox can touch me like this and stir excitement, but some part of me craves it even as he torments me.

There's no one here to stop him. Even if there was, I don't think it would change anything. No one holds authority over him. If he wanted, he could easily slide my school skirt up and do whatever he wanted. My clit shouldn't throb at that thought, but it does, *god*, it does. It's so messed up.

He doesn't choke me, but his hold is firm, pinning me to the tree in case I was planning to run.

I might be scared of what he could do to me, but I'll never run from him. The brooding jerk can have my fear, but he doesn't get my surrender.

Somewhere deep inside, there's a small part of him I recognize. I saw it last year, when I caught sight of him smiling at the holiday market in town. It was the same as the boyish smile that used to charm me to do anything when we were kids. I cling to that hope whenever I hear the rumors and whispers flying around about him.

"Fox, what are you trying to—"

"Why are you *here?*" he grits out furiously through clenched teeth.

Narrowing my eyes, I shove the fear aside. "I'm not allowed to exist now? Last I checked, you don't own the street or this field. I'm not trespassing. If I want to visit our tree?" I lean into his hand and my heartbeat flutters when his grip flexes. He's serious, but so am I. "I will."

Fox's dark blue gaze flashes at my defiance. He glances down the line of my body, lingering at the sight of his fingers wrapped around my throat. His mouth tugs into a smirk. "You never could resist trouble. You always loved the thrill."

He digs his thumb into my pulse point, making it crystal clear he could snap my neck with little effort. I struggle to swallow, fighting to drag in a full breath while he controls my air. He can probably feel my racing pulse. Then his thumb eases off to trace up to my jaw. The gesture is at odds with the contempt in his gaze, but it makes my hands grab at his leather jacket, curling into the supple material. For a moment he seems to freeze, like he's curious what I'll do.

Fox leans in until our lips almost touch, then waits another beat, watching me through his hooded gaze.

Is he going to kiss me this time?

This is the closest he's come to me since the party. I just want things to be right between us. If he's ready to move past his grudge, then I'll forgive and forget his cruelty so we can go back to how things should be between us.

Licking my lips, I strain toward him with want.

He releases a gruff, arrogant sound of amusement. "Do you seriously think I'm going to kiss you?"

The cutting tone makes me flinch.

"I..."

"How pathetic."

Oh god, I'm an idiot. The alarm returns, winning out over the fog of desire. I can't believe myself right now for losing sight of common sense. This is that damn party all over again, the intoxicating invisible tether cinching tight between us, but all it brings is heartache. How could I forget?

Fox scoffs. "You look so fucking desperate right now, little daisy. It's a terrible look on you."

Hurt stings the newly opened wounds and I shrink back against the tree. How could I think he was ready to move past why he hates me? He didn't that night he finally acknowledged me. I swallow the hot embarrassment and glare at him.

"Fuck you," I mutter.

His grin is scary. "You make me want to end you. Right here, right now. There's no point in dancing around it."

My eyes widen. The reality slams into me once more. Fox can and will hurt me without a second thought.

"Why do you hate me so much?" I whisper, despising the painful fire in my throat. "*Why?*"

Fox's lip curls and he brings his mouth to my cheek. "Stop acting like you don't know. It's making me sick. Everything about you makes me so goddamn sick."

My chest collapses with a hoarse breath. The acidic hostility in his tone is unmistakable.

A phone rings and he curses, tearing away from me. I lean against the tree, unsure of what he'll do if I move. Whoever is calling makes his sharp jaw tic when he clenches it. His glare finds me once more.

"Get out of my sight before I change my mind," he commands. "Don't let me catch you here again. You won't like what I do to you."

The thought of staying away from the tree drives a white-hot lance into my chest. I want to argue instead of letting him win, but I'm still reeling from allowing myself to think for a second that he wanted me. God, he's right. I am desperate, but all I want is to make things right between us.

When I haven't answered, he takes a threatening step toward me, his glare intensifying. "Got it?"

I hate this.

Heart lodged in my throat, I manage a stiff nod before I walk to my car on trembling legs. I won't run. I refuse to let him believe he can control me like that, snapping his fingers and barking commands to make me hop fucking to it because he said so. I deal with it enough from Mom and Dad, but no one gets that power over me.

Behind me, I hear the deep murmur of his voice as he answers the phone. "You got something new for me?"

Glancing over my shoulder, I watch him pace by the tree,

pushing a hand into his messy dark hair in agitation. The hint of a tattoo is visible at the neckline of his t-shirt. Curiosity tugs at me. I didn't get to see it at the party, but I caught a tiny glimpse of black feathers.

I don't stick around long enough to listen. Once I reach the SUV, I get in and drive away in a shaken daze. I don't even roll the windows down to let my fingers ride the waves of the wind whipping by the car. Dad would be really annoyed if he knew all his lectures about safe driving were flying out the window in the face of self preservation.

It doesn't make sense how Fox Wilder can simultaneously draw me in with magnetic force while also throwing off dangerous vibes that make me want to get away.

Nothing makes any damn sense to me anymore. It has to be the fact that there's so much history between us. Throw in his grudge against me and...whatever it was that went down at the party, the line between us is mottled and blurred by the ferocity of our feelings. One minute he ignores me, the next he's pushing me against the nearest flat surface to ignite a fire in me with his body, only to turn around and lash out at me in punishment. I never know what to expect from him.

Gripping the wheel hard enough for my knuckles to turn white, I head for Thea's bakery. My racing heart doesn't slow.

Fox is the only person who gets under my skin and riles up my easy carefree spirit. He makes me want to fight him. I'm more of a peace and love type of person, but when it comes to Fox, a fierceness I didn't know I possessed breaks free.

I should stay away from him—it's what he wanted. But I can't. Not until I know why he hates me enough to forbid me from coming to our tree.

FIVE

FOX

2 Weeks Ago

The party sucks. It's nothing like Wren Thorne's extravagant and hedonistic parties, but I wasn't expecting much from the spoiled brats of Ridgeview.

Whatever, that's not why I'm here tonight amongst the kids of the most influential and powerful people in town. Just need to blend in until the time is right, then I'm getting the hell out of here. Except right now I stand out too much to do what I need to.

People side eye me and mutter when I walk through the kitchen to another room where the pounding beat of music fills the huge house. No one will kick me out, though. They're all too chickenshit to cross me. If my fierce scowl isn't enough, the rumors about me are, so they let me crash.

"Bet he's got a dumping ground spot out at the old quarry," someone whispers loudly. "Buries all the bodies of people he's offed for the mob out there."

"No way," a girl responds, giving me a once over from the corner of her eye. "He's so hot. He can't be a hitman."

"He totally is! It's how he made all his money."

Rolling my eyes, I slip past them. The rumors in this town are getting stupider by the minute.

I grab a beer bottle to look less like an angry shadow and prowl around the party, keeping an eye out the entire time. People don't stand in my way because they recognize that I'm a predator who could tear them apart. When I spot the girl throwing the party—the daughter of the mayor, who has a habit of bringing his work home—I begin to make my way toward her. Her gaze trails me up and down, the heat flaring in her eyes easy to read. The corner of my mouth twitches in triumph.

Like a bad boy, do you?

"I don't remember inviting you," she says in a fake tone meant to entice me.

My shoulder hitches and I take a swig from the beer bottle. "I don't like playing by the rules."

She releases a breathy sound and inches closer, pressing her tits against my arm. If this all turns out to be a waste of my time, I'll be pissed I had to put up with her. Swallowing back the snarky comment climbing my throat at how she was making out with some dude from the football team thirty minutes ago, I give her a lazy smile that makes her flutter her lashes flirtatiously.

"You've got a sweet place. Is your dad someone important?"

Buying my act, she flaps a hand, leaning into me harder as she fires off questions rapidly. "I guess, but who cares? Did you bring your motorcycle? Can you give me a ride?"

I trace a thumb over my lip. "I did."

Didn't mean I was going to let her touch it. I barely let the guys back east touch my bike.

Girls like her have never interested me. That goes for most

of them, actually. Even amongst Wren's mismatched band of Crows, the girls that hung around never held my attention. There was only ever one girl who had my heart. Just one, but she crushed it to dust in her little fist.

The mayor's daughter keeps doing most of the talking and flirting while I stand there leaning against the wall, tuning out half of what she says to scan the room. Now that I'm blending in, the attention is off me. Good, that'll make it easier to get into the home office.

The plan is going fine until all the air in the room sucks out when I catch sight of who just entered through the front door out of the corner of my eye. Maisy fucking Landry, hair down from the ponytail she favors and dressed in a loose crop top that exposes her flat tanned stomach and tight blue yoga pants that hug her ass and her long toned legs. *Goddamn, daisy.* My focus splits, snagged by the need to watch Maisy's every move and stick to what I'm here to do—use this chick to gain access to her dad's computer.

For now I ignore her. It's been the best way to deal with the raging pain that sears my chest from the inside out every time I look at the liar. If I don't, I teeter on the brink of losing control and burning this whole fucking town to the ground.

Ridgeview, the town that turned on me and my family ten years ago. This was our home until it got my parents killed. I've waited this long and the time has finally come. I'm out for blood and I'm going to get it if it's the last thing I do.

Maisy scans the room and stops on me and the girl dragging her manicured nails over my chest. We lock eyes and I let my mouth quirk into a savage curve as I wrap an arm around the girl's waist, hauling her against my body. She squeals and releases the fakest moan.

"You want that ride now, baby?" I ask.

The chick doesn't notice that I'm not looking at her. She nods. "Let's go upstairs."

"Lead the way."

Maisy's nostrils flare and she rips her attention away, stalking through the party with an angry grace that makes my blood thrum more than the chick melting against my side. I force out a breath, trying to get my head screwed on right. I'm not here for games.

Once my decoy takes me into her room, I let her kiss my neck and I put on a show of throwing her on the bed roughly. She giggles when she bounces. I cover her body with mine and hold her hair while she writhes beneath me. She doesn't see it coming when I use Levi's trick with a pressure point to knock her out cold. I shift her onto her side in case she had too much to drink and put a pillow beneath her head. Sitting back on the edge of the bed, I smirk, glad I made the craziest of the Crows teach me how to pull that off.

I set a timer for twenty minutes on my phone and make my way into the home office at the end of the hall. The vibrating thump of music drifts up as I head straight for the expensive computer in the center of the luxuriously furnished room—just as swanky as the rest of the house. It shouldn't shock me after the years I've spent amongst the people the DuPonts associate with, but Ridgeview has this way of slapping their wealth in people's faces.

Reaching into my back pocket, I pull out thin gloves and get to work copying the hard drive. The computer has no password set, so I don't have to utilize the skills Colton taught me to get around it. I huff out an empty laugh. People are too fucking trusting that nothing can touch them when they're at the top.

I finish downloading the entire drive to a USB as a backup and pocket it before my alarm goes off. Making sure I haven't left a trace of what I've done, I slip out of the room and head for the staircase.

Maisy is waiting for me at the top of the steps, glaring down the hall. Damn it. She can't blow my cover. I return her glare as I stalk toward and she lays into me as soon as I reach her.

"So you'll talk to other girls, just not me. Right. Got it."

Sticking to ignoring her, I pretend she's not there as I shoulder her out of the way and head downstairs, tucking the copied hard drive deeper into my pocket. I got what I came here for, now I can get out of here.

"You can't even look at me anymore," Maisy accuses when we reach the first floor, gripping my elbow with an unexpected amount of strength.

I glance down at her hand. She always was strong. She used to hate it when Holden and I treated her like she couldn't do the same things we did because she was a girl.

This close, those blue leggings are even harder to resist. The urge to take a bite out of her ass is strong. Fuck, why are they so tight?

"I'm over this," she says, getting in my face while I hesitate. Her familiar determination and steel spine make me ache to crush her to me in a hug and push her away harder. "What have I done? Why are you so ready to throw our friendship away?"

It feels like as soon as I look down her body, everything I've ignored calls to me. I've rejected and avoided how beautiful she is—god, even more than when she had my heart ten years ago. I've disregarded how much my mouth has watered at her tight body for a year.

When I don't answer, her brows pinch and she keeps pushing. "Goddamn it, Fox. If you don't talk to me, then I don't know what I'm apologizing for. We can't keep going on like this. It's killing me."

The catch in her voice makes me ball my fists.

A thousand and one memories of when we were kids blind-side me. Her hazel eyes pierce through the intricate ocean artwork inked into my bicep and chest, straight into my heart. Then every inch of me turns to ash when I remember the most important thing—she broke her promise.

If she wants my attention so bad, she's going to fucking get it.

I slam her back against the wall. A few people look our way. The party has all but faded away, my focus narrowing down to my old friend.

"You can say you're sorry while you choke on my cock," I growl, face inches from hers as I cage her in.

Surprise crosses her face for a beat before it bleeds away, replaced by a look that has my dick hard in seconds. She slides her arms around my neck, watching me with as much arousal as I feel rushing through me, tempting me with her sweet scent of flowers and coconut. I bite back a groan and grasp her waist. My thumbs skate over smooth skin beneath the hem of her short crop top, exploring her bare belly. I brush the underside of her tits, unable to hold back a grin that she's not wearing a bra.

"That gets you hot, doesn't it?"

"Yeah, it does," she says without any shyness. She gives me a crooked smile when I stare at her. Leaning closer, she murmurs, "There's a lot that gets me wet. Going to keep going to find out?"

Holy shit. Heat pools low in my gut at the confidence she has. I thought she was going to cower and freak out at the rough treatment and dirty words meant to make her blush.

I picture her on her knees with those pretty lips wrapped around my dick, tears streaming down her face while I fuck her lying mouth until she's wondering whether or not I'll pause long enough to let her breathe before I come down her throat. Want crashes over me.

Ignoring her was stupid. Hate fucking her is so much better.

My hands drag down her sides to palm her ass. These yoga pants are sinful as fuck, skintight and leaving nothing to the imagination. I trace my tongue over my lower lip and picture peeling them off her with my teeth.

"Fuck, little daisy," I rasp in a smoky tone as my hands roam her body, claiming every inch with my touch. "You've grown up."

Maisy presses up on her toes, tilting her head. She wants to kiss me. Through the haze of lust, I shut down the way my heart thumps at an old dream coming true.

I stop her before her lips touch mine, holding her neck and jaw. Disappointment flashes in her golden eyes, but this isn't a romantic reunion of long lost friends. This is all physical, that's fucking it. Smirking, I direct her head to the side and close my mouth around her pulse point. I torture her neck until she's melting against the wall, releasing these soft sounds that drive me insane.

A few people have already seen us tangled together, but we're too wrapped up in an overwhelming flood of need to stop. The broken dam that held us back from this drowns us. Anger colliding with lust is a heady mix. The only thing I'm vaguely aware of is that we can't do this in the hallway at some house party, but I can't tear myself away long enough to take her somewhere private. Releasing a growl, I pick her up. She yelps, clutching at my shoulders as I grab her ass in a possessive grip.

Someone howls like a coyote, whatever the fuck that's supposed to mean.

I walk into the first room I find—a bathroom. Compared to the rest of the house, it's not that big, but I don't care. The enticing little monster in my arms digs her nails into my skin and it pulls all my focus back to her.

We knock over a decorative basket of hand towels as we get lost in the storm of each other. It's violent and passionate and fucking addictive. I drop her, pinning her hips against the counter as I return to biting and sucking at her neck. She arches against me, proving what those hours of yoga are good for. The thought of how my marks will be all over her neck make me grind my erection into her stomach.

Maisy pulls on my hair and wraps a leg around mine as she buries a cry into my chest. "I need you to—"

Before she can finish, I push a hand down the front of her leggings, finding her folds slick as my fingers glide across her pussy. I don't waste any time on teasing her, sinking a finger inside and leaning back to watch my fingers flex through the thin fabric of her pants and the way it makes her mouth opens on a breathy moan.

"Oh god!" Maisy moves against my hand and slides hers under my shirt to brush against my abs. She moves down to my black jeans, over my hard cock. When she rubs it, my eyes hood as I press into her. "We could've been doing this all year, you stubborn jerk. If you'd just talked to me. We've wasted so much time."

"Shut up," I command harshly, thrusting my fingers in with enough force to make her suck in a breath. "No talking."

"You're talking," she taunts with a gleam in her eyes.

I slow down for a second, gaze flicking up and down her body before I meet her eyes. "You want me to make you be quiet, or are you just hoping I'll punish that mouth by making you choke on my cock?"

"Promises, promises," Maisy snarks.

Sassy little brat.

I wish we had more time to explore. Breaking her until she submits would be something I'd want to do over and over.

The side of my mouth tips up. It's the only warning she gets before I push another finger in her pussy and fuck her hard with my fingers. She fists my shirt and grabs the edge of the counter, only able to hold on, head hanging back and small cries escaping her when I hook my fingers up. I'm relentless, not stopping until her eyes fly to mine, pupils blown wide from arousal.

"Fuck, right there, I'm—" She breaks off with a strangled sound and her pussy clenches down on my fingers.

I used to think I knew all of my favorite sounds and faces she made. Watching her come easily slots into the top favorite spot and it pisses me off even more that we can never have this again. We were made for each other, but she ruined that.

"Turn around."

Maisy's eyes flash. With a smug smile, I grab her chin with the same fingers I had buried in her pussy a minute ago. I touch her lips with my thumb and she licks it. The fact she likes it rough, likes my demanding nature makes me groan.

"Turn the fuck around."

I jerk her body around without waiting for her to do it. One of my hands runs up the back of her leg while my arm wraps around her shoulders to crush her back against my chest. I grab a handful of her ass in a harsh grip and dig my cock into her back. The want I feel for her is overwhelming to battle. My touch roams her body, squeezing her neck, then dropping to her waist as I pant against her temple and grind against her.

I hate Maisy, but god, I want to fuck her so badly. There's nothing I want more in this minute than to sink my cock into her pussy and make her scream my name.

Moving to tighten my arm around her, I drop my head to her

shoulder. "I could fuck you right now and you'd let me, wouldn't you," I rumble into her neck, enjoying the way her body shudders against mine. "That's what I thought. Let this be a lesson, because that will never fucking happen." She stiffens in my arms as my tone turns cruel. "This changes nothing. I still hate you."

I don't know if I shocked her into silence at last, or if she's reeling from the contempt in my voice, but she stays still as I unzip my pants and take my dick out. A groan vibrates in my chest as I pump myself, pressing the tip right against her ass. It doesn't take long for the heat in my gut to coil tight as my orgasm hits. With a hoarse sound, I come, painting her ass with it as I hold her hip hard enough to bruise.

She remains quiet as I stumble back, leaning against the wall to catch my breath. In the mirror above the counter I can see the pinkness in her cheeks, her lashes lowered to sweep against them. My gaze drifts down to her yoga pants stained with my come.

It's a fucking beautiful sight that will remain burned in my brain long after I break her. Pushing off the wall, I leave her to figure out how to clean up, banging out of the bathroom into the party. As I move through a crowded room, I get elbows and smirks from other guys who were wary of my presence here at first.

"Get this man a beer, he just deflowered the yoga prude," one of them says.

A round of cheers follows.

"Damn, bro, first Jenna, then Maisy Landry in the same night?" Another guy claps my shoulder, leaning in. "Jenna hasn't come back down to the party, either. What did you do to get that kind of stamina?"

"Screw that, I want to hear about Maisy." The first guy shoves a beer in my face that I don't take. "That yoga shit is hot. Was she flexible?"

As he asks, Maisy comes into the room. Her cheeks flush as all eyes turn on her. She folded down her yoga pants to try to hide the stain I left. A satisfying smirk settles on my face.

"Very pliant."

The guys in the room laugh while hurt fills her eyes. She hugs herself as they throw around more lewd comments, looking at her like she's their next meal.

It pisses me off, but I stare her down, drinking in her pain and humiliation.

I lied to her when I said it wouldn't change anything.

This changes everything. I'm done ignoring her.

SIX

MAISY

It took the entire ride over, plus one of Thea's magical soul-restoring hugs and her beaming smile before I was able to shake off the dark cloud of what happened at the tree. At least enough to resemble a well-adjusted, functioning person who isn't wrapped up in berating myself for falling for another one of Fox's tricks.

The look on his face...

Do you seriously think I'm going to kiss you?

Ugh, he needs to stop living rent free in my mind. Shoving him from my thoughts and locking the last hour away behind a mental wall of concrete, I shift my focus to painting this mural with my best friend.

Stevie Nicks' soothing voice serenades us from my phone as we work. I hum along to the melody of *Dreams* and laugh when Thea pauses her section of the mural to dance with her arms overhead, swinging her auburn curls around as she's feeling herself, no longer afraid to show off her curves. Minute by minute, I'm beginning to feel more normal, chilled out by hanging with Thea. I realize as I guide my paintbrush along the celestial mural design outline that I've been carrying so much negative energy in my heart ever since this situation with Fox escalated. It has me missing last spring, when Thea and I went to the yoga studio every weekend with baby goats.

Fox's dark shadow has infected the bright light in my life, shrouding me with his damn grudge.

"Yoga this weekend?" I suggest, rubbing the smooth piece of quartz in my brass bangle. I need something positive in my life to reset myself. A fresh nightly meditation plan is already forming in my head. I will get back to a zen headspace where Fox can't infect my bubble of happiness. "I've been slacking and your girl needs some serious best friend time."

Thea lights up. "Yes! I've missed going with all the stuff on my plate to get the bakery ready to open."

Her energy is so great right now. It's clear to see how happy she is, and that makes me glad for her. She deserves to glow like a goddess.

Smirking, I tip my head to the side. "Sure it's not because you get railed on the reg by that good D?"

Thea whips toward me, her cheeks pink as she fiddles with the engagement ring Connor gave her six months ago. The guy bought her a building because he wanted to support her goals, like what an incredible proposal. "*Maise.* Jesus."

I fall back out of my position on the floor, cracking up. I'm the most myself around her. It always surprises people who expect me to be quiet and prudish, but I'm not like that at all. Not the real me, anyway.

"You know I fully support your wild sex life. It's self-care. I just like living vicariously through you since it's just me and Righty." I wave my hand and waggle my brows when she releases a tiny shriek. "Well, and Sir Good Vibes."

"I still can't believe you named your vibrator that." She shakes her head in amusement. "You're so weird. I love it."

"Love you back, goob." I blow her a kiss. "Where's your man?"

"He's building me a desk in the office. There's still the city inspection, and the oven delivery got moved back, and, oh my gosh, the applications. I need to get those up, but I keep forgetting." She gets that overwhelmed look once her ramble ends, the one that happens when she takes on too much. She blows out a breath, lifting a stray curl from her face. "How am I ever going to open this bakery on time?"

All she's ever dreamed of is opening this place.

"Say the word, girl. My offer still stands—we can run away together and live our best life in Venice Beach. A shitty one bedroom apartment and the ocean, that's all we need."

I'm only half-teasing. The other half is kind of serious.

"That was always your wish." Thea purses her lips to the side. "You'll get to go on your road trip." She comes over and hugs me from behind. "They can't take it away from you, or any of your other dreams. You're going to do everything you want to with your life, and the choice is *yours*, not theirs. Don't forget that."

My breath catches and I latch onto her arms as she gives me a squeeze. Once again the truth of the words spray painted on my locker hit me.

Damn, she's too good at reading me. We've always had a strong connection, ever since I first found her bawling her eyes out on a hiking trail in the woods at the summer camp we met at. She was lost and I helped her find her way back to the campground. We've been inseparable friends ever since, from middle school onward. I can't imagine my life without her friendship.

"Thanks, dude," I mumble.

"Anytime." She holds up her pinkie and I lock mine with it. "No matter how much I'd love to go to California with you,

Ridgeview is my home. But I'm always down for a visit if that's where you go."

A heavy sigh leaves me. I play with the braided leather bracelet, touching the stones. "Yeah. You're right."

It's not just that I have this untamed need deep inside to leave at the drop of a hat, or even that I actually want to run from my problems. It's that the choice isn't mine, and that's what I crave when I fantasize about pulling onto the interstate and following it as far as it'll take me.

"That reminds me! I found a neat thing for you on Pinterest last night. I meant to text it." Thea grabs her phone and shows me a pin she saved on must-see cross-country road trip spots and tips for routes to take to make the most of the trip. "See? With this you can hit more places."

"Thanks, girl. This is good."

I haven't gotten that far, but Thea is more of a planner. All I know is I want to go. It's this hungry need that tugs at the inside of my chest whenever the wind moves my hair and I see a bird taking flight.

"Have you brought it up again to your parents?"

Shaking my head, I stare into my paint tray. "Not yet. Not since last time."

If I can't convince them to give me permission, I'm going after graduation. They can't stop me. No one can.

"It'll work out." She claps her hands. "Think good thoughts!"

My mouth quirks into a soft smile. "You're the best."

We get lost in painting again, singing along to the rest of the Fleetwood Mac playlist.

"Are you okay?" Thea asks after a comfortable silence.

"I—yeah," I push out, hoping she can't hear the strain in my voice. We both know each other too well to easily hide our emotions. Last year it was her hiding from me, but now the tables have turned. I think I'm starting to get why she kept quiet about her drama for so long. "Why wouldn't I be?"

She turns her big blue eyes on me and my heart leaps into my throat. Crap. She totally sees through me.

Reaching out, Thea takes my hand. "Are you sure? I don't want to push you, but it seems like there's a lot weighing you down. I've never seen you like this. I know your parents can be a lot to deal with, but you've been so quiet lately. Like your light's gone out."

My throat tightens. "It's nothing."

I force out a laugh and wince at how brittle it sounds, grating on my ears. It seems stupid to moan about rumors and someone spray painting my locker, so I haven't brought it up. Then there's all the stuff with Fox. When did my life get so complicated?

"You don't have to worry about me. There's a lot on your plate."

She frowns, squeezing my hand. "Full plate or not, you're my best friend. You can talk to me about anything. My therapist encourages me to picture pouring water out of a jug when I'm having trouble talking about my problems. We start with little things, and then it gets easier. I always feel a lot better after I've let it out instead of holding it all in like I used to, when..."

Thea trails off, but she doesn't have to finish. I know how hard last year was for her. It's behind us now and no one can hurt her anymore. She's shining brighter without the darkness that crept into her life.

Releasing a sigh, I shake my head. "It's not a big deal. Not yet, anyway." Just way too complicated to untangle. "I promise, or I'd already be spilling my guts about it. I'm just looking forward to graduating so I can get on with my life, you know?"

She nods. "Okay. Does this call for cupcakes?"

"My favorite kind?" I add hopefully. "And face masks when we're done with painting."

"Of course. I'll bake it all better after we finish this."

As Thea picks up her paintbrush again, I make a silent vow to tell her once I figure this out for myself. I fill in the sun and moon that make up the logo while she works on the Eclipsed Tarts lettering.

The song changes to *The Chain* and Connor dances his way into the room on the chorus, shoulders dropping to the drum beats as he lip syncs the lyrics into a hammer. His antics make us laugh.

"Your new office is officially sexy," he announces with a charming lopsided grin, winking at Thea. He shoots me a nod. "'Sup, little Landry."

I flip him off. "What did I say about calling me that? Dude, I will kick your ass, no hesitation."

Connor is as cocky as ever, the star ex-soccer captain of Silver Lake High with floppy hair and intelligent gray eyes. At first I thought he was an asshole with a bad reputation, too full of his own swagger who was going to break my girl's heart, but he turned out to be the perfect guy for my best friend.

His grin stretches and he gestures to my crystal bracelet as he sets down the hammer on the counter. "What happened to all that peace and love zen hippie shit?"

A smile threatens to break free, but I keep my expression serious to sell our usual song and dance. "I'll make an exception for you."

"Won't you two ever learn to play nice?" Thea asks fondly. "You're my two favorite people in the world."

"We just like to tease, sunshine." Connor draws her close for a kiss that makes her melt in his arms. He pulls back and smirks at the expression on her face. "She's family. A little ball busting is healthy."

He means it, too. Their group of friends that has absorbed me as a package deal with Thea consider themselves a family, one they chose. The guys can be somewhat intimidating with how intense they all are, but deep down they're good. They each love their partners and they're fiercely protective—that's good enough in my book to vibe with them.

"Oh, Dev got back to me in the group chat." He shows Thea his phone. "His summer break from college starts next Friday, but Oakridge College doesn't break until a few days after. He's going to wait until Blair, Gemma, and Lucas are done, then they'll all drive back to town together."

Out of all their friends, Thea and Connor both opted out of college. They don't need it when Thea's been baking her whole life and Connor is a loaded savvy computer nerd. The dude made bank because of a security app he created.

"Sounds good. Fam picnic in our favorite spot once they're all back?" Thea suggests.

"You know it, baby."

Connor steals another kiss while I grab my phone to change out the playlist. A text notification pops up at the top of the screen, sinking my stomach. Mom. My allotted amount of freedom is up for the day.

Mom: You have 15 minutes to get home before I have your father trace your location and pick you up.

"Shit," I say under my breath. It grates on my nerves the way she summons me. I can feel the damn bars of my cage slamming down. "I've gotta go. Sorry, girl. I'll see if I can come back tomorrow so we can finish painting, okay?"

Thea gives me an understanding look and I shrug. She knows my parents are overbearing. One of the reasons we bonded so easily as friends was because we both could commiserate over nosy mothers. She's managed to make peace with her mom, but I don't see that in my future. Not with how mine treats me like a doll—something to look at, a pretty prop to keep her reputation shining, but back on the shelf I go when I don't meet her expectations.

I hug Thea goodbye and fist bump Connor before heading out.

Lately it seems like it's more often than not she exerts control over me. At least last year I was allowed a longer leash.

Then again, that was before my parents knew Fox was back in town. Now I can't breathe without them needing to know about it.

*   *   *

The door slams behind me and I tense as it reverberates off the cream marble floors and the high ceiling of the foyer. Crap, I didn't mean to do that. I'm wound too tightly, annoyed at being called home before I was ready like I'm a damn child.

"Is that you?" Mom's voice drifts from the kitchen, where the savory scent of cooking fills the first floor.

"Yeah." Swallowing back what I really want to say, I add, "Sorry I cut it close. We were still painting."

Reluctantly, I go into the kitchen and take a seat at the large island in the middle with the same marble as the foyer. Mom was obsessed with making our new house look like it could be a palace from Greek mythology compared to our old one. It was nicer in my opinion since it actually fit us, unlike this oversized, too fancy monstrosity with a ridiculously over the top security system. It always feels cold and empty, no matter how many fruit bowls and flowers she puts out.

Mom has a folder with the Nexus Lab company logo on it,

standing at the end of the island. She flicks her eyes up at me briefly. "As long as you're not late. You need time to study."

My gaze cuts to our cook, who is preparing dinner. Lana doesn't pause in sautéing vegetables, familiar with these lectures she gets a front row seat to. Mom pays her three times the going rate for an in-home chef and made her sign an iron-clad NDA to keep her mouth shut about whatever she over-hears in the house.

It's yet another thing that changed when my parents got promotions. We used to cook meals together. Holden and I had a running contest to see who could catch the most food in our mouth when Dad would flick us a piece. We became obsessed with the game after a night out at a Hibachi restaurant. We haven't done that in years.

"I already have my acceptance letter to Northwestern," I say on autopilot, like I have ever since the thick envelope arrived a few months ago.

The words taste like ash on my tongue.

If I actually cared about going there, I imagine it would be really exciting to have an early acceptance. Impressing a college I don't give a damn about leaves me feeling empty. I can almost smell the salty ocean air and feel the warm sand—my imaginary happy place filling me with the kind of joy I should feel about college.

Mom turns a page of the report in front of her, releasing a quiet, unimpressed sound of acknowledgement.

I curl my fingers into my palms, concentrating on my breathing. "Isn't that what matters?"

"Of course. But so does finishing what you start. Are your latest grades in my inbox?"

The line of tension in my shoulders winds tighter. I stare at Lana's prim white chef uniform and focus on the snaps and sizzles of the vegetables in her pan. "Yup. I forwarded it when the student portal updated this morning."

"And you're still on track for Valedictorian?"

"Yes."

Not that I care. Finishing my senior year at the top of the class doesn't really matter to me. What I really want is freedom to explore this world, to go on an adventure where I don't know what awaits me next.

Mom turns another page. She looks the same as always. Her sleek light brown hair that Holden and I get ours from is cut in a fashionable bob, her lips painted red, and her pantsuit pressed to perfection. Even though she never changed her style, something about that summer ten years ago took away my loving parent and replaced her with this woman who hits me with one expectation after another.

I used to be free to run around untethered and untamed, discovering the world around me without a worry of the rules. Now my whims are silenced and if I don't think first before acting, I get an earful while I'm stuck in this gilded cage of a house.

LIAR. The inescapable words from my locker are burned into my brain.

Reputation. Respect. That's all that matters to her now, and Dad's gone along with it ever since he became chief of police.

If they get wind of the rumors and everything else happening at school, Mom will blame me. I don't want to know what else she can take away from me then, so I'm doing everything to make sure she doesn't find out.

"How long until dinner?" I ask.

"Twenty minutes," Lana answers.

"Great. I'm going to change out of my uniform."

"Tell your brother to come down for dinner," Mom says.

I can't escape the room fast enough, hugging myself as I jog upstairs to the landing above the foyer that leads to the bedrooms. At the third door, I knock loud enough to be heard over the thudding base beat vibrating Holden's door.

"What?" he shouts over the music.

"Dinner in twenty. You're cordially invited."

More like our presence is required or else.

"Whatever."

Holden's been in a pissy mood ever since his football scholarship was rescinded over the summer. He was all ready to fly the nest as fast as he could—something I don't blame him for—but his dream was crushed.

Part of me is relieved he's still here so I don't have to face Mom and Dad alone, but then guilt swarms in my stomach. Playing football at Ohio State was a big deal to him. I'm no stranger to desires being so close, and yet just out of reach when they're yanked away.

Now he's at Ridgeview Community College, the only school he could enroll at on such short notice. It's not a bad school, but for most graduates of Silver Lake High School it's a different world than a prep school that educates future politicians and lawyers. Power, that's what comes out of Silver Lake High.

I open my mouth to ask if he wants to do something this week after school, but his music turns up, drowning out the world. Leaving my brother alone to brood, I continue down the hall to my bedroom.

Once I'm inside, I lean against the door. This is the only spot in the whole house that feels like me. It's bright and airy, with a macrame wall hanging on a piece of driftwood over my bed. Above it on the ceiling, there's an old roadmap I tacked up there. I light the incense on my desk and breathe in the floral-infused scent. On a shelf above it, my crystal collection is lined up. A jar sits at the end of the shelf full of rocks, agates, and small geodes. They're all ones I found with Holden and Fox years ago. I've kept them all, including the ones I made into a bracelet.

I touch the old braided leather on my wrist, running my fingertips over the stones in the jewelry.

Heaving a big sigh, I peel out of my school uniform, dropping the blazer in a heap on the floor, followed by my skirt and blouse. I run my fingers through my hair, gathering it up into a messy bun.

Swapping out the lacy bralette and panty set I wore to school for a simple green strappy sports bra, I skip underwear and slip on a pair of gray flowy yoga pants with a slit in the legs that cinches with a cuff at the ankles. This is how I'm most comfortable and it's already working to relax me. I put on a meditation playlist, roll out my mat, and lose myself to a quick flow of stretches that ease the tension in my body from this afternoon.

As I breathe deeply and arch into a low lunge, my mind drifts where I don't want it to when I look at the old bracelet on my wrist.

Fox.

What is it about him that I can't ignore?

Ex-friends really do make the best—or the worst—enemies.

They know how you think. They know all your secrets. They know what will hurt you the most.

Fox hasn't known me for ten years, but he still understands how to cut me deepest. Except this time he's the one pushing me down in the dirt, not the one kissing my scraped knees.

I exhale and switch positions. Even if he was fine ignoring me for so long, I don't think I could ever do the same to him.

At first all he did was ice me out throughout junior year to push me away. I thought we would make it all the way to graduation like that, but then the party happened. After that, he's been everywhere, around every corner, always watching me.

A switch flipped and I finally have his attention—just not in the way I expected.

Fuck, little daisy. You've grown up.

The memory of his deep growl against my flushed skin makes me gasp and lose my balance from tree pose. I plant my feet on the floor and cover my face against the wave of heat traveling down my spine, thighs clenching.

Belatedly, Sam pops into my head. That should speak for itself that it took me this long to think of him. Pursing my lips, I tilt my head to the side. It's not like we're officially together, but it doesn't make me feel great that I was ready to kiss someone else before the guy who wants to be my boyfriend has kissed me, even if Sam doesn't get my heart racing like Fox does.

With his hypnotizing stormy gaze, his sharp jaw, mysterious tattoos, and those muscles he steals my breath. I can't deny that I'm attracted to him. My stomach twists in excitement, a coil of desire thrumming in my blood. His hands felt so rough on my neck and I liked it. He doesn't ask for what I want, he just takes unapologetically.

Heaving a sigh, I nod. It's time to be honest with Sam. It was never going to work out with us. He was a distraction that didn't even work. I shouldn't have used him.

I grab my phone, then hesitate. "Can't text him. That's too shitty. Ugh, phone call it is. This is going to suck."

My eyes close as the phone rings. He picks up.

"Hey, beautiful. This is a surprise. Did you miss me?" The flirtatious tone makes me frown.

"Uh, hey. Listen... Man, this is awkward, but I don't want to hold out on you."

"What is it?"

"I don't think it's going to work out between us." I chew on my lip, willing him to get it. "Like dating. I just wanted to be honest with you that I wasn't feeling it."

Sam lets out a sharp laugh. *"Wow, you really know how to let a guy down easy."*

I hate the swirl of guilt.

"This is probably a bad time to tell you I had a sweet date night planned for us this weekend. I already cleared it with your dad."

I blink. That was news to me.

Ugh.

Who the hell does that?

My parents eat it up. They're obsessed with Sam. This is exactly why he doesn't fit who I am. I know I'm making the right choice by stopping this before it goes too far. We haven't even kissed, though not for lack of trying to get into my pants on his part.

Who I date can't be a decision I make based on what makes my parents happy. My heart needs to be happy.

"Yeah, sorry dude. That's totally not happening."

"You'd really sleep on all this?"

The phone vibrates and I pull it back to find a photo of his shirt pulled off and his basketball shorts sitting low. I lift a brow. Yeah, nothing. Not a flutter, not a tickle, not a swoop. He does absolutely nothing for me.

"Um, yeah I guess I am. It frees you up to find someone who will appreciate, uh...all that."

Sam laughs again. *"Damn, girl. I'm trying to keep you and you're already setting me up with someone else."*

"Look, it's not really you, it's—"

"Don't." I startle at the force in his voice and the change in his easygoing demeanor. *"Don't do that. It's cool. Can we still be friends?"*

"Yeah, of course." I smile in relief that he understands. "I'm sorry we didn't work out as something more."

"Don't be sorry. You're too pretty for that."

I have no idea what to say to that. Awkwardly, I end the call after saying goodbye and drop back onto my yoga mat. One of the many weights on my chest evaporate, letting me breathe a little easier.

Thrown off from my meditation zone, I end up drifting over to the window to open it to let in fresh air. I reach for the latch and freeze.

A painfully familiar matte black Charger is lurking at the end of the street. Unease sits in my chest as I wonder if he's watching my house now.

Isn't there anywhere I'm safe from him?

SEVEN

FOX

Watching Maisy search through her bag three times the following week for the assignment due makes me want to laugh. It's a big one, a research paper worth a percentage of the grade. She's putting on a good show of appearing calm, but I can see the gears turning in her head going from confused to frantic.

Look all you want, it's not there.

I shredded that shit, then stashed it in the shiny white Audi Q7 she drove to school today. She's in for a nasty surprise when she discovers the gift I left her. It was child's play to swipe the research paper from under her nose this morning when she was pretending to pay attention to her preppy boyfriend's recap of what he plans to pick for his fantasy football league.

The teacher, a pinch-faced older woman who always looks like she just caught a whiff of dog shit, stalks back and forth along the front row of desks. Maisy tucks her head lower as she goes through her bag for a fourth time while I stretch out in my seat beside hers, swiping a hand over my mouth to hide my amusement.

"I know I put it in here," she mumbles.

A vicious streak of satisfaction shoots through me. I'm still angry she showed up at the tree last week. Finding Holden's car parked there as I turned down the road made me furious, but when I saw her long honey-brown hair blowing in the wind I saw red. She deserves this and more.

Our teacher stops in front of Maisy's desk and raises her brows. "Are you prepared for class, Miss Landry?"

"Yes."

"Then hand in your research paper. Everyone else is prepared. You're holding us up and I don't have all day to wait for whatever excuse you're going to give me next."

A round of titters sounds through the room. Maisy's shoulders hunch at the weight of their eyes on her. She's not familiar with being under a negative spotlight from the teacher and it shows in the discomfort radiating from her.

She drags her teeth over her lip. "Right. I just...seem to have misplaced it. Maybe it's in my locker."

The teacher rolls her eyes. "Like I haven't heard that one a thousand times in forty years," she mutters, crossing her arms and leveling Maisy with an unimpressed look. "This certainly isn't behavior I expect from you. Just because you've already been accepted to colleges doesn't mean you should slack off. Your final class rank and GPA will reflect in your transcripts."

Whispers break out among the other students in the class and Maisy shifts in her chair, clearly uncomfortable. All this humiliating attention is getting to her, showing who she is behind the curtain—not the girl at the top of the class who seems perfect in every way. The corners of my mouth tip into a callous sneer.

"I know." She rifles through her things again, brow furrowed. "It was really here, I swear."

As Maisy grows flustered over her mysteriously missing

research paper, she catches my smirk while I play with a pen. Realization dawns on her face and the curve of my mouth sharpens.

"I'll print off a new copy and turn it in tomorrow," she says in quiet defeat.

You can try.

I fiddle with my phone when it vibrates with a text I've been waiting for.

Colt: Hard drive is toast, nice and crispy [GIF of a marsh-mallow roasting over a fire]

A quiet huff of triumphant humor leaves me. It catches Maisy's attention and she flashes me another accusatory look, her hazel eyes burning. There's nothing she can do but take what I dish out to her. Even if she tried to get back at me for this, the faculty wouldn't touch me. She has no way to fight what's coming to her.

It almost makes me feel bad. Almost, but not quite. Because all I see when I look at her is my childhood best friend at eight, with her eyes bright and cheeks flushed as she fucking *promised*—

My fist clenches beneath the desk. No. There's no feeling sorry for the crybaby. She made her choice and now she'll pay for it.

"It'll be marked late," the teacher says before moving on, stopping in front of me. She lifts a skeptical brow. "I suppose you think you're above the final weeks of school as well, Mr. Wilder?"

"Not at all, miss."

She blinks in surprise at my response. The teachers here have grown to expect me being a silent dick all the time, but I'm not here for them. I'm only here for her.

Eyes locked with Maisy's, I hand over my assignment—which is really her paper, reworked a little. If she does manage to remember some of what she wrote and turn her project in, she'll be flagged for plagiarism and fail. It will be another hard hit to her class ranking and a black mark on her academic record that her college will frown on.

"Well." The teacher scans the first page and nods. "At least you finally put some effort into your school work. Better late than never."

That's right, miss. Maisy Landry does good work.

Not that I give a damn about the grade—it's just taking it from her that brings me the sick satisfaction I care about. Just like I'll take everything else away.

As our teacher carries the stack of papers back to her desk, Maisy stares at me. I rake my gaze over her. She huffs and turns in her desk to face the front, probably wondering what the hell happened to her assignment.

This is all petty shit in the grand scheme of things. Compared to what I've done when I lived in Thorne Point with Colton and Wren's crew, it's nothing. But it's all according to my new plan. Maisy is a rusted chain, ready to snap. I took care of Holden first, but she's more satisfying to break, slowly chipping away piece by piece until the fake good girl crumbles before me.

And she'll know without a doubt it was me crushing her to dust.

EIGHT
MAISY

This place is descending into madness, I swear. Eyes have burned into me in all my morning classes, eager for the show when I search my bag for assignments due only to find they aren't there. I've never been unprepared for class or turned my work in late once in my life, not even in kindergarten. Missing one paper is one thing, but every piece of homework due today isn't where it should be in my bag and I'm getting really sick of the muffled laughter behind my back.

At lunch I slip out to the parking lot, avoiding the snarky whispers that follow in my wake. I hope my research paper is there. It could've slipped out of my bag in Holden's Audi and I didn't notice. *Please let that be the case.*

Turning it in late is already going to be a hit to my grade point average. I'll still be in the top five percent, but Mom only cares about me maintaining number one. It makes her look good if I'm Valedictorian when I graduate, and if I lose that spot? Goodbye road trip I've been working so hard to convince her and Dad to let me take.

When I reach the car, I open the door and immediately rear back from the smell that hits me. "Ugh! What the hell?"

It's awful, the entire interior reeks of rotting fruit and sickly sweet soda, baked for hours in the car under the hot summer sun. This has to have been like this for a while, after I got to school. Sam met me at the car this morning and talked my ear off before we turned to walk inside together. It probably happened right after.

The driver's seat is covered in trash and rotten debris. Banana peels so ripe they're black are dumped into the cup holders of the center console and apple cores spill off the seat to the floor.

Holding my nose from the awful trash-plus-heat sauna stench, I pick up one of the banana peels and drop it to the ground with a revolted jolt. It's *sticky*. I wipe my hand on my plaid uniform skirt and scrunch up my face in dismay.

On closer inspection when I prod the black interior seats, they're soaked with the soda that was dumped over this whole mess. From the seats to the wheel to the dash, everything is covered in so much soda that whoever played this prank on me must have been prepared with several bottles. And mixed in with it all is a pile of shredded paper. One corner pokes out and through the smeared print, I can make out the title of my research paper.

Now I know where it went.

Groaning under my breath, I dig around in the back seat for a bag, then hunt down extra napkins from the glove compartment, glad Holden and I grabbed burgers at our favorite place yesterday. My nose wrinkles as I swipe the trash into the bag and clean up the soda as best as I can. It will need to go through a full detail service to really take care of it. Holden's going to kill me. I'll be lucky if he ever lets me use his car again. It will leave me completely stranded and at the mercy of others who can offer me rides.

Tears well in my eyes as I dump the trash in the can at the edge of the parking lot, right next to the vending machines where the culprit most likely bought the soda. What did I do to deserve this? Nothing warrants this.

There's only one person here who hates me enough to come at me like this. After swiping angrily at my eyes, my fingers clutch the braided leather bracelet, nails scraping over the stones woven into it. Stones I love because they're special to me.

Damn Fox Wilder. He's not going to beat me. He wants me to break and cry for him, but I'm not running just because he's put a target on my back.

Trudging back up the steps, past the school sign flanked by the SLHS coyote mascot statues, I head for lunch. As soon as I walk through the door, I stall. Every eye on the room is on me and conversations lull to a stop. It's weird and disconcerting knowing an entire room full of people were probably talking about you behind your back until you happen to walk in.

At the back corner of the room, Fox sits by himself, scowling at his phone.

My smile is wobbly, but I pull it into place like armor as I walk deeper into the room. The conversations slowly begin to pick up again.

Sam isn't in my lunch period, so I usually float around from table to table. I've always been kind and polite, but never made many friends in my own grade. The people I talk to are more like acquaintances. Today that divide feels more isolating than ever.

It doesn't hit me until now, with the rumors getting worse, how much I've kept myself separated from my classmates. I have no close allies I can trust because all of my true friends graduated last year. I miss lunches in the courtyard with Thea, Connor, Blair, and Devlin.

"Hey, Maisy, right? Come here for a minute."

I pause by the table of rowdy guys. Some of them are on the soccer and football teams, some are just jock by association. The one who stopped me is a guy I recognize from Jenna's party.

"Yeah, that's me," I say, tucking my wariness behind a mask of sweetness.

His friends elbow him and they shush each other, chuckling to themselves. I want to take a step back, but I hold my ground.

"So," the guy from the party drawls. I'm pretty sure he hangs out with Sam. "You free Friday night? I heard you and Sam Blake broke up."

"I have to volunteer at the library on Friday, then I teach yoga classes until pretty late." I shrug and tilt my head. "So I'm not free, sorry."

"That's cool, later is better for me." He gives me a flirtatious once over. "I'll pick you up and we can go up to Peak Point."

My shoulders stiffen as his buddies make lewd noises. Peak Point is Ridgeview's notorious makeout spot, a lookout point in the mountains where everyone parks in the shadows to hump in their cars.

"What?" My tone is frosty, but they don't notice, too busy congratulating each other while their friend propositions me.

"Don't be shy, baby." He stares openly at my breasts. What a pig. "I want the wildcat you were at Jenna's party. The easy one, not the prude."

There's nothing I can do to stop the way my body jerks in response. These rumors are out of control.

"You've got the wrong girl," I say, crossing my arms, no longer willing to play nice. "My answer is still no."

"Don't be a cock tease, those lips are begging to suck my dick."

Fuck this.

If I wasn't doing everything to make sure my parents let me go on the road trip, I'd deck this guy. Screw peace and love, he totally deserves a fist in his face to wipe off that smug look he thinks is so sexy. With a tight smile, I turn away.

"Hey! I wasn't done talking to you!" he calls after me. "Don't ignore me, bitch!"

Glancing around the room, I'm struck by the amount of attention on me from the surrounding tables. Beyond that, Fox watches all of this go down from the corner of the room, no longer occupied on his phone. His expression turns hard once my gaze sweeps over him.

How much did he hear?

The guy's friends at his rowdy table join in, slinging names at me. *Slut. Easy. Prude. Bitch.* The chants catch on until the whole room is shouting.

Which is it, guys?

Eyes stinging, I stare back at Fox.

Take a good look. You turned me into the crybaby. Are you happy now?

Again, I clutch my wrist, covering the leather braided bracelet carrying the stones he gave me. Neither of my bracelets make me feel strong right now. The one with the stones Fox found on the beach during our vacation used to make me believe in anything. After he was gone, wearing it felt like it was my last connection to him. I'd whisper my dreams to it at night as if I was talking to him. It made me feel close to him.

A tear slips down my cheek, then another. Mean laughter echoes around me, but I keep staring at Fox. He leans back against the wall in his corner, kicking one booted foot on the bench seat. His smirk is savage.

For the first time ever, I consider ripping off the bracelet I've worn since I was a little girl and throwing it down at his feet.

NINE

FOX

By the end of the day, it hasn't gotten old. We only share a handful of classes together, when I bother to show up. But this idea is way more gratifying than I first thought.

I'm surprised she's still standing after the lunch room turned on her. It just means she can take more and it sends a sick sense of satisfaction through me.

As Maisy sits in World History, staring helplessly into her bag like it'll give her answers, I stifle a silent laugh that shakes my shoulders. Petty playground bullshit or not, this is fun. More fun than I've had in years. The more she gets worked up, the more I enjoy the show.

"Did the dog eat your homework?" I taunt, making sure she's watching as I put another paper with my name and her effort in the basket on the teacher's desk.

Maisy stiffens, darting her gaze away. After all the other students hand in their assignments while she remains seated, red as a tomato, I saunter back to my seat, this time right behind her. I'm in such a good mood, I can't resist giving the ends of her hair a tug and she whips around to glare at me.

"What is your problem?" she snaps.

The corner of my mouth lifts. It's another crack in her calm, kind facade if she's showing some spirit to bite back. She waits, but I don't have anything else to say to her. Crossing my arms over my chest until my leather jacket creaks, I lean back and give her a cool stare.

Squinting, she leans toward me over my desk, hissing under her breath through clenched teeth. "You're behind this. It's got you written all over it. I'm getting sick of these pranks."

"Behind what?"

Her mouth tightens and her knuckles turn white as she grips the back of her chair. "You stole my homework. All of it. I thought you wanted nothing to do with me?"

A girl in the next row does a double take when she realizes there's drama stirring and who it's between. We're drawing more eyes on us as the teacher writes out the schedule for the upcoming final exams on the chalkboard.

"Or maybe..." Moving too fast for her to register before I'm in her face, I grab the side of her neck and clamp down hard so she can't move. The sharp inhale she sucks in is music to my ears. "You're just making excuses because you're tired of being such a fucking goody-goody all the time."

Hushed voices sound all around us while Maisy's breathing turns harsh and strained. I tilt my head, studying her. Her eyes have gone wide and she seems on the verge of breaking. Just one more push...

"Come on, you can't keep fooling us," I croon. "It's what everyone's thinking. They all know you're a liar. It's what your locker says this week, right?"

"No!"

Maisy shoves away hard, breaking my hold on her. Her desk topples to the side with the force. The room shrinks away, my world narrowing down to the girl who broke my heart and ripped my life apart.

I shoot to my feet and grab her shoulders, digging my fingers into her blazer. "What's wrong? Does the truth hurt?"

At all the commotion, the teacher whirls around with a shout. "What the hell is going on here? We're in class!"

Shock ripples over Maisy's features. She glances around, realizing how many phones are trained on us, probably recording. Paling, she turns to the red-faced teacher. He stalks down the aisle of desks to reach us.

"Get your hands off her, Wilder. What's gotten into you, Miss Landry?"

The teacher spares me a disgruntled look, then unloads all his disappointment on the little liar in my grip. I hold on for another beat, just to prove I'm in control. He doesn't ask me again. I let her go and she shrinks back a step while I stand my ground.

"I'm sorry, Mr. Brewer." Maisy's back to her fucking simpering mask, casting her gaze at the floor demurely. It pisses me off more than usual. "I didn't mean to make a scene."

"This kind of behavior is unacceptable. Disrupting class, fighting." He shakes his head, peering between us. "School policy deems fighting on school grounds a suspendable offense. But..." His glare softens when it leaves me and lands on Maisy. "Seeing as it's the first time you've been involved in this kind of trouble, I'll let you off with detention. That goes for both of you, everyday for the next week."

Barely resisting an eye roll, I stalk from the room. The teacher calls after me, but I'm done. I make it halfway down the hall before the sound of footsteps reaches my ears. I angle my head back and find Maisy following me. My brows lift.

Cutting class? That's a first.

"You're not even going to say anything, asshole?"

She grabs my arm once she's close enough and pulls hard to yank me around. It only works because I wasn't expecting it. As soon as I plant my feet, I become an immovable wall.

Cheeks pink, she takes a step into my space. "How'd you do it?" When I don't offer up an answer, air hisses between her teeth. "My research project that took me two months to do isn't on my cloud drive anymore. At lunch I found it—" She breaks off with a disgusted sound and glares at me. "How the hell did you do it, Fox? *Why* did you do it?"

I ignore her, staring over her head. Growing more frustrated by the minute, she pushes at my chest and releases an agitated little grunt when I don't move.

"Which is it?" Maisy demands. "I just want to know so I can stop getting whiplash. Cold shoulder and ignoring me again, or all your damn focus on me to toy with me in these demented mind games?"

That catches my attention. Smirking, I crowd her against the lockers, enjoying the startled but challenging look on her face.

"You want my attention again, daisy?" It comes out as a deep, threatening rasp. "Is that what you really want?"

Her mouth sets in a firm line. "Don't call me daisy."

I grab her waist tight, shoving a knee between hers to keep her pinned in place. Her legs clench together around my thigh and she buries her teeth in her lip, holding herself as far away from me as she can. A dark chuckle rolls through me. I trace my bottom lip with my tongue as I study her face for every reaction.

"Are you sure? Because the way you're squirming on my leg suggests otherwise. You like it when I pay attention to you, even if I make it hurt." Her face flushes and I edge closer, pinning her whole body with mine. A faint sound escapes her, but she lifts her chin stubbornly. The feel of her soft chest is familiar and draws a growl from me. "People say I'm a bad boy. Shouldn't that make you want to run instead of rub your pussy on me hoping I'll get you all dirty again?"

This close, her intoxicating floral and coconut scent tempts me to repeat what happened at the party a few weeks ago. Make fresh marks on her to remind her of me long after. Fuck, as soon as I allow the memories in, I'm drowning in her all over again.

"Fox," she whispers hoarsely.

Watching her face closely, my grasp flexes on her waist and I move my leg so it connects with the apex of her thighs. Her breath catches and she shudders. She digs her fingers into my shirt and manages to shove away from me by bucking her hips and twisting out of the hold I had on her. The only reason she gets away is because I'm momentarily impressed she handled herself so well when I had her cornered against the lockers.

The door to the bathroom a few feet away slams shut once she flies through it and a bark of laughter bursts from me at how easy she is to predict. But she doesn't get to run from me. I'm not done with her yet.

Not after she looked at me with all that forbidden want in her hazel eyes.

Stalking down the hall like a nightmare come to life, I follow her into the bathroom. It's straight out of a swanky hotel instead of a high school, with wood paneled stalls and granite countertops. Nothing like the grimy public schools I was bounced through in the system before the DuPonts came along.

"You finally figured out you should run when I'm around. Too bad I wasn't finished," I say as the door shuts ominously behind me.

Maisy jumps in surprise by the row of sinks. "Dude, this is the girls' room. You can't—"

"Well isn't this a familiar scene for us."

While she's caught up, I move, herding her. It cuts off her protest. She backs up twice for every one of my long strides. The edge of my mouth curls up when I have her where I want her, trapped in the far stall.

"I go wherever the hell I want."

Maisy's throat works on a swallow. She keeps a wary eye on me as I advance on her until her back hits the wall, my chest brushing hers. I can feel the rise and fall with each of her breaths. She's not backing down still. Interesting.

"You should get out of here. It's almost the end of the period. Someone will see you."

"Yeah?" I grab her throat, enjoying the flash in her eyes. There's something dark and depraved deep inside her that likes it when I'm controlling, dominant, and demanding. "You should be trying harder to get away from me right now." Leaning in, I brush my lips against the corner of her mouth. "I dare you to scream."

She jerks against me, whipping her head to the side. She speaks to the wall. "You're so messed up."

"Only because you made me this way," I mutter as I bury my nose against her temple, inhaling her sweet floral scent.

I shouldn't want you at all...but part of me still does.

My heart thumps and I cover the ragged breath that knocks out of me by pressing into her, taking her wrists and wrestling them over her head. I hold them in one hand and put my lips to the shell of her ear as she struggles and wriggles.

"Is that fight real or fake, baby?" I nip at her lobe and plant a hand next to her hip, tracing the edge of her plaid skirt. "Funny how you aren't screaming for me to stop. So either you want me to take whatever I want from you, or..."

I trail off and her expression says it all when I peer down at her. Defiant, but underneath it there's a hunger burning in her pretty eyes. One that calls to the same insatiable lust brimming inside me, making my dick hard.

It shouldn't. This girl destroyed me once.

I let her in that night at the party and used her body because it was a good cover. A moment of weakness I allowed because hating her in person rather than from afar was its own form of agony.

Yet my cock stiffens and I'm filled with the desire to taste her mouth, to swallow those breathy sounds she makes when she's close to coming. It's the one line I haven't crossed.

"If you were really going to hurt me, you would've done it by now." She's only half confident, but she stares me down. "I'm not afraid, so do your worst."

She's right.

This time I can't blame needing extra cover. I just want to take from her.

As I stare at those full lips, drawn inch by inch to close the small gap between us, the door clangs open. I still, remembering where we are. Maisy goes rigid, eyes wide as someone turns on water at the sinks. I release her wrists and grab the back of her thighs, lifting her. She manages to muffle a squeak, dangling until she realizes what I want her to do.

A smirk tilts my mouth when she's forced to wrap her legs around my waist rather than hanging there off balance. Adjusting so I can support her more easily, I mime a finger to my lips to tell her she better be quiet. She grants me the tiniest nod and the wicked sensation spiraling through me shouldn't excite me as much as it does.

Dirty, dirty girl.

No one at this school gets to see this version—the wild child. As I skim a hand down her side and bring my mouth back to her neck, I almost laugh, giving us away. She hides the vindictive little promise breaker well. Just like she hid the hickey I gave her. I'll just have to mark her all over again. I look forward to catching hints of my secret claim on her.

I bite her neck and hold her tight to absorb the force of her response, her back arching and her thighs squeezing tighter around my waist. Shit, she likes it rough. My cock throbs in my jeans and I send up a silent prayer of thanks for uniform skirts alongside the skintight yoga pants she favors outside of school.

Licking a trail up her neck, I stop at her ear, speaking in a smoky whisper. "If they catch you right now, they'll know you're not the good girl you pretend to be. I'll ruin that pretty reputation and show them who you really are."

She rests her forehead on my shoulder, whimpering as she places her hands on my chest. Sweeping her hair aside for better access, I nibble on her pulse point. Her nails dig into me hard and I grunt, reaching down to squeeze her ass through the skirt in retaliation. I find a new spot of her throat to torture, one that makes her writhe and mash her face into the muscled juncture between my shoulder and neck. Her lips brush over my skin inside the collar of my leather jacket and I falter from sucking on her skin at how good it feels.

Damn, I'm getting caught up in this, like last time. The line is blurring further and I need to bring everything back under my control.

Distantly, I'm aware of the running water stopping and footsteps leaving the bathroom. Thank fuck.

Once the person is gone, a wicked grin settles on my face. "You managed to stay quiet enough." I pin her back to the wall and slide my fingers up her leg, beneath her skirt while grinding my erection against her ass. "You must really hate yourself as much as I do to let me do whatever I fucking want to you. Does the thought of getting caught like this make you wet?"

"If you hate me that much, then why are you hard?" Maisy

accuses, spitting like an angry viper. "That makes you a liar, too. You said this wouldn't happen again."

My grin turns lethal and I crush my chest to hers to feel her shake. "You think I can't still hate you while I fuck you? Watch me."

As she trembles, chewing on her lip, my touch travels all the way up her smooth thigh to her hip. I blink, drawing a circle with my fingertips over her skin. Her *bare* skin. She's not wearing any underwear.

A brittle laugh forces out of me and I *tsk*, moving my hand between her legs to stroke her. She's wet as hell. I bet if I looked, she'd be glistening. My mouth waters without my permission and I clench my teeth.

"What a pretty mess you are for me, daisy," I murmur.

Mortification creeps into her expression. She can't deny that no matter what I put her through, she still would beg for more if it meant I would touch her. Desperate little thing. It just makes me want to double my efforts against her.

I pinch her clit between my fingers, keeping her on a razor thin line between pleasure and pain. She gasps.

"Fox, please—"

I interrupt her strangled cry with a hard tone. "Was this for him?"

She blinks. "Who?"

"Your boyfriend. That preppy idiot you're always with."

"Sam? No." She swallows and plays with the collar of my jacket, some of the fog of arousal fading. After a moment, she shakes her head. "I just...I prefer to be like this." Her challenging gaze darts up to meet mine. "It's not for anyone but myself. I like the freedom."

My chest grows tight and I force out a breath. I wasn't expecting that, or the honesty in her soft voice. This isn't supposed to be some sweet moment between a romantic couple. We're anything but that. We're the opposite, brutal heartache and wild destruction. Ruinous and destined for tragedy.

We'll never get back what we once had. I can't trust her and she should fucking run from me, because I won't stop trying to end all her perfect happiness, even now, with my cock hard between her toned thighs and her bare pussy dripping all over my goddamn hand.

I shake my head and rub her clit, intent on making her cry out for me. "What will he say about you allowing another man's hands on you like this?"

Maisy's eyes flash. "He's not my boyfriend. He never was." My fingers move in a circle, dipping lower. She struggles to get her words out. "We were just—hanging out. I broke up with him after...after the day at our tree."

Another laugh punches out of me as I fight off the wave of possessiveness that rises. She stifles a moan while I tease her slick folds and I lean in, licking a stripe up the column of her throat.

"Whatever you say." It doesn't matter. I don't care. She's not mine anymore—maybe she never was to begin with. As I attack her skin with my teeth, my tone turns meaner. "I'm still not going to kiss you, no matter how bad you beg me. I'm going to break you apart, and then leave you here."

"Fine. If you think that's what will hurt me, you're wrong." Fire burns in her gaze and she tips her chin up. "Bend me all you want, I'm flexible. But I won't break for you."

Her nails dig into my body again, right into the ocean and crowned crow inked over my heart. She's not going to be intimidated by me. I like it, her fight reminds me to see past her mask. As long as she understands this means nothing, then she can give me as much fire as she wants.

I shift her in my arms again, setting her ass on a bar on the wall for extra support. My hand goes to her throat, holding her while I slide my fingers through her wet folds. She releases a shaky breath, spreading her legs wider.

The determined, reckless look on her face sends me right back to ten years ago. That's my Maisy sitting before me. The one who isn't bound by anyone's rules but her own.

This girl...

I rake my teeth over my lower lip and sink a finger inside her without warning. She chokes when I squeeze her throat to stop her cry.

"Look at you. Feel that? You're soaking my hand. Getting off on the danger."

I thrust my finger deeper, adding a second. Every sensation feels new and heady, making me want to chase her down this rabbit hole to the very end.

Maisy wraps one hand around the arm at her throat and the other grips my leather jacket as she arches, riding my fingers. Fuck, it's a good look on her—cheeks flushed and lids heavy, she looks hedonistic. Free. Something I can't have anymore, a girl I vowed to never want. She broke her promise, and I'm breaking mine.

The grin I give her is sharp and ruthless. "What does it say about you that you'll let someone who despises you so much I can barely breathe around you do this to you?" I twist my fingers, hooking them into a spot that makes her lips part on a silent moan, her lashes fluttering. Her pussy clenches on my fingers as I drive them deeper. "How far would you actually let me go? Are you hoping I'll rip this skirt off and fuck you with my cock next?"

"God, just—shut up and make me come, Fox," she bites out. "Fuck! Don't stop, I'm really close."

An unhinged rumble vibrates in my chest as I grind my erection against her thigh so she can feel it. She claws at me, burying her face in my neck. A sharp pain makes me jolt, sending a spark of pleasure down my spine. She bit me back. When she tenses and comes with a muffled sound of ecstasy, I stare, just as struck by it as I was that night a few weeks ago.

The satisfaction of breaking her in a new way is tinged in bitterness because this can't keep happening—I want what I taunted her with too badly. Once is a mistake, twice is a bad habit. Fucking her is the one thing I refuse to give her, even if a thousand fantasy scenarios of making her scream by driving my dick into her tight heat rush through my head.

The bell rings as I step back, taking in how shattered she is. Her pretty features are twisted in orgasmic bliss at my hands. It drives a spike of ice into my heart. I slid too far down the slope, losing the upper hand by getting too wrapped up in this game.

Panting heavily and ignoring the throb in my hard cock, I take another step back. Her eyes finally open and she peers at me through her lashes. Another burst of possessiveness rears its ugly head and I grit my teeth, stuffing it back down to smother it before it can fully form.

I swipe the back of my hand over my mouth. My voice sounds hollow when I find my words. "Everyone here calls me a black shadow. They're not wrong, Maisy. When you call a boy a monster enough times, it starts to stick. What I touch turns to ash. Now that includes you."

I hold her gaze for a beat, then back out of the stall, leaving her exactly as I warned I would.

TEN
MAISY

The past several hours have left my thoughts a chaotic mess and my heart heavy.

After the bathroom door banged shut behind Fox, what happened hit me hard. I said I didn't care, but my bravado faded as soon as he was gone. I was disappointed in myself that I could sink so low right after he bullied me. Was it really worth it? Shame slid through me as I scrambled out of the stall, splashing cold water on my cheeks. It was no use, what we'd done was written all over my open face. I couldn't hide it, or how much I enjoyed it.

This was the same as the night at the party, down to the way he left. At least this time I didn't have to walk out to a gauntlet of people who knew just by looking at me.

I've never been someone who shies away from my desires, but it's the fact I keep fucking around with him when he's tormenting me that eats at me.

Today was such a shit show.

From the stinging humiliation of not being prepared for class with no explanation for how my finished assignments were gone from my bag, to the whispers and side eye looks that dug into my back as I passed. Discovering the mess in the car followed by the cruel taunting in the lunchroom. Topped off by the bathroom when I tried to face Fox head on because I wasn't going to just let him get away with it. I was done taking his crap laying down. His tampering with my school assignments irritates me way more than what happened after, but all of it is one big pile of suck sitting on my shoulders.

It was a miracle I made it through the last class period of the day on autopilot by keeping my head down until I could escape. I went through the motions of the yoga sessions I led at the studio in the health and wellness center, glad it was a day I was allowed to use Holden's car instead of relying on someone to give me a ride. Although if I didn't drive today, his car wouldn't have been the scene of one of Fox's disgusting pranks. I stopped to have it cleaned before my first class. He'll never know.

I'm staying behind as long as I can to work out my frustrations of the day, avoiding going home where I'm sure my parents have already heard about my detention. If they find out what else I was up to on school grounds, they'll blow their lids.

The last of my seven to eight late class trickles out, leaving me alone with a wall of mirrors and an emptiness eating away at my insides. I feel so adrift, and while that normally wouldn't bother me because I thrive better on the unknown, this feels different, like a heavy weight pulling me down, keeping me in the dark murkiness where it feels like I'll never get out.

It's getting worse the closer I get to graduation. Between Fox and my parents my problems threaten to drag me so far down I'll drown.

There's no way for Fox and I to be together. Maybe I was holding my breath in the hope we could still be friends—or *more*. His old promise of *someday* is something I still think about. I never forgot it, even if he has. Knowing his touch, I've been hoping to have that promise come true even more.

"No." I scrub my hands over my face. "Not in the cards."

My old feelings for him and the fact I find him hot can't cloud my judgement of how he's treated me. It's not okay.

That can't happen again.

After today at school and last week at the tree it's even clearer.

The harsh way Fox called me desperate echoes in my head. Is that why I let it happen? Why I didn't tell him to stop and allowed him to go as far as fingering me where anyone could have found us?

But you know what? No. It was a choice I made and I have to live with the fallout. In the moment, I wanted it and I refuse to let the guilt over it all fester. I'm not going to beat myself up feeling bad about anything. That's not my style.

Annoyed that this has taken over my mind for hours, I move into a flow, continuing even when the playlist switches off. I don't need the music to lose myself in twisting my body. I keep moving as my breathing syncs with my heartbeat, pushing away the fact Fox somehow destroyed my classwork so thoroughly, then violated Holden's car with it followed by the sinfully good exhilaration of his touch paired with his cruel words making me come so hard I couldn't move.

It feels good to keep pushing my limbs, stretching and arching through the flow.

My mind doesn't empty. Did I want to be caught, or did I just want to stay in his strong arms and let him torture me with his addictive pleasure?

The heat that floods my cheeks is searing and I cover them with my palms, closing my eyes while I concentrate on breathing. When I open my eyes, the fierceness I keep tucked away in my heart is there in my reflection.

I need a way to fight back against him so he sees I'm not the liar he's accused me of being. I won't be scared of him anymore because it's getting me nowhere. I thought he was capable of hurting me, but he's had the opportunity and hasn't taken it. That has to give me the only hope I can cling to. There must be a way I can find out how to get through to him so he'll stop hating me. I twist the leather bracelet around so I can see the stones.

If I can just get close enough to figure out if there's any scrap left of the boy I knew, I'd be able to break through his wall and fix this. Fix *us*.

Centering myself, I move into a handstand split against the mirror, using it for balance as I practice perfecting my inversions. My shoulders burn as I curve my spine and spread my legs.

The lights cut out.

My heart skips a beat as I suck in a breath, trying to adjust to the darkness. I keep working. It's not the first time the custodial staff turned the lights off on me. Besides, I have a key. Yoga in the dark is nice.

I work to get my breathing back in sync, feeling the exertion in my shoulders from supporting my weight. After I focus for a minute, I notice that something feels off. The hair on the back of my neck stands on end and a shiver travels against my exposed stomach not covered by my tight crop top.

The air thickens and my pulse speeds up, along with my breathing.

A touch comes from out of the darkness, nearly startling me out of my skin. It's a barely there, familiar brush of fingers right over my center that echoes the memories from earlier. My heart stutters in my chest. I tremble, but remain frozen in position. Is my imagination going wild? There's no way he's really here right now, no way he touched me.

I swear I hear a deep chuckle in the pitch black shadows. Then the lights flicker back on. Breathing hard, I carefully force my limbs to move out of the handstand split. My shaking knees make me crumple to the floor and I lean my forehead against the mirror, my breath fogging the glass. My heart is racing when I rest a hand over it.

Did I imagine it or not? It doesn't matter.

The message is loud and clear—*I can get to you anytime I want.*

It should terrify me. So why is there a needy ache between my legs?

* * *

Braced for hell when I get home a short while later, I'm met instead with a weird phenomenon. Mom and Dad aren't mad, they're disappointed.

"So, I'm not grounded?" I stand on the steps with my yoga mat under one arm and my gym tote, ready to escape to my room. When they met me at the door, Dad spared me a quick *don't make it a habit after you've worked hard* and left me alone with Mom. "The last time I got a detention you grounded me for a month."

The last and *only* time I'd ever gotten detention. It was freshman year, earned because I wanted to nap outside beneath the sun during the lunch period, which made me late for class. It was DEFCON 5 when Mom got wind of it, so I was expecting much worse this time.

She still hasn't yelled, or done the scary calm undressing that is even more terrible. She frowns at me.

"I'm not thrilled, don't misunderstand," she explains. "You caused a scene, and that is deeply disappointing."

Tiny invisible knives prick at my skin. "Sorry. I'll go upstairs and do my homework over. It won't happen again."

"I wasn't finished, Maisy Grace." She puts a hand on the banister, lines forming around her mouth. "I can't have you involved with that boy. I know he's to blame for this, just like his rotten drunk of a father."

My throat tightens and a hot lash of anger rushes through me. How can she talk about someone she was friends with like that? Mom and Dad believe every rumor about him.

"Fox? That's what you're pissed about? Not that I was fighting or that my GPA will drop because of my missed assignments and allow someone else to take the top spot you need me to have?"

Her mouth pinches. "Those things are important, but nothing is more serious than my warning to stay away from him. I thought I made that clear. Everything we've worked for to provide paths to success for you and your brother are wasted if you let that boy infect your life."

"*That boy*, Mom? Do you even hear yourself? He was my best friend. Holden's too. *Your* friends' son." I grip the strap of my tote bag. "Holden was allowed to hang out with him without you and Dad intervening, so why do I have to avoid him? It's impossible when we have classes together, and he—"

I cut off. I can't tell her about what's been going on because I don't want more rules from her.

My parents don't like Fox. If they find out there's more going on than me slacking on homework, they'll do something to get the school to expel him. I want to be able to handle this on my terms.

"Yes, and look where that got your brother," she says shrewdly. "Drafted to play for one of the top schools in the country, but he flushed it down the toilet by associating with trash."

A disbelieving scoff rips from my throat. "Jesus, Mom. Tell me how you really feel. You can't seriously believe that a college like Ohio State really looks that deeply into their incoming students, especially the athletes they accept."

One manicured brow lifts skeptically. "You're naïve if you think otherwise. This is what I've tried to teach you. The world is always watching. What you do matters—every move you make. Do not make the same mistake as your brother."

God, Holden and I really have become pawns to her if that's all she cares about. I open my mouth to protest, but she's not finished.

"You need to do damage control to get your life back on track. You're so close to graduating, Maisy. I won't let you throw it away because of your impulsive tendencies." Her nails tap on the banister as the gears of her mind turn. "What we should do is call that sweet boy, Samuel Blake. Invite him over for dinner. Why hasn't he been around lately to take you out? Your father and I like him."

"You've got to be kidding me," I mutter low enough she doesn't hear. "I don't think that's a good idea."

"Why not? He's perfect for you. He's a handsome and intelligent young man from a wonderful and well respected family."

"Mom, I broke up with him. It wasn't going to work. He's not someone I see myself with."

I'd tell her he doesn't make my heart flutter, but I don't think she'd give a damn about things like feelings.

"You did what? When was this?"

"Last week."

She gives me a look full of displeasure that calls on my urge to leave. Not just to run upstairs, but to get out of town.

"Maisy."

How she can make my name sound so cutting, I'll never know. I smother the urge to snark back and say *Mom*.

"You are such a disappointment. Go to your room."

Forcing out a breath, I turn to face her fully. "So which is it, Mom? Am I grounded or not?"

"Go," she snaps. "We'll finish discussing this later."

My feet slam on the steps, echoing in the foyer. The weight on my chest gets heavier and heavier.

"Maise," Holden calls from his open door.

I stop. He's sitting on the floor, leaning against his bed. Five o'clock shadow covers his jaw and his brown hair is a mess, but he doesn't look as down as he's been since my senior year started and his future halted in its tracks. Must be one of his rare good days.

He motions with his head for me to come in and I do, shoulders sagging as I dump off my stuff from the yoga studio inside the door. I collapse on the floor beside him, dragging my knees up.

"Did you hear?" I almost don't want to know.

"A little. Not all of it." He motions to his headphones sitting on the floor. "Just the last part."

I hope that means he didn't hear what Mom said about him. Acid sloshes in my stomach. Holden puts a comforting arm around my shoulder and I tip my head back against his bed.

"Do you wish things were different?" I ask. "That you'd gotten to go to Ohio State, like you wanted?"

He grunts. "Yes and no. Ridgeview Community College isn't so bad."

"Even though you've been sulking about it for two semesters straight?"

He chuckles and pinches my shoulder. I punch his leg in return and he smirks at me.

"I started talking to some of the people from my classes

instead of avoiding them and I realized the other day that it's pretty freeing actually. Not having to deal with the pressure they've put on us."

God, I want that. It's like this year Mom has taken what she divided between us and put twice as much on me as her last horse in the race.

"I don't think it'll work out like that for me. They won't even let me go on my road trip."

"So take it later. Who says you have to chase everything in your life now? You've got time."

I stare at the sports paraphernalia all over his room, wondering if he believed the same. "It's not even about the trip. I just hate being smothered and never getting to do what I want. Why does my life have to be so planned out?"

Holden ruffles my hair. "Just chill."

"Easy for you to say." I rub my lips together. "Can I ask you something?"

It feels nice to have my brother back after he's shut me out most of the year, but I don't want to piss him off.

"Shoot."

"Don't be mad."

He rolls his eyes. "Spit it out."

"When Fox came back last year, why did you hang out with him?"

"Uh..." Holden blows out a breath. "I don't know. We didn't really go back to being friends, he just sort of became my shadow. The guy grew up to be a real dick."

I suck on my teeth. "So what, he made you look good for the kids you shook down for money with your bets out at the quarry?" Holden's brows fly up. "Oh, don't give me that look. I knew exactly what was going on out there. It's not a great kept secret when it hits the Silver Lake High rumor mill."

He rubs at the back of his neck. "I guess. It didn't hurt and he helped enforce the rules." His mouth tips into a lopsided grin. "Especially when your friend Thea's guy showed up. Dude could really lay them out."

I didn't care about Connor's fighting skills, I was hungry for more about Fox. This is the first time I've gotten Holden to open up about him since his return. "What was he like?"

He shrugs. "Like I said, he was a dick. Didn't talk about much—only cared about the fights, his Charger and his motorcycle."

I'm quiet for a moment. "It's the same one his dad had. Remember?"

"Yeah," he says somberly, momentarily lost to the memories of our childhood. "Listen, I know you're not going to like this, but he's different. We were kids then. He's not that same kid we knew at all. Got it? You should avoid him. I don't want him messing with you."

I almost snort, but I keep it in. Holden has missed so much while he's been brooding over his own problems. I climb to my feet and grab my stuff, pausing at the door.

"Thanks for making me feel better."

Holden gives me a jerk of his chin on my way out.

I go to my room. Plopping on my bed, I stare at the roadmap I pinned to the ceiling, mulling over strategies for how I'll get closer to Fox without him realizing what I'm doing.

First I need to figure out why he only shows up to school half the time, or where he goes when he cuts out early. As far as I know, it's random. Determination settles in my bones. Before he knows it, I'll be inside his walls and we'll hash out the negativity between us.

ELEVEN
MAISY

Sneaking out on Friday night is the best idea ever. Another day of detention after school left me restless, and annoyed that I had to serve it alone—Fox didn't show. It was straight home after that. Mom's judgmental stare was too much at dinner and I was going stir crazy in my room while the sun was still shining outside, begging me to have some fun.

Luckily, Thea is best friend goals and loves me. When I messaged her, she and Blair helped me sneak out past our security system undetected.

As we peel away from my house, I reach forward to hug Blair from the back of Thea's Mini Cooper, arms wrapping around her seat to reach her. "You guys are the best."

Blair used to stiffen at my hugs—or anyone's affectionate touch who wasn't her boyfriend's—but now she gives me a husky laugh and reaches up to squeeze my wrist. "Who doesn't love a little jailbreak. Keeps life interesting."

I laugh. From the story Devlin tells of how they ended up together, she can get down and dirty, going as far as attempting to steal his car and earning a reputation for being a smooth pickpocket.

"I'm so glad you're back from school."

"Me too," she says.

We head for downtown Ridgeview, where the guys are meeting us to see a movie. My phone is off, so there's no worry of Dad tracking me down at Mom's command. Freedom feels damn good.

"Where's Gemma?"

"Her and Lucas and his parents drove out to Denver for the weekend to see her brother," Thea says.

I remember him. Our brothers both played football together for Silver Lake High. Gemma's really cool, someone who has an energy that matches mine and killer confidence I admire. It's no wonder her boyfriend Lucas, Silver Lake's ex-football quarterback, is off the deep end in love with her.

Once we reach downtown and park, the guys meet us in front of the theater. Connor and Devlin both have eyes only for their girls as the three of us head for them arm in arm with me in the middle. The guys look like the angel and devil that might sit on your shoulder, with Connor's lighter features and charming smile and Devlin's dark everything—hair, eyes, presence. When they're together, you know trouble is going down.

As soon as we're close enough, Devlin steps forward to cup Blair's face for a deep kiss that makes me and Connor whistle at them to tease. They both flip us off without looking or breaking their kiss. Chuckling, Connor slides his hand around Thea's waist and drops a trail of fluttering kisses across her cheek to her lips, lingering with a pleased hum.

Without meaning to, the memory of Fox's lips brushing against the corner of my mouth, but never connecting springs into my head. My cheeks heat and I clear my throat.

"All right, save the making out for the movie you're only going to half watch."

"Jealous? C'mere, I'll kiss you, too," Connor teases.

Rolling my eyes, I walk ahead of my friends. "I'd rather kiss Thea. She's way cuter than you."

Connor makes a sound like he's dying, then stops partway through to make an intrigued sound.

A round of laughter sounds behind me as we go into the theater. It's not that crowded inside, most of the seats in the dim room left open. Devlin immediately pulls Blair down one of the rows with only a few seats that will end up shadowy as soon as the lights go down. She smirks as he tugs her down into his lap. Two rows ahead of that, Connor leads Thea to a seat, whispering to her to make her giggle. I go one more row in front of them to give them some space to cuddle.

The movie starts and I get sucked in. It's about halfway when someone slides into the seat beside me.

It's Sam.

"Thought that was you I saw," he says, dropping an arm across the back of my seat.

"Uh, hey," I whisper.

I try to pay attention to the movie, but wariness sets in as he inches closer. At first he grazes his fingertips over my shoulder, toying with the thin straps of my summer dress. I don't want to cause a scene, but I'm not cool with this. We broke up.

"Sam," I murmur, shifting his arm off. "What are you doing?"

His hand lands on my leg and he shoots me a crooked smirk. "Don't be like that."

"Like what, dude?" I keep quiet, but an irritation edges into my tone. His fingers tease the bottom of my dress and I smack his knuckles. "Knock it off."

"I've been thinking. We should try again." He tips his chin

down—what is that, puppy eyes? "I don't think you gave me a solid chance. We only got to go on one date before you broke it off. I can't get you out of my head."

"That sounds like a you problem. Sorry, but I'm not interested in anything more than friendship with you."

"What's wrong, baby?" Sam's voice gets harder and he leans in to mutter in my ear so no one but me can hear. "You need a party atmosphere and an audience? Aren't there enough people in here to put you in the mood?"

Stiffening, I realize he means Jenna's party. I can't believe I thought this guy was nice.

Annoyance slides right into rising anger. "You weren't there. You have no idea what you're talking about."

He scoffs, twirling a piece of my hair. "All I need are the rumors. You pretend to be all innocent, but we both know you're not. Otherwise you wouldn't have had 'easy' spray painted on your locker. Quit playing hard to get because it's not cute anymore."

Now I'm really pissed off. "Sorry, Sam. That's not how I let my *friends* talk to me. We're done."

Slamming my hands down on the armrests, I get up and stalk out of the theater. He follows and it makes me grit my teeth. I'm vaguely aware of the rest of my friends—my real ones —trailing after us. They've got my back.

"Maisy, wait—" Sam puts his hand on my arm, but he's interrupted when someone grabs him.

"I don't think so. That's enough," Devlin bites out in a dangerous undertone, reminding me why he and Connor had full control of our school when they were seniors last year.

Connor closes in on Sam's other side. He has a terrifying gleam in his gray eyes that matches Devlin's. Blair and Thea come to my side, Thea taking my hand and squeezing while Blair levels Sam with a cool stare.

"Uh, hey," Sam says, losing some of his confidence. "I don't think we've met, I'm Sam. Maisy's boyfriend. If I'd known we were doing a group thing tonight, I'd have been here earlier."

Connor snorts, but there's nothing amused about it. "Yeah, no. I was watching the whole time. You ain't shit, touching her when she said not to. That isn't gonna fly, is it Dev?"

"Fuck no."

Despite what led to this, I'm fighting back a grateful smile. These guys treat me like I'm family. Like I'm someone they want to protect. This is what family does for each other, what my real one used to feel like before everything changed.

"Thanks for the backup, guys," I say, stepping forward to stand in front of Sam. "Listen, dude. You and I aren't happening. I don't know how much clearer I can be."

He clenches his teeth, nostrils flaring. "You're taking this slut's side? She's just a cock tease."

"Yo," Blair snaps.

"Slut shaming, wow," I deadpan, blinking slowly. "Cool. So hurtful."

His words don't sting at all, but now I'm glad I broke up with him. I knew I didn't like his vibe.

"Only a coward tries to tear a woman down with derogatory terms," Thea says.

"Just calling it how it is. She can fuck around at a party, but acts too good for it from her boyfriend."

Connor whistles low. "Look at that attitude. Don't you know who we are?" Sam jerks against Devlin's tight grip and Connor grins. "Girls? Meet us down at the bakery."

Thea takes my hand again and pulls me away.

I rake my fingers through my hair. "I don't need you to fight battles for me. He's not worth wasting your time on. I can do it myself."

Devlin glances at me. "We won't break him, but there's no avoiding this lesson. Want the first punch?"

Sighing, I shake my head. There's no saving Sam from his fate after he was such a dick. My gaze meets his.

"We're done, got it? There's nothing between us. No feelings, no friendship." I put my hands on my hips. "And definitely no fucking. I don't sleep with anyone who tries to use a woman's sexuality against her."

A deep laugh leaves Devlin as he and Connor drag a struggling Sam around the corner into an alley. The girls come to my side again.

"Are you okay?" Thea asks.

"Yeah. He's just an asshole. I thought he was nice, but... Guess not."

"The nice ones are always surprise douchebags because they hide it to get their reward," Blair says. "At least when they're a bastard up front, you know what you're getting."

"Right. And he had my parents so into him."

"They should've dated him then," Thea says.

We start to walk toward her bakery a few blocks away and I tip my head back to peer at the night sky. The early summer air is warm.

"So," Thea says, pulling out the sound. "Everything's fine at school?"

With a wry smile, I squeeze her hand. "Yes, Mom. The rumor mill is always looking for something juicy to tear someone else down, but it doesn't mean anything. You know that. People like Sam can be shocked I hooked up at a party, but that was my choice."

"Who with?" Thea leans close. "You didn't tell me this."

The growl of a motorcycle coasts down the street and I almost laugh. Impeccable timing. Fox drives by and it's like my whole body feels it when he turns his head our way. The helmet is blacked out, but I feel the sweep of his gaze.

"I hooked up with Fox." My heart is in my throat. *More than once*, but I don't add that. "Fox Wilder."

"What?" Thea gasps. "Oh my god. For real?"

"Yes." The memories flicker through my mind. The rich scent of leather, woods, and the tang of oil. The peek of his tattoos. His hands on me, rough and demanding, familiar and new. "It just sort of happened."

"Called it," Blair murmurs. "That dude is always looking at you like you belong to him and him alone."

"Hah, right. He still has a grudge against me."

Blair smirks secretively. "Hate sex is a wonderful thing."

I swallow. She's not wrong.

"It won't happen again," I say, staring down the street as his bike turns the corner.

Not until I fight my way through his misplaced anger.

* * *

It figures the first detention Fox shows up for is the final one of our sentencing for fighting in class. The teacher said nothing when he followed me into the room after the final bell, hooking my curiosity. The faculty never challenge him. They let him get away with everything.

The thoughts are short lived when Fox takes the chair next to me, surrounding me with his distracting masculine scent.

All week I've sat alone for detention, but now I can't escape his gaze as it locks on me. He watches me, tracking every move of my hand as I write out an essay explaining the school policy. He doesn't do the essay and the teacher isn't paying attention to us.

We don't speak, but it feels like he's saying a lot with the way he's focused on me. If he thinks it scares me, he's wrong. I'm done letting him intimidate me. Raising my head from my essay, I lift a brow. The corner of his mouth kicks up into an arrogant smirk.

"Such a good girl," he rasps, leaning into my space. "Perfect little daisy."

He can call me whatever he wants. I refuse to let his jabs hurt anymore. At first they were a shock, but they've lost their power over me once I decided I was stronger than he thought. I'm not a crybaby—never was. Unaffected, I turn back to my task and pretend he's not even there.

But he doesn't like me ignoring him. Bullies always get frustrated when their efforts are wasted. It's how to best them. I can feel his restlessness as he shifts in the seat next to mine, brooding gaze boring holes in the side of my head.

Which is it, I want to ask. *Cold shoulder or not.* He can't have it both ways.

Without warning, he snatches my wrist, making my pen drag across the essay. I turn a scowl on him, then freeze. His attention is zeroed in on my bracelet, tracing the braided aged leather and poking the stones woven into it. The stones he found for me on the beach.

My breath stutters out of me. "What are you doing?"

This time it's his turn to ignore me. His thumb slides beneath the bracelet, tugging the material taut. My heart clenches and fear tears through me, worried he wants to take it from me or break it.

"Don't!"

Slowly, those volatile dark blue eyes lift to me and his mouth tilts into a heartless smile. "Chill. You can keep your stupid rocks."

"You don't scare me anymore," I whisper, cradling my bracelet safely out of his reach. "No matter what rumors you spread, or what nasty pranks you pull, or the degrading names you spray paint on my locker."

Fox huffs sardonically. "That's what you think."

Going back to the essay, I don't take my attention off the notebook in front of me. "Shaking in my boots."

"You will be when I'm through with you."

I turn to him and smile sweetly. "Does it involve cornering me in a bathroom again?" I bite my lip. "I don't know, that turned out pretty good for me."

His jaw clenches, accentuating how sharply chiseled his features are while his gaze drags down my body, lingering on my lips when it travels back up. "*Tch*. What is it about looking danger in the face that gets you so hot?"

"Must be those handsome eyes of yours," I sass.

He swipes his fingers over his mouth and I hide a smirk. Some of the teasing nature leaves him as he leans closer, the harsh threat clear in his tone when he murmurs, "Watch it, or the next time you're alone in the dark in your yoga studio, I won't stop at a single touch."

My lips part. Abandoning the essay, I put down my pen and turn in the chair to face him.

"So that was you. I could report you for that."

"You don't have shit on me that would stick. And even if you did, I'd make it go away. You might have powerful parents, Maisy, but I'm no good boy. I like to live in the shadows." He grasps my chin and angles my face up. "I'll do anything to get what I want."

I swallow, steeling myself to keep from shying away from the ice in his dark blue eyes. Hearing him say my name in that cold, detached way drives a spike into my heart, leaving me bleeding out all over him and the table. I thought we were making some progress, but the banter from a minute ago has disappeared.

Leaning closer, Fox's voice drops lower with a chilling promise. "Or maybe you should be more careful of the roads you take." His mouth curves without a trace of humor. "You wouldn't want to get in an accident. You could get hurt...or worse."

"Are you threatening me to scare me?" I hiss, my eyes widening.

He squeezes my chin harder, bringing his face inches from mine. A tiny inkling of fear skates down my spine, followed by a spark of excitement. My body has its wires crossed.

"If you got in an accident, you could lose everything. The good grades, your perfect life, your future. How would that feel, to have that ripped away?"

My heart beats wildly as he pulls away. For several minutes I sit there trying to get my breathing under control. The danger in his gaze is burned into my brain. I feel his stare as I gather my composure.

I still don't know why he hates me so much. I have to find out before he crosses a line he can't come back from. So far his bullying and lashing out at me have been tough, but a storm I've weathered.

My mind shies away from the thought of him actually hurting me. That's not the Fox I know. No matter what people say about him, I don't believe he'd do it.

"All right. You're free to go," the teacher finally announces.

After I gather my things, he pauses in the door before he lets us leave. "I'll expect the behavior of model Silver Lake students from now on. Especially from you, Miss Landry."

I ball my fists against the unfair bias. "Yes, sir."

"I mean it. This is not the kind of thing we expect from you, like we do—" He glances at Fox warily. "Anyway, don't allow your personal differences to bleed into your time here on campus."

Fox huffs behind me, the strong lines of his chest practically pressed against my back. If he takes another step forward, we'll be touching.

Once the teacher moves out of the way, I hurry past. Fox passes me with a grunt, striding ahead with his phone pressed to his ear. Suspicious of who he's always talking to, I try to stay close to listen, but I can't keep up and he easily loses me.

On my way out, I remember that I don't have a ride home. I take out my phone and text Thea.

Maisy: Can you give me a ride? Detention just ended, but Holden has the car today.

Thea: Sorry, babe! We're both busy.

When I try the others, they're also unavailable.

"Crap," I mumble, glancing up from my phone when I reach the parking lot.

Fox straddles his bike, helmet in his hands. He cuts his gaze to me, then looks away. He's going to strand me here, too.

As I turn to head back up the steps to the school, his voice stops me.

"Get on," he growls.

"What?"

He can't be serious. The whiplash is killing me. One minute he's threatening me, the next he's barking commands at me.

"Too scared, crybaby?"

The corners of my mouth turn down. "Like hell I am."

Not when he tries his best to intimidate me, not in the yoga studio, and not now.

Fox narrows his stormy blue gaze and holds out the helmet. "Get on the bike."

His voice brooks no argument, demanding I do as he says. To get on his motorcycle with the one person in this world who claims he hates me. I breathe out slowly and rub my lips together in consideration.

I will not be afraid of Fox Wilder.

Mind made up, I close the distance between us and accept the helmet. He stares at me for a moment once I have it on, eyes drifting down to my skirt. A throb of heat pulses between my legs. Is he remembering my secret little rebellion?

He tears his attention away while I swing a leg over the rumbling bike behind him. It's more powerful than I imagined, vibrating through my legs and making a gasp rush out of me. I think he laughs, but I'm too busy thinking about where I have to put my hands.

Fox angles his head, giving me another challenging look over his shoulders. So today is one of the days he's fine with touching? Fine. I'm not backing down. He should really get that by now. Setting my jaw, I wrap my arms tight around his waist, our bodies melded together from hip to shoulder.

It feels...right. Like that warped piece I've been missing finally found a new way to fit us together.

"When you get wet from this, try not to get it all over the leather," he drawls in a sultry tone.

"I'm wearing underwear today, you ass."

A little scream leaves me as he revs the engine and takes off like a shot. I hold on tighter, riding the buzzing thrill that zings through me. The longer we drive, the more I drop my guard, enjoying the ride.

It's exhilarating, calling to my adventurous heart. I want to reach out and coast my hand along the sharp waves the wind creates as the bike moves fast around the bends in the road, but that would mean taking my hands off Fox.

Instead of taking the road that would lead to my house

faster, he takes the side of a fork that heads higher into the mountains. I release an excited yell into the sky and feel his shoulders shake with amusement.

I'm struck by the urge to tell him about the road trip I want to take, even though he was a dick in detention. He's the one who gave me the idea in the first place, back when our families took a vacation to California together. He and I found a roadmap and plotted out the way from Colorado to the coast, coming up with all these plans for how we were going to go on adventures when we were older. We were going to do it together.

Other than Thea, he's the only one who might understand why it's important to me.

The memories of our friendship always outweigh his actions of the present, reminding me of what we once had. Of who he can be when he's not hating me.

Riding on the back of his motorcycle, I press a smile into his leather jacket and wish it could be like this always.

This is how we're supposed to be. Just like this. Free and untethered, an open road ahead of us.

* * *

The exhilaration of being on the motorcycle clinging to Fox ends abruptly once he pulls up to my house. A line of tension stiffens his back as I step off and I freeze when I find Dad and Holden watching from the front step beneath the arched stone portico.

Dad's expression shifts from surprise to something I don't understand when he looks from me to Fox.

"Thanks for not leaving me stranded," I say, handing the helmet back.

Fox doesn't answer, just studies me for a beat before revving the motorcycle and speeding off.

I don't make it in the front door before my brother and father are in front of me.

"What were you doing with him?" Dad demands.

He's always been overprotective, it's why he often goes along with Mom's strict parental decisions, but he doesn't raise his voice like that to me. Between the two of them, Dad's remained more himself than Mom, but the weird edge in his voice has my steps faltering.

"We had detention. Remember?" I make to move past them, but they both plant themselves in front of me. "He just gave me a ride home. I didn't think you were here." Lifting my brows, I glance between them. "Um, can I go inside now? Seriously, you're giving me double vision with this whole 'grr men of the house' vibe."

"Don't give me the attitude, young lady," Dad grumbles.

"My maiden virtue is perfectly intact." I make a show of bowing. Holden coughs to cover a snort while Dad's graying brows flatten. "Chill, guys. It was just a ride."

They finally move when I nudge my way past them.

"I don't want you anywhere near him," Dad says, expression stern.

He used to smile so much. I miss it. Most days I just want back the man who would laugh with us.

"I agree," Holden says. "I told you, I don't want him to hurt you."

Everyone around here is a broken record. It's like they all forgot about Fox and just believe what the town says—that he's bad news and a twisted monster, troubled like his dad. It's all bullshit.

I whip around, tired of it all. "Why, Dad? Tell me."

The cagey expression doesn't bode well, turning my

stomach into a knot. Whenever I've pressed about Fox and his family in the last year, even to bring up good memories, my parents get like this. At first I thought they were just upset—they lost their friends as much as Holden and I did—but now I'm wondering if it's something more.

Could they be hiding something?

Maybe Fox isn't the only one who won't be honest with me.

"Why," I repeat more firmly. "I'm not a kid, so stop treating me like one."

He opens his mouth, then scrubs a hand over it, shaking his head sharply. Turning his back on me, he sets our Fort Knox-worthy security system. "Just stay the hell away from him, Maisy. Pretend Fox Wilder never existed in the first place and all our lives will be better for it."

My stomach swoops as I think of everything my family doesn't know about between Fox and I.

Too late.

TWELVE

FOX

Regret filters in and out as I pull into the garage at the warehouse. Once I park the bike, my thumb finds the old ding in the chrome and I rub it.

I don't know what made me fold and give Maisy a ride. Instead of stranding her, I hesitated. Something about that stubborn expression cracking at the thought of being stranded, alone. I couldn't take it, so I gave her the ride.

Her broken promise stole my dad away and I enjoyed driving her around for an hour. The feel of her arms locked around me and the echo of her body plastered against my back lingers. The sound of her joyful yell as my bike cut through the mountain roads plays on repeat. Every minute is burned into my brain. For a short while, it was like everything was how it should be.

Feelings I've suppressed and rejected for so long unfurled in my chest, refusing to be smothered completely.

A heavy breath leaves me.

The girl I used to climb trees with loved being on my bike. And I fucking liked it.

She still wears that same damn bracelet from when we were kids. I recognized it as soon as I snagged her wrist for a better look. My skin prickles with awareness. She wears the stones as a reminder of the ocean, and I tattooed it on my skin. I remember the day I found those stones for her.

The rocks and shells we picked have piled up in our bucket. My concentration was focused on the damp sand in search of more. Holden trailed behind me, climbing a rock jutting from the sand while Maisy poked her nose close to a tide pool at the base.

"There are tiny fish," she said. "Come look, Fox."

Before I went to her, a small cluster of stones caught my eye. One was white with black lines running through it, another waas blue, almost like seaglass, and another was orange with speckles. As soon as I spotted them, Maisy filled my head. I scooped them up, dusting off the sand. They were cooler than the finds we collected in our bucket, and I knew I had to give them to her.

"Here," I said when I reached her side by the tide pool. "Found these for you."

She took them with a murmur of thanks and her eyes lit up. "These are so cool."

There was a weird warmth in my chest and I rubbed at it. When her gaze lifted to meet mine, it was like the butterflies she loved to chase in the field at the end of our block lived inside my ribs.

"I love them. Thanks, dude."

"Yeah. They made me think of you."

She held up the blue one. "This one looks like your eyes."

Holden's laugh sounded behind me. "You gave the crybaby pretty stones?" He nudged my shoulder. "Lame."

"Shut up, Holden," Maisy said.

"You're jealous," I added.

"Am not." He shoved me harder. "Whatever."

Maisy and I snickered as Holden trudged down the beach, back to the area our parents were set up. Her attention returned to the stones I gave her and her mouth stretched into a wide grin.

Again, I try to suppress the same warmth trying to unfold and take flight. The past is better left buried. She needs to let it go...and so do I.

My mouth fills with a bitter taste as conflict plagues me. I keep allowing my judgement to be clouded, holding back when I should be enacting my revenge.

It's getting harder to keep my focus around her. Maybe I never should have touched her. If I didn't know what the coconut and floral scent tasted like on her skin, didn't know how to bury my fingers in her pussy and curl to make her breath hitch I wouldn't be in these situations where my goddamn dick takes over and makes me forget to hate her.

Every time I think I know what she'll do, she turns around and does the opposite. When I corner her, she lets me have her body. I threaten her and she...*flirts* with me. It's got my head all kinds of fucked up.

What is wrong with me? Why is there a part of me considering giving it all up if I could have another minute of those moments together on the bike?

Blowing out an exhausted breath, I get off the motorcycle and plug my phone into the speaker set up on the workbench. The song blares through the sound system, filling the garage with the heavy beat of drums and guitar riffs. Colton didn't have anything new that would help me out when I checked in with him after detention. Until he gets back to me, I'm at a dead end. The urge to work with my hands to clear my head wraps around me like a vice.

First I lose myself in tuning up the Charger, my thoughts swirling endlessly. As my fingers become coated in grease from changing the oil, I try to push Maisy's tempting body out of my mind. Those addictive hazel eyes aren't going to ruin anything, not when my goal is to crush her.

The only reason I came back to Ridgeview was because I'm out for blood. Nothing will stop my rampage against this town that turned on me. Time is running out for my plans. There are only a few weeks left until graduation.

It hits me then, after I finished with the car, while I'm making a piece of scrap metal bend to my will to become whatever my hands demand it create, that I've been more affected by allowing myself to touch Maisy than I was aware. I cut those thoughts off with a grunt.

I hate Maisy and everything she represents. She chose her parents over me. She lied to me and broke the promise she swore to keep the secret I showed her. There's no way I can trust her, forgive her, or fucking have her ever again.

I told her I could hate her and fuck her, but it was so much easier to hold onto that feeling when she wasn't in front of me all the time. Before those sounds began haunting my dreams, making me want old desires I burned out of myself years ago. Before I was faced with the same stubborn determination and wild spirit that I loved in her when we were kids.

Goddamn it. I didn't try hard enough to cut my feelings for her out of my heart. I can't want her. I won't betray my family's memory.

Longing for the misty ocean air at the cove in Thorne Point winds around me. I wish I could go there now. Instead, I rub at my chest where it's tattooed as a permanent reminder. The sound of the waves crashing against the rocks on foggy mornings always helped when I couldn't run far enough from the demons in my nightmares. Wanting Maisy Landry more than I hate her and her family is the worst nightmare I've ever faced.

When working in the garage isn't doing what it usually

does to clear my head, I head upstairs and spend the next hour pushing my body until I'm drenched in sweat and panting raggedly. The smack of my fists against the punching bag becomes the only sound I'm aware of as I picture Richard and Jacqueline Landry's faces, throwing hit after hit. With a fierce growl I throw another jab.

I put my body through hell, punishing it for my mistakes. My chest burns with each breath I drag in, but I keep going, sweat droplets rolling down my flushed bare chest. Damp tendrils of dark hair hang over my forehead as I take another swing at the bag. Each brutal punch is penance, an apology to my parents' ghosts.

Levi's gruff voice becomes my conscience when my form becomes too sloppy, reminding me of the time I spent in the boxing ring with him back east. Colton's friend would be pissed if he caught me right now. The guy is like a machine, with deathly focus on honing the weapon he's crafted his body into. Not all of us hit the bag to be the terrifying demon whispered about throughout Thorne Point—the rest of us just need to shut our brains up for a while.

Dropping my head back and propping my hands on my hips, I take heaving breaths and close my eyes. I scrub a hand through my hair and flick my gaze to the coffee table, where my laptop and the efforts of my hunt for the truth lay. I can't wait for Colt.

I grab a quick shower, leaning my palms against the wall while the hot water beats over my head. My dick gets hard because I let my mind wander again and Maisy's sexy smile and those fucking yoga pants taunted me even when she's out of reach. I don't touch myself, rejecting the attraction to her.

Once I'm out, I throw on a loose pair of joggers and sit on the couch, opening the laptop. It loads to the last thing I was working on—a PDF backlog of medical journals my parents have been mentioned in or interviewed for. They praise my parents and Jacqueline Landry for the advancements their research team achieved. My brow furrows in concentration as I continue to skim through them.

The other side of the screen has my efforts to track down an incident report. It's been a dead end so far, and what Colton was able to mine from Ridgeview Police Department's server isn't promising. If I can't pin Chief Landry with the incident report, it could be another dead end. I could look into CCTV to place the Landrys there, but there's no guarantee recordings from a decade ago were kept this long. Colton's working on hacking his way past firewalls to turn up old bank statements to find out when and how much they were paid off to keep quiet. For all I know they hired a hitman to do the dirty work for them while those greedy bastards reaped all the benefits of eliminating my parents.

I've been trying to remember what my parents were working on, but those memories are blocked by grief and betrayal. All I remember is wanting to show Maisy what I found in the garage, but no matter how hard I focus I'm unable to picture what was in the hidden stash and files I showed her that day I picked a daisy for her.

Something in my gut keeps pushing me to follow this thread. The key to what got them killed has to be in these journals and in their research.

THIRTEEN

MAISY

With a few weeks left until graduation, I'm no closer to figuring Fox out. After his threats during detention before last weekend, he's backed off. It's like being back to his cold shoulder again, his walls higher than ever whenever we're in the same vicinity.

It's crazy, but I actually miss his attention, even when he's promising my downfall. I also miss riding on the back of his motorcycle. Once was enough to make me fall in love with the thrill. I want to do it again to feel that rush of freedom. It didn't hurt that it was Fox I was holding onto, or that he didn't take me home immediately.

He still knows me so well and it makes my heart pang.

Instead of hunting me, he seems to be focused on the other thing that occupies most of his time. He acts increasingly shady —which is saying something given the way people in this town call him a black shadow—taking calls in the middle of class and disappearing. The teachers do nothing to stop him. They couldn't control him if they tried.

No one controls Fox.

School lets us go early on Friday for the holiday weekend.

We have off on Monday and one thought keeps snagging in my head—a three day weekend is plenty of time for Fox to stir trouble. My curiosity buzzes with the need to know what he's been doing and where he goes. If I can find out, it might help me get past his walls to finally make him listen to me so we can work through this thing between us—his grudge and the way our bodies are drawn together by a magnetic lure full of heat.

At the end of the day, I'm absorbed in texting Connor as I head for the parking lot. He's planning another crazy surprise for my best friend.

Connor: Don't worry about the tickets. I'm taking care of everything. What matters most is that our closest crew is there. [GIF of money raining down]

A grin crosses my face as I type my response.

Maisy: Dude, she's going to love it.

He is done with waiting to marry Thea. He's taking her to Paris to elope and bringing our whole group of friends as a surprise.

The way it calls up the need for adventure in my heart has me excited to pack a bag. I'm glad Dad is wrapped up in the parade logistics for Memorial Day in a few days, so I can duck him easily. Mom will be the tricky one to evade. If I can get far enough away, she won't be able to get me before I jet out of the country. Holden better help, because I'm not missing out on this chance to experience the world. I bite my lip as a giddy squeal works up my throat.

This gives me the same heady feeling as thinking about my road trip plans. The crush of excitement is a full body experience, tingling in my fingertips to my toes as I bounce with the happiness I can't contain.

Paris. Thea's always loved it and wanted to go. I'm excited just to leave the city limits of Ridgeview. I haven't been out of town since our family vacation in California.

The sight of Fox's matte black Charger parked not far from my car makes me pause in my mini mental celebration.

Glancing back, I find him on his way down the steps to the parking lot at the base of the hill. Keys in hand, the locks on his car disengage. He doesn't see me because he's scowling at his phone intently.

It's not like him to unlock his car from so far away without doing a sweep of his surroundings. Sometimes he acts like Dad does, on high alert for any threat, always checking the exits. I thought it was a cop habit, but when he does it, he doesn't look like a cop.

Opportunity calls to me. I rub my lips together, thumbing the corners of my phone case, a photo of the California coastline printed on the back. It's always reminded me of the day Fox gave me the stones on my bracelet. Instinct flutters across my awareness, whispering for me to take a chance. Mom hates my impulsiveness, actively working to rein it in, but I shove the thought of her aside as I close the short distance to his car and open the back door before the idea fully forms.

I'm going to find out where Fox goes all the time. Instead of following him, I'll stow away.

After throwing a quick look over my shoulder to check that he hasn't noticed me, I slide into his back seat. The rich scent of leather, wood, and that faint hint of motor oil that I secretly like best surrounds me, but I don't have time to appreciate it.

There's a big canvas duffel bag, a tool box, and what I think is a small drone. It's a really weird mix of supplies to keep in a car and none of it makes sense to me, making me burn with the need to know what he's been up to. It's a little cramped and I'm thankful for my obsession with yoga to help me twist my body into a comfortable enough position on the floor behind the passenger seat. Shrugging out of my uniform blazer, I use it and the bag to cover myself in case he checks back here.

Hopefully he doesn't look, because in my impulsive rush, I didn't think about a good reason why I'd be camouflaging myself against the dark interior of his muscle car.

There's no more time to think about it when the driver's side door opens and he gets in. I hold my breath, drawn to the powerful presence he exudes.

Fox isn't someone that doubts himself. He acts and expects the world around him to fall in line to accommodate him.

As the car begins to move, I wish I'd arranged myself so I could see him. It's disorienting to be shrouded in shadows beneath my blazer and the supplies he keeps in the back seat. I have no idea where we're going. He doesn't speak or turn on the radio, like he can't bother with any distractions. I imagine his expression—his sharp, handsome features locked in permanent grim determination, square jaw set, stormy blue gaze unwavering.

Wherever we're going, I sense that Fox will get what he wants. It's a palpable feeling that fills the car and almost chokes me in my hiding spot.

I try to track where we're headed by the number of turns, but he takes so many it's hard to remember the order. I'd never be able to replicate it. Dad wouldn't be happy after all the times he's drilled me with the necessary things to do if I was ever kidnapped, but I always write off his insistence that it could happen on his overbearing parental paranoia. It seems all the times he made me practice with him when I was younger, not long after the Wilder's deaths, haven't paid off because we could be anywhere in Ridgeview and there's no way I could pinpoint our location.

Despite the complicated route he takes, we don't drive for longer than twenty minutes. The car finally comes to a stop and I hear Fox release a weary sigh. I really want to peel back my blazer and peek at him, but I smother the urge. I doubt he'd be thrilled to find me sneaking around and spying on him from his back seat.

Belatedly it occurs to me that I left Holden's Audi at school and I have no idea where Fox lives. My eyes go wide, but I'll tackle the problem of getting home without anyone—Fox or my parents—figuring out about my little adventure later.

I almost jump when a door opens. The car shifts as someone slides into the passenger seat, the back of it pressing into me slightly. Whoever it is seems small, not heavy enough to make the seat crush me between the foot well and the bench seat. I regulate my breaths, glad again for all the meditation I do to know how to find my calm place as I strain my ears to listen.

"You're late," Fox grumbles.

"Sorry." It's a woman, her soft voice trembling at the edges. She keeps shifting in the seat and I guess she's not entirely comfortable around him. "It's not easy to leave in the middle of my shift without someone noticing. I did what you said so no one followed me."

"That's not my problem."

"You don't understand. They're—my employers aren't what they seem. If they find out about this, I won't just be fired."

Familiarity tugs at me as I concentrate on their voices. Something about her voice—I recognize it.

"I know all about what they're capable of." Venomous loathing drips from Fox's voice. He's silent for a beat, then his sharp baritone is closer and I picture him crowding into her space the same way he does to me when he wants to be intimidating. "And I don't give a fuck. Not my problem."

The woman squeaks and I think she presses back against the window to get away from him. "I don't want Mrs. Landry to find out."

It's an effort not to suck in a shocked breath. Lana. The person in his car is Lana, our family's in-home chef.

What the hell? What is she doing here? Why is she talking to him?

I want to burst out of my hiding spot and demand answers, but I corral the irrational urge in favor of self preservation and listening for more information.

Nothing makes sense. I swallow, being careful to inch around to hear better while Lana sounds like she's trying to get tears under control. My fingers clench around my school skirt as I try to understand what's happening.

"Are you going to give me what I want or are you going to keep crying about it?"

Fox's patience is running out. There's movement above me —he's digging through the canvas bag. It makes a little bit of light pierce the shadows I'm hidden in. Whatever he takes out makes Lana release a low, panicked sound. My mind races to figure out what he took out of the bag. A tightness in my stomach has me picturing a gun.

"I'm not playing around," he says in a deep, detached tone. "You're going to give me what I want, or I'm going to make your life harder than what they might do to you if they found out you helped me."

"Yes—yes, okay," Lana says hoarsely.

I've never heard her like this. She's afraid. Not just of Fox, but also of my parents. What she said before echoes in my head. *If they find out about this, I won't just be fired.* What more can they do to Lana other than fire her for meeting with

Fox? The NDA they've made the household staff sign is iron-clad, but I always thought it was because Mom cares so much about our public image with her prominent position.

Unease twists my insides into knots. Whatever is going on, it's serious. Once again I'm hit with the suspicion that he isn't the only one hiding things from me.

"Good. But I'm taking a thousand off the price we agreed on because you just pissed me off."

Lana makes a distressed sound. "No, please! I—I need it all for my daughter's treatment. We don't have the insurance coverage, *please*—"

Fox growls something too low for me to make out, but it makes Lana settle down. My heart lodges in my throat. Lana has a daughter? She's never told me about her. Not that we're close, but there are some days when Mom's lecturing me that she feels like the only one who knows my secret hell. Do I even know her at all?

I miss some of their conversation while I'm lost in my swirling thoughts, but when I refocus my blood turns to ice in my veins. Lana is giving him the details to our security system. She's telling him how to get past the one thing I thought protected me from him.

"It has to be this weekend," Fox says. "I can't get around the Landry's security system, it's why I'm paying you. They'll be at the mayor's Memorial Day party, like you said. I'll do it while they're there."

Shock filters through my system. He wants to break into our house in a way that we won't be able to detect while we're at Mayor Taylor's party? We've been going to the mayor's house for his holiday weekend celebration for years, ever since Mom and Dad got their promotions. It's stuffy to be around all the rich assholes in town gathered in one place compared to when it was only my classmates for his daughter Jenna's party, but I've always gone. How am I going to go while knowing he is trying to get into the house?

Fox would really go that far to get to me? Does he have any limits?

My throat thickens and it becomes hard to breathe for a moment, my vision going fuzzy at the edges from the force of the dizziness crashing into me. I close my eyes tight and try to breathe through the bout of panic without alerting them to me hiding in the back seat. An ache sears my chest.

When I get myself under control, the car is quiet again. Lana must be gone.

With the kind of access she sold him, he could get at me anytime he wanted. My stomach knots as I brush my fingers over my leather bracelet, touching the stones. I don't have anything in my room he could possibly be shocked to uncover. Nothing he could use against me to start more rumors about me at school. None of this is connecting the dots to make a clear picture.

We're moving again. Fox takes fewer turns as he drives. I stare through the sliver of light bleeding into my hiding spot without seeing. My throat stings with the questions swarming it, needing an outlet. I want to kick his seat and scream at him, demand to know what the fuck he's planning. To let me in.

This feels bigger than his efforts to bully me. It would be crazy for him to pay our cook so he can bypass our state of the art security system. He's able to get at me more easily than that, something he's proved time and again in the last few weeks.

He said something about my parents that sits like lead in my stomach. He knows what they're capable of. The way he said it makes chills break out across my skin. Hate like I've never heard before, deep and vicious and deadly.

"Shit," Fox spits before taking a sharp turn that snaps my attention back to him.

I'm jolted by the force of it, scrambling to brace myself so I don't go flying across the floor in the back. He curses again and the tires of the Charger screech as he speeds up suddenly. We whip around another bend. I can't hide anymore. I have to know what's going on.

While he's distracted by driving, I carefully move the bag and drop my blazer, remaining crouched low out of his periphery. Trees fly by the windows in a blur and the car speeds down an incline. So we were up in the mountains, I guess. Behind us, I hear the rumble of an engine. We're being followed.

Fox seems irritated, but not about to lose his head. He doesn't have his leather jacket on, the black t-shirt stretched around his powerful biceps. For the first time, I get a sense of his tattoos. The intricate design of a wave covers most of his left upper arm and disappears beneath his sleeve. It makes my throat burn and my wrist tingle against my stone bracelet to know he has an ocean tattoo. I want to see the rest of it, to discover what those feathers I glimpsed near his neck are.

He pushes a hand through his dark hair, tousling it. I can just make out his profile, jaw clenched. A muscle tics in his cheek as he flexes his white-knuckled grip on the wheel, the veins in his forearms protruding. He darts pissed off looks at the rear view mirror and clicks his tongue.

"Pain in the ass," he grumbles.

My pulse thunders as he drives away from the tail following his car. He's skilled but we're moving terrifyingly fast, whipping around corners. It makes my nails dig into the dark interior, but I'm only partly worried. The other part of me is flooded with the thrill. Adrenaline courses through me and I have to keep reminding myself to stay low and not jump up to whoop.

I doubt he would appreciate my enthusiasm for his driving

while he's being followed, and that's not even touching the fact I'm hiding in his car.

As he's taking another turn, his body twists to check over his shoulder.

The exhilarated smile falls and my heart drops into my stomach as his eyes lock with mine.

Fuck.

Fox sees me.

The growl that sounds from him might as well be the roar of an infuriated bear. His expression twists into a violent scowl as he faces front. He says nothing and my heart pounds.

"Fox," I whisper.

He ignores me, but I catch the way his whole body tenses. The wheel creaks beneath his grip. I fall silent, limbs stiff from being in my hiding spot for too long. Watching his profile, I ease off the floor onto the back seat. He makes another displeased sound that makes my heart thud, catching my gaze in his rear view mirror. It lasts seconds before he cuts away to look at the road, but it could've been an eternity.

Now that I'm not hiding beneath it, I see what's inside the duffel bag: dark clothes, some kind of techy tracking device, and binoculars. There's a gun and my heart clenches. The mental image I conjured was right and emotions collide in a confusing swirl. The only thing missing is fear. Fox has a gun and it should scare me, but it doesn't.

Glancing behind us, I see the tail. A big black SUV speeds up, gaining on us. It doesn't have any markings or a license plate from this angle. They're getting closer and my eyes widen.

"They're going to ram the back!" I shout.

Right before it happens, Fox makes a hairpin turn down an alleyway as we reach the outskirts of the residential center of town. The SUV can't follow with the same precision Fox has in the Charger. He takes advantage, making a series of quick turns as soon as we reach the end of the alley.

We're able to lose the tail, but my heartbeat doesn't stop racing because Fox doesn't relax.

I'm not out of danger yet.

FOURTEEN

FOX

Fury rockets through me, an unruly fire in my veins that draws on every violent tendency I have. I need to punch something, but first I had to deal with the fucking tail. People are starting to take notice of my digging. I expected it at some point, but I thought it would be later, when I had more proof gathered.

It doesn't bode well that they found me so quickly, whoever they are. Security for the Landrys, maybe. Or if I'm really unlucky, they could've been cops in the chief's pocket, as dirty as he is with a goddamn license to act under the guise of the law. It's possible the cook didn't follow the route I mapped for her exactly, or she's being watched. The specifics aren't important right now. I have a bigger problem in my lap.

I throw another furious look at Maisy in my back seat through the reflection in the mirror.

"I think you finally lost them," she murmurs, craning her neck to peer out the rear window like this is an afternoon joyride.

The urge to lock my fingers around her throat and squeeze for her goddamn actions has me damn near ripping my steering wheel off in a death grip. How dare she hide out in my car. Another surge of rage thunders through me, swallowing the long-dormant feelings that have been nagging me since our detention.

My lying daisy couldn't resist sticking her nose where it doesn't belong and now I'm screwed. The plan to get in their house to go through their personal computer for their secrets is a bust. I paid off the cook for nothing, because now Maisy will warn her parents of what I was going to do. It's what she did before when she broke her promise.

I drive for several minutes in silence, leaving the center of town and heading toward the shipping district where my warehouse is. I won't take her there, but I can't do this downtown where there are witnesses.

Once I find an empty parking lot near a hiking trail, I pull in. Maisy doesn't move while I cut the engine. The energy buzzing beneath my skin becomes too much. I explode from the car, yank open the back door, and grab her, ignoring the little yelp she makes as I drag her out.

"Hey—"

"No," I bark, slamming her back against the frame of the car. "*No.*"

Maisy has gotten too comfortable. Ever since I let her on my bike and gave her a ride home, she's becoming an insolent challenge, forgetting what I've promised to do to her. I shouldn't be that surprised, since promises mean nothing to her. My lip curls. I'll make sure she doesn't forget who I really am, just like I won't forget who she is—a liar.

"I'm sorry," she says in a rush, eyes wide and hands up in a defensive gesture. I want to rip that goddamn bracelet from her slim wrist. It's as much of a liar as she is, making me want things I can't have. "I just..."

My teeth grind and I pin her with my whole body. "You

just *what*? Thought it would be cute to sneak around with me? Think again. I told you, little daisy." My fingers flex on her upper arms, digging in. "Playtime is fucking over."

She tips her chin up, her favorite defiant move. "Why do you have a gun?"

I drag in a sharp breath. She never acts like I expect her to. Every fucking time.

"I told you. The rumors about me aren't wrong. I'm dangerous."

Run. I want to scream it in her face. But if she did, I'd chase her, hold onto her with every ounce of strength. I can't let her go.

How can I hate her so much but need her within reach at the same time? Is it the echo of the deep connection we once shared, or something more that twines us together?

"What made you think you had a right to get in my car?"

Maisy frowns and squirms against my immovable body. "I'm glad I did. You've gone too far," she accuses. "You can't get to me by going through Lana. Leave her out of this and just come at me."

A hollow bark of laughter punches out of me and I shake my head. It annoys me when Maisy acts like she doesn't know anything.

"I don't need your damn cook to get to you."

"Then why did you pay her for information on the security system on my house?" Her eyes narrow. "And you shouldn't have stiffed her, either. It sounds like she really needs the money for her daughter."

Now she pretends to care about others and wants to lecture me on bribing ethics. My brain can't even process the ludicrousness of it. The version of her that's kind and caring is another lie.

"I'm not telling you that," I force out gruffly.

There's a mutinous little pinch to her mouth that snags my attention to the shape of her lips. A harsh breath leaves me as a new need pushes at my senses. It takes more effort than I want to admit to tear my gaze up, fighting back the ridiculous desire to crash my mouth over hers.

What the fuck is wrong with me? I will not kiss her. I should be shaking her lithe body and demanding she never pull a stunt like this again.

"And more importantly," she continues like I didn't side-step her question, "why were you being followed like that? If you didn't take the alley when you did, they were going to hit you."

I don't have the answers she wants. I barely have the answers I want for myself. If I did, I wouldn't give them to her. But as my head clears enough for more thoughts to slip past the anger, one blaring truth becomes inescapable. I've been reckless with my life. It's never mattered to me if this hunt ends with my death. That's how far I'm willing to go to uncover the truth for my family.

But that disregard for life doesn't extend to Maisy. For all that I hate her and her family, the thought of her death is unacceptable.

The wrongness of it clangs in a jarring blare, still echoing in my head when I met her eyes in the car.

Whoever followed us is connected to the same sick people in power that have this town in their claws. They're dangerous, capable of making murder look like an accident. They don't care who they have to get rid of. If their greed is threatened, they'll go to any length to make sure they stay on top.

No matter what I feel for her, I don't want her dead. Hate is intense, but it's a passionate emotion that is as all-consuming as love. In some ways hate is love, equal in intensity from how deep it runs.

I loved Maisy before I hated her. Maybe it never fully went away, just shifted around to become this bigger, more complicated emotion that controls my heart when I look at her.

"I don't know," I finally say. It's like I'm hearing my voice from outside my own body, reeling a bit from the possibility I'm still in love with my ex-best friend. "They definitely weren't looking for a friendly chat if they caught us."

Her throat works as she swallows. Fear mixes with the bright exhilaration lighting up her hazel eyes. Something unlocks in my chest, a crack in my fortress that allows me to see her right now, separate from her parents.

For one too long, heartbreaking moment, my head fills with flashes of worst case scenarios. The SUV driving my car off the road, taking us somewhere to detain us, or skipping all of that to put twin bullets in our heads—all of it ends with Maisy dead in my mind.

No, my mind revolts against it. A tremor runs through my hands. She can probably feel it. The thought of her broken and gone from this world is wrong. My throat closes over and I blink against the staggering wave of refusal crashing down on my head.

This never started as an *us* situation, but now that I've had the thought, it won't leave. It's messed up as hell, considering the dirt I've been looking for on her crooked parents. But it was always me and her, back then and now.

Fuck it.

Something inside me snaps and I lose control of myself. I can't hold back anymore, taken over by a single driving need to kiss her, to hold her close and erase the images in my head of what it would be like if she was gone.

My hand fists in her hair and my mouth slams over hers. She stiffens for a moment, then makes a small sound as her lips part for me. A rough, broken noise scrapes my throat as I plunge my tongue into her mouth, claiming her in a way I've always wanted to but haven't let myself.

It was a line I wasn't going to cross, but that's out the window now that I'm kissing her. I never want to fucking stop.

Maisy wrestles her hands up from the crush of my chest against her and puts one palm over my cheek as I devour her in a soul-wrecking kiss. The other buries in my hair. My heart beats hard as I try to tuck her back into it, where she used to belong. She kisses me back, writhing against me like she's trying to climb into my body—or maybe draw my darkness into herself.

We kiss until we're breathless. It's pleasure and pain, teeth and tongue, and the wild sounds we both make. It's beyond perfect.

The only thing I'm aware of is how my world rearranges. I've existed like everything is upside-down for so long, but Maisy sets it right side up again.

And it kills me, because I can't have this.

* * *

In the end, I didn't use the information I got from the Landry's cook. I couldn't risk it, unable to trust Maisy not to warn her parents or stay home from the mayor's party to catch me. After kissing her, I ripped myself away and demanded she get in the car. Stunned, she listened for once, touching her lips. I drove her back to school in silence and left her by her brother's car before peeling out of there like my tires were on fire.

The kiss has plagued me all week.

I've avoided the Silver Lake High campus, thrown myself into my search efforts, alternated between working in the garage and beating the hell out of my punching bag, and punishing my body with more reps than usual on the bench press until I collapsed into bed.

The days bleed together, but she still won't get out of my head. The only saving grace of laying low is that whoever followed me hasn't found the warehouse yet.

Sleep brings no relief, my dreams full of the kiss on repeat and more, so much fucking more that I can't have. Old dreams that used to be all I wanted—a field of wildflowers, a white veil, and her glowing smile. Last night my subconscious trapped me in the bathroom from that party last month, only this time she wore her school uniform without underwear beneath her skirt and I fell to my knees to bury my face between her legs.

This world is too cruel, ripping my parents away and showing me exactly what I've always missed in Maisy.

The same damn girl who was my best friend and the catalyst to the destruction of my world.

She didn't have to be perfect for me, but the way she fits against my body and responds to every touch calls me down to my fucking soul. I've never looked at another girl the same way I'm drawn to her. It's something I can't deny anymore—I want her. Period.

It's only because of her social media I figure out she's not even in Ridgeview. She's in Paris for the weekend according to the photo of her and her redheaded friend in front of the Eiffel Tower. Her friend is in a flowing white dress and is flashing her ring finger. The caption reads *the bestie tied the knot in the most romantic place in the world.* I've been so wrapped up in my head, unable to stop thinking about her, that I didn't even notice when she managed to skip town thanks to her friends sneaking her out. Bet her parents love that surprise, judging by the cryptic comment Holden left on her photo to enjoy the fun while it lasts.

After another brutal workout that leaves me numb, I strip

out of my basketball shorts and grab a shower. The steam shrouds me and the water pounds over my head as I brace against the wall.

This shift in awareness has left me floundering in all my plans. There's nothing else I've wanted for ten years than to see the Landrys stripped down to the bone, but now I'm hesitating. I can't. I'm not giving this up. But realizing how much I want Maisy makes this harder.

I'm still pissed at her. She still broke a promise she made. Turned her back on our friendship. For so long that broken promise cut me deep.

Then the heavy-lidded look on her face after I tore away from the searing kiss floats to the surface.

Releasing a heavy sigh of resignation, I press my forehead to the tile and thump a fist against the wall to distract myself. Damn it. I'm so fucked.

I imagine her sweet floral and coconut scent, the way her skin tastes, and I'm a goddamn pathetic goner. Reaching down, I groan as I circle my fist around my erection. My cock swells as I remember how her tongue slid against mine with no hesitation, so fucking eager. If I'd kept kissing her, I would've slipped a hand beneath her skirt—no underwear again, I hope with a thrum of excitement racing down my spine—and found her pussy wet and glistening for me. Another rough sound passes my parted lips and my breathing grows heavy as I stroke my dick.

She's not afraid of me and still runs headfirst into danger once she sets her mind to it. God, why does it make me so hard that she's still defiant and wild?

Licking my lips, my eyelids fall to half mast as I stroke myself while the heat builds low in my gut. I picture everything at once, her on her knees until they're red and raw while I fuck her face, her lithe body arched in pleasure as she rides me in the back seat of my Charger, twisting her around on her hands and knees as I take her from behind with that damn school skirt flipped up to reveal her ass begging for my palm to slap it mercilessly until she's crying out, her flushed skin tender. I want Maisy every way my fantasies paint her.

"Fuck," I bite out as I come, the orgasm rushing through me.

I stand there for a moment, watching my release swirl down the drain. My throat is thick when I swallow. The guilt is only a mild throb, unlike how it used to be in the times I've given into my weakness for her and allowed fantasies to take over. I shut off the water and get out, scrubbing my body with the towel until my skin feels raw, as if I could wipe away jerking off to thoughts of her. No matter how hard I drag the towel over myself, it doesn't work.

Maisy Landry is branded on my fucking skin and she won't be erased without a fight.

My phone rings once I'm dressed. It's late on the east coast, but Colton and the rest of the Crows keep odd hours to carry out their misdeeds. I answer as I collapse on the couch, the apartment lit only by the dim glow of my laptop screen.

"Yeah?"

"Would it kill you to say hello?" Colt snarks.

"Probably." His husky laughter sounds at my blunt tone. "What's up?"

"No dice, they didn't have plates to run."

"Shit. Figures."

"They're professional for sure. They know the tricks to avoid CCTV and mask themselves when they can't. I lost their route when I tried to track it."

My fingers ball into a fist and my lip curls. Damn it. I need to figure out who was following me so I know what I'm dealing with now that someone is aware of my presence in Ridgeview.

"You'll have to lure them out on purpose to find out who they are."

"Or I'll just keep following the money. They'll keep coming out of the shadows to protect the empires they've built for themselves on the blood of others."

Colt hums in agreement. I put the phone on speaker and set it on the coffee table next to the laptop. The browser window I left open makes me hesitate. It's Maisy's Instagram page. I scrub a hand over my mouth as anxiety digs its claws into me. It unsettles me that she made it out of town without me knowing about it.

"Did your alerts go off when Maisy flew to Paris?" I ask hoarsely, fighting back the weird feeling in my gut.

There's a long pause. *"No. She's not in Ridgeview?"*

"No. She went to Paris with her friends while they elope or some shit."

Colt barks out a laugh and mutters, *"Bishop. That suave little shit gives me a run for my money sometimes."*

Who the fuck is that? A vague memory of the cocky asshole who knew how to fight better than anyone in Holden's amateur fight ring last year tugs at the back of my mind. I wait for Colton to elaborate, but he moves on, keyboard keys clacking faintly.

"Don't worry about it. I'll know when they're back."

The unease crowding my chest doesn't go away. If people know I'm digging around to unravel the secrets of the elite and powerful in Ridgeview, they could know she was with me the other day. Even her last name won't stop the greedy bastards from making sure their pecking order remains intact. It doesn't make sense, but I have to make sure she's safe. I can't drop everything here and fly out to France, but I have the connections to make it happen.

"Listen." I rake my fingers through my damp hair. "I need another favor."

"*A favor.*"

He drags it out, tone shifting from playful to something more serious. He's going into crow mode, treating me like one of their clients instead of his foster brother. My chest tingles with awareness where the black bird is inked into my skin, perched on a skull and hidden in the design of the waves. The detached, calculating nature creeps into his chuckle when I sigh.

"Yes. I want you to use the resources at your disposal. You guys have the reach. I just want you to do what you can to make sure Maisy is watched and gets home unharmed."

"*Helping you while you're in Ridgeview for your revenge is one thing, but outside of that, what you're asking...*" Colt trails off for a moment and clicks his tongue disapprovingly. "*You know the rules, Foxy. Can't break them, even for family.*"

Annoyance flares. "Don't call me Foxy, asswipe." I tug on my hair. "Come on, Colt. I'll owe you one again."

"*You sure you want to owe me more than once?*" I can hear his smirk in his tone. "*You know the price of favors owed in Thorne Point.*"

A gruff sigh leaves me. "Yes."

There's another long pause, then Colt laughs. "*Done. Your little flower is safe with me, brother.*" A low, sinister voice filters over the line in the background. Wren Thorne, the ringleader of their group. "*I've gotta go. You know how the big guy gets when he's in a mood.*"

We share a laugh and I picture Wren's fierce scowl. He's not someone to be messed with.

The anxiety fades away at last. I end the call and stare for long minutes at her social media pictures on the computer screen. There's work to do, but I don't move.

This is insane. I don't understand why I have this urge when I still don't fucking trust her. She's a goddamn liar, just like her parents. Yet here I am, selling myself out to a group of psychos with skewed morals and a code of loyal brotherhood I know the consequences of in order to keep her safe.

Forcing out a breath, I drag both hands through my hair and stare at the industrial rafters overhead. When I turn over the idea of giving it all up, everything in me revolts. Not happening. I've spent too damn long wanting to know the truth about my parents' deaths and I'm not done yet. Her parents are behind it and they have to be brought down.

Tracing my tongue over my lower lip, I nod slowly, mind made up.

I won't stop, but...I'll do what I can to protect Maisy from afar. I'll stop focusing my efforts on taking her life apart. Separate her from my vendetta against her parents. I'll quit bullying her at school. It's all I'll allow myself.

A hollow laugh escapes me at the weight lifting from my shoulders now that I'm acknowledging this. I can't outrun it anymore, or bury myself in messing around with scrap metal and engine grease, or pretend what happens when I'm around her is something else than what it really is. What it's always been.

For every minute I've spent hating her, I hate myself a little more because I've never been able to let her go.

The truth is, I never stopped loving her.

It's existed beneath the surface all these years. I can't cut her out of the hold she's kept on my heart since we were kids. It's why her betrayal sliced me open, hurt so much worse because I love her.

This damn thing I feel for her is still real, overwhelming and impossible to smother. Even my hatred is love for her, as fucked up as that is.

After the harrowing images my brain supplied of what could've happened if I didn't lose that tail and how things would end if we were caught, I know that even if I've been willing to ruin her life, I won't let anyone else do the same. I won't be the reason she gets hurt because she's impulsive and never learned to stay out of trouble.

The instinct to protect her is bone deep, woven into my being. She's mine and no one else can have or hurt her. Only me.

It scares me that I feel so deeply for her—the good emotions and the bad.

I have to stay away from her, or the things I've bottled up beneath the hate and my grudge all these years will explode out of me. I won't be able to control myself. The attention she's been begging me for will consume her like an untamed fire.

I'm in love with Maisy, but I can't ever trust her again. If I give her my trust, it opens my heart up to feel the agonizing pain of her betrayal once again.

FIFTEEN

MAISY

Once my whirlwind adventure in Paris to watch my best friend marry the man of her dreams ends, I face my front door with a sense of dread. Three days away from home was amazing. It was the trip of a lifetime, leaving my free-spirited, travel-hungry heart full. I made memories I'll cherish forever. Yet even amidst the splendor of a foreign city, Fox and what I learned last weekend never left my mind for a second.

The frantic kiss, the car chase, his rough hands on me, and his bribe with Lana—all of it demanded my attention. Even while Thea and Connor were exchanging their vows and rings while Devlin officiated, the thoughts were there, luring my attention away from being present in the moment. I kind of hated myself for being a crappy friend during one of the most important milestones in my best friend's life. We need to sort things out between us soon, or I'll go crazy from feeling like I'm living a double life.

My lips tingle at the memory of Fox claiming my mouth. All this time I've been braced for his storm to impact me. My heart wasn't prepared for what it would feel like when we finally collided.

He refused to kiss me for weeks, despite how he relentlessly took and took from me. Something broke and shifted at last. His walls are eroding and I have to slip inside before he builds them back up stronger than ever.

Staring down the door to the house, I clutch my bag tighter and breathe through the strong urge to turn around and go anywhere else in the world, as long as it gets me far away from this cage. But I can't leave things unfinished with Fox.

Not after everything I've found out.

Not after that kiss gave me hope that he's not out of my reach.

I've barely gotten past the security system and through the front door before the wall of judgement and anger hits me. My parents stand in the cold foyer staring me down. Holden sits on the staircase to watch over the mother of all lectures I can feel brewing. His light brown hair stands on end like he's been running his fingers through it repeatedly. I meet Mom and Dad's gazes and my heart gives a little stutter.

They're furious.

Deep lines bracket Dad's disappointed frown and Mom is so angry she's become a statue. It's a scary habit of hers to go as still as possible while her fury rises to the surface, pouring out of her in an unavoidable tirade when it crests.

"Hey guys," I say, clutching the strap of my travel bag like a lifeline.

Silence. Absolute and impenetrable.

Oh shit.

The last time she was so mad she couldn't speak was when I went camping and showed up late to a press conference for her company's new research project without telling her. Not only did I show up late, I was still sweaty and wearing the red dust of the trail instead of the smart business casual outfit she ordered me to wear. There's nothing Mom hates more than being embarrassed by my actions.

"Maisy Grace Landry," Mom finally says when I begin to shift my weight.

It's all she offers, making my name sound like a vicious curse. Dad pinches the bridge of his nose and takes over.

"What were you thinking?"

I blink. "I was thinking my friend invited me to his surprise elopement and I wasn't missing out."

"You couldn't have waited until their actual wedding in September?" Dad grumbles.

"Of course not." I narrow my eyes. It annoys me that they've never had close, genuine friendships in the last decade. They don't understand what you do for your real friends anymore. "I can't believe you'd ask me to skip my best friend's wedding."

Dad slashes his arm down, his voice rising. "And I can't believe you'd think it's okay to go gallivanting around the world without telling anyone."

The hurt racing across my senses is blistering. I duck my head and ignore the stinging in my eyes.

"I'm eighteen," I say in a low voice. "I don't see the big deal."

"You still can't do things like this without asking permission, Maisy. I thought someone kidnapped you." His expression turns haunted and I pull a face at his paranoia. "It's unacceptable. I can't prote—"

"Your road trip is officially off the table," Mom cuts in, folding her arms. I look from Dad to her, trying to keep up with why he'd need to protect me, but the road trip steals my focus. "Your childish actions have proven you're not a responsible adult."

My chest rises and falls with each strained breath. "How?"

"Running away from home. Do you know how that makes me look?"

The force of my scoff shakes my upper body. "Are you fucking kidding me? I went out of town for the weekend. Let's not alert the damn media over a vacation."

Mom's laugh drives ice into my veins. "You left the goddamn *country*, Maisy. Don't be cute."

"Guys." Holden's expression is troubled. "You can't baby her forever. What's the problem? She's home safe. Isn't that what matters?"

My throat grows thick with emotion for my brother standing up for me. We have our squabbles, but when it comes down to it, he's got my back.

"Stay out of it, Holden," Dad snaps. "This isn't up for debate. She needs to learn."

"What—that I'm expected to never experience life, just watch it from inside this glass bubble?" My voice is scratchy and the tears are falling freely now. Swiping angrily at my cheeks, I stare at them. I gesture to the security keypad on the wall above a video screen showing a grid of the house's entry points. "What are you going to do when I have to go to college, move off campus to watch me to make sure I behave?"

"Paris was your one wild trip," Mom says with finality. "So you definitely don't need to take the road trip you wanted. You will behave as I expect you to while you live under our roof. If you don't agree, you will be escorted by a bodyguard to and from the house, and all the security codes will be changed so you can't sneak out."

Holden's brows shoot up as air wheezes from my lungs. A bodyguard? That's crazy. This is the most excessive, overprotective, controlling decree my parents have ever set.

Pissed off beyond belief and at my limit, I spit out an agreement and push past them, running upstairs to my room. If they're so eager to treat me like I'm their prisoner, that's what I'll be. For now, while I make a plan for getting exactly what I want—my freedom from their insane expectations.

* * *

In the last week before graduation, Colorado is blooming with life. Bees and butterflies float on the fresh mountain air, kissing the wildflowers in the field around me. I stretch out on the blanket and turn a smile to the sun.

Since I've been home, I've been a good little prisoner. I stick to my schedule, not a toe out of line. I wear the good girl shell that appeases my parents, acing my final exams and filling my time with studying, feeling like I've given myself a lobotomy to shut off the adventurous side of me longing to go, go, *go*. It's boring as hell, sucking my soul out to smother everything that makes me who I really am. The time I spend at the yoga studio is my only outlet for all the frustration building up.

I don't look for Fox, even though every part of me is dying to get to him before he can shut me out again. It's been too long. I'm worried I'm losing my chance with him all over again and it pricks at my emotions. I won't lose him again, not when I'm so close to getting him back. He belongs in my life, and I belong in his.

Today is usually my volunteer shift at the library, but I got someone to cover for me. Once Dad dropped me off in front of the building, I hugged and kissed him goodbye, then ducked out the back doors where my friends were waiting in an SUV to pick me up. When I confided in Thea about what happened after I got home from Paris, she made it her mission to jailbreak me, offering to let me couch surf at her apartment with Connor. I'm not about to be a third wheel to the newlyweds, though. As much as I love and appreciate her support, I want to win this battle on my own.

My parents would be livid if they found out we're having a picnic near Peak Point in the mountains in a field that overlooks town. I'm probably chancing that permanent babysitter they threatened me with, but I needed to get out in nature to recharge myself.

Thea and Blair are stretched out on either side of me on the blanket, watching Connor and Devlin kick a soccer ball nearby while Gemma and Lucas share another one, snuggled together and murmuring to each other in a snarky tone. Those two love fighting each other, and I recognize it.

I think it's how my connection to Fox has evolved. Something in my blood sings when he comes at me and I don't shy away. Instead, I take him on and ride the thrill of surprising him.

We watch the guys pass the ball to each other. When they were at Silver Lake High, they were known as a wicked duo on and off the field, and those sharp skills are still evident as Devlin pulls a move with his foot that sweeps the ball from the ground to bounce on his knee while he smirks at Connor before returning it with a midair kick.

"You showy asshole," Connor taunts with a wide grin as he goes for the ball.

"Losing your touch? That one was easy to get," Devlin snipes back with a deep laugh.

"Never."

Blair shifts around and I laugh under my breath at the look on her face. It's one that matches Thea's as Connor dribbles the ball with some fancy footwork. These two are totally into their soccer player partners while I'm just admiring the athleticism and fluidity in their movements.

My blood only races when I think about calloused hands,

scarred knuckles, and the faint scent of motor oil mixed with leather.

Tracing my lip with my tongue while my cheeks heat, I roll over onto my back and flip my crop top higher to feel the warmth of the sun on my stomach, careful not to let the bottom of my tits out. If I was alone, hell yeah I'd take advantage and go for full nip freedom, but for now I'm content like this.

A playful growl sounds to my left and when I peek from the corner of my eye, Gemma is straddling Lucas, wrestling with him. The corners of his mouth kick up before he switches their position and pins her arms overhead.

"Caught you, sweetheart," he croons, kissing a path up her neck. He nips her skin. "I'll always catch you."

"Love you, caveman." She laughs, bright and happy. It's easy to see how much they love each other.

The guys come over to the blanket. Devlin reaches us first, tucking Blair's hair back before he kisses her. Connor flops next to Thea and tugs her half on top of him, cupping her face and drawing her down to press their lips together. Watching both couples, longing hits me and I pluck at the leather bracelet I always wear. I wish I could have what they've all found, but my heart is destined to weather the storm that is Fox Wilder.

I don't care what's happened between us in the last year. We can move past it all after I fight for him.

Maybe if I can find out who would follow him and nearly run an orphaned nineteen year old off the road, I'll be able to help him. I purse my lips to the side in consideration, glancing at Connor and Thea. There used to be a rumor about his reputation as a king of blackmail around school. It's how he got Thea involved with him in the first place, because he was blackmailing her when she accidentally sent nude photos to him thinking he was a lifeguard she flirted with at the summer wellness retreat we went to.

"Hey." I sit up. "Can I ask you something?"

Connor leans up on his elbows, relaxed in his sprawl beside Thea. "'Sup?"

"Do you know anything about Fox?"

His brow lifts and he ruffles his floppy hair. "Maybe." His gaze slides to Thea, and whatever silent thing she tells him, he nods, scratching at his nose with his thumbnail. "I've got a file on him. I keep tabs on everyone in town. If they've got skeletons, I find them."

"Cool. Well, can I, like...have it?" My friends all stare at me. They've seen how he used to glare at me while they were in school with me, but I haven't told them much about what's been going on since then. "You know we used to be friends, when he lived here as a kid. The Wilders were our neighbors and close friends. I've been trying to find out what happened to him after he left Ridgeview." I swallow. "After his parents died in an accident."

"That's so sad," Gemma murmurs.

Lucas gathers her close, rubbing her arms comfortingly.

"I know," I agree.

"I'm sorry," Gemma says.

I offer her a lopsided smile, appreciative of the sympathy for the hell Fox has been through.

"Yeah." Connor hitches his shoulder. He pulls his phone from his pocket and starts typing. "I'll get it for you. What I have is thin. I was never able to dig up too much on him, and since I was—" His gaze zeroes in on Thea again, burning in its intensity "—occupied last year, it was enough for me. It's mostly old stuff from an incident report, and half of it was redacted by your dad and his work buddies when I got it from him."

My brow furrows. "What do you mean? Why would my dad give you a police report?"

"Well," he hedges. "I mean, I'm no saint, you know?"

"Connor Bishop," Thea says with a chastising bite, elbowing him.

He coughs, murmuring to her under his breath, "All right, jesus, baby. You don't have to break out the elbows. I'll tell her." Turning back to me, he presses his tongue into his cheek. "So, it's not a very well kept secret. I'm surprised you haven't heard anything."

"About what?" I push.

"The chief is known for taking bribes and looking the other way. I held that knowledge over his head to get what I needed on your punk ass biker to make sure I could keep him in line if I needed to."

My brows fly up in shock. "Um, what?"

"It's true." Devlin shrugs and turns his attention to Blair and runs the back of his knuckles over her cheek in a loving gesture. She blushes, nuzzling into his touch. "I've had to utilize it before. It's probably one of the worst kept secrets in town."

"Yeah, even my dad tells me about it," Lucas says. His father is a lawyer. "He jokes with him about it when they get together for poker nights at my parents' place on the lake."

Dad has always been a good guy to me. He's protective, but deep down he's the man who used to smile and laugh with me. How could he take bribes? My world wobbles and I twist my fingers in the blanket. I gulp as I remember once again what Fox said to Lana—that he knows what my parents are capable of.

They're definitely hiding things from me. Now I'm sure of it. That's the only thing that makes sense to explain why they've always been so strict.

"You said his name is Wilder?" Devlin asks.

"Yeah."

"I recognize it. Is he related to anyone that worked for Nexus Lab?"

"Yes. His parents and my mom worked in the same research department."

"They used to be mentioned a lot in the science journals at my parents' house. I remember reading about the articles on their drug research," he says, somberness creeping into his voice.

For the most part, Devlin is relaxed and happy, but I remember before he and Blair were together. When I'd see him in the halls at school, he seemed to carry the weight of the world on his shoulders. His name is well known in this town for his parents' famous medical clinic. I've met them once or twice when Mom has corralled Holden and I to attend events for her company. They're a cold and unfeeling couple who barely seem like they're married, let alone parents.

Blair puts a hand on his arm and whispers something to him that clears the shadows from his expression. He leans into her for support, closing his eyes.

"Can I borrow the journals?"

Devlin snorts. "Sure. They're barely ever there, so I can get them for you if you want. I doubt they'd miss them."

"Thank you."

I'll take anything I can get to find out who Fox has become and discover what he's involved in.

SIXTEEN
MAISY

By the time I'm home, the file Connor sent is waiting in my inbox. I download it from the link he sent with the password he provided and settle in to learn everything I can about Fox.

He wasn't kidding, there really isn't much to go through. But what is there makes my breath catch. I rub the stones in my bracelet.

The first thing I read is the incident report from the accident, which is littered with bold black lines hiding vital information. It's hard to believe that mere days before this horrible thing happened Fox and I were playing with Holden and making one of my happiest memories in the field by our tree.

My brow furrows. Dad's signature is on the report, but I don't remember him being on duty that night. The harder I rack my brain, the clearer it becomes. We were out for dinner, which wasn't out of the ordinary for us. It was at the hibachi restaurant Holden and I loved so much. I think...we were celebrating Mom's promotion, but it wasn't officially announced until a couple of weeks after everything happened. How could

Dad be at dinner with us, but sign off as the officer in charge of the case?

"Why don't the page numbers line up?" I murmur to myself in confusion as I realize I'm reading page 8 after page 3. "Where's the rest of it?"

It doesn't seem right for pages to be missing. For a fatal car accident, there should be a coroner report and an analysis of what remained of the car after the fire was put out. A scanned handwritten note attached to the last page declaring the crash an accident states the rest of the file is sealed and the case is closed—signed *Chief Richard Landry.* I press my lips together.

I wonder if half of what's in the report are lies given what Fox said to Lana and what my friends told me about Dad taking bribes. I want to know why most of the report is missing, some parts redacted by thick black lines. What are they hiding if it was an accident?

There's another related document from the Ridgeview Police Department in the same file releasing Fox into the state's foster care system. This is signed by Dad, too. My stomach flips unpleasantly. Dad is the one who sent him away. How could he do that to his friends' son? We could've taken him in if he didn't have any other local family.

After the first placement, it looks like there was a trail of foster homes. The dates hurt my heart. Six months. A month and a half. Three weeks. Two days. One after the other, an endless revolving door kicked him out, mixed with two short stints in a detention center, painting a bleak picture of what an unstable upbringing he experienced after he lost his parents.

A letter catches my eye from one of the shortest times spent in a home. As I read, everything blurs from the tears filling my eyes. A few lines stand out.

Fox is a danger to himself and others...can't get along with the other children...extreme grief and anger. He is a troubled

child beyond help...getting into fights...the violence is too much
to have in my home, so I unfortunately can no longer act as his
state-appointed guardian.

After that it cuts off, leaving a weird gap between when he
was fifteen and now. It's like someone wiped him clean out of
the system.

This wasn't the life Fox was supposed to have.

All of this is heartbreaking to look at. I rub my forehead as I
click through, wishing there was more and glad that there isn't
because this is already a lot to handle. My heart sits in my
throat, aching as I think of what he went through.

He was all alone. He had no siblings or other family to take
him in.

A tear streaks down my cheek. It always used to be me,
him, and Holden against the world. Holden was the brother he
never had. I was...

You're my daisy.

My chest constricts at his voice in my head, but instead of
the way it sounded when we were younger, his deep, raspy
voice whispers to me.

That was torn away when he lost his parents. Everything
he had was taken from him.

Guilt twinges in my stomach for reading this about him
without him telling me directly, but I know from where we
stand right now he'd never let me in to tell me this on his own.
He's guarded now in a way he never was before tragedy tore
through his world. I had to know this. It's one more thing I can
add to my list of apologies he's holding over my head.

With some of the answers in front of me, I finally
understand enough to fit the jagged pieces of the new Fox
into the shape of the one I used to know so well. Of course
he's angry. I get it now. Who wouldn't be when faced with
so much grief and countless people who are meant to

protect him gave up on him, labeling him troubled and dangerous?

What he told me about calling a boy a monster enough times making it stick carries a heavier, depressing weight to it now that I know.

Taking a shuddering breath, I scrub my hands over my puffy cheeks. I wish he would've opened up to me instead of shutting me out when he came back. He didn't have to be alone anymore, but I understand. He's been alone for so long that he's learned to only rely on himself. What's the point in trusting the world around you when he has so much experience of it shitting on him to prove he's the only one who can look out for himself.

I jump when my door flies open, scrambling to open the window with a yoga YouTube video I had waiting to hide what I was looking at. Mom barges in without asking and I ignore her, throwing all my focus into the instructor stretching her body at sunrise on a beach in California.

"*Deep breath in, feel that energy filling your heart chakra, and let it out,*" the instructor narrates while she moves to the next pose in the flow.

"Maisy."

Releasing a small aggravated breath at the interruption, I flick my gaze to her. "Mom."

Jailer. I keep that to myself, not wanting to give her incentive to slap me with a freaking bodyguard to babysit me.

She narrows her eyes. "Why do you look like you were crying?"

"It's nothing," I lie, reaching for another to get her off my back. "I'm on my period."

Her nostrils flare, but she accepts the cover story. I pull my hair into a ponytail, but the next words out of her mouth have me freezing partway through.

"Get ready."

"For what?"

"We're going out to dinner."

"I'm not really hungry." I don't say it's because Thea made an entire feast for the picnic earlier since I snuck out to be there.

Mom gives me a triumphant look that makes me tense. "If you cooperate, I'll reconsider the road trip."

I wait for her to elaborate more, but she turns on her heel and leaves without closing my door. A bout of irritation skitters across my patience. Nothing agitates me more than her opening my door to bug me with her commands, then leaving it open on her way out. How hard is it to just close the door like when she found it?

Whatever, more importantly I'm going to do as she says because I want to go on my road trip. I've been making plans, but everything will be so much easier if I don't have to do it behind her back.

* * *

Understanding hits me as soon as we arrive at the ritzy steak house downtown. Tonight is all about image and reputation. Probably another lesson so I don't "run away" again. This is the worst way to teach me, stirring my resentment of my parents.

Because Sam Blake is here, waiting for us in front of the restaurant in slacks and a dress shirt.

"Samuel," Dad says warmly. "Good to see you, son. We've missed you."

"Chief. Mrs. Landry, you look beautiful tonight," Sam greets, saving me for last. His voice drops lower. "Maisy."

I watch in horror as he shakes Dad's hand. Boyish dimples

appear beside his broad smile as he puts his hand at the small of my back without my permission.

I throw an accusing glare at Mom, but her expression says it all—do not make a scene.

Road trip. Road trip. Road trip.

It's worth it.

Gritting my teeth, I shove down the urge to throw Sam's hands off of me. I wish Holden didn't have a paper due for a summer class so I wasn't here alone. Actually, I wish I could've done Holden's paper for him so he could be here, because at this rate I'd much rather stay home doing homework than sit through this torture. Mom and Dad finally got what they've always wanted from me. Who knew all they had to do was trap me at a public place with a douchebag almost-boyfriend?

"Shall we?" Dad suggests, guiding Mom inside.

Sam follows suit, nudging my back. I shoot him an unimpressed look, chanting about my road trip in my head. My feet feel like lead blocks as I trudge into the restaurant.

Of course Mom picked the most upscale establishment in town to set the stage for this puppet show. The mayor and his wife are dining at their table in the prime corner booth. Lucas' parents, the Saints, are nearby. So is Connor's mom that he doesn't talk to, the city council chair. I hear she's been angling for the mayor's office if her run for senate doesn't work out.

Every prominent face of the elite and powerful in town fill the steakhouse and they don't miss Mom and Dad's arrival. Several of them wave, or stop us to say hello while we're escorted to our table by a host. This is how the upper echelon of Ridgeview works. They all rub elbows with each other and pour on the smarmy charm, trading favors and securing deals outside of their offices. It makes my stomach turn, but when I take a step back from the mayor's table, I only put myself more soundly in Sam's embrace.

As we finally take a seat, I'm directly across from Dad and everything I've read up on Fox comes rushing back. Anger sparks to life in my chest and I use the menu folio as a cover to peer at my father over the top edge without him noticing.

He's aged, but maintains the handsomeness of his younger years, making him look distinguished, like someone who belongs in his position in the police department. Like someone who should be trustworthy that upholds the integrity of the law. Instead of the warmth of when I was a little girl, his clear blue eyes have become sharp, and his mouth sets into a more natural frown these days. Now all I see is the imposing man meant to protect this town.

But how much protecting is he really doing if police reports are suspiciously missing information?

The time he and Fox's mom took the three of us to an amusement park for the day flits across my memories. He was always ready to get us to smile, whatever it took. I still don't get how the guy who used to fling tiny bites of food in our old kitchen for Holden and I to practice catching in our mouths is the same man who could put Fox in foster care. That's not the man who raised me and I don't know how to process it.

Distrust tugs at my senses as I watch Dad's tight smile while Mom asks Sam about his college plans.

"University of Illinois in Chicago? How wonderful," she praises. "Maisy has an early acceptance to Northwestern University."

"You must be proud." Sam shoots me a smirk that's supposed to be nice. I want to punch it. He drapes his arm across the back of my chair, playing with my hair. "Northwestern isn't far from where I'll be. Same city."

"It's not," Mom agrees with a calculating gleam in her eyes. "You'll be able to visit each other without having to carry on your relationship long distance."

"Relationship?" I blurt.

That wasn't on the table. I will not sit here while my parents basically set me up in an arranged situation with Sam for the sake of my road trip. Literally, fuck that. I'll go on my road trip without their permission and give them two big middle fingers as I drive west without ever looking back. Screw college, screw their life plans and expectations, screw everything.

"I'm just glad I won't have to be far from you, beautiful," Sam murmurs, taking my hand and bringing my knuckles to his mouth.

It takes a monumental effort not to curl my lip at him. I succeed—*barely*—but I can't control the way my spine snaps straight. Sam notices, his eyes narrowing slightly. Seriously, how can he sit here putting on this nice guy act for my parents after the crap he said to me?

I'm sick of it by the time our salad course is cleared. There are only so many thinly veiled comments about our future together that I can stand before I'm on the verge of screaming in the middle of the restaurant. Bet Mom would love that.

Pushing back from the table with a graceful motion instead of the hard shove I want to give, I turn to Sam. "Can I talk to you for a minute? Outside?"

The arrogance in his gaze mocks me. Asshole. He checks with my parents before answering, making me fume even more.

He waits for Dad's nod before he finally answers. "Sure thing, beautiful."

"Excuse us."

I don't wait for my parents to respond before I leave the table. My simple, but elegant dress swishes with each purposeful stride to freedom. It's a pretty shade of blue with thin straps that braid together in the back, but I wouldn't have picked it up for myself, preferring to shop vintage when I can.

My style drives Mom crazy because I'm always in what's comfortable, like my workout clothes, or my favorite second-hand finds instead of the designer labels she wants me to wear.

The summer sun is just dipping behind the Rockies when I burst out onto the terrace in front of the steak house. It's chillier than earlier, the cooler evening air prickling across my skin. I rub my arms as Sam strolls out behind me, relaxed with a crooked grin and his hands in his pockets.

"You can wipe that smug look off now," I tell him. "There's no one around to watch the show."

He purses his lips like he's considering it. "I don't think so. I'm getting what I wanted." He closes the distance between us, snagging my waist before I can step out of his reach. He traps me against his body and murmurs in my ear in a low seductive tone that makes my skin crawl. "And if you play nice, I'll give you what you want, little slut. I've as good as got your daddy's permission to fuck you, so you're not getting away this time. No friends to step in for you, so just bend over and take it, yeah?"

"Get the hell off me," I snap, stepping on his toe hard to get him to release me.

"Ow! You bitch!"

Fury burns through me, hot and blinding. He clearly didn't learn the lesson Devlin and Connor inflicted on him. Screw peace and love in his case. He hasn't changed at all.

I stab my finger into his chest. "Tonight means nothing, got it? I'm only here so I can go on my road trip before my parents trap me in the life plan they've laid out for me." I look him up and down with disgust. "And if you ever think I'd let you touch me after calling me a cocktease and slut shaming me, you're dead fucking wrong. I will never let you touch me."

"You're the one who's wrong about that. They said you were easy and like it rough." He raises his hand to hit me, spewing vile bullshit as he swings. "I'll *make* you mine and have you screaming my name so loud—"

The blow doesn't come. I didn't realize I closed my eyes when I braced for the impact because I couldn't dodge out of the way, but as I open them Fox stands between me and Sam, digging his fingers into Sam's arm hard enough it looks like he's seconds from breaking the wrist if he squeezes harder. Sam's mouth hangs open in shock because Fox seemed to materialize out of the shadows with barely any sound.

Relief and annoyance spiral through me. On one hand, this is my fight and I will handle it myself. It wasn't cool when Devlin and Connor stepped in to defend my honor at the movies, and the same applies when it's Fox. On the other, a baser part of me is dancing around at his rescue.

"If you ever raise a hand to her again, I'll fucking kill you," Fox growls in a deadly undertone. His whole body is tensed for a fight, like a predatory animal ready to spring free of its cage. "There won't be any piece of you left for anyone to find." His grip tightens and Sam releases a pained groan as Fox leans in, speaking through clenched teeth. "I will make you disappear."

God, why does hearing him threaten Sam like that make my heart race and heat throb between my legs?

SEVENTEEN

FOX

I had to cut in. It's lucky I was parked in a discreet spot on my Harley, waiting to pick up a Nexus Lab employee ID badge at the back of the restaurant from a waiter I bribed to steal it for me. Maisy didn't notice me at all. The minute I saw her come out, followed by the guy she swore wasn't her boyfriend while I had my fingers buried deep inside her, possessiveness and protectiveness rushed through me. It's exactly why I've been avoiding her once Colton confirmed she made it back to Ridgeview.

Seeing the douchebag all over her drove fire into my blood, but the second he raised his hand to her, I was off my bike and catching his arm before he could slap her faster than I've ever moved in my life.

Maisy hovers behind me, releasing a tense breath. I grind my teeth. It doesn't bother me for her to see the true monster I'm capable of being, but a weak part inside of me that refuses to be stamped out flares with worry that she'll finally run away.

"Are you okay?" I ask.

"Fuck no, you're about to break my arm, you psycho," Blake bleats, contorting his body to get away.

With a grumble, I put more pressure on the tendon beneath my thumb. The corner of my mouth kicks up at the pained sound he makes, twisting to find relief that isn't coming. Levi taught me every trick he knows to make someone fucking hurt.

"I wasn't talking to you, shithead." My gaze moves back to Maisy, waiting for her answer.

"I'm fine." She steps forward. "But I had this, you didn't have to—"

"I did."

There's no room for argument in my bitten off response. The days spent avoiding her haven't changed a damn thing, the need filling my chest still very much alive. When it comes down to it, I won't let her get hurt. I'll protect her. It's instinctive, soul-deep, and undeniable.

The flood gates that kept these feelings at bay during the years I spent hating her with every breath have cracked and crumbled. They're open and there's no going back.

Maisy is mine, even when I can't have her. She's always been mine.

And I'll be damned If I ever stand by and allow another man to lay a hand on her like this fucker tried to. I wasn't kidding when I threatened him with death for touching her. That's how far I'll go for the people I want to keep safe.

The moments of Blake lifting his hand to smack her fly through my head again, and with a savage growl I maneuver his wrist to a painful angle.

"Dude!" he shrieks, free hand scrabbling uselessly at my leather jacket.

"Okay, scary tough guy, enough," Maisy grits out. "I appreciate your help, but I can take care of my own problems."

"No, daisy," I mutter, dragging Blake by my hold on his

wrist so I can step closer to her. Flowers and coconuts touch my sense of smell and my mouth quirks up at the sides. I bend my head down so she can hear my low promise. "He wanted to touch you. That makes this my problem, too. You're my problem."

Her breath catches as her eyes fly up to meet mine. The seriousness evident in my gaze makes her lips part. My attention falls to her mouth and an intense yearning to kiss her right now pours through me.

God, I want to steal her away, put her on the bike behind me, take her back to our tree to pin her against it like before while I peel this dress up, and—

"How touching," Blake snarls, breaking the moment. He struggles to escape, but I have a good grip on him. "Is it the leather that does it for you? His motorcycle? You hide it well, pretending you're this perfect ideal. What will your daddy say when I tell him?"

"Tell him what?" Maisy cuts him off with a glare. She holds out her arms. "This is the real me. You have no idea what I'm really like because you didn't want to get to know me. I don't care what you or anyone else thinks of me. I thought you wanted to be my friend, but you're such an asshole, Sam."

He releases a caustic laugh. "Friend? Bullshit, I just wanted to fuck you after all those rumors that you finally stopped being such an uptight good girl. That's the only reason I was nice to you, I fuckin' earned the right to—"

Before he can spew more shit, she cocks her arm back and punches him. Blake can't move far thanks to my iron grip on him, so he takes the full force of her fist to his cheek with a groan. Laughter puffs out of me at the fierce expression on her face.

"Like hell you earned anything with me, you entitled dick," Maisy says furiously. "What I do with my body and who I decide to do it with is my business, not yours. So stop trying to comment on it like you have any right to my body because of some fucked up notion you got in your head that if you were nice to me I'd reward you."

"You should use your whole body. Turn your hips and torso with your momentum," I suggest, raking my gaze over her.

"What?"

She turns to me, still spitting mad. It's a damn good look on her, sending another bolt of heat shooting to my groin.

"Your form is good, but you're smaller than him with less muscle tone to power your hits." Her eyes narrow dangerously, and another chuckle leaves me. "I said less tone, not that you aren't strong." A beat passes as I take her in. Every stunning inch. I can't hide the reverence in my voice. "I know you're strong. If you do it that way, you'll pack a harder punch without sacrificing speed."

Her eyes soften and a pretty pink color tinges her cheeks at the compliment. I swallow back the happy rumble that starts climbing my throat, cutting it off before it can escape. She keeps making me forget, drawing me in with magnetic force to something I can't have.

"I can't believe you'd rather spread your legs for this bad boy act, slu—"

We both release irritated sounds. Blake doesn't get to finish, breaking off into a scream when I twist his arm in my punishing hold, yanking hard to stretch it, and then angling up until there's a sickening *pop*. A vicious grin crosses my face as he stumbles away from us in agony.

"Holy shit," Maisy whispers, staring wide-eyed at the sight of Sam Blake's dislocated arm.

This time she doesn't look ready to run. There's no fear in her hazel eyes, only a bright intensity that echoes the violence brimming in me.

"What the fuck?!" Blake yells, trying to cradle his injured limb. "You—Your dad is inside. When I get him and report you for assault, it's over for you, Wilder."

I stare at him with an unwavering threat that makes him freeze. "Fuck off, Blake, before I do something more serious to your car than making sure it doesn't start the next time you get in it." When I take another step toward him, he scurries backward like the coward he is. "A dislocated arm will be the least of your worries. Be glad I didn't break it."

"Get out of here," Maisy says. "And don't ever come near me again, or I'll file a restraining order for harassment."

Blake looks between both of us standing side by side and mumbles, "Screw this."

Then he leaves us alone in front of the restaurant in the fading twilight. I turn back to her, unsure of what I should do or say. It's unlike me. I swallow as my head fully empties for the first time in a long time. She looks beautiful tonight, her soft light brown hair framing her face and skimming the bare skin of her shoulders. My fingers twitch with the urge to reach out and thread through her hair.

"Next time, you need to leave it to me."

I blink out of my stupor. "Not happening."

Her lips purse and she crosses her arms. "Yes it is. I don't want you to fight my battles for me. I appreciate the help, and the..." She trails off as a flush creeps into her cheeks. Coughing, she darts her gaze away, brushing her fingers over her leather bracelet. "The thing you did. Not that I think violence is the answer, even though I decked him. I mean, he deserved it by that point," she hastily tacks on, throat working as her lashes lower. "But I don't need a man to save me, you feel me? I can stand up for myself."

Fuck me. A rush of heat races through my body. Maisy is turned on by what I did to him. I drag my teeth over my lower lip and file that away to fantasize about later—the only way I'll let myself have her. In my fantasies, I don't run the risk of her betraying my trust.

"Let's get one thing straight here." I step close enough that the soft material of her dress brushes against my chest. Grasping her chin between my thumb and finger, I tilt her face up. "I have no problem with a woman fighting her own battles, but don't expect me to stand idly by if I'm around. Either I show you how to protect yourself, or I do it for you. Like I said, you're my problem. So if someone threatens you, I will step in to take care of it."

Her hazel eyes are luminescent, almost gold in the amber glow the restaurant casts off. Her breathing turns shallow and her pupils dilate at my dominant tone. For a beat, she looks at my mouth with so much longing, all I want to do is crash my lips against hers.

"Even if the threat is you?" Her voice is soft and alluring, but her eyes harden when I begin to close the small distance between us to claim her mouth. "Or do you not count in taking responsibility for your actions because of double standards? That would undermine every sexy word that came out of your mouth."

Well, shit. She's got me there.

"You're right," I rasp, caressing her bottom lip with my thumb.

Now that she's safe, I can walk away. I need to, before I slide further down the treacherous slope and do something stupid again, like kissing her within an inch of her life.

"Maisy."

We both turn at the sound of Jacqueline Landry's bitchy tone. Her parents stand outside the restaurant's doors. It's the first time I've come face to face with them directly since I moved back to Ridgeview.

I don't release Maisy right away, fighting against another wave of possessiveness. It's stronger this time, latching onto me and making me want to never let her go. Richard Landry looks about ready to pop a blood vessel at the sight of his precious daughter standing so close to me, and his wife actually looks annoyed she didn't plot to make sure I was in the car with my parents that night so she could've avoided this moment. Maisy tenses, grasping my shirt in her fist as a tremor runs down her spine. What was once a simple revenge plan has gotten complicated by what I feel for her.

She presses gently against my chest and steps away from me. My hand falls to my side, chest burning with an acute tightness.

"Where is Sam?" Jaqueline demands in an icy voice, because asking anything is beneath her.

"He had to leave," Maisy says. Lowering her voice so only I can hear, she adds, "Crying shame."

I snort.

"You've been out here too long and you left before the entrees were served," Jacqueline says. "People inside started to take notice."

Maisy shrugs. "Sorry. I'm not that hungry now."

Jaqueline's detached gaze flicks to me for a moment. It's hard to believe those eyes are the same color as Maisy's, which are full of life. "Then I guess you don't feel like going on your trip."

Maisy bristles beside me. I take a step, but she shoots a hand out to stop me.

"Don't," she murmurs. "I have to take on this fight for myself, too."

I look back to Jacqueline and Richard. The coldness in her eyes is awful. I remember when she would buy us ice cream, and the time she drove us to the aquarium for a class trip when my parents were out of town. She used to look at me with the same fondness as she had for her own children, like I was another son to her. The malicious way she looks at me now harbors no warmth, like if I say something she doesn't like she won't hesitate to end me if it threatened her greed.

Meeting her gaze, I know beyond a shadow of a doubt this is who took my family from me.

EIGHTEEN

MAISY

"Fox, wait!"

After staring at Mom for several tense heartbeats, he turned and walked away toward the shadows past the pool of light outside the restaurant. I'm not finished with him yet, not by a long shot. I need to talk to him before he shuts me out again. I want to know what he meant about me being his problem and why he stepped in between me and Sam when he was actively tormenting me not that long ago.

"Maisy, get back here!" Dad calls as I go after Fox. I move faster to outrun him, expecting him to restrain me if he has to, but it doesn't come. "Please! Jackie—"

"We won't make a scene here, Richard," Mom says cryptically.

I'm not turning back, not even for the desperation in Dad's voice. They can't keep me from him. I'm fighting for him and they won't stop me. For once, Mom's insane need to control every aspect of her image is working out for me to escape so I can chase Fox.

I'll deal with the fallout when I get home later. I'm sure I'm in for hell from her for ruining her meticulously orchestrated night by running off. Let people start another rumor, see if I care. There are more important things happening right now than maintaining the image she's obsessed with.

When I reach the shadows, I don't see him. Crap. Did I miss him? How does he move so quickly and quietly so it's hard to follow his path?

A pair of strong arms circle me from behind and I'm whirled around. I release a tiny gasp before my back hits the brick wall of the restaurant.

"What are you doing, Maisy Daisy?" Fox rasps in a smoky tone, lips brushing my temple while his hand closes around my neck.

Unlike before, this time his hold is almost...gentle. His thumb swipes the underside of my jaw, guiding my face up.

For a moment, I can't speak. My throat closes over with the emotions choking me up. He's called me daisy, and by my name a few times, but never the full nickname from our childhood. My hands automatically rest on his chest, clinging to the material of his signature black muscle shirt beneath the leather jacket to anchor myself so I don't float away in the sea of memories attacking me. I didn't expect how it would make me feel when I used to hate it so much, but hearing it now infused with so many things—wry amusement, sultry teasing, *affection*—I have to swallow a few times and force out a ragged breath.

"You're more interesting to be around than my parents." I want to pull him closer. A snort shakes his shoulders and a hot puff of air travels over my neck. "I need to talk to you."

"No."

The arrogant way he decides it makes me bristle.

"Yes," I insist, twisting my fingers and tugging on his shirt. "I didn't plan on you."

I don't know what he means by that, but it sounds like the admission cost him.

He sighs in resignation, tracing his nose down the side of my face, as if he can't keep away from me anymore than I can stay away from him. It's impossible. The world knows we're meant to be like this, so it gave us an invisible cord that ties our hearts together.

My whole body protests when he pulls back, allowing the cool night air to get between us. It feels like he's putting the cavernous divide back in place. His eyes are hard to read in the dark, but they still pierce through me.

"I have to go." His mouth twists. "There's something I'm late for."

"So take me with you. We really need to talk. You said I was your problem and I want to know what you meant."

He pushes out a breath, cutting his gaze to the side as he drags his long, calloused fingers through his tousled dark hair. His jaw works while he shakes his head.

"No."

That damn refusal again. I tighten my grip on his shirt, ready to jump across the deep invisible crevice he separates us with.

"Don't."

"What changed?" My words come faster and my voice cracks. "Why did you hate me so much and do everything you could to make my life hell, but now you decide you'll protect me?"

The more I push, the more I feel him closing off. My one chance to get past his walls is slipping away. He steps back, prying my hands from his shirt. He won't even look at me.

"Why?" I yell. "Just tell me!"

Fox moves aggressively, pinning me to the wall. "Why?"

A harsh sound passes his lips as he grips me by my upper

arms and cages me against the bricks with every inch of his hard muscles. His controlled composure breaks and everything he keeps locked away pours out of him.

"*Why?* Because you broke your goddamn promise, Maisy!"

There's so much anger bleeding out of him, I expect the red stain to be all over my dress and shoes when I return to the light.

His voice grows hoarse and gravelly. "You know that! Stop acting like you don't!"

"What?" I sputter, caught off guard as confusion swarms me. "What are you talking about?"

"You promised me. You swore not to tell Holden or your parents when I showed you what was in the garage."

Fox breathes heavily, digging his fingers into my upper arms. The brick bites into my back through the thin designer dress. I ignore all of it, because what he said triggered my memories. It's all coming back in a visceral rush that threatens to swallow me whole.

"The day you gave me the daisy," I whisper, my eyes widening.

There's something else I want to show you. It's in my dad's garage. The image of Fox at nine floats to the surface of my mind as we stood in the field by our tree. *I wasn't supposed to find it. You have to promise not to tell anyone.*

I remember that day now. I haven't thought about it in so long because it was too close to when I lost Fox.

He took me into the garage and I thought he was going to show me something to do with the mechanics he was learning from his dad. But I was wrong.

His excitement was infectious, and I loved following him into trouble. It gave me a thrill like no other. He never told me I couldn't do something because I was small or a girl. He liked it when I came along on our adventures.

Everything looked normal at first. Fox jogged over to his dad's motorcycle and ran a proud hand over it. "I'm going to take you for a ride on this once I'm allowed to drive it."

I nodded eagerly. I wanted to feel the wind in my hair while I got to hug him really tight.

Then he took my hand and led me to the other side of the garage where his dad usually kept a stash of his favorite beer in a mini fridge. We opened the door and instead of beer bottles, there were trays of small tubes with labels on them. As far as I knew, our parents weren't allowed to bring their work home from their lab.

"A science experiment?" I asked.

He shook his head and carefully prodded one of the tubes. "I think it's this." He let the door to the refrigerator shut and moved a box of tools out of the way on the workbench, pulling out the folder hidden there. "It says it's a patent."

"Synthetic opioid formula trial," I read aloud on one of the section headings. The page had a scientific diagram on it. I couldn't pronounce some of the longer technical words, even though I read a lot for my age. "How come they have it here? Why is it hidden?"

"Dunno. Cool, right? We never get to see their work. They always say I'm not allowed to visit when I beg them to bring me to their lab for take your kid to work day."

We only spent a few minutes marveling at Fox's discovery of his parents contraband drug trial stash. I remember one of the pages in the packet having a long list of numbers that I wrote off at the time, but now that I'm thinking about it, I remember dollar signs and lots of commas. Whatever they had been hiding in the garage was worth a huge amount of money to the company.

"I-I did promise." And I did break it. "I'm so sorry."

The echo of guilt flares as fresh as it was when the words

slipped out of my mouth in my excitement to tell my parents about my new favorite day at bedtime. Once they tumbled out, I couldn't steal them back.

The memory of the weird, tense look they exchanged makes my breath catch. They told me not to tell anyone else what I saw. To forget it even happened. It was the first time Mom ever became controlling with me, but we're so far down the path now that I'd pushed the memory far behind all the other bad blood between me and Mom. The expression on her face scared me that night.

Grabbing onto his biceps, I will him to hear out my explanation. "Wait—I did tell my parents when I said I wouldn't, but they already knew." I felt really bad about it, but our parents were close friends and it made sense that they knew, because Mom worked with them. "They didn't seem surprised by what we saw in the garage."

He's angry all over again. It rolls off of him, nearly suffocating me. I sense he's ready to shove me back out behind the iron walls he built around his heart once more. How could I have forgotten about that day?

"You picked them over the promise you made me."

"I was too excited to tell them about my day. It wasn't on purpose, it just slipped out."

"The secret of what they were hiding got them killed," Fox grits out through clenched teeth. I can feel the vibration of his deep voice through his chest against mine. "Their car crash wasn't an accident. They were murdered along with my baby sister."

Another wave of shock crashes over me. I'm on the verge of shattering, stuck between the old memories and the truth coming out.

"Sister?" It comes out strangled.

"Mom didn't want to tell anyone yet, but they just found

out she was having a girl." His voice is shaking. "I was supposed to have a baby sister."

Did I unknowingly contribute to his family's death? Even if my parents knew, did I put everything in motion to get them in trouble by spilling a secret that wasn't mine in the first place?

Ice freezes my veins and I slam my eyes shut to block out his expression. It hurts my heart too much. This is why he's hated me. This is how our friendship was destroyed.

Fox hasn't only been living with the grief of losing his parents to tragedy all these years. It's so much worse than I ever could have imagined.

"Murdered." The word tastes like ash on my tongue, but I force it out.

My eyes open slowly and I stare at his unyielding jawline as my thoughts turn. The police report. The investigation was ruled an accident, the coroner report missing. I knew it was suspicious that there was information missing from it and that Dad's signature was all over it. Fox's weird behavior and the way he's been lurking around town bribing people makes sense now. I've finally figured out what he's been up to.

"You're trying to prove it."

It takes him a long time to answer. He studies me, not letting up on his punishing grip.

"Yes."

"How? You're nineteen."

"That doesn't concern you. I have to do this. I won't let the people that did this to my family get away with it. They don't get to enjoy the power they got by killing my family." His conflicted tone breaks my heart as he breaks off, swallowing audibly. The sorrow threatens to drag me under. "You helped them by breaking that promise. No one would've found out what they were hiding."

"That's not true. I told you my parents already knew!" I

have to believe it's not true, rejecting the idea that I inadvertently helped hurt them.

Fox grunts as he bears down on me, finally releasing my arms in favor of locking his fingers around my throat as he gets in my face.

"Why do you think your Mom was promoted to CEO out of nowhere? Check the damn dates. That's the level the people behind this are working at." His hand flexes and I struggle to draw my next breath. "That's what your broken promise did."

My heart crushes under the weight of guilt. "I was eight! We were just kids!"

"Tell that to my dead parents!"

Fox smacks a palm against the brick over my head and backs away with a frustrated noise. I reach up to rub my neck. My throat burns like I've swallowed thousands of knives, but not from his rough handling.

"So you hate me because you think I helped the people that did this?"

The question hurts because part of me actually wonders if I'm remembering the events of that day wrong and I did inadvertently have a hand in it all, but I force it out. Fox gives me a low rumble in response.

"You seriously believe I would hurt you so deeply when I've always lo—" I clamp my mouth shut as he crushes me against the wall with his body once more. Both of us are breathing hard. I lick my lips and tilt my chin up. His searching gaze tracks the movement. "I would never hurt you like that."

"Then why did you break your promise?"

Fox sounds gutted and it stabs a knife into my stomach. I shudder at the way everything about him seems torn to shreds. He's carried the weight of this pain on his shoulders for ten years and it's killing him.

It makes me want to take all of his anger and grief and hurt.

I'll bear the weight of it for him. I just want to take it away so he doesn't sound so utterly damaged by the world.

Reaching up, I cup his face. His cheek turns hard, a muscle jumping beneath my palm. But he doesn't pull away. I dig into the flare of hope that gives me.

"I'm so sorry. I didn't mean to." Determination fills me, giving me strength. I wait until he meets my gaze in the dim shadows. "My heart knows yours, Fox Michael Wilder. It always has. I never ever forgot." I lower my voice. "Did yours forget me?"

"No. Never." It comes out on a broken growl.

"Then you have to know I wouldn't betray your trust to hurt you on purpose. I'm not your enemy. I'm sorry, Fox."

As soon as the words leave me, I wind my arms around his neck and hug him. He remains stiff for a long stretch of seconds. I close my eyes tight, hugging him harder.

Slowly, his muscular arms come around me until he's crushing me into his embrace. He buries his hands in my dress and holds me.

It's like he's not used to the touch anymore, as if he hasn't had a real hug for ten years when I last threw my arms around him for having my back or making me laugh. My heart squeezes when a barely there tremble shakes his broad frame.

A soft, rough noise leaves him, then he breaks away, putting distance between us. He scrubs a hand over his jaw while I lean back against the brick wall so my knees don't give out. I can feel the shift, the energy cleansed from the decaying thing that used to hang in the air like venom between us.

But when he speaks, low and gruff, my heart finally splinters.

"I won't mess with you anymore. That's done now, so you can go on to live your life." He pauses, tugging harshly on his messy dark hair. "But we can't get back what we had before."

NINETEEN

FOX

The undeniable sincerity in Maisy's apology caught me off guard and I still feel the echo of her hug hours later in the middle of the night. It's created a deep-seated yearning in me. A wish that I didn't pull away so soon, that I kept holding her and got to kiss her one more time.

All these years I thought she knew she lied and broke her promise, but she swears she didn't remember until the truth came out.

I trace my thumbnail over my lower lip as I stare at the laptop on my coffee table.

Can I really believe her? My heart riots against my rib cage, telling me I can't trust her so easily. She could turn around and stab me in the back again. It's not something I could survive a second time.

I tamp down those thoughts and squeeze the back of my neck. She couldn't fake that sincerity.

If I accept her apology...she could truly be my daisy again.

As soon as it crosses my mind, my chest caves and I lean back against the couch. Focusing on what I got from the waiter at the restaurant is impossible. I'm supposed to be using the duplicated ID badge to gain access to Nexus Lab from the inside to dig up dirt on Jacqueline. Every time I try, I circle back to Maisy, as inevitable as the shifting tides of the ocean I miss so much.

And her.

Because I still miss her.

"Pathetic bastard," I murmur to the industrial walls surrounding me.

Something did hit me hard earlier tonight while standing outside the restaurant. For the last ten years I've formed my vendetta around the entire Landry family. I punished Holden and Maisy as ruthlessly as I want to go after their parents. But as I had her chin grasped in my fingers and stared them down, everything sharpened with clarity.

The real problem has always been Richard and Jaqueline. Not my old friends.

I've been so stubborn and sure of my grudge against the entire family that I might have sabotaged my own efforts to bring them down. Instead of wasting my time with the school-yard shit I came at Maisy with and the strings Colt helped me pull with Holden's college football draft, I should've been focusing all my attention on the two people who actually had a hand in this.

Hating Maisy for breaking her promise was the old pain of a kid broken by loss and torn away from the only friends I had.

I swallow past the lump in my throat and rub at the burning sensation in my chest.

Without being clouded by anger and anguish, I'm able to think back on the day I found the wild daisy for her and took her to the garage. I remember how much I wanted to learn to ride dad's Harley as fast as I could and imagined all the places I would drive Maisy. We had so many adventures planned, including the most important thing I promised her.

I'm going to marry you someday.

I swipe my fingers over my mouth and let the old love I felt for her crash with the love it's grown into in the background, behind every intensely passionate thought I've ever had toward her.

Hate. Love. Betrayal. Longing.

The secrets of this town tore into the path we were set on, but somehow it couldn't fully destroy how deeply connected I am to her. If I told her that, she'd probably have a name for it, like fate or destiny. My mouth curves into a lopsided smile as I picture scoffing and telling her fate was for fantasy stories.

Knowing now that she never meant to hurt me makes a sludge-like sense of guilt settle deep in my gut. I've been such an asshole to her. I hunted her for sport, like the psychotic bastard I've honed myself into, put my hands on her, and sabotaged her grades and social standing. I wanted her to hurt and I made it happen, driving her fear and tears when she's been resilient against my efforts to take her life apart. All because she's fucking brave and wanted nothing more than to earn my friendship back.

My throat works on an uncomfortable gulp. I don't like the feeling creeping through my veins as I consider all the horrible things I've done and said to her. It makes what I told her tonight ring more true—we can't get back what we had because I'm afraid to trust her, but also because I can't look at myself in the mirror for what I've done to her for the sake of revenge.

I rub my face and release a sigh, sagging deeper into the aged leather of my second-hand couch. I do want to accept her apology. It's lifted a solid weight off my shoulders and I finally feel like I can breathe easier without every breath being tinged with so much darkness.

But some part of me still hesitates. Once trust is broken, it's hard to heal it. Even if I want to erase it with her apology, the withered parts of my heart are wary, more comfortable behind thick walls of impenetrable stone to remain hardened. It's the only way to protect it from reliving the pain.

Instead, I need to do what I said I would—stay the fuck away from Maisy. She can go on with her life, and I'll keep living this half-formed existence, destined to spend my days missing the girl who makes my heart feel like it could beat without hurting. I'm no good for her.

Decision made, I turn my attention to the information on my laptop leading me to a shipping warehouse. I have work to do and it's time to stop hesitating. Jacqueline and Richard will pay for what they've done.

TWENTY

MAISY

Healing a broken heart is impossible, but self-care keeps me going. I throw myself into my routine. That means plenty of yoga, face masks with the girls, and hanging out with the rest of our friends at Thea's apartment when I'm allowed out. Plus I spend time centering myself in nature when I can convince Holden to go on a hike. A nightly session with Sir Good Vibes helps to blow off steam and I totally don't picture calloused hands running over my skin. Absolutely not.

It all recharges me, but I'm still trying to find a way to breathe without Fox again.

He doesn't think we can even be friends. It's worse than the first time I lost him, because now I know why he couldn't even look at me when he first came back. This time he wasn't ripped away from me, he made the tear himself.

I haven't seen him in days. He never showed for finals and hasn't come to any of the graduation ceremony practices.

After what he said to me, I didn't bother looking through the medical journals Devlin dropped off a few days ago. They've been sitting by my rolled up yoga mat in the corner of my bedroom, mocking me. Instead of reading them myself, I want to give them to him, but first I'd have to pin the stubborn elusive jerk down to offer them to him.

As predicted, I caught a load of shit for running off from the restaurant and causing an unwanted scene for my parents the other night. Since Fox left me there alone, I called Holden to come pick me up. I've never seen Dad look so mad. He was livid, more angry than Mom, who regarded me with a cool and dispassionate look the minute I walked through the door. She didn't even bother berating me, like I expected, simply announced that the road trip was off the table again. I stood there grinding my teeth, quelling the desire to stand up to her as she informed me that if I didn't get my impulsive, childish urges under control then she'd send me to a private disciplinary school that specializes in rehabilitating troubled brats of the influential and wealthy instead of the college they made me apply to. The admissions paperwork was already completed. I wanted to call bullshit, but the threat in her empty gaze was very real. After she was satisfied with my stunned silence, she spun on her heel and went into her office.

Then Dad tore into me for putting myself in danger for a solid twenty minutes. He wouldn't hear any of my arguments in Fox's favor or that the most danger I was in was stubbing a toe in the dark. He's the one who decided I wouldn't be leaving the house except for school and my yoga classes, and that I couldn't go anywhere on my own. I'm not even allowed to do my volunteer shift at the library. Dad made me pick—yoga or reading to the kids, and as much as I love their little faces, I need yoga or I go crazy from bottling up my energy every day.

The reminder of their ability to control my life stung.

It could've been worse. They could've actually shipped me off to the mysterious disciplinary school. I'm at least glad that Holden is my new warden, escorting me everywhere now that his summer class is over for the summer. He told me he feels bad, so he's been far more lenient than my parents expect. If they had hired a bodyguard, like they threatened before, I definitely couldn't have pulled sibling sympathy for an easier time. My brother doesn't say anything when I spend half our time together with my nose glued to the map app on my phone, dropping points for where I want to go on my road trip.

I'm biding my time until the moment is right to make my move.

On the day of graduation, I'm one step closer to freedom. I just have to get through the ceremony, then I'm hitting the road. Mom can threaten me all she wants, but there's no way I'm letting her send me to a disciplinary school. The cage they've kept me in for so many years is becoming too much, suffocating the wings I need to spread. An itch crawls across my skin, growing worse by the day.

"Stop fidgeting and stand up straight," Mom hisses so no one else will hear her perfectionist nagging.

We're standing off to the side of the school on the path that splits to lead to the football field, surrounded by a sea of green and white graduation gowns that match the one I'm sweating in and the families of the graduating class.

It's my high school graduation and I feel...nothing.

Shouldn't I care more? I can't find any reason to. Thinking back on my last four years, I'm troubled by how little of my own interests I've explored. My senior year was a complete bust. The only bright spots are the times I spent with my friends when they were still here with me before they graduated, and the only memories worth reliving that give me a thrill are the times Fox was focused on me.

"The ceremony hasn't even started yet," Holden says. I shoot him a grateful smile and he winks. "Give her a break for five minutes, Ma."

"Like the break I've given you, Holden?" Mom says sharply. "It's been such an awfully long break."

He clenches his jaw at the reminder he's missed the mark on how high she expected him to jump by ending up at a public community college. A few people glance our way curiously and Mom's spine goes ramrod straight while she plasters on her CEO smile.

"We're so proud of you," Dad says.

Really, I want to ask skeptically, *even though I didn't make Valedictorian?* As if she can hear my thoughts, Mom's mouth pinches.

"Thanks, Dad."

"Well, at least you're graduating. We would have liked to see you earn the top spot in your class." She speaks out of the side of her mouth as she nudges me toward the group of students lining up by one of the teachers. "It's disappointing that you've deviated so much from what your goals were."

I couldn't hide my grades when she has a rule about keeping her updated with them, but I'm not even that annoyed anymore at Fox for messing with my class rank. It's just a grade, so what's the big deal? My life isn't over or ruined because I got an A minus instead of an A plus. It took a deep meditation session to come to that realization and once I did the weight lifted from my shoulders, leaving me lighter. I should thank him for making me face it.

"Valedictorian wasn't ever something I'd pick for myself anyway," I mutter.

Mom flashes a severe look that warns me to back up. *They're all your goals,* I want to snap, but I drag in a measured breath and let it the fuck go. *Just make it through the ceremony,* I remind myself. Then I can finally get a break from their dog and pony show.

"We'll meet you after, sweetheart," Dad says. "We'll be cheering for you."

They leave with Holden to find seats with the rest of the families heading for the football stands.

Fox still isn't here. My brows draw together and my heart gives a pained little pinch. I don't know if his number of absences this year disqualified him from being able to walk in the graduation ceremony, but I was hoping to see him.

I'm still hurt that he could give up so easily on friendship, or the fiery thing building between us. When I'm around him, he makes me feel safe, despite being a stubborn asshole. He's always seen my wild side without telling me to tone it down. He's the only person who makes me feel alive and I want him in my life, no matter what that looks like. After the initial despair from my shattered heart dulled, a new grief formed a pit in my stomach.

My fingertips find the old braided leather and smooth stones of my bracelet.

Fox shouldn't have to do what he's doing alone. I want to help. If I can do that, maybe it will be enough to make amends for breaking my promise. Even if I was just a kid, it's been eating at me that I had any part in hurting his family or him.

My thoughts continue to drift as I follow the rest of my classmates into the school to line up like we did yesterday in practice. Glancing at the rows of lockers and classrooms as we're led through the hallways, sadness trickles through me. My parents might be proud, but can I say the same thing?

High school should be a time where I started to learn who I could be. I should've been making memories and discovering my own voice. It's the chance to start to explore independence and shape my values and goals in life. But I didn't get to do any of that.

A boy bumps into me that I don't even know and it only

makes me regret that we never got the chance to be friends. I frown and mumble an apology that he waves off, picking up his animated conversation with his buddies.

If I could do it all over again, without all the rules and pressure to perform in the precise way my parents wanted, what would I have picked for myself?

As soon as I think about it, I'm hit with a realization that almost brings me to my knees. Air rushes past my lips and I clutch the polyester gown hanging off my shoulders. Someone gives me a funny look, but I barely register it.

Mom and Dad haven't just controlled me for years to make sure I follow a life plan they set out for me—I let them. I helped them by not fighting back hard enough. I gave in and went along, strangling my impulsive urges and curtailing every whim I've ever had.

Whims are for children and you're a grown woman now.

Mom's favorite criticism fills my head. Funny how I could be a grown woman but also still be treated like a kid by my parents. Whatever manipulation they had to pull to keep me in line, doing what they thought was best for me—what made them look good—was fair game to them.

How many times have I cut away pieces of myself in order to do what I've been told so I'd be seen as this perfect goody-goody?

Big parts and small, ones that didn't seem noticeable and ones that hurt to shave away from who I really am. Everything from not dying my hair a fun color to only picking classes they wanted me to take, instead of choir and women's history and a rock climbing elective introduced last year—because anything I wanted wasn't as important as maintaining the path they wanted me on. I did it to keep the peace, in the hope I'd one day be granted the reward to take control of my own life. I did it because deep down, I didn't want to disappoint them if my good behavior was the only reason they paid attention to me.

Because I was afraid.

I put myself in my cage as much as my parents did. That needs to end.

My throat closes as I glance through the open doors to the stands where families are seated, trying to search for my parents and my brother.

The ceremony is about to start. My fellow graduating classmates stand with me in line, waiting to be led out onto the football field on a bright, sunny summer day.

I'm supposed to be here. Expected to. But this is not where I want to be right now.

Time to stop pretending to be the good girl. That was never me.

"Where are you going? We're about to start," Jenna Taylor says when I step out of line.

I glance over my shoulder at her. This is the first time she's ever spoken to me directly. She's the mayor's daughter, the one that threw the party Fox was at two months ago. It feels like a million years ago now. I was so jealous when he took her upstairs. The emotion swept through me like an angry tide, overtaking me to the point I just couldn't stand by and take his crap anymore because that wasn't who I was. I guess I should thank this girl for pushing me to find my backbone.

"I have to go to the bathroom," I lie. "Be right back."

She pulls a face. "Don't you care if you miss the beginning? This is like, your thing."

"What is?"

"School. Smart nice girl shit? I don't know, you've always seemed like a huge priss since you never partied all four years here and only focused on school."

I lift a brow. "Assume much?" Hitching a shoulder, I gaze

past her at the other students in line. Most of them don't know the real me and never bothered to look beyond my reputation or the rumors. "If you'd ever taken the time to talk to me, you'd know that isn't me at all." Her brows jump up and an embarrassed blush creeps across her cheeks. I wave a hand. "I'm pretty glad this is all over. I don't actually care about any of this, or missing the beginning."

Or missing the entire pointless thing, I think as I leave to sneak off campus.

As much as I want to smash out of my imaginary cage and take what I want—hitchhiking if I have to—there's something more important I have to do first. *Someone* more important.

Once I make it around the corner to the side hall that leads to a terrace, I fish out my phone and text my brother. He drove separately from me and our parents, so he's my only hope of getting out of here in a hurry.

Maisy: Meet me at the courtyard by the north building.

Holden: Uh, that's not the football field. Why, what are you doing? Are you okay?

Maisy: I'll tell you when you get here. Hurry!

Holden: Fine, on my way.

I blow out a relieved breath and lean against an Aspen tree. It doesn't take Holden long to arrive. I ignore his confused expression and rush over to him.

"Holy shit, are you okay?" he blurts as I grab his arms. He cups my elbows to balance me. "Isn't the ceremony about to start?"

"Yes, fine," I say in a hurry. "Forget about the ceremony and give me your keys."

His grip on my elbows tightens. "Why?"

I hang my head back and swallow my annoyance. I don't have time to explain this, but he's never going to help me if I don't give him something.

"There's no requirement that says I have to walk in the ceremony. I'd rather go hang out at Thea's bakery instead of go through all the stuffy traditions."

Holden gives me a flat expression. "Right," he drawls. "Except, I totally recognize the look on your face. Cough up what you're not telling me, or I'm not giving you shit."

I sigh. "Holden."

"Nah-uh. Give me the real reason you want to ditch."

Damn it. Fine. "I'm going to see Fox."

His gaze hardens. "Seriously? I don't think that's a good idea. After he's been treating you like crap, you just forgive him? You should listen to Dad and just stay away from him."

"Well, I can't." Staying away from Fox was never in the cards for me. The desperation flooding my voice makes him pause. "Just—Can't you trust me that I know what I'm doing? He needs my help and I'm going to give it to him."

Holden lets go of my elbows and steps back, scratching his chin. "I still don't want to let you go." He holds up his hands when I open my mouth. "God, you're annoying when you get your head stuck on something. Are you sure? Mom and Dad will be pissed and you're already skating on ice so thin it's cracking. I think they're serious about that disciplinary school."

"I know. But I'm sure." I offer him a half-smile and hold out my hand for the keys. "It's time I stop letting what's expected of me dictate my life. It's making me miserable and I'm done with feeling like crap to make everyone else happy."

Conflicted emotions flit across Holden's face, but after a

few moments he nods. "Okay. I don't want to, but I hate seeing how unhappy you've been this year. Just be careful around that guy."

"He's not a threat to me. He never really was." My throat burns as I think about those case files again for the accident and what I've learned from Fox. "I'm going to fix what broke between us."

And help him prove his parents were murdered.

Holden drops the keys to his Audi in my hand and the taste of freedom bursts on my tongue. For a second, I wish I could just *go* and never stop, but I fight back the familiar urge. First, I have to find Fox and help him. My road trip escape will have to wait indefinitely until then.

"Maise," he calls out as I turn to go, already tugging off the polyester graduation gown over my dress. When I look back, his brows dip and he scrubs a hand through his light brown hair. "I'm sorry I've been a shitty brother."

"You haven't been. You've just been dealing with your own stuff."

"Still." His shoulders sag with his sigh. "I could've pulled my head out of my ass for five minutes to see how hard this year has been for you, too. Or how all your smiles are fake. I've been a selfish bastard, but that stops now."

I swallow past the lump in my throat. So someone did notice, he was just too torn up about his own problems and crushed dreams to let me in for some solidarity. "It's fine. We'll talk later. I've got to go."

"I'll cover for you with Mom and Dad."

"Thanks, Holden."

TWENTY-ONE
MAISY

Skipping out on my high school graduation ceremony to search for Fox—and most definitely pissing my parents off in the process if Holden can't make up a good excuse for why I'm not there to receive my diploma—is all good in theory.

In practice?

I have no idea how I'll find him. It's hard enough to trail him whether he knows he's being followed or not—he's good at covering his tracks. If I hadn't stowed away in his Charger, I never would have gotten the slip on him. My fingers tap out a random beat on the steering wheel of Holden's car as I drive aimlessly for a few minutes through the rolling hills on the winding road at the base of the mountains.

You can figure this out. Think. Where would he go to look for the pieces of the puzzle he needs to prove his parents were murdered?

Nexus Lab. It's the best I can start with for now, considering what Fox showed me in his garage when we were kids.

On my way to the pharmaceutical company where Mom now holds the highest position of power, my phone dings with a text notification. The bluetooth connection shows it's from an unknown number on the console screen in the dashboard. My brow furrows. Maybe it's the fact I know Fox is trying to prove his family was murdered, or maybe it's the adrenaline rush still buzzing from making a decision for myself to leave my graduation ceremony, but a random text from an unknown number has my stomach rippling with suspicion.

Once I reach a red light, I snag my phone from the cup holder and check it.

Unknown: 1207 Rolling Rock Drive, Ridgeview, Colorado 80304

"Huh."

The address isn't for Nexus Lab. It's the opposite direction, on the other side of town near the shipping district full of warehouses and not much else. Is this Fox's number? It has to be. I suck in a breath, the horrible thought crossing my mind that he could be in trouble and this is his way of asking for my help.

As I input the address to the GPS feature on Holden's car, a fierce determination settles in my shoulders. *I'm coming, Fox.*

The first thing I notice when I arrive is that I don't see his Charger or his motorcycle. But an SUV that looks just like the one that tailed us the day Fox met with Lana is here, along with a whole matching fleet.

I hope Fox is the one who found them instead of the other way around since they didn't seem all that open to a friendly chat when they tried to run us off the road. But I have no clue how he managed to locate these guys when I didn't see any identifiable plates in the chase. I pull the car into an open spot and look down at the outfit I'm wearing—another one of Mom's designer picks, paired with my lowkey rebellious disregard for wearing underwear or a bra.

"Just gonna roll with it and hope for the best," I mutter as I leave the car.

The warehouse is isolated on a no outlet lane with no others nearby. I don't come to this part of town often, but I follow the row of SUVs around the corner. An eighteen wheeler is backed up to an open bay door and I catch sight of Fox. My steps falter as I head for him and the man with a clipboard he's talking to.

Always aware of everything, he spots me before I even reach them and his eyes tighten at the corners. Hot and cold tingles run across my skin and I suppress a shudder from the intensity in his gaze.

He's not wearing his usual leather jacket, ripped black jeans, or the heavy combat boots. Instead, he's dressed in a sharp suit and it's actually pretty distracting because he looks hot. Warmth pools low in my stomach, and I can't decide if I prefer him rugged and rough, or clean cut with the sinful edge lurking beneath his hard blue eyes.

I glance between him and the warehouse employee, plastering on my brightest smile. The older guy seems wary of me despite my nice dress, studying me with a small frown as I stick my hand out. This isn't my world at all, but I'm not letting that stop me from getting sucked in if it's part of helping prove the Wilders were murdered.

"Hey! I'm M—"

Fox sucks in a breath and takes a small step forward. It's a subtle move, but I catch it and correct myself.

"Millie. Intern," I add when I spy the Nexus Lab ID badge clipped to his jacket. The guy with the clipboard raises a brow. I gesture toward Fox with my thumb. "Sorry I'm late. They keep sending me for coffee runs when I'm supposed to be assigned to his side to learn about the department."

Fox relaxes slightly, but is still wound tight. "Right. I forgot to mention her when I called to arrange our meeting." He pauses and shoots me an assessing glance that seems to go straight to my soul. "She's new to all this."

I almost laugh, but stop myself, keeping my friendly smile in place as I sink into the role of eager intern. The clipboard guy shakes my hand, then strokes the trimmed stubble growing around his mouth.

"You were saying," he prompts.

"The higher ups are looking to double check and tighten communication between departments," Fox says. "I'm here to audit that and confirm the shipments through each distribution network."

While they talk, I let half of my attention drift around the warehouse. There's not much to see. Only a few employees mill around packing boxes and transporting them on forklifts into the truck waiting at the bay door. The logo for Nexus Lab is all over the place and I realize this is a shipping warehouse for the company's manufactured product. This is the first time I've ever been to one of the other sites of the company. Usually I only go right to Mom's corner office at the sleek building nestled at the base of the mountains, but something nags at me as I take everything in.

The quantities are off from what I would expect. Most of the boxes carry the same label for a synthetic opioid rather than a variety. The company is supposed to be one of the top pharmaceutical manufacturers in the country, so why would they be making such large amounts of the same thing? And if this is the shipping department, shouldn't there be more here than the sparse equipment and a handful of employees? It's all weird.

"This hasn't been an issue before," the older guy says. "As far as I know, the company likes it this way."

I glance between the skeleton shipping crew and the number of boxes full of synthetic drugs being piled into the truck. There's no way there's such a high demand for only one drug when they're meant to be making all kinds of things.

Fox holds up his hands with a crooked smile that makes my knees go weak. "Don't shoot the messenger. I'm just doing my job, same as you, man."

"Right. Okay, come this way."

He takes us through the procedure they follow at the warehouse and shows Fox his clipboard so we can match it to what Fox has in a list on his phone. A large portion of the shipment is heading for the same two places—an address on the west coast and one in the northeast. That doesn't seem right. I wish I knew more about Mom's company to know if there are medical companies in those locations that would order such a large amount of the same drug.

"So, as you can see," the manager says, slapping his clipboard. "All in order."

"Right," Fox agrees. "Thanks for your cooperation."

He nudges the small of my back and we head for the bay door. The manager stops us before we make it out.

"What department did you say this was for again? I'll need to write it in the log. Protocol and all, you know how they are."

Fox barely reacts, but I go rigid, thinking we're caught. He calmly offers his ID badge for the guy to copy the information to his clipboard. Whatever is on it, the manager is appeased and sends us on our way.

"Thanks for your cooperation," Fox says.

My thoughts race as I try to work out the puzzle in front of me. What is Nexus Lab really up to? Isn't it illegal to flood the market with this much of one drug? There are regulations for what they're allowed to produce, I'm sure of it.

If this massive supply is making it to the legitimate market at all, that is. I don't like the thought as soon as it crosses my mind.

Fox grabs my elbow and leads me outside, his grip hard and unyielding. He doesn't slow his long strides and half-drags, half-carries me out the door and around the corner behind a pile of shipping palettes.

"What the hell are you doing here?" he demands through clenched teeth, dropping the cool and collected act.

"I came to help. The address sent to my phone... I was already skipping the grad ceremony to find you, but I thought it meant you needed me."

"Needed you?" Fox drags his fingers through his hair and jabs his finger back toward the building. "You almost blew my cover."

I cross my arms and frown, eyeing him up and down. "Which looks flimsy at best." I flick his badge. "This doesn't look fake or anything, even if it passed for a legit one. How did you get this anyway?"

He grumbles something under his breath and pinches the bridge of his nose, ignoring my question. "How the fuck did you even get here?"

"The address sent to my phone, I told you." I show him the text. "You haven't given me your number, but when you sent it I knew it was you."

"You thought—" He breaks off with a curse, pulling a face as he glares over my shoulder. "I'm going to kill Colt for bringing you here. I told him to stop surveillance tracking," he mutters. I have no idea what or who he's talking about. Turning his attention back to me, he shakes his head. "I didn't send for you, Maisy. You can't help."

"Like hell I can't. I want to."

Standing my ground, I silently dare him to tell me what I can and can't do. I've had enough of playing by the rules and doing what's expected of me.

Fox blows out a breath, treating me to the same once over I

gave him. Except his eyes drag much slower over my body, lingering at my chest for a beat before lifting to meet my gaze again. His head jerks with the force of his snort.

"Always so fucking stubborn."

Somehow he makes it sound like it's a trait that gets under his skin and makes him fond of me at the same time.

"You shouldn't be here." He rubs his mouth. "I can't let you get involved in this."

"You can't do all this on your own," I reason. "I know you said we can't be friends, but I want to help. Two heads will be better than one."

It sounds like he mutters that he already has an additional head, but he continues pinning me with his stare, working his jaw as he considers my offer. I have to sweeten it so he sees how much I need this as much as he does.

"With me, you get more access. I have the incident report from the night your parents..." I trail off, not wanting to say it. An ache of sorrow moves through me for the little sister he never got to meet. Licking my lips, I go on. "Look, helping you is the only way I can think to make up for my broken promise. Will you let me?"

The shadows in his eyes kill me. As soon as the impulse grips me, I take a step, bringing our bodies close together. I touch his chiseled jaw lightly and press up on my toes to kiss him.

Fox allows it, releasing a low rumble as my lips slide against his. He doesn't let me in, so I start to pull away, but then he grips my waist and unleashes his storm on me. My heart sings when my back hits the wall of the warehouse as he claims my mouth with a deep kiss that sweeps me up in its possessive force.

This time when I pull back, lips swollen and tender, the shadows have cleared.

We gaze at each other and his thumb moves back and forth at my waist. With a sigh, he rests his forehead against mine. "There's so much you don't know still."

"So tell me. Don't push me away again. Let me in."

Fox's throat works with a swallow. "You want to help so bad? Fine," he murmurs in resignation. "Just remember—you asked for this."

TWENTY-TWO

FOX

Continuing my search for the truth with Maisy at my side wasn't the plan, but she does everything her way. I almost laugh because I should've known better than to try to control her free-spirited nature. Maisy is only controlled by her wild heart.

After leaving the warehouse, I led her to a place to stash her brother's car. As soon as she slid into the passenger seat of the Charger, my grip tightened on the wheel as my mind jumped back to the last time she was in my car. We drive to the diner near the interstate where I want to stake out a meeting Colt intercepted the details of.

The whole ride over, she had the window down with her arm hanging out to ride the waves of the warm air with her hand. More than once my attention snagged on the old leather bracelet she wears, the one with stones I gave her. She still never takes it off.

"I've never been on a stakeout before," Maisy says after we've been parked for twenty minutes. She digs through the glove compartment. "We should've stopped for some snacks."

I run my tongue over my teeth. "Stakeouts usually require quiet and concentration." I gesture with the hand resting on the wheel to the target. "So keep those pretty lips shut before I find a way to make you be quiet."

Maisy shoots me a look full of heat at my threat and I bite back a groan. God, this is torture after so many days away from her. The faint scent of sweet coconut on her skin is killing me.

"All right, grumpy." With an impatient huff, she falls back against the seat and props one leg up against the door to get more comfortable. "You don't have to be so bossy."

"You don't have to help," I remind her, trying to find something to distract myself from admiring the length of her toned legs as the hem of her dress lifts higher from her position. "You're only here because I'm allowing it."

Letting her in is probably my worst idea ever.

After what she said at the warehouse, I considered that I'd been going about this wrong by pushing her away. She should learn the truth about her parents. Besides, by keeping her close I can keep an eye on her. She'll either be an asset I can use against her parents, or if she picks them over me I'll be aware of it before she betrays me again.

My gaze drifts to her for the third time in five minutes instead of where my focus needs to be and I bite down on the inside of my cheek. If she slouches anymore, I'll be able to see right up her dress. A bolt of heat shoots to my dick. Damn little temptress...

Maisy draws me in with this crazy force made of the fabric of the universe. I drag my teeth over my lower lip and give her a subtle once over, wondering if her habit of forgoing underwear leaves her pussy bare beneath that dress. The last time I had her in my car, I couldn't stop the fantasies from coming and they're back in force now as the arousal builds, clouding my head with a hunger for her to ride my cock until she screams for me.

This time the want is even more intense, now that she's forced her way back into my life, demanding to help after I kept her at a distance. She won't let me go and it does things to my heart that make it twist around on itself and thump hard.

Blowing out a breath, I rest my hand on the gearshift between us and barely brush my fingers against her smooth thigh while fighting off the desire to drag her across the center console into my lap where I could kiss her.

After a couple of minutes, she adjusts in her seat, bringing her closer to me as she scans the area we're staking out. "So what are we on the lookout for?"

"I had a tip off for a meeting going down here today. I don't know who with, so I'm prepared for anything. Whoever it is, I'll document it."

"Cool. Got it."

I consider how dangerous it is to poke the sleeping bear while I hunt for the truth, but she would only prove to me once again that I have zero chances of keeping her out of this anymore.

"When the meeting goes down, I want you to make sure you duck out of sight. You understand?"

She peers up at me. "Why?"

"You know why," I mutter, clenching my fists. She lifts her brows questioningly and I sigh. "To keep your face hidden. That will protect you if we're spotted. I'm less recognizable in this suit, but I'm not taking a chance that anyone will recognize you and connect your face to your parents."

"Okay." She stares at me and reaches over to put her hand on my leg. "We're doing this together. You and me, the way it always should be."

I look at her from the corner of my eye, resting my elbow

against the window while tracing my lip with my thumb. "Yeah."

A bone-deep truth settles in me. I never should've blamed Maisy. We were just kids back then. The breath I release feels like it yanks away the last dredges of my years-long grudge, leaving me lighter and less shrouded in so much pain.

The car goes quiet again as we settle in to wait. I pass the minutes by running through everything I've learned so far in my head. The accident was covered up and Richard Landry helped with his new position as police chief. Jacqueline Landry becomes CEO mere weeks later. Both of them became richer and Nexus Lab grew from a small regional lab to one of the nation's top suppliers in the last decade.

Maisy's breathing slows as her head droops, hitting my shoulder after a few minutes. She's asleep. I still for a moment, then adjust my position to support her head better. She'll complain if she gets a stiff neck from falling asleep that way. Her floral and coconut scent wraps around me the same as her hug did the other night, making my lips twitch with the urge to smile.

This time instead of being a distraction, I find myself centered like she's a guiding light. I watch her sleep for a minute, then shift my attention to wait out the meeting.

For a while there's no activity, then two cars pull up. I shift around carefully without dislodging Maisy from my shoulder. Surprise lances through me. The first man, I don't recognize. He's a big, mean looking guy with a barrel chest and buzzed hair in a cheap suit. The other is Richard Landry.

Shouldn't he be with Maisy's family? I check the time and guess the graduation ceremony ended.

Richard is agitated, hands jerking sharply as he talks to the man he's meeting with. There's a quick exchange of something when they step closer together. Money, probably. And I caught him in the act of accepting a bribe.

Using my phone, I discreetly record everything. Colt will get the footage and analyze it on his system for me. Instead of leaving as soon as the coast is clear, I wait, allowing myself to watch her again. Her lips part and I want to trace them. Unable to help myself, I caress her cheek, careful not to wake her.

"Mm, sorry," Maisy says in a husky whisper as she stirs not long after. "I didn't mean to fall asleep."

"It's fine. I got what I needed while you were out."

"Did you?" She sits up, taking her warmth and comfortable weight with her. I have to restrain myself from drawing her head back to my shoulder. Her expression twists into an adorable pout. "Man, I didn't want to miss it. This totally ruins the badass cred I'm working on. I've got undercover work down, but choked on the stakeout."

I snort. "Yeah, you're definitely ready to take on corruption with those skills."

Colton would get a kick out of her. For the first time ever, I picture what it would be like to introduce my foster brother to my daisy. It puts a smile on my face as I start the engine and pull onto the road. Maisy's hand goes out the window again, coasting on the air as I pick up speed and race around the winding road.

More than once, my attention darts to her. She seems content with her hand in the wind and her hair. It's times like this I see the girl who held my heart in her small hands when we were kids.

"Do you remember California? When we went on vacation?" she asks after a short stretch of peaceful quiet. I hum in response, flashing her a curious look. Her attention is on her hand, expression distant and tinged in sadness. "That was such a good trip. I still have the shells and rocks we collected.

Remember when I turned the stones you picked out for me into this?" She holds up her wrist with the leather bracelet. "I miss the ocean."

A pang hits my tattooed chest with the same ache I've felt. "I do, too."

"You do?" There's a catch in her voice that lights a fire inside me.

Licking my lips when I feel her gaze on me, I rest my hand over the top of the wheel and willingly open up to someone for the first time in years.

"When I lived in Thorne Point on the east coast, there was a cove I would go to when I couldn't sleep. I stole my foster brother's car to get to it, and he caught me." I laugh at the memory of Colt squinting at me and calling me a punk-ass little twerp. "He let me borrow it anytime I wanted after he saw the haunted look in my eyes."

"Nightmares?"

"Yeah. They come and go, usually around the anniversary, but going to that cove helped. I miss the salt air on my skin. So much so, I tattooed it there."

Maisy leans toward me. "Exactly! I've been planning this road trip. I want to hit up as many national parks as I can between here and the west coast. I'm going to do sunrise yoga in each one and really connect myself to nature."

As she explains, I'm struck by nostalgia, remembering how many hours we'd spend pouring over roadmaps and making plans for the adventures we would go on. It was me and her, ready to take on the world. All of our dreams used to intertwine until we didn't know where hers stopped and mine began. We were so close.

I find myself smiling. "You're finally taking it. I remember how important it was to you."

"Yeah." She bites her lip around a smile, hazel eyes bright.

"Not yet, though. First I'm helping you, then I'm hitting the road."

When the impulse strikes to punch the gas, I follow it, shifting gears and opening up the engine. Maisy yelps as her back hits the seat, then throws her hands up. It's clear to see what the thrill does to her as it rolls through her whole body, as alive as she is. She smacks the roof overhead and lets out a whoop while I take a bend.

We drive like that until we hit the shorter roads that twist around the boulders dotting the hills.

"Will you give me a ride on your dad's bike again? I loved it."

Air catches in my throat. "You knew it was his? Not just the same model Harley, but *his*?"

"Yeah. I'd recognize it anywhere. You used to idolize it." Her eager smile softens. "I'm glad you have it."

"It was hard to track down."

There's a beat of quiet where we're both in our heads.

"I'm sorry you were alone for so long. I wish you never had to leave here." She pulls her hair out of her face and glances at her lap. "I missed you every day."

"I wasn't always alone," I admit, throat constricted from the pain in her tone. "For a long time, it felt like all I had was me." My life has gone so wrong, but not every second of it was bad. "The foster system wasn't good to me, it was like my past followed me like a bad smell." My grip flexes on the wheel. "Most of the families were afraid of me."

"Why?"

"I was so angry all the time. I fought anyone I could." I clench my teeth, then relax when she reaches out to take my hand. "It wasn't until I was fifteen that the DuPonts took me in after I'd been bounced around so much. Then things finally started turning around."

"They were good to you?"

"Yeah. Kind of socialite snobs, but they had an older son. Eventually I found he was in my corner, and with him, there were others."

"I'm in your corner," Maisy says mildly, squeezing my hand.

I grip her small hand in mine. "I know that now. Colton, my foster brother, had friends. They brought me into their circle and treated me like family. Honestly, after so many years of what I went through, I was against it at first. In the system you learn fast that nothing belongs to you and no one really wants you."

Her fingers tighten around mine. "Fox..."

My shoulder lifts in a shrug. "That's the system. These guys, though, they cracked through my *fuck you* shell before I realized that they'd accepted me as one of them."

"Are they who you were with at the holiday market last year?"

I blink. "What?"

Last year Wren, Colton, Levi, and Jude had rolled into town out of the blue around the holidays. I thought the Crows had come for me, but Wren said it was strictly business and I understood the lethal hardness to his eyes. His sister. He'd been on the crusade since she died, searching for her fucked up teacher that preyed on her not long after I started living with the DuPonts. We met up briefly at the local holiday market downtown, but I only saw them for a few minutes before they left in a rush when they finally found the bastard.

"Yeah. How did you know?"

"I was there with my friend Thea." A complicated expression contorts her beautiful features. "That day was pretty crazy, but before that I was looking for her and saw you with those guys. It was the first time I'd seen you smile genuinely since the last time I saw you, before..."

She doesn't have to finish, I catch her meaning. I haven't smiled much since returning to Ridgeview. It seems I only do when it has to do with her.

Curiosity brims in her gaze as she studies me. I can sense her hunger to learn more about what my life has been like in the time we've been apart. When the connection between people is as deep as ours was, there's this sense of possessiveness that's hard to kick. I know I've felt it around her, too.

It's not until we're almost at my warehouse that I realize I wasn't on guard with her, driving on autopilot. That more than anything else tells me I'm ready to trust her again, when I rarely let anyone in. The patched up wall around my heart finally crumbles.

"I want to show you something."

"Okay."

I take the turn off for my place. She's the first person in town I've brought here. Once I pull in and park the Charger in the garage, she gets out.

Vulnerability burns in me as I follow her around my workspace while she takes in my abstract pieces.

"This is where you live."

"Yes."

She brushes her fingers over the bike and glances at me. "I'm serious about that ride."

Some of the vulnerability bleeds away and I smirk, dragging my gaze over her body. "As long as you promise not to get the leather dirty, little daisy."

A flush colors her cheeks and she finds the steps leading to the studio apartment. I follow her up, sinking my teeth into my lip as her ass sways.

"Love what you've done with the place. Big Batcave vibes," Maisy says with a crooked grin. "Down to the workout corner."

I chuckle, glancing around to try to see what she sees with her fresh eyes. "It serves its purpose."

She hums and explores, examining the coffee table and skating her hand over the back of the couch. While she looks around, I take off the suit jacket and toss it on the arm of the couch and pull the tie loose. Her gaze tracks my movements, lingering on the flex of my arms. The corner of my mouth lifts and I slow down.

It's so clear now, with her fitting right into my space as if she's always belonged here. I never should've blamed her. Anger blinded me and festered in my heart until it was an unruly beast. It's still there, but she tempers it with the way she balances me. The hope that I haven't fucked myself over by hurting her arrows through me.

I want to make this right. I have to.

Reaching for her hand, I sit her down on the couch and park my ass on the sturdy coffee table I made with my own two hands. My knees bracket hers. "There's something I need to say."

The apology doesn't come easily. I prefer actions over pretty words, but for her I try to get it out.

"I'm...sorry. For being an asshole to you, for hurting you, and all the times I tried to scare you." Her brow creases, but she doesn't pull away, giving me the strength to go on. "I see how wrong I was now. I never should've put the blame on you." I meet her gaze and swallow at how much could be showing in my eyes, not hiding from her anymore. "If you can forgive me, I want to do better. I want to trust you. All the rage and grief and pain blinded me for so long—years. I couldn't believe you were as good as you seemed when I came back when I formed this picture in my head, but you are. You've shown me time and again that you're still as good-hearted and kind and real as when we were kids."

"Fox," she whispers, stroking my knuckles with her thumb. "It's okay. It's behind us now, right?" I nod and she smirks. "Good. Because I'll kick your ass if you try to push me away or treat me like crap again." She holds up her fists at the ready. "Use the momentum from my core, right?"

Lips twitching, I scrub my face. "I'm sorry I wanted to destroy you. It's all I've been planning for years—you and your parents and Holden. All I could see was that my parents were dead and your family had this great life. I wanted it to hurt as badly as I did, but I...I couldn't do it." I clear my throat. "When it comes down to it, I can't truly hurt you. I would rather protect you or die, because I..."

My words dry up. Good thing, too, because I was likely to let it slip that I'm still in love with her. Always have been. As much as I want to rush and take everything I want with her, I know I can't scare her off. This is my one chance to keep her and I'm not giving it up.

When Ridgeview is in ashes, it'll be Maisy at my side.

"We're a mess, huh?" She gives me a soft smile. "I'd rather have you in my life than go back to living another day without you, no matter what it means to keep you."

A rough sound escapes me because I feel the same way. My heart never stopped belonging to her.

Maisy leans forward, winding her arms around my neck as her lips find mine. She tastes sweet when my tongue pushes into her mouth. My fingers bury in her hair and I yank her forward so she has to straddle me. Fuck, how did I ever think I could live without this perfect girl?

I groan when I slide a hand up her dress to push it up so it's out of the way and find out I was right about her naughty secret. No panties stop me as I palm her ass. She moans into the kiss, grinding down on my cock as she tugs on my hair. I haul her closer and nip at her lip, growling when she gets me back by digging her nails into the nape of my neck. My girl is wild and untamed and my dick is so fucking hard for her.

Leaning back, she licks her lips. "There's something I want."

"Yeah?" I trace her lips with my thumb and curse under my breath when she takes the tip into her mouth.

She nods and speaks against the pad of my thumb. "I want you to fuck my mouth. Like you promised before. I want you to take control of me."

"Shit." It tears out of me and my grip on her ass flexes. I didn't promise, I threatened. "You want me to stuff your mouth with my cock, baby?"

Instead of answering, she takes my hand and swallows two of my fingers, keeping her eyes locked with mine. Heat rockets through me and in one motion I stand, bringing her with me. Glancing around the room, I spot a towel on the floor by the bench press. It'll have to do. I want her on her knees, but I don't want the concrete to hurt her while she takes me down her throat.

Carrying her to the corner of the room, I let go so she slides down my body in the most sinful, sensual glide. There's a damp spot from how wet her pussy is on the front of my suit pants and I drop a hand to rub my erection, grinning with a feral edge. Maisy steals another kiss and grabs the towel, folding it a couple of times and dropping it on the ground. She follows, gazing up at me from the floor.

Holy. Fuck. That is a beautiful sight.

"Fuck my face, Fox."

I hiss, pausing in unbuckling my belt to grip myself. If she's not careful, she could send me over the edge before we get anywhere. I never let other girls in, because they weren't her, and now that I get to touch her again it's got me worked up as hell. She reaches up to help.

Gripping her hair, I tilt her head back as I glide my cock across her lips. She grins up at me with this wicked look that makes my hand flex in her hair. Without warning, I force my way into her mouth and she accommodates me, opening wide to take me. My head tips back, but I keep my gaze on her, testing her limits with a few shallows thrusts. It feels so goddamn good, the perfect amount of heat and suction.

She curls her tongue around me and bobs her head in time with my thrusts. I let her lead for a minute, fascinated and turned on by the sight of her perfect lips wrapped around my cock. My fantasies have nothing on the real deal.

A sharp pinch at my hip makes me blink. She lifts her brows as if to say *are you going to do it?*

Grinning, I tighten my hold on her hair. "Open wide, daisy."

Warmth floods her gaze as I take my first sharp thrust. She likes this. The rough treatment, the way I take control—it gets her hot.

"Bet that pussy is fucking drenched for me, isn't it?" She nods as best she can while I control the pace. A savage need overtakes me. "Show me, baby. Stroke that pretty pussy and show me how wet you are for me."

Maisy's pupils dilate and her hand flies between her legs, diving beneath her rumpled dress. Her lashes flutter at the first touch and she spends a little too long fingering herself. I yank on her hair to get her attention and punish her by going deeper, hitting the back of her throat. She chokes and sucks in a breath when she can, adjusting to the new depth.

"Show me," I growl.

Tears cling to her lashes as she lifts her fingers to show me. They're glistening, her hand covered. With a rumble vibrating in my chest, I capture her wrist in my free hand and bend down to suck her taste into my mouth. Next time we do this, she's going to suck my cock while I make her sit on my face and I won't stop eating her until she's a sobbing mess for me.

I release her wrist and speed up my thrusts to the point she has to concentrate on when to suck in air before she passes out. Her hand goes back to rubbing her clit and her thighs shake. Pleasure races down my spine and my balls draw tight. I'm close.

Maisy moans, tears leaking from the corners of her eyes, one hand gripping my leg for balance and the other buried between her thighs as she takes her own pleasure. My thrusts pick up and I gasp for air as I drive my cock into her mouth. It's too much. Fuck, it's *too much*, and I release a loud groan as my orgasm hits.

Her nails dig into my thigh and she swallows my come, throat working as she meets my gaze with hazy pleasure burning in her gorgeous hazel eyes. The flush in her cheeks darkens and she bucks her hips, crying out around my cock as she comes.

It takes us a minute to come back to ourselves. When we do, I scoop her up from the floor and kiss her, holding her against my body.

I never want to let her go. Even if it meant never getting the justice I've been seeking, I'd live in this moment for eternity if I could.

She pulls back with a dazed smile while I tuck my dick away and pull the suit pants up. As she's wiping the corners of her mouth and catching her breath, her phone goes off on the table. She grabs it and her eyes go wide. "Shit. Can you give me a ride back to Holden's car? He just warned me that his distraction didn't work out so well."

I want to say no. I need to taste her. Strip her down and lay claim to every other inch of her—spend hours rediscovering my daisy. But I nod.

Smirking, I strip out of the suit pants she stained and grab a pair of jeans from by the bed across the room. "Let's take the bike."

Maisy's hazel eyes light up and it calls to a deep part of my heart to bring that side out of her.

TWENTY-THREE

MAISY

There was no sense of dread when I returned home, like I've already burst from my metaphoric cage and allowed my wings to fly free. Maybe it's the lingering thrill of riding on the back of Fox's motorcycle, or maybe it's how unchained and right I felt taking him in my mouth. Either way, I won't let them put me back in the miserable place they've kept me for years. And when it comes down to them and helping Fox? I pick him.

Once Holden texted me, I knew I had to get away from Fox's studio apartment fast so Dad couldn't track my phone and know how to find him. It was just as exhilarating as the first time to ride on the bike, my arms locked around him as we zoomed down the roads.

Before I got off the bike, he took my phone and put his number in, kissing my cheek before he drove off.

My parents and Holden aren't home yet when I get past the security system. I don't waste a minute, seizing the opportunity to get what I can to help Fox before they get back. My best bet for snooping on what my parents could be hiding is in the home office.

Mom uses it more often than Dad, but I know he's brought home his work before. He's the one with more power and I can't get the sight of his signatures on the Wilder case files out of my head. His secrets might have lurked in our house for years. It makes my suspicion spike as I sit down in the expensive leather office chair, turning on the computer. I wonder what else I can find on Nexus Lab that Mom might keep on this computer as the busy CEO.

I tuck my phone against my shoulder and ear as I wait for the computer to boot up, calling the one person I know who can walk me through this fast. I've never been more thankful for my best friend to have married a computer genius than I am right now.

"*Sup, little Landry?*" Connor answers, like the cocky ass he is.

"I don't even have time for you right now," I say with a smirk. "Walk me through copying a hard drive. The fastest way you've got, preferably ."

That piques his interest. "*What are you up to?*"

"Clock is ticking here."

"*Are you doing something illegal?*" There's a grin in his tone. "*I'm in.*"

"You'd better be." I throw a glance at the door with no idea how much time I have before they get home. "Come on."

"*Aight, relax. I've got you. It's easy.*" It sounds like he's stretching. "*Do you have a flash drive or an external?*"

I search the drawers of the large desk and come up with one. "Yes."

"*Good, so here's what you need to do.*"

He walks me through the steps and it goes faster than I expected. A question occurs to me as the progress bar hits the halfway mark of copying the drive to the flash drive.

"Will I be able to access everything?"

I know Dad's password because he let me buy concert tickets for a show Thea and I went to. I didn't want Mom to know. Hers are a mystery to me, though, and I'll need them if I want to get into the pharmaceutical company's files on the drive.

"All the settings will copy, so anything not encrypted or password protected is fair game."

I bite my lip. "So I'll need the passwords."

He laughs. *"Maybe. Depends on the level of security on them. What are you getting up to, hippie chick?"*

"None of your business, Bishop. Keep this to yourself."

"Cool, cool. Your little snooping secret is safe with me."

For now is left unspoken, because Connor loves collecting information and has a penchant for blackmail. Not that he'd actually use it against me. He collects information to protect the people he cares about, too.

The computer dings when the hard drive is copied. "It finished. Thanks."

Swiping the flash drive, I go to my room and stash it in a vintage blue suede purse with fringe. I catch sight of myself in the mirror and pause. My lips are still pink and slightly swollen from earlier and my dress looks like a mess. I shift, rubbing my thighs together and still feel the tingly echo of how much I liked what Fox and I did.

The front door opens and closes, low murmurs from Dad and Holden drifting through the foyer.

"Maisy Grace Landry," Mom calls ominously. Her voice only raises enough to carry without outright yelling. "Downstairs. Now."

Sighing, I head for my execution.

When I reach the top, Holden shoots me an apologetic expression. I give him a subtle nod. It's fine, I knew it was going to be tough to avoid this, even with him running interference.

Leaving my high school graduation ceremony probably meant when my name was called, there was a wave of confusion when I didn't get up and walk to the stage to accept my diploma. Bet Mom really loved that embarrassment. I picture the other parents in the stands whispering.

"Get down here," Dad snaps.

Oh good, they're both upset. Mom I expected, but Dad's always acted out of an overbearing sense of protectiveness. I don't make it down the steps before they tear into me.

"Where were you?"

"What were you *thinking*?"

They both speak at once and my gaze bounces between them. Mom narrows her eyes and shoots Dad a look that has him stepping back. Lines form around his mouth with his severe frown as he folds his arms.

"What ridiculous notion did you have that made you think you could get away with walking out on your graduation ceremony?" Mom hisses. "They called your name for five minutes before they finally moved on. Why would you do this?"

Jutting my chin, I cross my arms. "There's no rule that says I had to attend. They'll mail my diploma. Why is that so wrong?"

"You are so childish," Mom says coldly. "Go to your room."

"Go to my room?" A sound of disbelief escapes me. "I'm not twelve. You have to stop treating me like a baby."

"When you stop acting like one, you'll be treated accordingly," Mom shoots back. "Your actions today reflect on all of us."

"So what!" I explode, descending another step. "Who cares so much that you got a side eye for five whole minutes? There are more important things than reputation!"

"Reputation is *everything*," she argues, gesturing between me and Holden. "One child can't maintain his college acceptance and ends up in a public community college, and the other is a goddamn wild child I can't control no matter how many rules I have to lay down for you to become a proper example."

"I actually like my classes," Holden mutters, expression clouding. "I'm...glad I lost the football draft to Ohio State."

I could hug my brother right now. This is the first time he's stood up to their tyrant rule over us, too. I think we're both done with the bullshit. The anger is expanding in my chest, climbing my throat. I won't swallow it back or let this go. I'm eighteen and I've done every single thing they've ever wanted—studied hard, gotten the grades they demanded, and put myself in the boxes they wanted.

"Oh, shut up, Holden," Mom says haughtily.

My laugh is caustic and bitter. "God, Mom, do you even hear yourself? Who fucking cares!"

"Maisy," Dad barks.

"No, Dad! Seriously, the world isn't ending because I skipped out today. You guys are the ones acting crazy for thinking that."

"We didn't know where the hell you were or if someone had taken you," he says angrily. "I looked all over."

"You didn't try to track my phone, like usual, warden?" I shout. "Shocker, it's usually your go to."

His expression darkens. "That was to protect you."

"From what?" I rush the final steps and throw my hands out. If I get him worked up enough, maybe I can make him admit the things he's done. "Where is the threat? If you can be honest with me about why we have such tight security and why you think it's okay to track my whereabouts by my phone, I'd be willing to listen. But I can't do this blindly anymore. You're suffocating me." The breath I take is sharp and painful. "I can't be a doll anymore. I have my own feelings and thoughts."

He opens his mouth, conflict flooding his gaze. He's going to tell me something important.

"Every choice and sacrifice we've made for you has been to set you on the best path to have a good future," Mom cuts in, exchanging an unreadable look with Dad.

Damn it.

I face her and am struck by how much I have bent myself into whatever shape she demanded. "If you really loved me, you'd let me pick what I wanted for myself. Everything you've forced on me I've hated. And none of it has ever been good enough to satisfy you, just makes you demand more and more of me. The grades, the clothes, then you forced Sam on me as another way to keep me under your thumb. Why are you so obsessed with him?"

"He's a perfectly good match for you. He's from a well-respected family on our level. We're in talks with his parents and we all agree, you'll date and after you both graduate from college we'll talk about marriage plans."

"You expect me to marry him? Hell no! I'm not having some arranged marriage. Dad, are you seriously going to let that happen?"

Dad can't look me in the eye.

"Mom, come on. That's too much," Holden says warily. "You can't make her to do that."

"Maisy will do what I think is best," Mom says.

"I can't anymore. You can't control every aspect of my life."

Her mouth pinches. "You're just a child. You can't possibly know what's good for you."

"That's the point I'm making here! I need to make these decisions for myself." I stand up straighter. "Starting with this one—I'm not going to Northwestern. I never wanted to go there. I want nothing to do with Sam Blake, so you can toss that

232

out, too. I'm going to make my own life plan instead of following the one you forced on me."

It feels good to finally get that off my chest.

Dad shoots a worried look at Mom and she steps into my space, putting her hand on my shoulder. Her nails dig in slightly.

"Jackie—"

Dad doesn't get to finish.

"Well. Then pack your things." Her voice is so cold. It's hard to believe she's my mother with how little emotion is in her voice when she stares at me. "If you don't have any plans to go along with these choices, then the disciplinary institution it is."

I grit my teeth and jerk away from her. "No."

"Yes."

"You can't make me. Holden gets to go to community college, but I have to get shipped off to some shady finishing school because I had an original thought instead of one you fed to me? No fucking thanks."

"Yeah, that's not fair," Holden says. "Why can't she just pick?"

"Because I said so," Mom says.

"Let's not be hasty, Jackie. I don't want to force that on her."

Dad tries to reason with her, but I've never seen her like this. Ruthless, that's what she looks like. She was playing nice before, but now the gloves are off.

"Shut up, Richard. This is necessary."

I back up, inching toward the stairs. "You're insane if you think I'll let you send me anywhere I don't want to go."

"You will do as I say," Mom says.

"I won't! I'll get a lawyer. I'm eighteen, you can't do that to me!"

A vein pops out in her temple and a flush creeps up her neck. "If you won't obey my rules, then you'll be cut off." She's livid now, her threatening voice shaking. "I give you enough liberties as it is. If that's what it takes to make you behave, then that's what will happen."

"Go ahead," I challenge, putting a foot on the first step. "I'm leaving. You won't listen, so I'm gone. I'll cut myself off." Swinging to Dad, I add, "If you track my phone, I'll throw it away and get a new one because parents don't invade their kids' privacy and lives like that."

"Maisy Grace!" Mom yells after me.

I'm so fucking done.

With my chest heaving and adrenaline from the fight rushing through my veins, I run up to my room and slam the door. I need to make this quick, or Mom will pull something crazier, like putting a security lock on my door or overruling Dad to send me to the disciplinary school against my will.

I grab the first bag I find in the closet and throw clothes inside with my laptop, then snag my purse with the flash drive. The medical journals from Devlin go in next, followed by my jar of rocks and my favorite crystals tucked carefully between my clothes. Glancing around the room, my throat goes dry. I can't fit everything in my bag.

In one motion I strip the rumpled designer dress overhead and fling it onto the floor, standing nude in the middle of my room with the evidence of what I did with Fox two hours ago dried on my upper thighs. It feels good to stand there like that, like I'm shedding a skin that was too tight and I've finally burst free through the constricting seams.

For a minute, I consider going to stay with Thea, but I don't want to intrude on her and Connor. They're still enjoying their time together as newlyweds. As much as I love my best friend, there's somewhere else that's calling me.

As I pull out my favorite yoga pants with slits in the sides that cuff around my ankles, I call Fox, searching for a shirt with my breasts out and proud. Nothing will keep me down anymore.

He answers on the first ring. *"Hey. You good?"*

I don't have a penny to my name. No savings, no car, no phone if my parents cut me off for this stunt.

And I've never felt more alive.

"Yup. So, is it too soon for me to move in?" I joke, grabbing a fitted crop top. "Come get me?"

There's only a brief silence before his deep voice filters through the phone. *"I'm coming."*

Nothing has ever made me smile wider or made my heart soar as high.

TWENTY-FOUR

FOX

Two coffee mugs clink on the table when Maisy sets them down next to my laptop in the morning. "Walk me through what you know so far."

For the second time yesterday, her arms were wrapped around me on my bike after I picked her up at the end of her block when she left her home. She told me Holden helped her out after a blowout fight with her parents.

The sensation of her embrace created a steadfast ember of warmth in my heart. I've fought on my own for a long time, even struggling to let Colton in completely. But with Maisy, it feels like the world has opened up from the blinders I've had on.

Once we got back to the warehouse, I kissed her, then went down to work in the garage. She watched, perched on the steps until it got late. We ordered pizza that I went to pick up and stayed awake until the early hours of the morning talking. I told her more about what it was like growing up in foster care, about my favorite cove in Thorne Point, and the story of how I managed to track down my dad's Harley and bought it back.

My heart ached when she described what it was like after I had to leave town, then told me the story of when she met her redheaded friend, and how much her road trip plans meant to her.

At some point we finally passed out in the middle of the conversation, trying too hard to soak in each other and make up for all the lost years.

This morning I woke up with her tucked against my side, her face smashed into my shoulder and I spent several minutes gazing at her, lightly brushing her tangled hair aside. After getting up, I heard her rustling in the sheets and she joined me in the workout corner, running through yoga poses and stretching her lithe body while I went through my own routine. I thought I'd hate having someone else in my space, but with her it just fits as if we've always been like this. When we were done, she showered and I ended up on the couch with my laptop.

Instead of taking the coffee, I pull her down into my lap on the couch and get distracted for a moment, kissing the side of her neck as my palm skates over the strip of her stomach exposed by her tight crop top. I can't decide if I like this version or one of her loose flowing ones better, but I'll never get tired of having easy access to her tits. She arches when I push beneath her shirt to tease a nipple.

"Mm, focus, or we won't get anything done today," she says in a husky tone.

"Can't help it," I rasp against her neck. "I resisted everything for so long, but it's like putting a starving man in front of a buffet."

Her lips meet mine in a lazy kiss that has my arms banding around her waist. "Come on." She speaks against my mouth. "Lay it all out."

"I want to lay you out."

Her shoulders shake with her laugh. "Later."

"Fine."

Releasing a calming breath to encourage my erection to go down, I adjust her so she's not teasing me with every tiny move, settling a hand on her hip. She grabs the coffees and offers me one while I gesture to the laptop.

"I always knew that the accident was faked," I start. "I was with my dad when he checked the car, it was only a day or two before. They weren't supposed to go out that night, but they'd been arguing about something. I tried to listen, but they dropped it when they saw me trying to sneak down the steps. It wasn't until I started to dig into everything to connect the pieces that things didn't line up and I started to get suspicious of the circumstances surrounding their deaths."

"Why do you think they had those samples hidden at your house? Is that what they were arguing about?"

"I don't know. The best guess I have is they were trying to protect their patent. My working theory is Jacqueline must have gotten there first and the company rewarded her for it by appointing her CEO. It's quite the promotion."

She nods with a troubled look. "We went out to dinner to celebrate her promotion that same night. It wasn't announced publicly, but she already knew."

That's news to me. I nod slowly, swallowing. She puts down her coffee cup and laces her fingers with mine.

"When I started looking into Nexus Lab to find answers connecting back to my parents, I found something weird that gave me the first clue something wasn't right. The previous CEO just disappeared off the face of the earth. Officially he took early retirement about twenty years too early—he was in line for Forbes 40 under 40. It's like someone got rid of him in order for Jacqueline to take the position, jumping straight from R&D to the top. It was the same when I looked into your dad with a miraculous promotion. I've been trying to follow the money to trace it back to what happened and how my parents ended up dead because of it."

Maisy listens attentively, asking questions for clarity as I take her through what I've gathered. I let her in on what I was doing at the restaurant the other night before school ended, bribing a waiter to give me a stolen employee ID badge, which led to finding the remote shipping facility Nexus Lab uses when I accessed the employee's schedule. I show her photos Colton enhanced for me that I took discreetly at the warehouse. I'm only slightly surprised when she doesn't shy away from the facts I've found that paint her parents in the worst light.

"Someone else was supposed to become the chief," I explain. "He was in the process of taking the position when suddenly your dad was sworn in. Your dad's been known to take bribes and has maintained a corrupt office as chief. He was who showed up at that meeting we staked out. I think it's because he already knew how to play dirty that someone put him in that position of power."

She sits up. "I know. I brought stuff that might help fill in the blanks. I copied the computer at the house before I skipped out. And the police report from the accident, although some of it is redacted."

My brows jump up. Colt assured me he'd wiped most of the important things from the system so that I could dig before someone covered their tracks more than they had. "How did you get that?"

"My friend Connor. He knew about some of Dad's corrupt ways and used that knowledge to squeeze it out of him to get information on you, or he was going to expose Dad as a bribable cop."

I'm starting to get why Colt has taken such a liking to

Connor Bishop. The two of them are practically cut from the same cloth.

"So Richard really gave it up?"

"I guess. I don't think Dad thought anyone would look too closely at a closed case accident report, or maybe he thought it would be more suspect to withhold it like he was trying to hide something. My dad's signature is all over it, though, even on the night of the accident when he had an alibi because we were out to dinner."

"That's the problem I have. I can't prove their involvement without proof of payment or something more concrete. The alibis put them in the clear."

"As smart as the alibis are, there are still holes. It didn't make sense why pages were missing. Why hide things when it's supposed to be an accident? It's what first made me suspect his involvement in covering it up because it was closed so fast." Her brow creases and she looks at the laptop. "But this explains why Mom was always so uptight and a total bitch to me. She didn't want to risk anything casting doubt on her if it threatened her power. They've both changed, but she's so different from when I was little."

Frowning, I pull her closer, tucking her hair behind her ear and brushing my fingers down her cheek. I used to resent her for growing up with her parents and her brother, but I can't imagine how much Jacqueline and Richard's greed has poisoned their relationship with Holden and Maisy. I don't see the woman who was sweet to me when I was a kid anywhere in the soulless woman she is now.

"Do you think my parents actually killed them, or were they the ones who covered it up?"

I've asked myself that same question over and over. "I don't know. I just know they were involved somehow."

"I'm sorry," she whispers. "I hate that they could hurt you."

"It's not your fault." I know that now and I don't want it to weigh on her.

Opening up to tell her this feels like I'm in a twilight zone. It's not just that I've let very few people know the full story— only Colton knows the full extent. But sharing it with her makes it feel like I have someone I can lean on. I bump my nose beneath her ear and squeeze her tight in an embrace.

"The truth is coming out," I murmur. "One way or another."

She makes a soft sound in agreement, turning to kiss me.

"I also brought these," Maisy says, getting up to rustle through her bag at the foot of the bed. She comes back with a stack of magazines and perches in my lap.

It's the science journal I've been looking up online. I lift a brow.

"A friend of mine, his parents run that medical research clinic in town. He got them for me."

"You have helpful friends. I should've gone after them instead of you."

She smacks my chest and puts the stack of magazines on the table. "Maybe I can scope out the company if I play it like I'm stopping by to see my mom? She had an important meeting on the calendar that she's spent a month preparing for. Maybe I'll convince the guard to let me wait in her office since I'm her daughter. I can snoop around and see if I can get us more."

"Let's find out." I adjust her in my lap, reaching around to switch windows on the laptop. My brows furrow at the map. "That's weird. I have tracking on her phone, but she's not there."

Maisy's brows dip. "She's really strict about her work hours, she should be there."

"Hang on."

I type a few keys to trigger the tracing Colton hooked me

up with. It takes a minute for the scanner to pinpoint her signal, but once it does we both lean in. The address she's at isn't anywhere near where she should be, on the opposite side of town in the middle of nowhere. It's not far from the shipping warehouse I snooped around at, but further off from the rest of the shipping district.

"Switch to street view on Google maps," she suggests. "I want to see where she is."

I plug in the address and Maisy tilts her head as we take a virtual tour. It's another warehouse, this one much shadier looking than the shipping facility. The tin siding is covered in rust and the roof looks in disrepair.

"Wait. Go back, I recognize that logo."

"This?"

I navigate back to the front of the building. On a rolling bay door in faded, peeling letters is SynCom.

"SynCom," Maisy says in a dull tone. "Fox, that logo is on her paychecks."

"What? Why wouldn't Nexus Lab be the ones paying her?"

"They are. It's done through this, I think. I was with her once at the bank and she had me hold a stack with this stamped on it."

"There must be some kind of investor or something that owns Nexus Lab privately. I'll find out if this SynCom is a holdings company and see what this means."

"We make a good team." She beams at me.

I rub my mouth. "I should've been working with you instead of against you this whole time. I would've gotten more answers sooner."

"I told you at that party, jerk," she teases, elbowing me. "We could've been doing so much this year—kissing and kicking ass—instead of wasting all this time."

I hum at the memory of my wild daisy at that house party. That first taste was everything. "Did you keep those pants?"

"Maybe." She blushes. "I was going to throw them out because they're stained, but..."

A slow grin stretches across my face. The tight leggings she has on now are similar, hugging her legs in a deep green color. Only a thin barrier separates her ass from my lap.

Cupping her face, I draw her in for a kiss that quickly turns dirty as our tongues glide together. She twists her flexible body to reach me, ending up straddling my lap and grinding on me. I groan against her lips.

"There's something we didn't get to do yesterday and I can't hold out any longer."

Her lids are heavy. "Do your worst."

The echo of the last time she said that to me when I cornered her in the girls' bathroom sounds in my head. I hoist her into my arms and carry her to the bed, dropping her down hard enough to bounce. She stretches, lifting her arms over her head. With a wicked grin, I crawl over her and kiss my way down her neck, over her hard nipples, biting them through her cropped shirt to earn a cry. I continue lower, licking into her exposed belly button on my way to her waistband.

Peering up, I take in the incredible sight of her propped up on her elbows, watching me. "I'm going to taste your pussy."

"Yes," she whispers, her knees falling open to allow me room to settle between her legs.

A hunger that's nearly feral overtakes me as soon as I hook my fingers in the waistband of her snug yoga pants. I yank them down with rough tugs and fling them behind me while she giggles. Smacking the outside of her thigh to quiet her, I use my grip to pull her leg open for me. Once again she's not wearing any underwear. My mouth waters as I sink to my elbows between her thighs.

The first swipe of my tongue over Maisy's wet folds makes me groan and dive in for a second taste. It's better than I imagined when I pictured doing this for the first time. She arches off the bed with a high-pitched cry as my tongue drives her wild. I grab her hips and find every way to make her pant and moan. When I slide two fingers into her, she clenches around me, gripping me with her tight heat, making me want to drive my cock into her right now.

"Oh, fuck!" Maisy hooks a leg over my shoulder, hips bucking as she rides my fingers and my face. "I'm so close!"

I growl against her slick and swollen folds, sucking and licking until she clenches her thighs around my head with a hoarse cry. I don't stop. I keep feasting on her like I have to savor every single taste, curling my fingers inside her and pumping them. At first she tries to get away, only to let her legs drop open while pushing her pussy against me, coming undone again. I force orgasm after orgasm out of her until she's trembling.

"I need you," she begs. "Please, I need you right now. Don't keep me waiting anymore. We've wasted too much time on waiting."

I still don't stop, not until I'm good and ready to take my mouth off her. Maybe it's to put off what I have to tell her for a few minutes more. Her begging turns into a delirious litany. When I do sit back, my face is a mess. I pull my fingers free and make sure she watches as I lick them clean.

"I want you inside me," she whispers, her gaze full of liquid heat. "Right now. I need your cock filling me up."

My heart clenches and my stomach dips.

"I—"

I break off, running my gaze over her body. It's not like I was waiting specifically for her, but I didn't go out of my way to do it either.

The truth of my love for her hits me right in the chest.

She's the only one I've ever cared for, the only one I've pictured doing this with. I swallow thickly. The times I've been with girls have been far and very few between, and even then it never felt right to do more than get them off with our clothes mostly on. Meeting her gaze, I lay my secret on the table.

"I haven't... There was only ever you. It was always you, Maisy."

TWENTY-FIVE

MAISY

My heart sits in my throat as the deep aching need intensifies between my legs. I never thought... He's always been so dominant the few times we've hooked up, I didn't even think he wasn't experienced.

Leaning up to cup Fox's jaw, I smile. "It's okay. I want you. You just made me come like four times. You can't do it wrong, just do what feels good."

Relief melts the lines of tension that I'm not judging him for never having sex before. That kind of stuff doesn't matter to me, it's all society pressure anyway. He crashes our mouths together in a wild kiss. We wind up in a tangle of limbs as we peel out of the rest of our clothes.

A huff leaves him when I push him back to study his inked chest. The tattoo of the ocean is amazing, the intricate waves rolling and rippling along his muscles, stretching across his heart and down his arm in a half sleeve. Hidden amongst the details is a second tattoo, this one a crow wearing a crown perched on a skull with its wings spread. My lips part as I trace it with my fingertips. A hoarse noise vibrates in his throat as I touch the ink I've been dying to see.

"It's beautiful."

"I told you I missed the ocean, too."

Grinning, I steal another kiss. His powerful thighs drive me crazy as I trap one between my legs. I have half a mind to rub my clit against his thigh until I come again, but I want to feel him inside me.

Fox breaks the kiss and curses under his breath, glancing at his discarded jeans with a dismayed look. "I don't have a condom. The guys...they used to tease me and slip one into my wallet, but I got rid of the last one when it expired."

A laugh rolls through me. "Good. Don't use expired condoms. That's as bad as being unprepared."

He grunts, pulling away. I lock my arms around his neck and keep him in place, with his cock gliding along my folds.

"I have a contraceptive hormonal implant and I'm clean."

My cheeks burn hot with the admission. I'm not ashamed or anything, because I own my body, but the implant wasn't my first pick for birth control. Mom didn't want to risk any kind of scandal, including teen pregnancy. Always controlling me in one way or another. As soon as I was old enough, she made me ask the doctor about it and signed off her *permission*.

I force her and the awful sensation crawling up my throat from my mind and bring myself back into the present. "We're good to go."

Fox licks his lips, desire flaring in his gaze at the prospect of having me bare. "Are you sure? I've only touched you, but—"

I cover his mouth and smile. "I'm sure."

He studies me for a beat, then lowers himself over me, wrapping me in strong arms as he tortures the sensitive skin on the side of my neck. I moan as we rock together, his dick rubbing my clit instead of slipping inside. I open my legs wider in the hope he'll fuck me sometime this century, but I'm fine with doing this at his pace.

"Have you ever...?" The question is rumbled into my flushed skin.

I bite my lip, partly wishing I could tell him this was my first time, too. But I can't change the past and I don't regret that I've had sex before.

"Yeah. Last year during a yoga intensive retreat." I run my fingers through his hair when he shifts to peer at me through dark lashes. "It was fun, but that was all."

He tenses, shoulders flexing as he holds me tighter. "I kind of want to kill him for—"

"*She* isn't important right now," I stress, keeping my expression open. I've only come out to Thea and a tiny flutter moves through me.

Fox stills, blinking. "She? You're—"

"Bi, yes. But what matters is that I'm with who I want to be with right now." My fingers tighten in his messy hair at the back of his head. "Who I've always wanted to be with. You."

The relaxed, open smile he gives me pierces into my heart. It feels good that he accepts who I am just as much as I accept everything about him. "I'm going to fuck you now, Maisy Daisy."

A hot blush creeps up my neck, heating my cheeks at the nickname. I tuck my lips between my teeth and nod. He skims a hand up my leg and adjusts our position so I'm straddling him. When he lines up and presses inside, he watches my face as I sink down his length. The concentration in his expression makes my chest expand. He fills me inch by inch and I tip my head back, parting my lips.

"Good?"

"Yeah," I breathe, circling my hips. "So good."

"Thank fuck," he mutters, the concentration clearing as he thrusts up. "God, you feel incredible."

Fox holds onto my thighs as I move above him. I watch the emotions play out on his face, my breathing becoming strained as arousal pours over me from the way his blue eyes darken with pleasure. He groans and thrusts sharper while I ride him. He keeps the pace slow and careful. As good as it feels, I need more.

Bracing one hand on his tattooed chest, I grab hold of his hair and tug to get his full attention. The side of my mouth kicks up challengingly. "What are you doing? Sweet and gentle is fun, but it was never going to be us. Those times you were hate fucking me with your fingers?" I lean down to whisper hotly against his ear, pulling his hand to my neck. "I liked it. Don't treat me like I'll break, because I won't."

He releases a growl, grinning as he flips me over to take control. His hips snap and I gasp as his cock hits me deeper. His fingers wrap around my throat and hot and cold shivers run across my skin.

"Yes, like that," I hiss as the heat builds. "Don't stop."

"Look at me when I fuck you, daisy. Don't take your eyes off mine." I snap my eyes open at the command. He looks wild, dark hair hanging in his face, full lips parted, possessive gaze locked on mine. He punctuates his words with thrusts. "I want you to know it's me doing this to you. That you're *mine*. You always have been."

I nod, wrapping my legs around his hips.

Fox grunts, fingers tightening on my neck as he pins me to the bed. I'm getting wetter the harder he fucks me. Collapsing onto an elbow, he stops choking me in favor of holding my jaw in a firm grip. My nails rake down his back. He pants against my cheek, alternating between kissing and biting the side of my face as he drives into me.

"Fuck, Maisy," he chokes out. "I'm going to come hard enough to paint your goddamn insides so deep no one will ever claim your pussy after me."

"Never," I agree, arching against him as pleasure erupts in my core. "Oh god, I'm coming. Fuck, harder."

A rough sound tears from him, his thrusts speeding up with even more force as he chases me to orgasm. He pushes up far enough to watch my dazed expression with a hungry focus as I tremble from coming so hard. Moving his hand to grip my hair in his fist, he snaps his hips and stiffens with a low rumble. His cock throbs deep inside me and I gasp from the sensation.

We're both panting, coming down from the ecstasy racing through us. Fox pulls out and collapses beside me, reaching out and tugging me against his sweaty side. With his other hand, he reaches down and pulls my thigh across his torso. My pulse is throbbing between my legs and I shift just to feel the dirty gratification of our mingled come coating my inner thighs.

After a few minutes our breathing evens out.

"Damn," I murmur, lacking the brain power to say much more.

Fox chuckles, the low, raspy sound sending warm tingles over my skin and wrapping around my heart. He squeezes my thigh and turns to place a kiss in my hair. I tilt my head up and his lips find mine, the soft kiss at odds with how wild we were together. When we part, our gazes lock and we stare at each other.

It's comfortable. I don't feel the need to fill the silence, and neither does he. We simply exist in this moment. I'm bared to him down to my soul and feel like he's allowing me to look into his. There are no more walls between us.

He traces random patterns on my skin, holding me close. I feel like I'm right where I belong, the old warped piece that was gone from my heart for so long now firmly back in place.

* * *

When I wake up in Fox's bed, the apartment is empty and quiet. I stretch, enjoying the aches from yesterday and last night. The sight of Fox's belt still tied around a pipe above his bed where he restrained my wrists for round...who knows last night makes my mouth stretch in a delicious smile.

Music drifting from the lower level reaches me when I get up and drag one of his t-shirts over my head. It's big on me, hitting mid thigh and slipping off one shoulder. I skip everything else, pour a cup of coffee from the still-warm pot, and go off in search for him.

So far I've lucked out. My parents haven't done anything to find me. I wasn't kidding about smashing my phone if they tried to track it, but part of me is surprised they let me go after how controlling they've been. It leaves me waiting for the other shoe to drop. I need to check in with Holden and see what things are like at the house.

All other thoughts fly from my head when I creep down the stairs to the garage. Fox is in the middle of working, covered in a light sheen of sweat and grime. He's shirtless, tattoos on display, ripped black jeans hanging off his hips as he crosses to the workbench to grab a tool before heading back to the piece of metal he's bending to his will to form something. I park my ass on the step, watching in fascination with my coffee cup cradled in my hands.

It's as if the materials he uses have no choice but to obey his command to become what he wants. I don't know what it was originally, or what it will be, but it's beautiful. He hammers out a piece until it flattens, then uses another power tool to cut off a raw edge.

Fox looks up when he realizes I'm there, catching me out of his periphery. I grin when his gaze rakes over me from head to toe, the want obvious as he drags his teeth over his lower lip. Damn, a girl could get used to that.

"Hi." I keep eye contact as I take a sip of coffee.

Without a word he wipes his hands and crosses the garage, taking the steps two at a time until he reaches me halfway up. He slides his fingers into my hair and tilts my head back for a deep kiss.

Pulling back slowly, his eyes dip to what I'm wearing. "Nice shirt."

"I thought so," I say with a smirk. "You been up for a while?"

"I was under the impression people who did yoga got up with the sun. It's almost ten."

"That's when they aren't fucked within an inch of their life by an insatiable monster," I sass, indicating the finger-shaped bruises on my thighs to prove my point.

His gaze turns heated as I tease the hem of the shirt higher to follow the pattern of marks he left on me—bites, hickeys, and bruises covering my body. He takes my hand and sets my coffee aside on the step.

"Come here."

He tugs me down the steps, leading me to the Charger. Spinning me around, he captures my mouth again, nipping my lip before swiping his tongue over the sharp burst of pain. His large calloused hands fit to my waist, almost encircling it. I run my fingers over the scar on his knuckle as he guides me back until he has me splayed on the hood of his car.

"My dirty, rebellious little daisy," he murmurs, gaze pinning me in place as he slides a hand up my hip, pushing up his stolen shirt to reveal I have nothing on underneath. "You know what this means, right?"

I sink my teeth into my lip and shake my head.

With a crooked grin that's all mischief, he grabs the bottom of the shirt and rips it up so my lower body is completely bared to him.

"It means it's time for my breakfast. You don't wear panties around me and I'm going to fuck your pussy with my tongue, fingers, and cock. Got it?"

A bolt of electric heat races through my body as a moan escapes me. Fox pushes my legs wider and his sinful mouth descends on me. He sucks my clit into his mouth, chuckling at the noise that rips from my throat. My hands fly to the back of his head, holding on as he tortures me with his talented tongue.

The bay door is open, and though it seems like there isn't anyone else around in the row of warehouses where Fox has made his home, anyone could catch us if they drove up. It only makes the carnal exhilaration soar higher, calling to a deep hidden piece of myself I've suppressed for so long.

I'll never be able to look at his Charger again without blushing and thinking of this, him eating my pussy on the hood of his car.

"Yes," I sigh, threading my fingers through his hair as his tongue swipes with the perfect amount of pressure.

He doesn't shy away when my hips begin to rock, riding the sensual wave of building arousal. His face buries deeper between my legs and he lures me over the edge into an orgasm that ripples through my core. Damn, Sir Good Vibes has nothing on waking up to this first thing in the morning. My chest heaves with my panting breaths and I skate my fingers lazily over my nipples through Fox's shirt, enjoying the lingering aftershocks.

"That was amazing," I murmur.

"We're not done." Fox leans over me with a feral grin, planting his hands on either side of me on the matte black hood. "I love the way you look right now."

"How do I look?"

The question comes out breathless. A shiver wracks my body. Fisting the t-shirt I stole, he tugs me up.

"*Mine,*" he rumbles against my lips before kissing me.

Tearing his mouth from mine, he turns me around and pushes in the middle of my back to encourage me to fold in half over the car. "Bend over."

Once I'm where he wants me, he lifts one of my knees up onto the hood. A breath shudders out of me from how turned on I am. The tip of his cock rubs up and down my folds as he teases me. He does it until I squirm.

"Come on," I plead, desperate for him to give it to me. For as much as I've awakened a beast in him, he's ignited a fiery need inside me. "More. Want you in me."

"Ask for it, baby," he demands, smacking my ass.

The words can't climb up my throat fast enough. "Please fuck me."

Fox slams into me, making my back arch and a cry catch in my throat. I manage to suck in a breath as he pulls out and thrusts again. My legs tremble, unable to move a lot in this position. I have to just take it and I love it, giving in to the feeling he stirs in me when he takes control. Tingles deep in my core have me close to coming again and we've barely started.

"You like it when I fuck you like that?"

A choked noise of assent escapes me. He grabs hold of my hair, just hard enough to feel it and his skin slaps against mine with his next thrust. I come hard, screaming as I ride it out.

"Mm, you squeeze my cock so good when you come all over it."

He leans over, kissing my spine as he slows down. The change hits me at a new angle and I squirm beneath him, trying to press back into each thrust. He chuckles, dragging his lips up my back. Long fingers reach around and press into my mouth. I curl my tongue around them and suck, loving this new sensation of being full with his muscular body stretched out over mine.

"Get these good and wet, wildflower, because I'm going to fucking own every part of you," he rasps against my hair.

Air gusts out of my lungs at the filthy promise. How does he know exactly what I want without me having to voice it? We've been apart for so long, but the ways our connection has matured into this intense compatibility almost scares me. No one else can give me this kind of fulfillment like he can. I know that deep in my bones.

I moan, slurping around his knuckles when he pulls free. With a quiet rumble, he changes the angle again, slamming his cock into me while he traces his wet fingers down the crack of my ass, circling around my hole. My breath hitches.

"I wish you could see how good you look right now, Maise." He massages my hole as his cock fills my pussy. When I relax enough one of his fingers enters my ass, he releases a low, satisfied groan. "Fuck, you're sucking me right in. Feel that?"

My head feels light and hazy, but I manage a nod as his finger sinks deeper. The sensation is strange, but my insides coil tight in excitement. He gives me time to adjust as he fucks my pussy and my ass, then adds a second finger after leaning down to spit in my crack. It's so vulgar, but it gets me obscenely hot. I can hear how wet I am as his cock pounds into me.

"Fox," I beg hoarsely, not even sure what I need.

"I've got you, baby. Just keep taking it." He squeezes my hip, pumping his fingers in time with his hips. He owns every inch of me, just like he promised. Body, heart, and fucking soul. "Good girl."

It becomes too much and I shake apart beneath him as I take it. The orgasm shatters me, unlike any I've had before, even better than all the things we did last night. My throat is scratchy as I scream through my release.

"Oh shit," Fox grits, his fingers digging into my hip as his dick pulses deep inside me, filling me with his come.

Carefully, he pulls his fingers free and braces his hands on the hood, caging me in. I can't move, still too delirious from such a mind-blowing orgasm, and he seems to be the same as his hot panting breaths coast over my damp skin. He stays inside me while he helps guide my leg off the car, then folds over my body, gathering me in his embrace. His lips press to the side of my face when I turn it to try to see him.

"You okay?"

"Yeah. That was... Wow. Good wow." I make a small noise and he understands, lips finding mine in a sweet kiss.

"Want me to carry you upstairs for a shower?"

"That sounds amazing, but not yet. Let me up?"

He peels away, our skin sticky. His hands hover over me as I stand, the large t-shirt falling down to cover me. Reaching overhead, I draw in a deep breath while stretching and focus on the energy moving through my body while he tugs his jeans back up his hips. I go through a couple other poses to get my blood flowing that leave me with only the delicious lingering aches of sex.

The first two times I saw the garage, we didn't stay long. Curiosity has me exploring, wanting to know more about Fox through the things he loves.

First I touch the motorcycle, finding the ding in the chrome. The memory filters through my head, making me smile as I think of his face when he sought me out to hide him before his dad killed him for the damage. We spent hours hidden away in my room watching cartoons. While I look around, he studies me, thumbs hooked in his jeans. I get distracted for a moment, admiring the hard planes of his sculpted body glistening with sweat.

"What?"

"Nothing, just admiring the excellent view," I sass.

He snorts, ruffling his dark tousled hair so it ends up even messier.

Biting my lip around a secret smile, I turn toward the workbench. Half-finished projects and his tools cover the surface, along with the piece he was working with when I came downstairs. I touch it, feeling the cool metal and trace the curve he's twisted it into.

"What are you making?"

"Not sure yet. I don't always have a plan when I'm making something. I usually just go with it until it feels done."

Thinking of the equally scrappy furniture pieces in his apartment, I glance over my shoulder. "Did you make the stuff upstairs too?" He nods. A soft smile tugs at my lips. "I like it. It's amazing that you can make something with your own hands. Your stuff has so much character. It's like I can feel you in them."

The compliment makes his handsome features morph into a perplexed expression. I don't think he thinks about sharing it with others. Warmth expands in my chest because he's sharing it with me.

"I remember how much you liked working on cars and learning about the mechanics, but this stuff is cool. How did you get into doing it?"

Coming around the Charger, he backs me against the workbench, bracing his hands on the edge. I take advantage of his proximity to trace his abs, grinning when his stomach twitches. Still ticklish. I file that away.

"It's mostly a hobby now. Something to keep my mind busy when it's too loud. I like working with my hands and tinkering with shit until it shapes into something. Sometimes it's useful, like the coffee table, and others it just is what it is." His gaze turns distant for a moment and he holds my hips, tugging me against his body like he needs me close enough to climb into his heart. "At first it was a habit I needed to survive. Once I went into the system, I wasn't used to having a lot."

I swallow at the melancholy in his tone, winding my arms around him to give him a hug. Resting my chin on his tattooed chest, I peer up at him while he tells me the story.

"Nothing belonged to you. That's the first thing you learn. It eats away at the hope most of those kids have that they'll find some damn stability in whatever home they're shoved into. But I already had everything ripped away from me, so it wasn't new." He sighs, rubbing my back like he needs to comfort me instead of the other way around. He laughs. "After I started living with my foster family in Thorne Point, Colt's mom caught me messing around with scrap metal from a junkyard on the outskirts of the city and tried to put my pieces in an avant garde art show. Eventually I stopped doing it because I had to, and kept at it more because I wanted to. I enjoy it."

"I'm glad," I murmur.

The smile he gives me makes my heart stop. I love the curve of it and I give him one of my own as I reach up to trace it.

When his lips connect with mine, I forget everything for a little while, existing where it's just the two of us without any of the pain of our past tarnishing this moment.

TWENTY-SIX

FOX

After making good on my offer to carry her upstairs, we cleaned up in the shower together. She protested that she could still walk, but a primal part of my brain needed to take care of her after she let me fuck her so roughly. I lose myself in running soapy hands over every inch of her body and massage her skin until she melts into me. My cock is ready for another round, but we have time.

"Stay in as long as you want. I have to call Colt to check in. I'll get him to mask your cell signal so your parents can't use it to find us."

She murmurs an agreement and I drop a quick kiss on her forehead before getting out.

"Let's go through the journals first, then we'll check the flash drive you brought," I tell her on my way out of the bathroom.

"Okay."

There's a part of me that wants to get back in under the hot spray of water with her. The part where she's entwined into my soul, tattooed on my heart. It takes effort, but I manage to force my feet to cross the room, discarding the towel around my waist to tug on a worn pair of jeans with rips in the knees.

Moving to the couch, I open the laptop and call Colton, setting my phone to speaker so I can work handsfree. I pull up the screenshots I took of the shady place we found Jacqueline at yesterday.

"*Foxy,*" he greets cheerfully.

"Fuckface," I shoot back in the same tone.

Colt makes a cooing sound like I'm adorably amusing. I roll my eyes and push my fingers through the damp hair curling over my forehead.

"*There was a warrant for impound out on your car and your bike. Two more popped up after I took care of the first one. I dropped a little present in their reporting system that'll crawl for any others and scramble them. You're welcome.*"

It figures Richard is trying to flex his power now that I'm getting closer.

"Thanks. I found something new. Jacqueline Landry skipped out on her normal schedule and when I traced her, she turned up at this remote address. It was another warehouse, looked shady as fuck. There was a logo on the place. SynCom."

"*Maybe a meeting?*"

"That's my thought. I sent it to you. See what you can pull on it? I'm thinking it's some kind of silent investor Nexus Lab doesn't want anyone to know about. Maisy confirmed it's connected when she told me Jacqueline's paychecks are paid through this company instead of the public front."

"*Oh?*" Colt's tone goes light and teasing. I can clearly see the kind of expression he has right now—grinning with his tongue stuck in his cheek while he spins around in his stupid fancy gamer chair. "*Your little flower is playing ball now?*"

I grunt and he chuckles. I haven't told him yet about how things have changed for me, but he's always teased me about her, especially when I found her on Instagram before I came back to Colorado. Staring at her photos for hours was so I could learn what I needed to, but he always thought it was more. Now I realize he was probably right. Asshole always sees through people, picking up on what they don't want found out.

"She's...yeah."

Luckily he lets it go instead of picking at it because he's a nosy bastard. The conversation jumps around for a few minutes while he gives Maisy's phone the same treatment he's given to mine and the Crows, making it untraceable. The water shuts off in the bathroom.

I trail off mid-sentence, gaze zeroed in on Maisy walking out of the bathroom in a cloud of steam. She's wearing one of my t-shirts again and I fucking know she's not wearing anything underneath because my wildflower likes her freedom. Her damp hair falls around her shoulders and she shoots me a crooked grin that makes my pants feel tighter with just one look. God, she's heaven and a curse wrapped into one perfect girl.

"*Fox?*" Colton prompts when the silence has stretched for a minute.

"Uh, yeah." Shit, what was I saying?

Maisy circles behind me on the couch and wraps her arms around my shoulders, giving me a kiss when I angle my head toward her like a moth to a flame, unable to focus on anything but her. She hums into it and I can feel the curve of her smile.

"Is that your brother?" she murmurs when we part.

"*You've got company,*" Colt says knowingly. Fucker probably has the biggest shit eating grin right now. "*Hey sweetheart. You sound hot. Tell me you're hot.*"

Maisy snorts, shooting me an amused glance as she comes around to sit next to me. I leave her be for a minute before giving in and dragging her onto my lap.

"Sure."

She says it without any shyness, owning herself. My arms tighten around her middle and my love for her expands in my chest. I inhale and the corners of my mouth twitch up. She still smells like flowers and coconut, but now there's something else.

Me.

After the shower and spending hours together, she smells like she's mine. It sends a pleased jolt through me.

"*Confident*," Colt says with a hum. "*I like it.*"

Her light laughter makes something tug with want in my stomach. "It's not for you, sweetie," she says slyly. "I do it all for me. Everything else is bonus points."

"*Oh, damn. I think I just fell in love. Marry me?*"

A brief rush of jealousy flares, but I tamp down on it. My brother isn't a threat, but I can't help how possessive I feel about her—how possessive I've always felt around her. Maisy as a kid knew her worth and spoke out when she had an opinion, but as a woman her matured sense of self-assuredness is sexy as fuck.

"Sorry, Fox promised he'd marry me when he was nine. It was a proposal complete with a flower. You'll have to get in line."

All the air in the room feels like it's sucked out. She remembered my promise to her?

My throat bobs as I swallow and absently stroke her thigh, inching my fingers beneath the shirt and finding nothing but her warm skin. I squeeze a handful of her ass and nuzzle my face into her neck, trailing kisses and fighting the urge to leave another mark to claim her. I can't help how tactile I've become with her around, like I have this constant need to touch her in some way.

Colt makes a distressed sound like he's fatally wounded.

"So, he's told me you're his foster brother." Maisy leans toward the phone. "What was he like?"

I slide my lips together. If things were different, she wouldn't need to ask because she would've been with me. I never would've been separated from her. I picture it for a second, like I have many times, what it would be like if we remained close friends. How we'd have our first kiss by the tree we loved to climb as our friendship grew into something else.

"*He was a grumpy little shit,*" Colton says with a chuckle. "*Definition of doom and gloom. It was hilarious. Spill the tea, girl. What was he like before all the angst got to him?*"

Maisy launches into a story about the time me, her, and Holden swindled our entire block out of money on our lemonade stand racket so that we could buy a video game we wanted, a plan I masterminded. I huff out a laugh. It was my idea, but she's the one who organized us and brought all the customers in. Her whole body moves as she tells the story animatedly, her golden eyes lit up with fondness at the memory.

As they talk, I stay quiet, listening to the girl I never stopped loving and the first friend—family—I let in past the thorns stabbing into my heart meet each other. The way it makes my heart thud catches me off guard.

Colton shares another story of his own of the first time his parents dragged me to a Thorne Point high society party with their socialite friends and how he caught me sneaking canapés in my suit pocket.

It feels right that they're meeting and sharing these halves of my life that make up the whole, like my shattered life is colliding back into itself to mend the broken shards.

"*I'll update you when I find out,*" Colton says, breaking me out of my musings. "*Later.*"

The call ends and I stop playing, removing my hand from beneath the shirt she stole so we don't get sidetracked again.

"He seems great," she says, leaning against my chest as she curls up in my lap.

"Is this going to be a thing?" I tug on the material that looks way better on her than it does on me.

She grins. "Yup."

The corner of my mouth lifts. Good. When she wears my clothes it makes something hot and possessive slot into place inside me.

Maisy gets up, collecting the stack of magazines she had in her bag and hooking an arm through her hippie style purse before coming back to the couch. She splits the stack in half and nudges it toward me.

She settles in the corner of the couch with her own half, tucking her bare toes beneath my thighs while she leans against the arm. "What are we looking for?"

"Anything. I tried to look these up before online as PDFs to see if they talked about what they were researching, but I couldn't remember what they had samples of."

We work in a comfortable quiet as we begin scanning through the medical journals.

"Wait, I think this is it," Maisy says after getting partway through her share. She sits up, shifting to her knees to show me the magazine article. "Right here. I recognize it from the stashed patent files you showed me in your garage. Do you have the photos from that shipping facility?"

Tossing aside the magazine I was reading, I pull the laptop closer and bring up the images I took when I posed as an auditor assessing the company internally. I click through images of the shipping operation until she stops me with a hand on my wrist.

"The synthetic opioid! That's it."

"Looks like they didn't get to file the patent paperwork and the company pushed forward with producing it in large quantities."

Is this why my parents were killed? All over this drug?

"This is what they were shipping out," she murmurs. "A lot of it. When you were talking to the manager, I thought it seemed weird that they were only shipping out this. And only, what, five guys loading it onto the truck?"

I make a low noise of agreement, my heart thumping at this new development. For years I've tried to remember what those hidden papers in the old garage said, but my memories were too foggy from grief. It's been right in front of me this whole time.

Rubbing my jaw, I glance at her. "We should go back there to see if we can find out more."

TWENTY-SEVEN

MAISY

The shipping warehouse turns out to be a bust. We've circled the building twice, but after Fox lifted me onto his shoulders to peer in through a high window it became clear we were too late.

"It's empty." My shoulders droop. "Everything's gone, like they cleaned house as soon as they finished loading the outgoing shipment."

"I was afraid of that." His grip on my thighs flexes. "Damn it."

"We'll figure it out. You have those pictures. We can use them hopefully."

Fox sighs raggedly, lifting me down from his shoulders like I weigh nothing. His sharp jaw is clenched, a muscle quivering in his cheek. I reach up and smooth my thumbs over his face until his attention is back on me. He relaxes and lowers his forehead to rest against mine, hands finding my waist.

"Sorry," he rasps. "I thought maybe we'd be able to learn something more after such a big break."

"It's okay."

"Let's head back. It looks like it might rain."

Taking my hand, he leads me back to the low-hanging tree where he parked the Harley to hide it from anyone who might catch us here. He gets on and hands me the helmet before I swing my leg over the bike and take my place behind him. The leather of his jacket is cool to the touch as I slip my arms around him. Once the engine roars to life, we speed away from the mysteriously wiped shipping warehouse Nexus Lab used to distribute drugs they made.

We're only on the road for a few minutes before Fox tenses.

"What is it?" I shout to be heard over the wind.

He angles his head back to surreptitiously glance behind us, then faces front again. If he's uneasy, it can't be good. I want to look back, but his voice stops me.

"Hold on tight," he commands.

It's the only warning I get before he takes a sharp turn onto a gravel cut through that connects to another lane. As we hit it, heading in the opposite direction from Fox's warehouse studio apartment, I see it—the blacked out SUV tailing us.

My heart thuds loud enough in my ears to rival the growl of the motorcycle's engine. I hold on tight as Fox weaves us through the roads. This isn't like the last time he was followed, when we were in his car and had the cover of the more popu-lated downtown area to get away. This time there's only long stretches of road surrounded by foothills and random ware-houses in the shipping district.

Behind us, the SUV revs its engine as it speeds up, keeping hot on the bike's tail. Fox curses and takes another route. My fingers are sore from how tightly they're clenched in his leather jacket. We whip around corners and fly down roads, climbing up higher into the mountains where the motorcycle maneuvers faster than the SUV can.

When we finally lose the tail, Fox spends another twenty

minutes taking us on a winding path, still not fully relaxing. We eventually make it back to his place. My limbs are stiff when we climb off the bike. His big rough hands help me by removing the helmet. He tugs me into his chest, locking his arms around me in a hug.

"Close call," I murmur, slipping my hands into his open jacket.

"Too close." He squeezes me tighter. "Come on. We have to see what your parents had on their computer."

As we take the stairs up from the garage, the clouds open up with a heavy rain that pounds the gravel lot outside, quickly creating puddles and rivers. Fox shrugs out of his leather jacket and pushes a hand beneath his muscle shirt, lifting it as he chases an itch. The downpour creates a white noise amplified by the metal roof and the large industrial windows that wrap around the second floor.

We return to our spots on the couch from earlier and I hand over the flash drive I used to copy the hard drive of the computer in my parents' home office. Fox plugs it in. My phone vibrates with a text and I pull it out of the back pocket of the cutoff shorts I changed into before we left for the shipping facility.

"It's Holden," I say when Fox shoots me a curious glance. "He's just checking in. Wants to make sure I'm okay." I run my fingers through my hair and give him a sidelong look. "You know, since it's my first time running away and all."

He snorts. "You're eighteen, not eight. I don't think they call that running away anymore."

"Semantics."

While Fox gets everything set up, I text my brother.

Maisy: I'm all good [peace sign emoji]

Holden: Where are you though? I hit up Thea because I assumed that's where you went and she said she hadn't seen you.

Maisy: I thought about it but she's been busy with her own stuff, I didn't want to dump more on her. She should just enjoy being married and focus on her bakery right now, not letting me couch surf.

Holden: So where are you then?

Maisy: Safe. That's all you need to know. Keep me posted on if Mom and Dad seem like they're going to send out a search party because I'm being "over dramatic" [eye-roll emoji]

Holden: Actually I overheard them last night. They didn't know there wasn't music playing on my headphones when they were talking. They were acting kinda weird and Mom said she didn't think you knew anything and wasn't worried. She's sure you'll come around before things get out of hand.

I bite my lip and tell him thanks, tossing my phone onto the couch.

"Everything good?"

"Yeah." I scoot closer. "Holden's going to keep an eye on my parents and let me know if anything is up."

He nods while clicking into files from the copy of the hard drive. "Looks like there's a backlog of financial records and they kept track of meetings."

"That's good, right? Maybe there's a suspicious payout, like you said. Follow the money."

"Yeah." Fox's thick dark brows flatten over his stormy blue

eyes. "Jesus, this says they met with the mayor at the time to bribe him to overlook Richard taking that other guy's place as chief. There's more, too. Mostly at that steakhouse, but sometimes random addresses."

I lean in to see what he points out on the computer screen. Seeing the proof of how deep the deception goes fills me with disgust. The steakhouse is known to be a hotspot for lucrative business deals and meetings amongst the power players in this town, but to find out they were doing stuff like this right out in the open doesn't sit right with me. I had no idea any of this was happening.

"This is like insurance. They keep track of it so that if they were ever caught, they could bring down the whole house with them."

Fox murmurs in agreement. "Whatever is going on, I think it funded a lot of the wealth in this town behind closed doors. Nexus Lab wasn't as big back then, but since it's grown to be one of the top producers in the last ten years, anyone connected got richer."

I slip my hand into his when his shoulders go rigid. He holds it like a lifeline and I want to take away all the pain he's carried.

Anyone who cooperated got richer, but people like his parents wound up dead. Could they have been trying to stop whoever was pulling the strings and blow the whistle on the whole thing?

"Do you think they did it to anyone who didn't play along? What happened to your parents, I mean?"

"Maybe. It's likely, but I...I've only been looking for anything connected to my parents."

"Hey," I say softly, encouraging him to turn his face to me. When he meets my gaze, my heart aches at the lost look in his eyes. "It's not your responsibility to solve everything. Whatever we find, we can send it somewhere. Like a tip line. But you're not a superhero, okay? Don't feel bad because bad things happen in the world."

His jaw works, but he nods, then tugs me closer. I climb into his lap and shield him from the computer by winding my arms around his neck for a hug. His strong arms band around my waist like a vice and slowly the tension in his body bleeds away while we sit there comforting each other. I comb my fingers through his thick hair and he leans into me with a rumble that vibrates in his chest.

We stay like that for a long time.

My heart feels heavy after going through what was hidden under the same roof I lived by my own parents. The deeper we dig, the more corruption and deception we find. It unsettles me that my parents had a hand in what we discovered.

Lies, bribery, death. All of Ridgeview is soaked in blood and it shakes me to my core that my parents are at the center of it all.

* * *

Colton calls Fox two days later with more answers. While he answers the call, I get a text. Grabbing my phone from the coffee table, I find a message from Thea and the girls in our group chat with a photo of Thea, Blair, and Gemma making silly faces.

Thea: We miss your face!!! Holden said you got in a fight with your parents. We're staging another jailbreak kidnapping and demand girl time. We've got your back!

A pang hits my chest. I want to go be with them. On any other normal day, I would be, but I've been sucked deep into this world Fox exists in, one that lurks beneath the bright surface. I can't drag my friends into this mess. Thea went through a scary situation last year and I won't be the one to put her in danger again. And while Blair and Gemma are total strong badasses, this isn't their problem either. It's mine and Fox's and it goes back ten years at the start of all of this mess.

Maisy: OMG excuse me, I just lost my heart to three beauties [heart eyes emoji]

Gemma: [Blowing a kiss emoji] We're a fine bunch.

Blair: [smirking emoji] [black heart emoji] Come hang, we're doing a beach day at the lake.

Maisy: I miss you too, babes. I'm laying low. You know how Dad gets track happy with my cell signal. Promise I'll swing by the bakery this week though.

Thea: [GIF of a puppy dog face] You sure you're okay?

Maisy: I'm good, I swear! I'll see you in a couple of days.

Thea: Okay, be safe and remember we love your bright face!

Maisy: You all better do a face mask for me [heart emoji] Put it on Dev, you know he secretly loves it [laughing emoji]

Gemma and Blair text back GIFs of laughing. The last time I roped him into doing face masks with us, I put his thick black hair in short little pig tails that looked like horns, making him live up to his old nickname as the school's dark devil.

I vow to tell them everything—including that I'm sort of with Fox now. As soon as we find the answers he's looking for to prove his parents murder, then I'll do the whole introduce him to my friends thing. The thought of Fox meshing with the rest of my friends almost makes me laugh. Despite being my oldest friend, he's totally different from everyone else's vibe in our social circle.

Putting my phone down, I tune into what Fox is talking to Colton about. He paces behind the couch, phone pressed to his ear while he rubs the back of his neck. It makes his t-shirt ride up, but I drag my attention off his body to focus. I don't know if it's good news or bad that's making him pace.

He catches me watching and sighs, switching to speaker phone and holding his phone out. "Repeat that."

"It's definitely a shell company. They bought out Nexus Lab eleven years ago," Colton's voice filters through the room. *"I dug up financials and it lines up with the growth Nexus Lab has had in the last decade. It wasn't until this shell bought them out that they became a national supplier."*

Fox and I exchange a look, his expression matching mine as my brows pull together.

"So who owns that?" I ask.

"That's the kicker." Colton uses a light and joking tone, but I sense he's as displeased by what he found as Fox. *"SynCom is traced back to a bigger company called Stalenko Corp. It's rumored to have Russian ties. I've heard some chatter about them in different hacker circles on the web in the last couple of years."*

Startled, I blink, turning to Fox. "Russian ties—like the mafia?"

"Yeah," he says gruffly. "Probably. It makes sense, how easy it's been to build a small pharmaceutical research and development company up into what it is today from the shadows.

Direct supply chain if they're flooding the market with the drugs from the source, either dealing on the black market or maybe using their hold on such a large piece of the market pie to drive up the costs to legitimate buyers by astronomical amounts."

My eyes widen. "They'd also have access to control how much is made and where it's sent to."

"Cartels are probably pissed they didn't think of it first. Now the Russians have spent ten years building a nice little nest egg for themselves right alongside the opiate boom. Who needs to worry about product when it can be cooked up synthetically in a lab and be twice as potent."

Blood pounds in my ears. I'm vaguely aware of Fox ending the call with his brother as my head swims.

Criminals.

That's who my parents are working with. Working *for* probably.

All of Dad's smiles and his deep belly laughter and all the ways Mom used to be completely different flash through my head. They used to love their life and Holden and I back when they were a bright-eyed scientist and a cop with a moral code. Where did that go so wrong?

"Maise." Fox catches me by my shoulders with a worried expression. "Are you okay?"

"Yeah. I think...that was a lot to take in."

His mouth flattens to a grim line as he rubs my upper arms. A chill skates down my spine. "I know."

"How is this our lives? How are my parents working for a shell corporation with Russian ties?" My throat gets scratchy and hot when I consider that I still have my parents, even if they're secretly evil lapdogs for a foreign mob. He doesn't have any of his family left. "None of this is fucking normal."

"That's the point." Sighing, he pulls me closer and I lean

my head against his chest as he rubs my back. "It makes it so much easier to manage an empire and carry out illegal business when they can pull strings through powerful business people with good public standing. No one suspects an ambitious woman with two high-achieving children and a husband who upholds the law in the middle of the country compared to a thug packing heat doing business in the middle of the night. It's how the most powerful crime families operate now. They'd probably make Forbes for their damn innovation and advancements wherever they've dipped their dirty hands to operate their puppets from the shadows."

I take comfort in his touch, melting against him. His heartbeat drums beneath where I rest my head and I listen to it, allowing it to center me with each deep breath I take to clear the dizziness.

Wanting to forget for just a second, I lift my head and seek him out. He meets me halfway, our mouths crashing together with a burning intensity beneath the kiss. His fingers tangle in my hair, cupping the back of my head as he holds me so tight I'm almost breathless. I press up on my toes, chasing the exhilarating feeling of his kiss with a desperate edge.

Fox rips his mouth from mine and cups my face, gaze bouncing back and forth as he meets my hooded eyes. I swallow back the wild woman I almost let take over.

"It'll be okay," he says in a strained tone.

I really hate that my parents could turn on their friends like this because of their own greed. Whatever the extent of their involvement is, they allowed it to poison everything in their life, all for the sake of the power it gave them, even if it meant people died for them to get ahead. It fills me with this urge to act and I follow the impulse.

"We have to go down there," I say.

"If they've got their people watching the shipping place, they probably have them on this, too."

It's not like him to want to be cautious. He's a take action type of person.

"We'll be careful."

The corner of his mouth kicks up and he tilts his head, giving me a once over that sends heat racing through me again. "Always in it for the thrill of trouble."

I grin. "So we're going?"

"Yes. But we need to blend in better than your scraps of fabric pretending to be yoga clothes and my ripped jeans in case people are there. We should make it look like we could be Nexus Lab employees again."

"It looked abandoned on Google street view."

"Still."

"I didn't bring much, but I'll see what I can throw together."

Luckily, I did put a pair of slim fitting black pants in my bag when I was throwing random things from my closet into it. They'll have to do. I pull them on as he dresses in a pair of dove gray slacks and a shirt. Once again I'm tempted by the sight of him dressed up from his usual rough appearance.

Fox's gaze trails the bare curve of my spine as I put my hair up in a sleek high ponytail, then put on a lace bralette and steal one of his few button down shirts from a rack he keeps in the corner. He lifts a brow, but says nothing. I get the message from his smirk, it amuses him that I keep stealing his clothes.

"This is more business chic than the vintage blouses and casual workout clothes I brought with me when I left my house," I point out once I'm ready. "I didn't account for how much undercover work I'd be doing when picking out my quick getaway wardrobe."

"Whatever you say," he says lightly, gaze traveling over me again. "You look good."

Kneeling by the black duffel bag that was in the back of his Charger when I stowed away, he takes out a handgun and checks the amount of bullets before slotting the clip back into place and tucking the weapon in the back of his pants. He puts his hand at the small of my back and guides me down to the garage.

"You think we need to be armed for this?"

"We have to be prepared for anything."

A chill skates down my neck at the ruthlessness in his tone. I change the subject.

"If you have suits, why didn't you ever wear the school uniform?"

"Because I don't play by the rules." He huffs out a laugh, putting his arm around my shoulders to draw me closer once we reach the bottom of the steps. "And because it helped people fear me if I looked like I could kill them with my bare hands. A preppy blazer wouldn't have done me any favors."

I sink my teeth into my lip. Is it wrong that what he said turns me on? Probably, but I don't care.

Chuckling, he plants a kiss on my cheek. "The rain let up. Let's go."

The ride there isn't long. It's closer than I expected to Fox's place. We take the Charger instead of the bike this time.

Instead of pulling in, we park on the no outlet lane and walk over. The place seems as deserted as the shipping facility was after it was wiped of any evidence of Nexus Lab using it. The building is run down, overgrown weeds doing their best to take over.

"Doesn't seem like anyone is around," I say after we test the front door and find it locked with a padlock.

"But Jacqueline definitely came here for something. It had

to be important. She wouldn't break her strict routine and risk the way she likes to portray herself for something random."

"Something she didn't want to be seen doing," I add.

"Right. What about around here?" Fox's fingers circle my wrist and he takes us around the side of the building. "They might want it to put off this vibe like it's nothing important, or abandoned, but then have a back entrance or something on a sub level."

We barely make it ten steps before we're spotted.

"Hey!"

A sharp voice calls out, making us whip around. My stomach takes a nosedive. Fox moves quickly, putting me behind him protectively, one hand going to the back of his pants to grip the gun he tucked there.

"What are you doing here?"

TWENTY-EIGHT

FOX

The adrenaline racing through my veins doesn't slow when I spot the man who called us out. Once he's close, I see he's only maybe five years older than us in his mid-twenties with reddish brown hair and glasses with thick plastic frames. I'm still on the defensive, ready to protect Maisy from any threat. My grip on the gun doesn't ease.

"Who are you?" he demands.

"Who are *you?*" Maisy shoots back, inching out from behind me. She flicks her ponytail with confidence and gives the man a once over. "We're doing an internal audit and this is the property we're checking out today."

I want to smile, but I keep a stern expression. She's jumped to the cover I used when I snooped around the shipping facility.

The man raises a brow and adjusts his glasses, gaze flicking between us. "Really? Funny, because the internal records department is where I work and I've never seen either of you."

We both tense and I move close enough to grab her wrist, ready to fucking run if this guy calls backup.

"So let's try again. Who the hell are you kids and what are you doing here?"

"Kids?" I scoff. "You're not much older."

"I'm Maisy Landry. My mother is the CEO of Nexus Lab."

I swallow a curse. Damn it, Maisy.

She steps in front of me full of confidence like she's going to protect me with her family name, propping her hands on her hips.

This gets the guy's attention and he gives her a crooked grin that makes me growl under my breath. His gray eyes flick to me for a moment before his shoulders shake with a silent laugh. "I see. So, not internal auditors then."

It makes him relax that we don't work for the company.

"No. Now answer my question—who are you and why are you here?"

He holds out a hand. "Ethan Hannigan. Records department, as I said. Unlike you little sneaks, I'm seriously an employee."

I take in his casual shorts and button down. "Why would someone from the records department be out at an abandoned warehouse practically in the middle of nowhere on a Saturday? Doesn't seem like it should be in the job description."

Ethan turns his lopsided grin on me. "Observant. And you are...?" He leaves the question hanging, then smirks. "Miss Landry's bodyguard? The suit's a nice touch, definitely makes you seem older. And you're armed. Smart."

"My boyfriend," Maisy says firmly, putting her hand in mine.

A stupid flutter fills my chest at the term and I have to work to keep my mouth from curving. For once, I pull on the pain of losing my parents and all the shit that happened to me after to help me keep from grinning like an idiot that the girl I love might feel the same about me.

Together we form a united front against Ethan. My gut tells me he's not what I first thought. If he was, we'd already be in the back of a blacked out SUV on our way to face whoever keeps trying to take me out just like my parents. It's enough for me to release the gun. But I'm still wary of trusting strangers and taking them at face value.

"How did you find this place?" Ethan asks, tucking his hands in his pockets.

"Followed my mom here when she was supposed to be at work," Maisy says, only partially lying.

Ethan hums like that makes total sense. "This is the first time I've been able to get out here. Every time I tried to follow, I'd lose the car taking her here. It's a little underwhelming from how suspicious it seems, huh?"

For whatever reason, he trusts that we aren't going to relay his admission of digging around to Jacqueline. He scans the tree branches waving over the damp concrete behind us and his expression shifts.

"We should probably get out of here before the security patrol comes around," he suggests. "They're a punctual bunch and they don't like uninvited guests."

"There's a diner nearby," I say.

Ethan nods. "I'll meet you there in twenty minutes. Grab a booth."

As I pull Maisy back toward the Charger, she keeps her voice down. "Are we just going to trust he's chill?"

I glance over my shoulder at the direction Ethan heads. "Didn't you see how much his demeanor changed once he found out we weren't official employees? I think he guessed we're snooping around like he is."

"What do you think his deal is?"

"That's what I want to find out. Come on."

We climb into the car. The drive to the diner is only a few

minutes. It's mostly populated by truckers with its proximity to the interstate. The lunch rush is dwindling, the parking lot half full. We head inside and ask for a booth near the back. Maisy sits on my side and I keep an eye on the door while she chats to the waitress about our friend who will be joining us. It's not long before Ethan arrives with a leather satchel hanging off his shoulder, ambling over to our booth after a quick scan of the diner.

"So who are you really?" I prompt before his ass hits the fake red leather bench seat.

Ethan chuckles. "Damn, kid. Hasn't anyone taught you anything about the art of subtlety?"

"Don't really have time for subtlety." My fist clenches on the table, my other arm draped across the back of the seat around Maisy's shoulders.

Ethan holds up his hands as the waitress brings over a menu for him. He perks up and takes his time browsing over the specials. Maisy's elbow catches me in the side and I grunt. She lifts her brows and gestures toward Ethan with her head.

"I'm starved, aren't you?" She picks up her own menu, muttering out of the side of her mouth. "Let's order something so we don't stick out."

Ethan hums in approval, darting a look at us over the top of his laminated menu. Sighing, I flip mine open and order the first thing I see when the waitress comes around to collect our orders.

"Talk," I say once she drops off our drinks, unable to fully relax until I know what his deal is.

Pursing his lips, he stirs his Coke with the straw. "I work for Nexus Lab, but it's because I'm an undercover journalist. I've been investigating a network of elites tied to it. Politicians, other businesses—the works. The network stretches across the states."

Maisy's lips part and she leans across the table. I want to tug her back and keep her close.

"What have you found out?"

Before he tells us, there's something else I want to know. "Why are you telling us? You met us less than an hour ago."

"Your name is Fox Wilder," Ethan says matter of factly. "You look just like your dad. I've got access to employee records and your parents' files were some of the first that tipped me off to some of the bigger things at work when I first began infiltrating the company."

My jaw clenches as I slump back against the seat. It's gratifying to know there are others who found what happened to my parents suspect. Maisy's hand lands on my leg beneath the table and she squeezes, leaning into me. I curl my arm further around her, catching a strand of her ponytail between my fingers.

"It's taken time to gain access, but I've been able to gather a good look at the history of the company," Ethan explains. "The money records are something else. Something changed a little over a decade ago that really put Nexus Lab on the map compared to its more humble beginnings."

We all pause when our food comes out. Ethan makes heart eyes at the burger set in front of him while Maisy digs into a breakfast special with a side of sausage links. I don't have the appetite for the sandwich I ordered, but I shove a chip into my mouth anyway. Maisy reaches over and steals one, making me smile reluctantly.

"So," Maisy prompts.

It takes Ethan a minute to continue, too busy taking a huge bite of his food and sighing in delight. "Gonna miss this."

Maisy and I glance at each other. She hitches a shoulder and presses her leg against mine, knee to hip.

"In the last couple of weeks I've been able to dig deeper

without raising alarm now that I've built up my reputation and respect at the company. I came across a sealed file on employee termination. It seemed weird. I haven't had any luck cracking it —computers aren't really my thing." He meets my gaze directly and my stomach drops. "What caught my interest was the date. I checked the local papers and it lined up with your parents getting into an accident."

Everything he's telling us lines up with what Colton has found out for me, so I know what we're chasing is real.

"I have someone I trust who's good with computers. I want to prove my parents were murdered," I say. "That's it."

Ethan nods. "Of course. Take this." He rummages in his satchel and pulls out a flash drive. I palm it and tuck it into my pocket. He sticks another fry in his mouth. "The trail's leading me to the east coast. This is my last week at the company. I've already given notice because I've burned through my resources here."

"Why can't you stay and see it through?" Maisy asks.

"This is just one piece of the picture. I want the whole thing when I break this story. Everything I've got so far is on that drive."

"Thank you," Maisy says. "I'm glad we ran into you, or we might've missed out on knowing this."

"Probably would've gotten yourselves caught by the patrol, too," Ethan says with a pointed look as he drizzles ketchup over the rest of his fries. "Seriously, watch out for them. You'll find what I've pieced together on this in what I gave you, but when someone from their parent company has a meeting with the Nexus Lab board, it throws off this shady vibe. My co-worker goes white as a sheet whenever they come around."

I don't mention what we learned from Colton earlier about who owns the shell corporation that owns Nexus Lab. "Yeah. We'll be more careful."

"You'll have to be to prove what happened to your parents. Here's my number if you need me. Good luck."

With that, Ethan wipes his mouth with a napkin, slips me a business card, and tosses down enough cash to cover his meal before he nods to us and leaves.

Maisy sits back against the fake red leather. "Kismet."

"Bless you?" My brows dip. "The hell is that?"

She blows out an amused breath, lips curving. "It means fate, that something was meant to be. We seriously got lucky crossing paths with an undercover journalist who's been digging into the same thing you have."

"I don't believe in fate," I mutter, glancing out the window to watch the vehicles on the interstate fly by the exit for Ridgeview. "Shit's for fairytales."

"I believe you and I were meant to find each other again." Her hand finds mine and she leans her head on my shoulder. I almost laugh because I knew she'd call us fate. "You and me, that's how it's supposed to be. Just like we used to say."

That I can't argue with. It's the only way to explain the way my heart beats harder when she's around. How much less I'm ruled by the anger of my past because she keeps me grounded from spiraling out of control. How much better I fucking sleep without nightmares clawing at my mind because she's in my arms with her soothing floral and coconut scent wrapped around me.

"You're right." I turn back and drop a kiss on top of her head, inhaling her sweetness mingled with my shampoo. "It was a lucky break. We could've missed him and then we wouldn't have more information to comb through."

"See, the power of positive thinking." She sits up. "That's what Thea always says."

"The one with the bakery, right? Eloped in Paris?"

She nods with a fond smile. I'm hit by a pang of guilt.

Maisy deserves to be enjoying her summer with her friends and living a normal life, but instead I've dragged her into my shadows and uncovered the seedy underbelly rotting this town from the ground up.

"Wait, how did you know about Paris?" She narrows her gaze. "I didn't tell you about that."

The corners of my mouth curl up in a smug smile. "I told you, daisy. Any move you made, I knew about it." Grasping her chin, I angle her face up and kiss her. She grins into it. "Ready to get out of here?"

"Yes. I want to know what Ethan's found in the time he's spent under the radar."

"Me too."

We leave the diner and I press Maisy back against the side of the Charger for another kiss before I hold her door open for her. She laughs as she slides in.

On our way back to my place, I grow quiet, contemplating everything we've learned in the last several hours. I can tell she's worried about me by the thousand and one looks she's shot at me in the last ten minutes alone.

She must finally reach a limit, because she reaches across the center console and takes my hand.

"What are you thinking?" Her soft voice is a balm to my aching soul.

I lick my lips, staring ahead at the road. My hand hangs over the wheel and I twitch my fingers, thinking how to put it.

"I have a bad feeling. All of this is bigger than I thought." I shake my head. "I only set out to prove the truth about my parents being murdered, that it was covered up. I never expected to discover this intricate web of lies and corruption. This shit runs so deep its roots burrow into Ridgeview."

"But now we can make it right."

Her optimism is a buoy to reach for in the churning sea I

feel myself being pulled further into. I thread our fingers together, knuckles turning white from how tightly I grip her smaller hands. I just need to hold on and let her light guide me out of the darkness threatening to swallow me whole.

"I don't know what to do, Maise," I admit hoarsely.

Christ, I sound so goddamn broken and beat down by the hand I've been dealt. I wish more than anything nothing bad ever happened so she and I could've been two kids who grew up together and had a good life. But I know that's not how the world works. It's a cruel reality.

"No matter where this goes, I'm with you," she assures me with an admirable steel in her tone.

I manage to loosen my death grip on her hand and bring it up to my mouth for a kiss. That's when I see it in the rearview mirror. My body stiffens and time seems to slow in the seconds it takes me to suck in a sharp breath and focus on one thing: *drive*.

A loud bang goes off and Maisy screams. The back window blows out in a shower of broken glass. Fuck, this can't be happening!

"Get down!" I shout, trying to shield her while I drive.

There's no time to grab for the gun I stashed in the glove compartment. Instead of fighting back, I want to get us away to keep her safe. I slam my foot on the gas pedal, flooring it as I weave back and forth to make us a harder target to hit. The wind is loud, whipping into the car from the damage. I let my guard down and it might get us killed.

"Oh my god! What's happening?"

The blacked out SUV tries to close the distance and I see the shotgun again in the side mirror.

"Shit!"

Another bang rings out as I yank the wheel, but I'm not fast enough. The driver's side window shatters, sharp pieces catching me across the cheek and neck as I instinctively shy away with a grunt. Ignoring the pain, I grit my teeth and push the car harder to get us the hell out of there.

"You good?" I demand, praying no buckshot spread flew through the car.

Maisy tries to lift her head as my tires screech across the road when I take a turn too fast.

"Down, Maisy!" I press down on her shoulders and she curls up in a ball. "Someone's fucking shooting at us!"

"I figured that out," she yelps over the wind of the two destroyed windows. Reaching up, she latches on to my arm that's shielding her, grip desperate and scared. "They must have been watching and followed us."

"Hold on tight. I'll get us out of here."

My heart thumps hard as I white knuckle the wheel. I will get us out of this or we'll meet the same fate as my parents. I'll never let them take anything away from me again.

Especially not my daisy.

TWENTY-NINE

MAISY

Fox winces and I scrunch up my face in sympathy as I clean the cuts he got from the broken glass. He's sitting on a low stool shirtless, hair wet from the quick shower we took when we got back. His hands grip my hips as I dab at freshly dried blood on his cheek. He hasn't stopped touching me once, like he needs to physically know I'm safe by keeping me within reach.

"Sorry," I murmur when he grits his teeth from the sting of the alcohol wipe.

He grunts, jaw locked. I know he's not mad at me, but the force of his anger is a palpable thing. His body ripples with the need to tear something apart.

Someone fucking shot at us. If it wasn't serious before, it's clear how dangerous this is now.

I'm shaken by what happened on our way home from the diner, but staying strong. This is no time to lose my head. Neither of us got shot, thank god. I really hope Ethan wasn't followed. We made it away safely thanks to Fox's fast driving, managing to lose the blacked out SUV by luring them into the

293

residential part of Ridgeview where they couldn't shoot at us without witnesses. That's what matters.

I peel open a small bandage and stick it over the long wound on Fox's neck, fingertips lingering on his warm damp skin. My body shakes with a shudder and air rushes past my lips. It hasn't stopped doing that, even after the shower. My pulse has calmed, but there is still something simmering beneath my skin. For now I ignore it, focusing on getting Fox patched up.

His dark blue eyes watch me with something like recognition reflecting back. I think he knows I'm more rattled than I'm letting on. He uses his thumbs to trace patterns on my hips and with a subtle press he guides me closer between his spread knees, near enough that I feel his breath coast down my chest and across my bare stomach.

My nipples tighten in response. A pulse of heat throbs between my legs and I swallow. I didn't bother to throw on more than a pair of tight workout shorts and a sports bra after the shower while he only tugged on the jeans he had on this morning.

When we stumbled up the steps to the second floor of Fox's warehouse, him half-dragging me, we stripped out of our clothes at the door. Pieces of glass clung to my hair, hitting the concrete floor with little pings as I shook it free. Fox pulled me right into the shower to wash off the danger and any lingering pieces too small to see. He took his time running his hands over my body first with a look of deep concentration and protectiveness until he was satisfied that I was glass-free. I did the same to him, carefully pushing my fingers into his thick hair while he silently watched.

Fox ended up with minor scrapes and one deeper cut on his neck. I was sore from how tensely I'd curled into a ball, crouched low and held in place by his arm as he drove us to safety, but the worst I'd end up with is some bruising from smacking into the center console from the tight turns. It's a miracle neither of us ended up with buckshot embedded in our skin.

Actually, it's lucky we made it away at all.

These are the people my mother and father work for. People willing to kill Fox, willing to kill *me* because I'm seen with him.

Do either of them know that I was shot at today?

Would they care?

They're willing to look the other way and go as far as covering up their friends' murder so their dirty bosses will keep paying them, so how far is too far? I don't know if I want to find out just how much they'd sacrifice for their greed.

"Hey." Fox grasps my wrist and cups my nape, bringing our foreheads together. The waves of anger subside a little as he focuses on me. "Stop thinking for a minute."

"How do you know that's what I was doing?" I whisper.

"Because you're shaking." He soothes his hand down my arm and rubs until the trembling passes. "It's okay. I'll keep you safe."

It's the most he's managed to say to me since the danger descended on us, like he had to work through everything clouding his own head too.

I close my eyes and slide my nose along his in a gentle nuzzle, taking comfort in his protective nature when it comes to me.

"Are you cold?" he asks in a low voice tinged in the shadows of his anger. "You could go into shock."

"No. I'm good."

Fox puts his big hands on my back and smooths them up and down every inch of my exposed skin. I can't help the way it makes me arch against him, a tiny sound catching in my throat.

He keeps up the slow touches, stroking the curve of my spine with his calloused fingertips. My skin isn't cold, it's the opposite —I'm burning up inside and each tender touch nudges me closer to a cliff edge I feel like I need to dive off.

A strange hunger eats at me, one unlike any I've ever experienced. I've always had a healthy sexual appetite, but it's never been like this. My mind fills with images and I scrape my teeth over my lip, pushing aside the wish for Fox to pick me up by my thighs and toss me down on his bed.

"We should see what Ethan gave us on the flash drive," I say instead of entertaining the fantasies.

I move to go fish it out of Fox's pants, but his hold on me tightens, keeping me in place. Leaning back, I peer at him curiously, but he doesn't let me get far. He adjusts on the stool and pulls me onto his lap. There's so much conflict swirling in his dark gaze when he cups my face and brushes his thumbs over my cheeks.

"I think we should stop," he finally says.

"Stop?"

Fox sighs heavily. "This is dangerous. I don't want you to get hurt." He pauses, throat bobbing. "That's the last thing I want now. If I have to choose between you and my revenge on this town, I choose you. My parents are dead, but you're alive and I'm not letting you go."

My heart cracks open and my breath hitches. I grasp his wrists as tears sting my eyes. Hearing him ready to give up on everything makes me ache, but at the same time hearing that I mean more to him than anything else makes me happy.

"Fox," I whisper. "I..."

His gaze pierces mine. It seems like he's holding his breath, waiting for me to confess how I feel about him. He has to know I'm in love with him, right? I think I always have been, since we were little kids.

"You said you've been searching for these answers for so long," I say.

"I know." He forces out a breath. "It's driven so much of my life, but it doesn't matter. I'd rather let it go if it means keeping you safe."

He's saying he's giving it up, but his body is wound tight, like it hasn't caught up with his head. He might be ready, but I'm not. He's pulled back the veil that shrouded my life and I'm done with the complacency. What's going on in this town is wrong and I want to see the consequences come down on them all.

"What if I say I'm not done?"

His brow wrinkles. "Maisy..."

"I'm serious. I think we should still keep going." I sit up straighter in his lap and set my jaw. "I'm not afraid and I want to see this to the end with you."

Fox studies me for a long stretch, cupping my shoulders like I'm something precious to be cradled and cherished.

"Are you sure?" His hands drop off my shoulders and skate down my back, stirring the heat in my center. The deep rumble of his voice is its own seductive and sensual temptation stroking my skin. "We could just leave. Follow the road wherever it takes us." Leaning in, he places an open-mouthed kiss on the column of my throat that makes my thighs clench. "Just you and me."

God, I want that. It's been my biggest dream for as long as I can remember. Damn him for dangling it in front of me.

We're so close to uncovering the truth, though. I can feel it. Fox needs that closure to be able to truly move on with his life.

I purse my lips. "I'm sure. We can't let them keep getting away with it all."

He stares at me for another moment, then nods. "The

minute you're in danger again, we're stopping. Chasing ghosts isn't as important as you are to me."

A flutter moves through my chest and I smile. "Deal."

Pulled by the force of the thing still itching beneath my skin, I cover his mouth with mine. A sound sticks in his throat as he parts his lips for my tongue, holding my hips. The temperature in the room rises fast and I break off, panting and breathing him in. Zaps of the adrenaline that hasn't fully faded skitter across my body and I shudder. It's been building since we got away, since the shower with his hands on me under the water, since he kissed my neck and offered to give into the urge that always sits in the back of my mind to get in a car and drive.

It's all too much to ignore anymore and I need him.

Fox's eyes are heavy-lidded, tracking my tongue when I dart it out to wet my lower lip. My nipples harden, feeling sensitive with every tiny shift of my body in his lap.

"Is it..." I try to catch my breath. "Is it weird if I say I'm really horny right now?"

He chuckles, the sound dark and inviting, then captures my lips again, hands roaming freely. I moan into the searing kiss as pushes beneath my sports bra to squeeze my breast while teasing me with his tongue. The wild edge of his passion matches mine and seems on the verge of breaking free.

"Fuck me?" I breathe against his lips.

Fox leaves a lingering kiss at the corner of my mouth while grabbing the back of my thighs and lifting me into his arms as he stands. "You never have to ask twice, baby."

We leave the kitchenette area on one side of the converted warehouse space, but don't make it far. He drops me on the back of the couch and wastes no time peeling my tiny shorts off, tossing them aside before popping the button on his jeans. I watch in fascination as his powerful thighs are revealed and my breath grows short at the sight of his cock, hard and ready.

He slants his mouth over mine. Taking a fistful of my hair, he angles my head back so my neck is bared for him and breaks the kiss to lick a stripe up it. I shiver as he trails hot biting kisses back down.

"We could've died today." It's sinking in. The thrumming beneath my skin reaches a fever pitch. I meet his hooded eyes. "Make me feel alive?"

He keeps hold of my gaze as he releases my hair and drags his fingers down my body, over my folds, eliciting another shudder from me. He flicks his attention down briefly to watch his finger sink into me and I bite my lip, almost crying out in protest when he pulls it out. Holding up glistening fingers between us, his mouth curves into a seductive smirk.

"Thought so. Look at that, you're fucking soaked."

My cheeks prickle with heat, but I won't avert my gaze or hide from my arousal. Fox's smirk stretches wider and he kisses me hard, pushing my legs further apart.

Balanced on the back of the couch, I don't have much to hold onto, so I cling to his muscled shoulders and shudder as his cock enters me with one sharp thrust. My mouth falls open at the intense heat coiling in my core.

"Fox," I gasp, nails digging into his tattooed skin as I wrap my legs tighter around his waist.

There's a gleam in his eyes as he lifts one of my legs, stretching it high enough it drapes over his shoulder. He tests my flexibility and swipes his tongue in a slow arc over his lower lip when he finds the position is within my limit. Holding my hip with one hand, he grabs my nape with the other, trapping my leg. His thrusts are powerful and something dark and feral swirls in his eyes that stokes the fire burning in me. When he hits a spot that lights me up, my back arches and my nails rake across his skin, making him groan.

Our movements are passionate with an undercurrent of

roughness that I crave.

His fingers clamp tighter on my nape as his skin slaps against mine. He pulls me closer and kisses me demandingly. I lean into it, a strangled cry sticking in my throat.

We almost died. Someone shot at us. But we're alive. *We're fucking alive.*

I break the kiss first, tilting my head back and closing my eyes. Fox curses, lips pressed to my neck.

"God, yes," I push out. "Don't stop."

"That what you need, baby?" His teeth scrape a sensitive spot on my neck, followed by his tongue. The vibration of his low laugh drags me closer to the edge. "Yeah, that's what I thought. Your pussy is begging for my cock."

I level him with a look, grabbing a fistful of his hair. He grins at me when I pull his face up from my neck. "Then keep going. Make me feel good."

"You want to come?" He snaps his hips to punctuate the question.

I nod, a moan escaping me as he hits that spot again.

"Hold on tight, or I'm going to fuck you so hard you fall off this couch."

Air punches out of me and my stomach dips with the spike of desire racing through me. The force of the next thrust makes my eyes roll back in my head. My entire body lights up, needing more, more, more. He takes me hard and fast, controlling and commanding my pleasure, and I have no choice but to obey.

A scream tears from my throat when I come. Fox's grip flexes on me. His thrusts turn more powerful as he chases his release. With a deep rumbling growl he stiffens and his cock pulses, filling my pussy.

This is what I needed—him making me feel how alive we are.

THIRTY

MAISY

Fox wasn't about to let me out of his sight for the foreseeable future, but I convinced him I needed to leave his converted warehouse or go stir crazy if I didn't get out for a bit.

The itch under my skin was killing me and I wouldn't tame myself or hold back from what I need anymore. My usual yoga routine wasn't helping. I needed fresh air and something normal to beat back the memories of being shot at yesterday. I promised to be careful while I hung out with Thea at her bakery. He tried to shove his gun in my purse, but since it wouldn't fit and I refused to carry it on me, he told me with finality that I had an hour before he picked me up.

"An hour and that's it," he reminds me when he drops me off on the main street lined with shopping boutiques, galleries, and a coffee shop. "I don't like leaving you here."

"I'm grabbing smoothies with my bestie, not walking into a life and death situation." He growls in displeasure and I bend to give him a quick kiss. "I'll be fine. Look, see? There are yoga moms. Totally safe."

As I gesture at the cheerful storefronts and the women I

usually see in my classes pushing their kids in strollers amongst the other shoppers enjoying the summer day, his chiseled jaw works. Some people look our way, pausing to stare at him while they whisper to each other, probably spreading more lies about him.

"You should always be prepared," he says gruffly. "Be careful and keep an eye out. We still have no idea if they know you're with me. I'd rather no one found out if it keeps you safe."

I point to Thea's bakery in the middle of the block. "I'm going right there. Nothing's going to happen."

If I say it enough times, I'll believe it.

He brushes my waist. "If you need me, you call right away. I'll be back in an hour to get you."

I nod and watch him drive off, admiring the sight of him on his motorcycle. A pair of women in LuLulemons and trendy corduroy baseball caps wave to me as I head down the sidewalk.

"We missed you in class this week," one of them says.

"I know, sorry. I'm on a break for a while," I offer with a smile. When they exchange a glance and tilt their heads in silent yoga mom language—aka totally judging me—I add, "Figuring out stuff for my freshman semester."

"Oh," they drawl in unison.

"Keep working on your crane pose, you'll get there." I infuse cheerfulness I don't feel into my tone. "It's all about practice, ladies."

I leave them behind and keep heading for the bakery.

A familiar voice nearby stops me in my tracks. *Mom.* Ducking under the shaded awning of a boutique, I hide behind a rack of clothes and pretend to browse until I spot her up ahead with Mayor Taylor and another man in tow. I've managed to avoid my parents around Ridgeview since I left, but I didn't think I'd run into her downtown in the middle of the day. Shouldn't she be at her office instead of having lunch with the mayor?

Then again, Fox and I traced her to that shady abandoned warehouse when she was supposed to be at work for an important meeting. Thinking of what happened after we went there yesterday sends a shudder rolling through me. I came out here to get away from the thoughts rattling around in my head.

It's weird to look at her now that I know she's working with criminals.

For a moment, I wonder if the mayor is in on their scheming. The old mayor was in some way, since they got him to overlook Dad's promotion with a bribe.

This is an opportunity I can't waste. I take out my phone and send a quick text to Thea letting her know I'm running late. She won't mind and this could be important to help us figure out more of what's going on.

Keeping my movements casual, I sneak my phone through the rack and snap photos of the three of them as they talk. They're too far to hear clearly. Mom seems tense and the guy with the mayor is frowning. I don't recognize him and it only tugs harder at my suspicion.

They turn and head my way. Crap. I shift around the boutique's sale racks and fake being absorbed in a vintage red suede number that, actually, I would love to have.

"Maisy." Not a question, barely a hint of surprise at running into me, and no trace of worry or remorse for the things she said to me the night I left.

I meet my mother's cool gaze. "Mom." My attention shifts over her shoulder to the mayor. "Mayor Taylor."

The third man stands close to the mayor. He has cropped hair and looks rough, even in a cheap suit stretched to its limit by his barrel chest. His steel gaze sweeps over me, making my skin crawl. Must be a new bodyguard.

"Nice to see you, Maisy," the mayor says. "I hope you're feeling better. Your mother mentioned you caught a bad stomach bug when I saw you last at the steakhouse."

"Right," I say, glancing accusingly at Mom. Any lie she can spin to keep her from looking bad is fair game. "I was sick to my stomach."

Partially true, since my parents tried to force sleazy Sam Blake on me as yet another way to control my life. Now I know all their dirty skeletons they hid from Holden and I.

It's subtle, but the corners of her mouth pinch in disapproval. She does a good job of acting like everything's normal while each slight gesture tells me I'll be sorry if I make a scene. Years of learned behavior rises in me, calling me to her will because it can't be unlearned overnight. I clench my teeth.

Do you know? I want to scream. *Do you know that the psychos paying you shot at me and Fox?*

"You should be at home," Mom says with a well-practiced casual air. She's a pro at doublespeaking to get her meaning across without raising alarms to anyone who doesn't know what she's really like. "It's too soon for you to be out and about after how seriously ill you were."

Translation: *stop fucking around and do as I say.*

Pressing my lips into a thin line, I stretch my arms overhead in a show of defiance. "I feel a lot better now."

"All the same, I'd rather see you go home, sweetheart."

The mayor's bodyguard is eerily transfixed on me. He gives me a yellow-toothed grin when I catch him staring at me for the third time instead of keeping an eye out for any potential threats, like a bodyguard is supposed to.

I roll my shoulders back. "I don't think I will."

Mom's eyes flash in annoyance. "Well. If you insist on being difficult."

Is it difficult or am I just thinking for myself? Not that she'd care. Her world only consists of what she wants to control.

"Jacqueline," the mayor says. "We should..."

"In a moment. We'll make it on time for the..." She pauses and her sleek bob swings when she turns back to me. The body-guard shifts restlessly and she sighs. "Investors. I just want to make sure my daughter makes it home."

She grabs my wrist, nails digging in hard. I suck in a breath, shocked that she would do it in front of an audience. There isn't a shred of empathy or compassion in her gaze. If she doesn't know I was shot at, I doubt she'd be moved.

The truth of it is a punch to the gut. After seeing proof of her dirty business dealings, I can barely look at her. We haven't had a great relationship, or even an okay one for years, but it hurts to know she feels little for my well being.

A rumbling around the corner snags my attention. Fox's motorcycle turns down the road and relief washes over me. He must've stayed nearby. With his leather jacket, tousled dark hair, and the fresh cuts from our run in with the criminals my parents are working with, he looks every inch the dangerous bad boy whispered about throughout town. Mom and the others stiffen at the sight of him.

Oddly, she exchanges a look with the bodyguard, as if he's the one in control rather than her or the mayor.

"Bye, Mom."

Yanking my wrist from her talon-like nails, I keep my gaze locked with hers as I move toward the curb. The bike stops behind me and Fox's stony presence envelops me like a hug, warding off anyone else who dares get close while welcoming me into its embrace. Mom watches, enraged, as I get on the back of the bike and wrap my arms around Fox's waist.

"Maisy," she hisses.

Fox revs the engine, arrogantly cutting off whatever she

tries to say next to save face and puts a hand over mine for a beat.

Mom cuts a sharp glance to the bodyguard, then the mayor, before looking back at me and silently commanding me to get off the motorcycle. I set my jaw. All I hear is the sound of glass shattering and the angry blast of gunshots.

Without another word, we peel away from my mother, the mayor, and his bodyguard. Later I'll apologize to Thea for ditching, but Fox couldn't have come at a better time.

It's like he knew I needed him. No matter what, he'll come for me.

THIRTY-ONE

FOX

Bright light filters through the industrial windows, making Maisy's hair shine in the summery morning rays. It's fanned out on the pillow as she sleeps. One of her hands is tucked beneath her cheek and the other reaches out to me, draped over my inked chest. Carefully, I roll toward her with a content, sleep-tinged sigh.

Having her in my arms, in my bed, to chase away the tortured images my mind fills with in sleep is wonderful. They haven't been bothering me as much. It's the best sleep I've gotten in years.

As I watch her, she cracks her eyes open groggily. My lips twitch and my heart turns over. For someone that loves to move and stretch her body with yoga, she doesn't love mornings. Maybe yoga is what helps her accept being awake.

"Morning," she whispers huskily.

With a cute little grunt, she snuggles closer and smiles at me. I caress her back and enjoy the feeling of her head resting on my chest. It's quiet and comfortable for a few minutes. This is nice, not having to worry about my problems or a plan or what happened two days ago, nothing but enjoying the beautiful girl in my arms.

"You feel okay?" she asks a while later.

"Yeah," I say, touching one of the scabbed over cuts on my cheek. "They'll heal in a few days. Not the worst I've dealt with."

She lifts her head, propping her chin on my pec to peer at me with her sleepy hazel eyes. "What do you want to do after all this is over?"

I go to answer, then pause. Do I have a life plan? My life has only been focused on revenge for so long. I never thought past it.

"I don't know," I say slowly.

Her calf slides against my leg beneath the sheets. I like it, all the little ways she touches me. She hums and shifts, folding her arms over my chest to rest her head on, her bare tits pressing into my skin. I lick my lips and skate my fingertips down her sides.

"What about the stuff you make? You could do something like the work you do with reclaimed materials. People would buy the things you build. Or do you like working on cars better?"

Her lips pucker in thought and I'm too busy breathing through a wave of fondness mingled with the tug of arousal low in my stomach when her body moves while she talks.

"You could open a workshop that gives you the space to do both." Her eyebrows waggle. "Y'know, because you're so multi-talented."

As her voice dips with double meaning, she slides her soft body over mine, straddling me. Shit, I'm liking where this is going. My hands automatically find her hips and a pleased rumble vibrates in my throat.

"I...yes, I like that idea. Never thought about it much before."

I can barely string together a sentence, too distracted by the way she looks with the sheets pooled around her waist, hair mussed from sleep, hunger burning in her gaze. Proud of her body and happy to have me admire it. Her lashes flutter and she puts her hands on the ocean and crow on my chest as she continues in a hushed voice, painting a dream of the future.

Her skin is soft. I move one hand from her waist, pushing my palm up from her stomach, through the valley between her tits, not stopping until my fingers wrap around her throat. The corners of her mouth lift in approval. Using my hold on her neck, I pull her down to steal a kiss.

Mine, I think with a flare of possession.

"It'll be close enough to the beach to hear the seagulls," she mumbles against my lips between kisses. "Venice Beach, I think. Just a couple blocks away. And nearby, I'll have a beachfront yoga studio of my own. I've been thinking that's what I want to do, after my road trip. Just picture it."

I'm liking the idea more and more, but my thoughts haze over as she sits up and sinks onto my cock with this wicked half-lidded bliss on her face that has me ready to blow my load the minute I'm fully inside the wet heat of her pussy.

"Anything you want," I rasp, fitting my hands back to her waist and groaning when she starts to ride my cock. "As long as I'm with you."

All the things I thought I had to do seem less vital to living right now. This is all I need. When I'm with her, everything else fades away.

Victory gleams in her beautiful golden eyes and, god, I love her. I fucking love her.

* * *

It takes a few days, but I managed to get what I needed to fix the blown out glass on the Charger. After the repair is done, I climb the steps and find Maisy in a nest of sheets on the bed in a sports bra with the laptop, squinting at the screen. We hit a snag with the sealed employee file Ethan gave us that even Colt has had trouble decrypting, so she's combing through the copied hard drive from her parents' place searching for a way to get in.

I scrub a hand over my jaw as I watch her for a second, pushing away the thought of what happened the other day. Putting her life in danger is unacceptable. I'm still pissed those fuckers took a shot at her just to get at me. Even though she said we should keep going, I'm wondering if I should pull the plug on this.

Again I'm hit with the idea to put her on the back of the bike and just go. Leave Ridgeview in the dust while I take her wherever we want. Go find the life she talked about for us. I've spent so many years on this, but being with her makes me rethink what's important.

I cross the room and cup the back of her head, kissing her hair. "Any luck?"

"Not yet."

Maybe that's a good thing, I think grimly, partially hating myself for being so disrespectful to the memory of my dead parents.

It takes her another minute to give me her attention. I rub her shoulders and neck until her lashes flutter and she makes an appreciative noise. She's tense and I don't know if I'm good with her running herself into the ground like this. My mind whispers with the idea again, we could just leave and find the ocean. I slide my lips together and sigh. I miss the damn salt air and I want to breathe it in with her by my side.

"Don't forget to take a break. You've been at it for days."

She nods, tilting her face up to accept the quick kiss I drop on her mouth before I pull away. "I'm going to workout."

I put on some music and lean my head side to side as I warm up, loosening my muscles until my limbs are ready. The first hit against the bag always feels the best. I let myself go, channeling all my rage at Nexus Lab and Stalenko Corp into my workout.

Feeling her gaze roaming over my form not long after, I smirk to myself. I'm not one to puff out my chest and preen, but it feels good to show my girl what I'm capable of as I unleash hit after hit to the punching bag. Sweat rolls down my body and I push myself harder for her benefit. The air in the room thickens. I have half a mind to abandon my workout and pin her to the bed instead, vent out the rest of my frustrations with my cock buried deep in her body.

It's a temptation that's always there, but I refocus on my breathing and go again.

Almost an hour later, Maisy sucks in a sharp breath and punches both her fists in the air. "I did it! Holy shit, I found it."

My gaze swings around, instinct always drawing me to her, and the heavy bag thumps into my side. I grunt, lifting my hands to steady it, then swipe an arm across my face to clear the sweat.

"You got in?"

"Yeah. There was a passcode with a number sequence tucked away within a subfolder." She rolls her lips between her teeth as she pushes the laptop away on the bed. "Um, the numbers line up with the date of the crash."

I scoff.

Of course they do.

Smug assholes, hiding everything in plain sight like they can't get caught for what they covered up. I blow out a breath and stalk across the room. Anxious ripples move through my stomach the closer I get to the bed, to Maisy, to the laptop with the answers I've been waiting for.

"So what's in the termination file?" I brace one hand behind her, leaning over to see the screen.

She pulls the laptop close again and scrolls through. "It's a notice of resignation. Your parents signatures are both on it."

I squint at where she points. "That's forged. Mom never made a loop for the L in Wilder. I remember because I used to try to copy her signature."

"It looks like other than that there's a PDF email thread, like it was printed out." She clicks on it, but the screen prompts her for another password. She tries the one she used to open the file and her shoulders relax in relief when we're granted access. "I think this IP address at the top means it was on a private company server. Look, it's from your dad's email at Nexus Lab, but it isn't with the company."

"That's your mom's email." I jab at the screen, unable to stop seething. Another email address catches my eye. "Wait, it was all of them and someone from Stalenko Corp. Why would they keep that if it connects them all? Password or not, if anyone found this it's solid proof. Scroll down."

My eyes fly back and forth, reading so fast the decade old email conversation blurs. The words jump out at me as I try to process what I'm seeing.

Previous payment is insufficient...risk of the supply chain tracing distribution of controlled substances back to the source... file a patent if our demands aren't met...

The responses from Stalenko Corp are clipped and unrelenting. They don't say it outright, but the threat between the lines is clear: cooperate or face the fatal consequences.

My fingers dig into the sheets and I lean over far enough that Maisy ends up almost folded in half beneath me while I try to get closer to the screen. As if being closer will change what's in front of me.

"Fox, are you okay?"

Maisy twists to put a hand on my chest. It caves as I stumble back from the bed, shoving my fingers into the sweaty roots of my hair.

"Fox." Her voice is gentle and tentative. She reaches out to brush my back. "Talk to me."

Thoughts collide in my head one after another. The undeniable truth is right there in black and white. Even Colton couldn't find it out.

My parents hid the samples and the patent paperwork they started in the garage because they were extorting Stalenko Corp for more money in the middle of helping them plan for Ridgeview to become the main manufacturer for the Russian syndicate's drug empire. They were in on it the entire time with Jacqueline Landry. Modern day criminals, working out their business deals over email instead of meeting in back alleys on foggy nights.

Memories from my childhood reshape and crystalize, moments where I saw them as innocent viscerally replaced with the harsher clarity of their whispers at night when they thought I was asleep.

Money.

They were always arguing about money and what they were going to do.

No.

In a swift move I grab the laptop, intent on throwing it through the goddamn window.

"Fox," Maisy says sharply, placing a hand on my inked arm.

My grip flexes as I drag in labored breaths. Red floods my vision and my heart pounds. I let her pry the laptop from my grip and she sets it aside. The ache in my jaw makes me rub at it and it takes effort to unclench my teeth. Spinning away from her, I begin to pace in time with my furious heartbeat.

A lie.

That's what I've chased for ten fucking years.

A lie.

That's what broke my heart and tore away my childhood strip by bloody strip until all that was left was what I am now— cold, savage, hellbent on going after what I want, what I thought was right.

A lie.

That's what plagued me with nightmares.

A goddamn lie.

Air burns my lungs as I struggle to catch my breath. Everything I thought I knew is a lie—lies on top of lies, that's all my life is made up of. An awful, broken sound echoes off the industrial windows and I realize it came from me.

"I thought," I choke out.

They were innocent. My family was murdered.

"I know," she murmurs with this sympathetic look that wrecks me.

"Fuck. It was just a dirty business deal gone wrong, so Stalenko took them out. I've fought to make this right for them for so fucking long."

I dedicated every ounce of energy to this. Fueled my thirst for vengeance with hatred for my best friend over a broken promise that didn't even matter. Because my parents were in on it all.

I knew corruption ran deep through the streets of Ridgeview, but I never thought it poisoned my parents.

"Fox, come on. You have to breathe."

She hovers close at the edge of the trail I'm burning into the concrete, unafraid of the violent fury coming off me in waves. I can't even look at her. I came back here ready to destroy everything in her life. All because I believed for so long that her family caused the destruction of mine—believed I was making things right when they've never been more wrong.

I should've pushed harder to let it all go when I was ready, because then we wouldn't be here. I wouldn't know the truth about my parents. Wouldn't know what really happened to them.

"Fuck!"

The yell bursts from me and the dam breaks. As I pace, the anger and hurt spill over, my heart beating faster and my vision tunneling. I kick hard at the couch and the heavy furniture scoots several inches. Maisy backs up a step and another rage-filled shout from me echoes off the walls.

Grabbing the next nearest thing blindly—the twisted scrap metal I worked on that she brought upstairs, calling it a conver-sation piece with a proud smirk—I hurl it across the room. It crashes somewhere in the kitchenette, the sound of breaking glass and carnage still not enough to make any of this better.

It's all I'm good for—destruction.

"All the goddamn shit I've done to get here! So many things, all of it bullshit. I dragged Colt into this. Dragged you in." The words slip free with each ragged gasp. The fragile control over myself is a whisper away from snapping entirely, leaving me dangling close to becoming unhinged. I feel myself dangerously near the edge as my thoughts take on a manic energy. "Destroy lives, that's what I came to do and I fucking did it. I fucked with yours like it was a game, plotted to take down your parents, made sure your brother's future crumbled. What was the goddamn point?!"

Maisy freezes. The patient concern for me disappears as her spine straightens.

"Wait, hold up, what?" Her voice rises. "What did you just say?"

Fresh betrayal shines in her hazel eyes.

It rips me from the precipice of losing control, reality crashing back over me as some of the overwhelming anger clears from my head. Panting and disoriented, I replay what I said and curse silently.

Holden was the first friend I ever made, before I became friends with Maisy, too. He taught me how to ride a bike when I was jealous Maisy learned before both of us. We'd race home from the bus stop, run into our houses, and meet back up to trade Pokémon, or play any of the latest games. He knew all my secret fears, and I knew his. We grew up side by side, partners in troublemaking.

We were best friends. Brothers before I had Colton and the Crows.

The rushing tide of memories of my childhood with the Landry siblings makes my chest constrict. Each one is more bittersweet than the last. I lost every good thing I had. Lost them. And what do I do? I come back and make enemies out of them. Because I wasn't satisfied with Jacqueline and Richard. I wanted to punish them all for the years I suffered.

Invisible shards of glass rake my throat and acidic self-loathing swirls in my stomach. "I took away his future by having his draft offer reversed. To make sure it stuck, I sent the college video clips of the fights he organized at the quarry in high school. He's...his face is clearly visible in them and some-times he'd wear his letterman jacket."

"What the hell," she whispers. "You hung around him because you wanted to blackmail him? I thought... Damn it, Fox, I thought you were his friend."

The hurt lacing her tone is like being shoved onto hot coals with no protection from the blistering heat.

This was a long game. He used me as his enforcer and put me right in position to unravel the strings of his life. I took the video myself last fall in his senior year while making sure everyone else abided the rules.

Shaking her head, she begins to pace. "You know, when you messed with my grades, I didn't really get all that torn up about it. The grades, the life plan—that wasn't my dream in the first place. The rumors you stirred, even breaking into the yoga studio to freak me out, I moved past it. The car prank was disgusting, but it's just stuff. It didn't physically hurt me. I mean, whatever, right? You tried to break me with all that, but I'd have to care about those things for it to work. I was more hurt that you wouldn't talk to me for so long, but hung out with him. That's where your damage finally hit me hard."

Hearing her lay out my mistakes steals the rest of the air from the room.

"I believed they were innocent," I bite out, scrubbing my face. "Everything I did was for them and my sister. It didn't matter what I had to do."

I immediately want to take the explanation back. The words came out wrong. She doesn't take my defensive tone well, halting and narrowing her gaze. I open my mouth to apologize and explain better, but she beats me to it.

"You know, Holden really did love football and wanted to keep playing. He hasn't touched the game once all year. Hasn't watched it, either. You really fucked him over. He's told me he's happy, but that was when he thought he didn't earn that opportunity to play for a school he loved." Her mouth purses in frustration and she flings out an arm. "How could you do that to your best friend? I get that I broke my promise and understand why you hate my parents, but Holden? He didn't do shit to you and you destroyed his future as collateral damage. Don't you have limits? There's a difference between innocent people and the ones you think deserve to suffer."

Guilt rakes over my nerve endings. I was willing to do

anything—whatever it took to get my revenge. Holden wasn't an innocent guy. He organized that fight ring and made money. Partied hard and lived his life wild. But he wasn't part of this. I could've spared him.

Maisy folds her arms over her chest. The distrust flashing in her gaze cuts deep. My jaw clenches, even as my heart splinters with a thousand fissures, the damn thing on the brink of implosion.

This is it. She should've run from me from the first moment and now it's happening. She finally sees the truth—what a monster I've become.

This time I can't chase her. I need to let her go if that's what she wants. I betrayed her and this is what I deserve for it.

I love her, but I went after everyone in her family. We don't get to ride off into the damn sunset together with the ruinous outcome of my actions laying between our feet.

"I'm sorry."

It's gruff, jagged around the edges, but what more can I say? The damage has been done for over a year.

She stares at me for a long moment. "I want to believe that, but I think this made me realize something really important. I've jumped from living my life under my parents' rules to living it for someone else. I got too caught up in all this. I don't want anyone to control me." She darts her gaze away, unwilling to look at me when she goes on. "I need to live my life for me."

My throat constricts. Fuck. Everything in me revolts. I don't want to lose her. Not like this. Not ever.

The confession of what I feel for her pushes to the surface, but I swallow it back. I have to respect her choice.

"I never want to take that away from you," I mutter. "I'm not holding you prisoner here."

She looks so lost for a moment that it eats me up inside. My stubborn, headstrong girl has spent too many years under someone else's control. I swallow, throat working as I close the distance between us. Regret tastes sour, sitting in the back of my mouth as a reminder of everything I've ruined for ghosts that didn't deserve my fierce loyalty.

Maisy touches my face and I close my eyes, breathing in deeply so I'll always remember her sweet, soothing scent.

"Take the Charger." A small gasp escapes her at my offer. "I don't want you to feel stranded. It's yours for as long as you need it. Go."

Across town, across the country, go wherever you want, little daisy.

"Okay." She sounds as wrecked as I am. "Thanks."

Her touch drops from my cheek and I already miss it. She rummages around the bed for clothes, her shoes. Keys jingle across the room, the sound ominous and final.

I keep my eyes closed the whole time because I can't stand to watch her go. Not when this is my fault.

As soon as I hear her drive off in my car, I sink to the floor, leaning against the back of the couch, and stare at nothing. The energy drains from my body like I'm slowly bleeding out. I expect to look down at the dusty concrete and find a pool of blood, but there's nothing there.

Just emptiness, like the hollow feeling carved out in my chest.

THIRTY-TWO

MAISY

It's weird driving Fox's matte black Charger. The windows have been fixed, but I can still hear the sound of the rear and driver's side windows shattering from over the weekend.

The muscles in my stomach tighten and I focus on taking measured breaths, rubbing my thumb over the quartz inlay in my brass bangle bracelet. Once my heart rate calms, I step out of the car and climb the steps to Thea and Connor's apartment with nothing but my phone because I left everything at his place like I'd be back.

Except his converted warehouse is the last place I want to be right now.

I need to get my head and my heart back in balance before I fall under someone else's control. I can't jump from my parents' rule to his.

First I drove around for a few hours, stopping at a peaceful grassy field to watch the sunset dip behind the Rockies while I meditated. Nature has this magic power and sitting there centered me. Once the warmth of the summer day bled away, I texted my best friend and she welcomed me with open arms because we always have each other's back.

Thea and Connor live in a chic, newer part of town in an apartment building built near the shopping district in the center of Ridgeview. The black metal railings leading up to their unit are modern with tension wire.

Letting myself in with a key Thea gave me, I shout, "Don't be naked!"

Thea's laughter rings out from the kitchen, her favorite spot in her home. She pokes her head around the doorway and beams at me. My heart swells at the sight of her, auburn curls piled on her head with flyaways framing her face.

"I thought you have no problem with nudity," she says as I kick off my shoes in the hallway, relishing the feeling of the cool tiled floors on my bare feet.

So much for letting her and Connor enjoy their private time as newlyweds. At least they welcomed me to couch surf with open arms. I definitely can't go home.

Not just because I don't know how I'll look my brother in the eye knowing I'm partly to blame for his college football draft being stolen from him. I'm still disgusted by what Fox and I discovered about my parents and I don't want to see either of them. There's no way I'm putting myself back in their clutches to try to control me again. Never.

Thinking of them only reminds me what I uncovered earlier in the afternoon that sent Fox flying off the handle. As mad as I am at him for keeping what he did to Holden from me, my heart is heavy for him. That was a shitty way to learn his parents were just as corrupt as mine.

"I don't. Bodies are totally natural." We go into the kitchen and I light up at my favorite batter in the mixing bowl, swiping a finger through it and sticking it in my mouth while Thea gives me a look. "But I don't want to walk into your home and watch while Connor dicks you down, babe. I'd rather be the main show than watch one."

Her cheeks turn a pretty shade of pink and she busies herself putting away ingredients. I fake a gasp and my mood lifts when a tiny squeak leaves her.

"You were totally doing it when I texted to say I was coming here, weren't you?" When she opens and closes her mouth, darting her blue eyes to the doorway I nod. "Knew it. Sorry for interrupting."

"It's fine. You know our door is always open for you. Want me to invite everyone else over? We can make a night of it."

"No, please." Some of my easygoing bravado fades and I rub my hands over my face. "Can it be just you and me for a bit?"

"Of course, Maise." Thea comes around the sleek white island to wrap her arms around me. "Connor's in the shower, but he can go to Devlin's if you need him to."

"Thanks."

A wave of gratefulness crests over me. I'm so glad I have such great friends and I feel more than a little bad I've kept them in the dark for so long. It's only been a little under two weeks since I went to live with Fox, but how much I've been missing after getting sucked into his dark world hits me like a punch.

"How's the bakery?" The opening is this week. God, I've been such a crappy best friend. "Everything ready?"

Thea lights up. "Yeah. I'm nervous as hell, but Connor's been keeping me distracted whenever I go off on a tangent."

I smirk at the loving curve of her mouth and the faraway look that fills her eyes for a moment. "I'll bet he has."

After she pours the batter into a baking tray and puts it in the oven, she washes her hands. I watch, leaning against the counter. She dries off, then nods toward the living room.

"What about that beach day you guys had?" We collapse on her couch, my head in her lap. "Tell me everything I missed while I've been laying low from my parents."

"About that," she says. "What's the deal? You normally come stay with me when they suck."

Biting my lip, I stare up at her. "I went to stay with Fox."

Her brows jump up, but she makes no judgements. "Blair and Devlin called it."

An amused breath gusts out of me. "Of course they did. Nothing gets by those two."

"So you worked things out from all his broody staring, I take it?" She leans over me and her voice lilts with excitement. "Did you ride his motorcycle?"

It's my turn to flush and I almost snort at the heat flooding my cheeks. I'm not embarrassed, but thinking about how we went from being at each other's throats to how it's been since he let me in makes me warm all over.

"Pretty much. And yes, it's... I can't even describe how amazing riding it is." I pause, waggling my eyebrows. "It's not the only thing I was riding."

Thea makes a scandalized noise that has both of us laughing and shoving at each other playfully.

I sigh, touching my leather bracelet as the amusement fades. "Until today."

"What happened?" Her voice is soft and soothing. She's always been nurturing and I close my eyes, letting her comfort me by running her fingers through my hair. "Tell me whatever you're comfortable with sharing."

I start at the beginning, explaining my childhood friendship with him in more detail than I gave her last year when he came back. Then I take her through his cold shoulder treatment, to everything changing after that fateful hookup at Jenna Taylor's party and how he tormented me but I sought him out anyway. I couldn't stay away from him if I tried. When I get to the story about sneaking into his car going from bribery to a car chase she yelps.

"Holy shit, Maisy," she says with wide eyes.

"I know. Things have been crazy and I'm sorry I didn't tell you. There's more."

Now that I've started unloading this, it feels good. I don't realize Connor is listening to me explain about all the corruption Fox and I have unearthed until he chimes in from the doorway where he's propped against the frame, fingers tucked in the waistband of his basketball shorts.

"You've been doing all this under our noses? Shit, I could've helped you. I know some guys."

Connor doesn't elaborate, but I guess from the mischief in his gray eyes the guys he knows are probably like Colton and the friends Fox has described. The type of people that skate outside of the law.

"So does Fox. We haven't been totally alone, but I didn't want to interrupt up your lives with this mess. You just got married and after all the crap you both had to deal with last year, I didn't want to add to any stress on top of opening the bakery."

Thea squeezes me. "You can always lean on your friends no matter what, okay?"

"Thanks babe," I murmur, soaking in the restorative energy of her magic hugs.

"Just let us know if we can do anything," she says. "We're here for you always."

"You know we've got your back. You're family and we protect our own."

I snort. "Has anyone told you and Dev you sound like mob bosses when you guys say that?"

His wide smile is full of wickedness. "Gotta keep our reps striking fear in the hearts of our enemies."

This time a laugh rolls through me, but it passes and I'm still left with the confused mix of feelings that haven't really left since Fox confessed about Holden.

How can he still own my heart but make me want to tackle him for hurting my brother? If I did, would I fight him or kiss him?

"You still seem tense. Want me to roll a joint?" Connor offers.

"No thanks." I shake my head, wanting to be clear headed more than relaxed right now. "Can Thea and I chill on our own for a bit?"

He gives us a charming crooked grin and nods. "You got it." He comes over to the couch, bracing against the back of it to kiss Thea above me. "I'll go see if the guys are all good for the opening, sunshine."

"Thank you," Thea murmurs, face tilted up for one more kiss.

My chest cinches tight watching them. It makes me miss the rich scent of leather and earthy woods mixed with motor oil. Makes me miss *him*. How can someone become necessary for breathing in such a short time?

He gave me my own freedom by letting me take his car. I could go back there...or I could get on the highway and drive until the road runs out. My dreams have always been focused on traveling, but I keep shoving it aside.

But this is where I should be right now. I can't run from anything. My best friend is opening her bakery in two days and we've been planning the opening day for months.

"Peace out," Connor calls as he leaves the apartment.

"I'm in love with him." I don't wait, pushing the admission out and staring up at my best friend. Fox is the only person who makes me feel so alive. "But he did something bad. Well, a lot of bad things."

Thea puts a hand on my shoulder and helps me sit up. "We don't get to pick who we fall for. Did he hurt you? Because if he hurt you, then—"

"Yes, but not the way you're thinking." I curl up next to her and let her drape her arm over my shoulders. Playing with the hem of my loose shirt—god, another shirt I stole from Fox without even realizing—I exhale and tell her the rest of what happened today. "When we finally worked through the grudge he had about me, he kept this part about Holden a secret. I forgave him and we got each other back. I want to trust there's good in him, but when things get bad will he always take things so far?"

"Maybe. But that's him before he had you with him." She tilts her head. "It's a partnership. Connor's taken things too far, but together we find the balance."

Balance. That's what I want. If Fox didn't push me away, I could've pulled him back from the edge. I could've saved my brother from the heartache of his dream disintegrating right in front of him.

"What would make it better?"

I worry my lip for a moment. Holden still doesn't know. He's been better in the last few weeks now that he's settled at Ridgeview Community College. Not just better, he's been happy for the first time in a long time. I don't want to ruin that by telling him the truth. Maybe I'm overreacting to all of this. For once, I wish I wasn't so impulsive so I could've confronted Fox instead of leaving.

"Talking it out, I guess. But I don't know, Holden's been pretty chill. I'd hate to rehash it if it's going to leave him reeling without the chance to reverse it. Fox said he sent incriminating video."

Thea frowns. "Does he still wish he could have gone there to play? Because if he doesn't, that might tell you the answer."

I shrug. "I don't know. He said he's glad it worked out, but it was taken from him. Given the chance? Maybe. But I think he met someone in one of his classes this semester."

"I think you should start by asking your brother since it has more to do with him."

Nodding, I slouch further on the couch. I'll text him later to broach the subject.

Thea's always been the logical one between the two of us. Now that I have the space away from the emotions racing through me when Fox angrily spit out what he did, it doesn't sting as badly when I prod at the memory. Betrayal still flares, but it's the same as when Fox explained the reason he hated me. An indignant sort of ache, but not such a deep cut I'll never move past it.

I try to picture if I had parents I idolized, would I end up like him? Every relationship poisoned by the demolition site of my heart? God, as angry as I was at him, my heart wobbles in sympathy.

I wonder what he's doing right now and hope he managed to calm down or find a better outlet for his anger than throwing shit around. Today was a shock for him, too, and I left him alone to handle it.

"If I love him, why does it hurt so much?"

How can I love someone that is capable of turning his back on my brother? How can I be ready to forgive him?

Thea wraps me up in another hug. "It's just how love is, messy and intense. Love is good and bad all at once."

She's right. More than that, I came here because I want to figure out what my priorities are. I jumped from standing up to my controlling, shady parents to throwing myself into Fox's crusade for the truth. Now that he has it, do we keep going or does it stop here?

Did I let myself bounce from one thing to the next because I'm afraid to take something I want for myself? I've pushed off my road trip indefinitely for so many reasons. It's scary to think I barely know my own self underneath all the layers I've put on over the years at my parents' command.

As I turn it over in my head, it rings true. That's been my problem, finally teased out from the murky shadows.

I'm scared. Too worried what happens if I make a mistake because I'm not used to making my own choices. And I used my shock about Holden to give the fear bigger wings.

My throat constricts and it takes a few tries to swallow past the lump that forms. I twist my fingers in Fox's stolen shirt, bringing the oversized neckline to my nose to take comfort in his faint scent lingering behind, like I've brought a piece of him with me.

It's still wrong, what he did. But Holden is happy and just like me, he's not physically hurt by Fox's manipulations.

"What do you need?" Thea prompts, breaking into my internal reflection. "Do you want to leave town for your trip? I know it's been hard to work it out, but you can take my car. We'll go together to your house and pack up all your stuff into the back."

A pang hits me hard. My first thought is Fox. I need him. I feel most like myself, my true self, when I'm with him. But I don't want to be the girl who can only be like that with him. That's why I asked him for space because everything was getting too crazy.

I need to live for me and make my own choices. But am I doing that if I stay for him, or should I stop letting excuses keep me from taking the road trip and moving to California?

As soon as I consider it, I know that's not what I need. The thought of leaving him behind hurts as much as it did when he was gone from my life. When I think of going to California now, I picture what we've both been talking about—both of us on the road together, him opening a workshop and me making my own path with a yoga studio of my own. I never wanted to do it alone, but I didn't realize I was waiting for the right person to do it with. Someone who knew from the beginning how much I dreamed of it.

I brush the old stones of my bracelet. When he gave them to me, he said they reminded him of me. I always thought the blue one looked like his eyes.

Fox is woven into my heart and soul, bound by our years-old connection and strengthened by everything we've been through together in the last couple of weeks.

That's what I needed to figure out. I couldn't see it until I stepped back. I was afraid I wasn't ready to discover myself, too scared to do something on my own.

While I search my head and heart for what I need, Thea waits patiently.

"I think living for myself doesn't have to mean that if I'm with Fox, I'm forgetting myself," I finally say.

Thea's eyes crinkle with her smile. "No one can outshine your light. Only enhance it."

"Yeah, you're right. It's about making my own choices."

Something I never had the luxury of with my parents breathing down my neck. Now that I know why they've been so meticulous my stomach turns in disappointment.

Screw them, though. They can't control me anymore. No one can, only me.

It's my choice to be with Fox and I'm not giving that up.

"Thanks for letting me talk it out, dude. You rock, forever and always."

Thea huffs in amusement and cups my cheeks. "I just asked the questions, you did all the heavy lifting."

I raise both arms and flex my biceps, enjoying the sound of her laugh. She pops up from the couch and disappears for a few minutes while I breathe through the lifted weight off my chest now that I found some clarity.

When she comes back, she has freshly baked cupcakes and holds up a bag of chips. "Want to gorge ourselves on snacks and marathon Bake Off until we pass out? I promise, you can eat all the cupcakes this time because I love you and you need it."

"Yes," I say, dragging it out in a lazy drawl. "You're the best."

"And don't you forget it."

"Never," I swear.

THIRTY-THREE

FOX

Darkness fell over the warehouse before I moved from the spot where I collapsed.

I could lose everything all over again. Revenge set me on this path, and if I hadn't followed it I would never have known the truth about my parents and what happened to them. It led me back to the girl who has always made my heart feel whole. But...it could be what poisons our relationship before it starts.

She never said we were done, even left most of her things behind, yet the dull ache in my chest has been a constant reminder of her absence as soon as I offered her the keys to the Charger.

There's a row of crystals she lined up on the windowsill near the bed. I pick up a pink one that looks the same as the other bracelet she wears, then put it back. Pushing my fingers through my hair until it's sticking on end, I sigh raggedly.

I should've told her everything at the start, as soon as I trusted her again and let her in. I'm an idiot for hiding what I've done. The last secret I kept from her never should've come out because I was in pain and losing control.

It's been two days since she left and every minute has been an agonizing blur of self-loathing, pushing my body past its limit so I pass out, then waking up drenched in a cold sweat in the middle of the night from a nightmare, bed fucking empty. No matter what I do, my demons come for me anyway. I keep at it. All so I don't chase after her and beg her to look at me, to see past the monstrous things I've done.

Keeping her was a pipe dream. I knew I was someone she should run from, but I swallowed her in my darkness anyway.

In the short time she'd been here, she filled this space with her light. Now it feels as empty as I do. I *miss* her. The rhythm of her breathing when she stops, drops, and does yoga at all hours of the day. The shape of her next to me in bed. The amused little curl of the corners of her mouth when I steal the coffee she can't ever finish. Damn it, the bright look that fills her eyes when she talks about how much California felt like a home she didn't know she'd miss even though she's only been once.

When she busted her way back into my heart, she put me back together. I've been broken for years, damaged beyond repair, but she made it better. She made me want more out of my life. As long as it meant having her by my side. I want to see her seek out every dream she has.

Taking in the state of the studio apartment, my stomach clenches. Destruction is all around me. For the first time in a long time, I don't want it. Any of it.

I go to the kitchenette in the corner and pick up the twisted scrap metal. My fingers follow the curved shape and if I squint, I can see the shape of a flower. I didn't know what this was before when I made it, one of those pieces I followed instinct instead of a plan.

I was making her. Making what I feel about her.

Swallowing past the roughness in my throat, I put it down

and clean up the broken mugs and a bowl that shattered when I threw the thing I made across the room. Once I'm done, I move to the couch, bringing the abstract metal flower representing my girl with me. I put it on the coffee table and trace the shape with my gaze, seeing the curve of her smile, the arch of her back, the indescribable and intangible feeling of her excitement when she's on the back of my bike.

No wonder I followed the pull to create, willingly leaving her in my bed to get this out of my head. I was a man possessed until she crept down those stairs. I lean forward and curl my hand around it, imagining it's her under my palm.

Every single thing went into this piece and I feel naked staring at it.

Fuck, I can't live without her anymore. I don't want to. Learning to do it in the last ten years has been the worst kind of hell.

Maisy gave me back something I haven't had in a long time by reminding my heart it could still beat and feel—and it's always been for her. She's it for me. I can't let her go without a fight.

She's what's most important to me now.

Not my parents' ghosts.

Not taking down her parents for condemning me to a life of gruesome nightmares, emptiness, stripped of everything. The life my own parents had a hand in damning me with. But they couldn't take everything away from me. I fought and survived and found my way back to her.

You and me, that's how it's supposed to be. Her voice echoes in my head. We said it to each other as kids. We're not soulmates, not fate—nothing poetic like that. But we do fit together.

I was surviving before, but I wasn't living until Maisy Landry was mine again.

My hands flex at my side. Why am I sitting here pretending

I'm a gentleman when I'm anything but? I'm not a good man. Maisy is *my* daisy and I'm going to go fight for her to prove it.

Determination settles in my bones and I grab my keys for the motorcycle while putting my phone to my ear. As soon as the call connects, I'm talking without waiting for a greeting.

"I need you to do something for me," I say, swinging a leg over the leather seat. "And I need it done yesterday."

My thumb swipes over the smooth material. Everything around me reminds me of her.

Colton's laugh filters through the phone. *"Really making a habit out of breaking the rules. If Wren finds out about these IOUs, he won't be a happy camper."*

That guy hasn't been happy since his light left this world. There's nothing left in him but brutality.

"I don't care." My voice doesn't shake as I give everything I have to make this right for her. "I'll pledge my entire life if I have to in payment."

Colton grunts, then goes quiet when he realizes I'm deadly serious. After a minute, he asks, *"What do you need?"*

I start the bike's ignition, mentally mapping every field of wildflowers I know of. I'll start with the one by our tree, where I found the purple daisies ten years ago.

"Holden Landry's admissions acceptance and football draft. Reverse it. Erase the blackmail evidence we sent."

"Uh, why?" Colt drawls. *"That's the opposite of what you've been working on."*

"It's important," I snap. Pausing to draw in a deep breath like Maisy was showing me this week before she left, I lower my voice. "Please, Colt. Just help me out with this. If I don't fix it..."

I don't finish, shutting down the thought. Life without Maisy isn't something I'm going to think about, which means failure is unacceptable.

"*I'll see what I can do.*"

"Thanks. Text me."

Hanging up, I take off in search of the flowers that always remind me of Maisy with fire burning in my blood. I'll pick every wild daisy I find until there aren't any left. She deserves that and more, and I'll give her the whole fucking world before I'm done proving to her how much she matters to me.

* * *

By the time I make it to the bakery, I have to nudge my way through the opening day crowd spilling onto the sidewalk. A few people give me sharp looks and wide berth, the Wilder name still hard at work, but I ignore all that when I hear her laugh ring out inside. The light, airy sound ripples over me.

Maisy.

It's impossible to stop the way my heart stutters.

"Let me through," I say.

People move aside, glancing curiously at what I'm carrying and I reach the door. My hands shake slightly as I step over the threshold into the bustling bakery.

The fresh scent of cookies hits me first. Maisy's friend Thea stands behind a wood counter overflowing with treats beaming at the people waiting in line with Connor nearby, pride filling his gaze. A few conversations slow to a stop and I almost have to laugh. Everything is bright and cheerful in this place, and I'm darkening the door in ripped black jeans and a dark t-shirt, probably looking like a damn psycho.

All of that fades the moment I lay eyes on her across the room, perched on top of a table with Holden and one of her friends, heart-stopping smile wide and hazel eyes lit up with life. She's wearing a pair of cut off shorts with bleach splatters and a white stretched out muscle tank over the sports bra she had on the day she left. Her eyes meet mine and she stops. I want to cut open my chest and hand her my bleeding heart right then and there.

Because it's hers. It's always been hers. The damn thing beats only for her.

It sits in my throat as I take one staggering step toward her, then another. In three long strides I'm in front of her and for a second I hate this place because I can't pick out her floral and coconut scent. The irrational feeling passes after a beat.

Is this what love is? This crazy madness that latches onto the body?

"Fox," she says.

Holden shifts in his seat, away from the girl who seems to be with him to slide between me and his sister. I bite off the urge to snap at him to get out of my way.

"If you think I'm going to stand around while you hurt my sister some more—"

I cut him off. "The last thing I want to do is hurt her."

"Dude, move," Maisy says instead, nudging her brother aside. "I've got this."

Holden's brows flatten. "You're good?"

Maisy rolls her eyes. "Yes. Shoo. Go enjoy your date over there."

He swings his gaze back to me and I recognize the protectiveness in his expression. The girl with him takes his hand and tugs him toward the bakery counter.

"I'll be watching," Holden promises before turning around to hug the girl from behind, lifting her off her feet to make her laugh.

"So will we," mutters another of Maisy's friends with dark hair and a sharp gaze.

"Oh my god," Maisy says in exasperation, taking my wrist

and tugging me closer to a mural of the sun and moon painted on the wall. She peers up at me with a worried pinch between her eyebrows. "Is everything okay? Did you find out something else?"

God, this girl. I hurt her and she still asks if I'm fine first.

Words fail me. They've never been my strong suit. The carefully thought out apology I planned while I picked flowers for an hour flies from my head.

Licking my lips, I try. "I brought you these."

Her gaze falls to the flowers in my hand. At least two of them are crushed from my choking grip, their stems bent. In my head it was a more romantic gesture than the reality, but her lips part.

"Purple daisies," she whispers.

"Yeah, I... They've always reminded me of you, Maise." I carefully touch the petals of one of the blooms sticking out. "Wild, stubborn, beautiful, and free."

Her eyes fly to my face, bouncing back and forth as she drinks me in greedily.

"You are. Doesn't matter what keeps you down, you'll overcome it. You bend to grow where nature will let you, but you also crop up wherever you want because nothing holds you back. You're a wildflower."

My wildflower.

A small sound escapes her and I want to reach out to bring her closer, but if I do I won't get this out. I rummage in my pocket for my phone and open the screenshot Colton sent me as I was pulling up in front of the bakery.

"I'm sorry. I know I fucked up, but I'll do whatever I have to so I can make it right."

"Fox, is this—?" She reads the text again, fingers curled around my phone.

"Yes. I reversed it. Well, Colt did, but if he still wants it, it's his. They'll take him next semester. I'm working on yours next."

"Don't bother," she mutters. "I'm not going to North-western."

Blood rushes in my ears and I focus on not crushing the daisies in my fist. "Are you going to leave?"

"Someday soon. Not by myself anymore, I hope."

"No."

It's out before I can hold it back. Because I don't want her to see the Pacific ocean again for the first time without me being there to watch her face as she takes it in.

"No?" She tilts her head and narrows her eyes. "What makes you think you can control what I want?"

"I know I can't. But I hate the thought of you with anyone else."

Just thinking about it makes me want to wrap my fingers around the neck of whoever would dare touch her and squeeze. A flash of possessive anger spears me as I take in the muscle tank hanging off her body and I hate that it's not one of my shirts. She laughs, breaking me out of the dark, murderous vision.

"Good thing I wasn't planning on that then."

The words that failed me before burst out of me in one breath. "I love you."

"You do?"

Maisy's throat works and I hold her gaze.

Nodding, I say it again. "I loved you back then and I love you now. It never went away, even when I believed you lied. Even when I thought I hated you, the whole time I was in love with you."

Taking another step, I close the distance between us, bending close enough to graze my lips over her temple. I touch the stones I gave her on the bracelet, a piece of me that she carries with her everywhere. She tilts her face up and all I want to do is wrap her in my arms and never let her go. I hold up the fistful of wildflowers between and offer my heart to her.

"You're my daisy," I rasp. "It's always been you."

THIRTY-FOUR

MAISY

Hearing him say those words starts a riot inside me. My heart skips a beat, tripping over itself like it wants to burst from my chest into his arms, where it belongs. Where *I* belong.

I draw in a shaking breath.

The second he walked in here I wanted to go to him, but I had to wait out the urge just to see what he would do. Since I left and talked it out with Thea, I knew what he meant to me.

Holding myself back from touching him, hugging him, kissing him was a sweet form of torture building the anticipation until I can't take it anymore. Now I can give in.

There are smudges beneath his eyes and stubble shadowing his jaw. He hasn't been sleeping.

Oh, Fox. I hope his nightmares haven't returned.

The daisies are choked in his desperate grip, some wilting and a little sad. But they're the same color as the one he gave me all those years ago when he promised I was his daisy and that he'd marry me someday.

I'm still his daisy.

Warmth blooms like the flowers he brought me, unfurling in my chest bringing a sense that feels a lot like happiness.

"I'll walk away from everything if it means you'll forgive me. I choose you, Maisy. I know how much you want to see the ocean. I know because the ocean is in my soul, too. We'll go together. I'll take you to California." He puts a hand over his heart where the ocean is inked into his skin. "I just needed you to know all this. I'll wait for as long as you need, forever if I have to. You and me, remember?"

My heart turns over and before he can say more, I press up on my toes, fisting his shirt before I kiss him. People around us cheer, but all I'm focused on is the slide of his lips against mine, the scrape of his stubble on my jaw, the soft relieved groan he pushes into my mouth when he wraps his arms around me.

The wobbling axis of my world rights itself in that moment.

Fox was never going to hold me back from what I want. Deep down, I knew that. I was scared to love him as much as I do because I worried it meant I'd lose myself in his black hole.

I was going to go back to his place after the opening to talk things out with him now that my head is clearer, but he was one step ahead of me. I didn't ask him to reverse Holden's ruined college draft, but he still made it better. He took action for his mistakes and it makes me fall for him even more than I already have.

Fox makes me feel alive. He's always known who I am and encouraged the wild streak I can't tame. He's who I'm meant to be with, who my heart sings for.

Pulling back from the kiss, I rest my forehead against his jaw, simmering with the joy bubbling through me. "I wasn't going to leave without you. You're who I meant I wanted to go with, like we said. Your workshop and my studio. Our own little adventure."

He squeezes me closer, probably crushing my handpicked

bouquet of wildflowers even more. A laugh huffs out of me and I hug him back.

"I want you if it means the good and the bad. I'd relive the years of missing you, the pain of you coming back, all of it because it meant after all that my heart would be whole again." His lips touch the top of my head and I sink further into his strong embrace. "We found our way back to each other."

"We did," he murmurs.

Fox releases me and seals his lips over mine in a searing kiss I feel down to my toes. I smile into it. He pours so much into it that I sway slightly and he catches me. Cheers sound around us again and I recognize my friend's voices among them.

A throat clears and I lean back to find Holden hovering with the girl he met at school that he's been wrapped up in. I lift my brows in question.

"You're good?" he asks, glancing from me to Fox.

"I was until you interrupted."

The girl with him snorts and hooks her arm in his. "I told you to let them be, big guy."

Holden's cheeks fill with color and he rubs the back of his neck, muttering an apology under his breath. This girl is good for him and part of me is glad he ended up at the community college, or they'd never have met.

"Come on." I take the bouquet of flowers Fox picked for me and slip my hand into his. "I still haven't been able to introduce you to everyone."

I take him to the table where Devlin and Blair are. Gemma and Lucas joined them while Fox and I were working things out. When Connor sees us at the table, he pulls Thea away from the customers and they come over, too.

"You've grown a shadow," Devlin deadpans, making Connor snort.

"Dude," I say mildly. "Guys, this is Fox."

They introduce themselves and he keeps a hand tucked in my back pocket.

"That's your bike out front?" Lucas asks.

"Yeah. It was my dad's," Fox says. "I had to rebuild most of it until I got it back."

Lucas whistles low in understanding. "I have a 1990 Jeep I rebuilt. It's a labor of love." He throws a sardonic look at Gemma and plays with her hair. "Something some people don't appreciate."

A low laugh rolls through her. "That was one time, babe. One time. Besides, you were a dick then and you know you deserved it. Let it go."

"Never," he mutters, leaning in to kiss her cheek, making her smile affectionately.

Blair smirks. "Nothing wrong with stealing a man's pride and joy."

"I beg to differ," Devlin says, but there's fondness lacing his tone.

Thea comes around the table to size Fox up, hands on her hips. She's half his height, if that, but the fierce look on her face makes him stand at attention.

"Do I have to give you the shovel spiel?"

"The what?" Fox asks in bewilderment.

"The best friend, you-hurt-her-we-bury-you warning," Blair supplies with a gleam in her brown eyes.

"Oh." A short laugh leaves him and his hand flexes on my ass in my back pocket. "I'm pretty sure she'd bury me before you had the chance."

Thea's expression melts into a smile at the pride in his tone and Fox relaxes. "Good answer. Be right back."

She disappears into the back and returns shortly after with a fresh plate of cookies shaped like suns and moons baked in honor of her bakery opening. I'm so proud of her and as my friends all chat, I lean into Fox and feel a true sense of happiness. He doesn't exactly fit in with them easily, not when the rest of the guys have the bond of knowing each other from childhood, but he's not out of place either. He stays quiet, listening to us as we tease each other.

Holden joins in for a while, he and Fox talking in low murmurs while Gemma shows me photos of a hike she and Lucas drove north of their college for in the spring. I glance up and see them laughing together. It feels good, like the broken things between the three of us aren't beyond repair.

Our parents might have done irrevocable things, but we aren't them and we won't make their same mistakes.

Fox brushes his lips over my ear several minutes later. "Ready to get out of here?"

"Yes."

I say goodbye to my friends and congratulate Thea for the millionth time on doing what she always wanted. She hugs me tight in one of her magic embraces and tries to wink at me—tries and fails because she can't actually wink for shit—and I promise to check in with her later. Fox takes my hand.

Outside, the summer sun shines down on us, glinting off his motorcycle.

He hands over the helmet and closes his fingers over my wrists before I put it on. "Who's shirt is that?"

"This?" I look down. "Mine. Well, Holden's first, but I stole it from him three summers ago. He brought me clothes over at Thea and Connor's apartment yesterday since I didn't have anything."

He visibly relaxes, grabbing a handful of the material and tugging me in for a quick kiss. "Good," he rasps against my lips. "I don't have to kill anyone today."

Snorting, I push him off with a playful grin. "Were you going to deck Connor if I borrowed it from him?"

He mulls it over, jaw moving side to side. "Maybe. He'd hit back, but it would be worth it."

"No hitting my friends, even if they know how to fight."

"Fine." He smirks, raking his gaze over me. "No wearing anyone else's clothes. Only mine."

When he claims me like that, my stomach dips pleasantly. I've always liked when he wanted to be possessive of me, even when we were kids.

"Fine," I agree easily. "I like your shirts best anyway. Just a shirt and nothing else underneath, best feeling in the world."

The sound Fox releases is part-groan, part-growl and he grabs my hips. "Careful with that mouth, Maisy Daisy, or I'll fuck you right here in the middle of town."

My mouth curves and satisfaction rolls down my spine. "Promises, promises," I murmur in a seductive lilt that makes heat flare in his dark gaze. "Take me home?"

"Yeah. Get on."

Fitting my arms around him with the rumble of the motorcycle between our legs feels like home and freedom all at once.

"Hold on tight," he says over his shoulder.

Grinning into his back, I squeeze him. "Never letting go."

* * *

We're barely parked in the garage before I hop off the bike, needing to have his lips on mine after two days of being apart. He catches me in his arms, still straddling the bike as I grasp his face between my hands and capture his lips. Heat races over my skin as his palms drag over my body. At the needy sound that escapes me, he pops the buttons on my cut off shorts and stands from the bike in the same motion.

Yanking my body against his, he attacks my neck with his mouth, finding that sensitive spot that makes my thighs rub together against the pulse of heat in my core. His cock is a hard line against my stomach, but his focus is completely on me as he buries his big palms down the back of my shorts and pushes them off, rumbling in approval against my neck when he finds I don't have anything on beneath them.

"My wild girl," Fox rasps.

A grin tilts my lips at the reverence in his tone and my heart swells in my chest. *His wild girl.* That's who I am. Untamed and free and *myself*.

The shorts fall to my ankles and I kick them off without stopping my own exploration, hands roaming beneath his shirt and pushing it up. He reaches behind his head with one hand and tugs the t-shirt off. Lifting me by my thighs, he guides my legs around his hips and carries me up the steps. My palms roam over his biceps, tracing the half sleeve tattoo on the left one.

We're barely through the door when his mouth captures mine again. His grip flexes on my ass and he seems like he doesn't want to let me go.

"Gonna make you mine," he says.

A light laugh shakes my shoulders. I feel like I'm floating on a cloud. "I never stopped being yours."

"Doesn't matter. You deserve to know I love you every second of the day."

He puts me down on the coffee table and flattens his palm in the center of my chest, pushing me down until I'm spread out for him across the reclaimed wood. He kneels at the edge between my thighs, placing hot kisses at random across my thighs.

The conversation piece I brought upstairs from the workshop stands next to my head. I'm glad to see its hypnotic curves haven't been damaged from him throwing it clear across the room when he was upset.

I reach up to touch it and Fox releases a rough sound.

"It's you."

I prop up on my elbows. "What?"

"I was...making you. I didn't realize it until you were gone." His thumbs trace tiny circles on my hips. "It's you, Maisy. How I see you. How I love you."

My breath hitches and I look at the mixed materials, the metal that shouldn't bend in that way but it does—both strong and fluid at once. Rooted in wood, but reaching for the sky. No one but him has ever taken the time to see me so clearly, to take that and create something beautiful. I lick my lips and lift my gaze to him knelt between my thighs like I'm something he cherishes. Worships.

"I love it," I whisper, setting it aside and combing my fingers through his dark fringe. "I love you."

The corner of his mouth kicks up in a crooked smile that makes my heart stutter. The fondness in his gaze melts into something more sensual.

"By the time I'm done, you'll never doubt that you're mine again. Because I've only ever been yours, Maisy Daisy. Since you were six years old, trailing after your brother and jealous he got to go to school before you. Let me show you."

Holding my gaze he lowers his mouth to my center and takes me to oblivion with my head thrown back.

The sexy smirk he shoots up the length of my body after I come should be illegal. He swipes the side of his mouth and licks the taste of me from his lips. Scooping me into his arms, we move to the bed.

"Not done with you yet," he says in a smoky whisper. "Sit on my face."

My stomach bottoms out. He doesn't wait, tugging me where he wants me and my fists scramble in the sheets at the swipe of his tongue on my pussy, my folds still sensitive from the first orgasm he teased out of me.

"Ride my tongue."

The command is muffled, his deep voice vibrating against my clit. It rips a gasp from me, but I rock my hips and tip my head back on a cry. He knows exactly how to bring me to the brink.

Not only because he's fucked me all over this warehouse, but because he *knows* me. My heart knows his and his knows mine. The truth of it wraps around me.

"Oh god," I breathe, dragging my nails over his tattooed chest and folding in half when my thighs start to shake. "God, I'm going to come again."

He chuckles against the swollen folds of my pussy and I tip over the edge, the waves of pleasure echoing from my core. He's not done. In fact, he shifts around like he's getting comfortable for the long haul, palms smoothing over my thighs and squeezing while he licks and sucks my clit with a deceptively sedate focus.

As much as I'm enjoying his pampering, my mouth waters at the sight of his erection straining against his jeans. I want to make him feel good, too. I lean over and plant a trail of kisses down his abs, licking a spot I know is ticklish. He grunts and I smile into his skin as I rub the front of his jeans. He slows down his tongue and brushes his fingers over my side.

"Let me make you feel good, too." I stroke him through his jeans. "If you think you're the only one allowed to lay claim, you're wrong, babe."

Fox hums against me and I unzip his jeans. He lifts up to help me shove them down far enough to free his cock. He's thick and hard, already past the point of ready to go. I waste no time swiping my tongue over the head and he groans in appreciation when I slip my lips around him. He returns to eating my pussy while I suck his cock and our moans become a symphony of pleasure filling the converted warehouse.

He kisses my folds slowly, then puts pressure on my clit that makes me draw in a sharp breath as I ride out the tingles racing over my skin. The vibrations of the noises I make have him thrusting his cock into my mouth and I relax, letting him fuck my face.

"Shit, your mouth is heaven," he chokes out as his thighs tense. "Fuck. *Fuck!*"

His come floods my mouth and I swallow it down while his arms wrap around me. He goes boneless after his orgasm and a primal sort of pride burns in my chest for making him come hard. After a minute, he strokes my back and guides me onto my side. He props up on an elbow to kick his jeans the rest of the way off and helps me out of my tank and sports bra so we're both naked.

I collapse against the sheets and stretch, rubbing my thighs together lazily to enjoy the lingering sensitivity.

"You think you're all done?"

I crack my eyes open and quirk my brows. Fox shoots me this sinful look that sends a shiver down my spine as he smooths a hand up my side.

"Just because I came doesn't mean I'm finished giving you orgasms, baby. Gonna keep fucking your pussy with my tongue while I finger your ass until my cock is ready to go again. I want you to be a filthy mess for me, little daisy." He bends over to kiss my hips, punctuating his next words with teeth and tongue. "Every. Single. Inch."

Air leaves me in a rush and I don't get the chance to respond before he does exactly what he promised. And after, when he enters me in one smooth thrust, he cradles me close until our bodies become one.

* * *

Sitting up in bed later, I suck on my swollen lower lip. It's tender from the hours Fox spent kissing me long and slow and unrelenting while I shook apart in his arms countless times until I didn't have another orgasm left in me. He's sprawled on his front beside me, one arm thrown possessively over my lap. We haven't stopped touching since we got back to the warehouse. He's worn out from how many rounds we just went.

"We have to get my dad out of office at least," I say.

He makes a barely audible sound, cracking an eye open to study me. "Are you sure?" He rubs my hip. "We could just let it all go. I have the answers, whether I wanted them or not. These people pulling the strings are dangerous. Fuck them."

"Yes, fuck them. That's my point."

He must see the determination in my expression because he drags himself up, curling around me so I'm resting against his chest. I hold onto the forearm banded across my chest and twist to see him.

"I don't want this town run by corruption. My friends will still live here when we leave. My brother still lives here." His chest moves with his sigh. "I can't stand that the person who is supposed to protect everyone and uphold the law is as dirty as the criminals he's arresting. I don't care if he's my dad. We can still make some of this right."

"So you still want to tangle with a criminal organization and a corporate drug operation?"

My lips press together. This is what we have to do. It might have started as Fox's crusade, but now his war is mine. I'll see it through until the end.

"Don't you? We can't run away yet."

His fingers thread through my hair. "It's not running if it's what we want."

"It is what I want, but we can't go to California without doing something about it first. Not when we know what they're doing."

His expression darkens, but he nods. "You're right. So, we do this, then we go?"

"Yes. No one else is going to stop them."

We might be young, but we're the only ones willing to do something to uproot the corruption in Ridgeview.

THIRTY-FIVE

FOX

The warehouse is more crowded than I ever expected with Maisy's friends here to help. I was wary of letting more people into my circle, but she trusts them and I trust her. They showed up this morning and took over the space that didn't really feel like home until Maisy came to stay with me.

"Listen, you crow bastard," Connor Bishop snarks, stabbing a finger at his laptop where he's working with Colton over Face-Time with the video connection off. "You can't tell me you prefer clickjacking attacks over trojans. You just can't. Not after you were an asshole and infiltrated my shit."

They agreed to combine their tech skills to pin down the money trail we need to follow once and for all to connect Stalenko Corp to Richard's promotion. It turns out that Colton knew Connor and his wife better than we thought. They were tangled in the same mess that brought Wren and the Crows here last year as he hunted down the bastard that took his sister away from him.

"*Just admit it's better!*" Colton laughs over the call. "*Your firewall had a nice sized hole in it and I put my dick there. It was more than a year ago, get over it.*" Connor sputters, but Thea brings him a piece of the cake she brought with them and he forgets to be angry because he has eyes only for her. She kisses his head. *"Now quit trying to distract me with your opinions, peasant, and let the master work."*

"Master?" Connor scoffs playfully with one arm around Thea. "Bro, you couldn't even crack this rotating cryptographic encryption sequence until you had my help just now."

"Play nice," Thea says.

"Listen to your little cutie, Bishop."

Thea stops his growl with a kiss.

"Was it the smartest idea to let those two become friends?" Maisy murmurs to me as she takes a marker I was using to write on a white board. "They seem..."

"I know." Shaking my head, I give her a wry smirk. "I didn't know there were two of them."

She snickers and we turn back to the white board where we've laid out our strategy. Connor and Colt are stealing the secrets we need from the inside. Once we have those, we're bringing in the big guns. Ethan gave us his contacts, including federal investigators with a tip line. We have the incriminating email thread from ten years ago between my parents, Jacqueline Landry, and Stalenko Corp detailing their dirty plan. Plus the evidence I recorded during our stakeout of Richard accepting a bribe.

On top of that, Connor handed over his entire blackmail file on Richard Landry—which he made me pay for, the little fucker. When I told Colt, he cracked up about it and called it good business practice.

What's important is that Richard can't get out of this. They were idiots to keep track of their meetings and bribery over the years, and now we'll use it against him. Maisy and I are going to nail his ass to the wall and force him to resign, or every news outlet in Ridgeview will have a juicy new scandal to rock the town's idyllic mountainside foundation.

After I found out my parents weren't who I thought they were, I was ready to wash my hands of all this and walk away, but Maisy was right. If we don't do something about this, they get away with murder and continue to make money off the drugs they're funneling into the world.

"It's done." Devlin Murphy moves like a shadow, creeping up behind us.

It's unsettling he could sneak up on me. Blair pulled the same trick on me an hour ago when she showed up at my elbow and almost gave me a fucking heart attack. I think she knew it, too; she gave me this smug little smirk and I heard her husky laugh as she turned away.

He pushes fingers through his black hair and hands a legal pad to Maisy with notes from the phone call he's been on for most of the morning. "The DEA and FDA contacts your journalist friend gave you believed I was my dad on the phone and were pretty disturbed to hear about synthetic opiates being cooked up for sale to the black market. They insinuated there was an influx of the hard stuff flooding the streets and their west coast offices haven't been able to trace the source. They took down my number and said they'd be in touch if they needed to go over more questions."

"Thanks, Dev," Maisy says. "That gives this more credibility if it comes from someone as well known in the medical field as your dad is."

Devlin grimaces, like hearing it pains him. He shrugs. "Lucas and I are writing up testimonies, too." He motions with a nod of his head to the couch, where the guy who told me about his Jeep at the bakery sits with his girlfriend and Blair. "I paid your dad to keep Blair's arrest off the record when I bailed her out, and Lucas is recounting the poker nights at his house where your dad accepted bribes."

"Good," I say.

"Love a good takedown before lunch," Devlin says with a glint in his gaze that says everything I need to know about him. "Too bad there wasn't a need for any casual B and E this time around." His gaze cuts to Blair and fills with fondness. "I have missed a certain little thief's wily ways," he murmurs more to himself than us.

"Yes!" Connor cheers with his fists in the air while Colt makes a racket. He pulls Thea into his lap to celebrate. "Boo-fuckin'-*ya*, baby!"

I hope their celebration means good news. If they found the payout that has eluded the searching Maisy and I have done in the last few weeks, we'll finally be set.

It's strange to let this many people in, to have all this help when before it was hard enough to let Colton sniff out my secrets, to let Maisy see the full extent of the pain infecting my life. Yet somehow it feels right. I don't know her friends very well, but they dropped everything to help us.

"Think it'll be enough?" Maisy asks once Devlin goes back to the group on my couch.

"It'll have to be."

We're more than covered with incriminating proof to take Richard out. What remains to be seen is how it will affect Nexus Lab to operate without one of their obedient pieces on the board while we wait for the federal investigators to make their move.

* * *

It's sunny and bright the day Richard Landry faces the implosion of his career. The Ridgeview Police Department is quiet when I park the bike out front. The old Gold Rush era architecture makes it look like it belongs in a movie, matching many of the historic buildings in town.

Maisy gets off the back of the bike and holds her hand out for me to take. I grin as I lace our fingers together. Her and me, us against the goddamn world. She joked once about my warehouse being like the Batcave, but this is the first time I've felt a little like a hero.

Imagine it—me, the black shadow nightmare in this town, the hero of the story.

One thing's for sure, I've got the girl and I'm not letting her go.

"Let's do this," she says, spine straight and head held high. She looks like a firecracker, fierce and determined, set to go to war. I can't help pulling her into me for a kiss, sweeping my tongue into her mouth. The curve of her smile against my lips owns every beat of my heart. "Ready to fuck some shit up?"

It's taken us a few days to coordinate the proof we've gathered between what we already had and what her friends helped us dig up, but now we're ready.

"Yes. Let's go take a swing at an ugly empire."

Maisy pretends to fire off pistols with her fingers and winks at me, stirring a flutter in my chest. Hand in hand, we walk into the station. It's so obvious to me now, watching her slip into the good girl mask everyone around her saw her with. That was never the real her, just the way everyone expected her to act. She takes us right up to the front desk and tilts her head with this coy smile on her face.

"Hey, Officer Dean. How's your cat doing? I hope he adjusted to the diet."

"Maisy," the officer greets without suspecting anything. His gaze guts to me once with a hint of wariness, but returns to her. "Waffle is doing good, thanks for remembering."

"I'm so glad to hear it." She folds her arms over the high countertop. "We're supposed to meet my dad for lunch. Is he in his office?"

"Oh. I don't think he remembered." Officer Dean frowns. "He stepped out in a rush for a meeting."

"Can we wait for him in his office?"

She practically bats her lashes and has this guy eating right out of her hand. I have to fight back a smile.

"Well, you're not supposed to, but..."

"Oh, you're right." Maisy sighs. "I just wanted to surprise him."

The officer softens. Pushover. "You know what? Go ahead. He's been stressed lately and I think it'd cheer him up."

Maisy lights up. "You're a gem, Officer Dean. Thanks."

We leave the front desk behind and I lean close to murmur in her ear. "You're like a dangerous little honey trap."

"I'm saving the honey all for you," she says with a sly grin.

Richard's office sits in the corner of the building with big windows overlooking downtown Ridgeview. It's cushier than anyone would expect, even for a chief. I peer around while Maisy keeps an eye out for her dad.

A large polished mahogany desk sits in the center with an expensive leather chair. There's a family photo on the desk. I pick it up and the corners of my mouth tighten. It's from the trip both our families took to California. I'm in it, right between Maisy and Holden with our arms all linked around each other. We're grinning with sunburnt faces while Richard and Jacqueline stand off to the side. My mom is on our other side, but my dad isn't there. Instead of looking at the camera or his wife, Richard's gaze strays surreptitiously toward Mom. She's looking his way, too, peeking out of the corner of her eye while she tucks her hair behind her ear.

My heart thuds as I stare at the old photo. There's no

way. I refuse to believe the hints of what I'm seeing, forcing my mind to shy away from the whispers of memories scratching at the edge of my awareness, that back up what my gut is telling me. Times the two of them would take us on outings. No. No fucking way Richard and my mom had a thing.

Swallowing hard, I put the photo down. It's the only one on the desk. For someone who wants to seem like a family man, he doesn't have anything else to remind him of them in here. The rest are photos with the mayor and with other prominent members of Ridgeview society. It's easy to guess money ties each of these men together. Favors. Bribery.

This is what Richard sold his soul for.

Muffled footsteps approach through the closed door. Richard comes in and his cheeks turn red when he realizes he's not alone. He rushes toward Maisy.

"You—I've been so worried!"

Before he reaches her, I step between them and shove him against the wall. "Don't touch her. You don't have the right."

Maisy calmly shuts the door. He fights against me. Despite his broad stature, I'm stronger, easily able to keep him in place.

"Why are *you* here? What do you think you're doing?"

Richard's face reddens more as he struggles to free himself. He goes for his holster, but I cut him off, twisting his arm.

"Were you just about to pull your weapon on your daughter and another civilian?"

"Civilian?" He barks out a harsh laugh. "With the whispers going around town about you, I'm sure you've probably done something to warrant an arrest."

"I thought you'd be happy to see me, Rich. No love lost for your old friends' son?" My lip curls and my fingers dig in harder to his designer three piece suit. I move to grab him by the throat. "I guess you did have me shipped off and figured I'd disappear so you didn't have to look at me to remind you of your sins."

His lips move, but he can't get any words out when I tighten the chokehold. His eyes bug out.

"Fox."

Pushing out a breath, I ease off from squeezing the life from Maisy's dad. He puts on a show of coughing and fighting me. It's futile. I'm bigger and stronger from the years I've spent keeping in shape while he sat behind a desk and enjoyed steak dinners with a side of cash under the table. Knowing he won't crack me, he appeals to her.

"Maisy, what is this? I told you to stay away from this boy. You're standing there while he assaults me? Sweetheart, look at me."

She won't. In my peripheral vision she keeps her gaze locked on me, remaining silent while he becomes increasingly agitated.

"Maisy!" Richard blusters. "Answer me, damn it. I've been lenient since you left the house, but this is too goddamn far. You need to come home. Your mother and I—"

"I just have one thing to say, Dad. *Arthur Jones.*"

Richard jolts at the name of the man who was supposed to be chief of police before Richard was hastily installed into the position instead. Color drains from his face and he turns a sickly shade of gray. Maisy huffs and a humorless smile twists my lips.

"Yeah. The one who was supposed to have your position right now." I grab him by his silk tie and jerk him against the wall. "Funny, he had a heart attack about two months after you were sworn in. Shocked his family, since he was healthy before that. Weird, right? I have the obituary."

"You shouldn't be looking into this. You don't understand," Richard warns when I go for my phone.

Maisy turns away from us and I listen as she plugs the flash drive she brought into Richard's computer. I drag him away from the wall and sit him down at one of the seats in front of his desk while she turns the monitor around. All the evidence we've gathered is on the big screen. He releases a sound as if someone punched him in the stomach, shaking his head.

He's pathetic, unable to face what he's done. All the years I've spent imagining retribution, I never pictured him blubbering like this. The Richard Landry I remember from my childhood had a backbone, but it seems to have been whittled to nothing in the last decade. The single family photo is next to the screen, but I focus on him.

"Here's how this will go," I say, deceptively calm with an undercurrent of deadly fury lurking beneath the surface. "Resign, or this gets out. Everything you've done, the bribes you've taken, the blood on your hands—the people of this town are going to find out exactly who you are and your precious reputation will be ruined." We point out each piece of damning evidence we have against his years of being a crooked cop. Grabbing him by the collar, I lean down to snarl, "Your bosses don't like scandal, do they? And to be clear, I'm not talking about the taxpayers of Ridgeview. They might pretend to operate like a corporate investment firm, but we both know that's not what they really are."

"You're in over your head," he says hoarsely, picking up the photo I don't want to look at. Staring at it, his shoulders tremble and his throat bobs with a swallow. He turns to me with dead eyes. "You don't know what you're talking about."

"Don't I? You put me in the fucking foster system after my parents died, Rich!" I drag a hand through my hair as bitterness pricks my throat. "You signed off on the incident report, closed the case for the crash. You had to have seen the coroner's report. You knew my mom was pregnant. You helped cover up their murder."

Richard explodes from the chair, the photo clattering on the mahogany desk. He turns into a different person, shedding the flimsy remorse. Grabbing fistfuls of my leather jacket, he gets in my face.

"You're not walking out of this fucking station. I'm charging you with assault and then you're going to go away." His voice shakes with rage. "You'll never see my daughter again and poison her head with your lies. We've worked too hard to have it go up in smoke because you doctored proof."

I catch Maisy's disgusted expression from the corner of my eye as I stare down a man so different from the one I remember as a kid. His spittle hits my chin, eyes bloodshot and angry graying brows drawn into a deep wrinkle. This is not the same man who taught Holden and I how to hold and throw a football when we were seven at a block party in our old neighborhood.

"Dad!" Maisy shouts, coming around the desk. "Stop!"

He swipes an arm behind him and catches her off guard as she stumbles back, grabbing the corner of the desk to keep her balance. From the shock on her face, I guess he's never raised a hand to her before. I jerk, wanting to kill him for it.

"You think you solved the mystery?" Richard laughs, the sound dark and chilling. "You've got shit. This will go away. No one will believe biased testimonies."

Releasing me, he snatches the flash drive, drops it to the floor, and crushes it beneath his heel. Triumph has him standing tall against us.

"That's not the only copy, Dad. We've got backups of the proof. You can't run from this."

"Proof? Sweetheart, I know you're smarter than that. Don't be an idiot. Having your friends sign letters without witnesses to corroborate the story isn't proof of anything. There's no hard-copies of anything."

"What's your soul worth, you greedy bastard?" I ask coldly, stopping him in his tracks when he rounds the desk.

Confusion crosses his aged features until I throw down the final nail in the coffin, the payment buried in the Landry's financial records from an offshore account. Colton and Connor came through when they uncovered it after months of searching.

"Three quarters of a million." Richard's shoulders stiffen. I set my phone on the desk with a photo of the statement. He stares down in horror at the damning evidence. "Not a bad payout for murder, but you're still scum. Resign. Go away silently, or I'll make sure what the guys at Stalenko have threatened you with to keep you obedient will sound like a goddamn island vacation."

"How did you get that?" His voice is barely above a whisper. To himself, he stumbles over his words. "They swore no one would find it. Couldn't trace it back to us."

"It doesn't matter. If you don't resign, we're going to the press with this," Maisy says. "Step down, Dad. It's the right thing to do."

"Maisy," he says brokenly when he sees her clenched jaw. "Sweetie, I didn't... We had no choice. If we didn't follow orders, they'd kill our whole family."

"So you let them kill Fox's parents?" Her features twist in an appalled expression. "How did you justify that to sleep at night and look Holden and I in the eye for ten years?" There's only a faint tremor in her voice and I'm proud of her for standing up to him. "You're nothing more than a pawn and a coward. So you're going to do this, because if you don't I won't stop until you're behind bars where you belong."

Defeated, he sinks into the expensive desk chair and drags

the discarded family photo, tracing his thumbs over the frame. The emotions flitting across his face sour the satisfaction I get seeing him knocked down to his knees. He touches my mom's side of the photo and my stomach revolts. *No.*

I snatch the photo from him and toss it aside. "What's it going to be, Richard? Do you have a shred of decency left in you?"

With a sigh, he begins to type. I move to stand over his chair from behind when he pauses to look at Maisy.

"Do the right thing," she says as she picks up the photo. "I remember this day," she whispers, gaze flickering. Richard flinches. "It seems like it was the last time we were all happy before..."

Before my parents died and everything changed.

Richard says nothing until he finishes drawing up his resignation letter. It's not until he signs it that I release a breath it seems I've been holding for ten years. Setting it aside, he turns to me with regret filling his gaze.

"I'm sorry, Fox. I never wanted it to be like this."

It's too little too fucking late.

"I loved your mother."

The room goes deadly silent and I stand rigid as another bomb drops on me. Maisy's eyes widen and she comes to my side to hold my hand as I grit my teeth.

"No," I bite out. "No you fucking didn't."

If it were true, how could he let her die. He's lying.

"We were...we wanted—"

"No!" I slam a fist down on the desk.

Richard swipes sweat from his brow and his shoulders slump. "It's the truth, son."

"Was the baby yours?"

"No. We were waiting for the right time."

It doesn't bring any relief.

"What are you saying?" Maisy demands, squeezing my hand.

Keeping his gaze pinned on me, he continues in a mournful voice. "It destroyed me when I found out about the crash. It wasn't supposed to happen. I wanted to protect her, too, but your dad just wanted more and more money. He wouldn't leave it until he got what he wanted. They weren't going to budge, so they eliminated them and made us cover it up."

"Stop it," I growl. "Just shut up."

I can't listen to this, or I'm going to explode. I don't know whether to wring his neck or deck him.

"How do you live with yourself? I don't even know you anymore," Maisy says. "I only wish I'd known sooner."

"Sweetheart," Richard begs. "I swear to you, everything I've ever done was to protect you and Holden. I just wanted to give you a good life. Please, please go home." He gets up, clearly intent on trying to patch things up with her. As he reaches out, Maisy takes a step back. "You're going to get hurt being around him. Just listen to me, honey."

"No! You think anything you say is going to make it better? I wanted my dad back!" Breathing heavily, her nails dig into my hand and it grounds me. I can't drown in my own misery when I have her at my side. "You lost me and Holden the minute you agreed to this insane deal. You and Mom destroyed our family. I don't want anything to do with you."

"Maisy, no, please—!"

She turns away from him. When he charges, my protective instinct takes over and I block him, hauling him by the lapels of his suit as I push him back.

"You'll never be able to hurt or control her again," I swear. "You'd have to go through me to get to her and I'll die before I let anyone touch her. Do you understand?"

"Maisy!" he tries again and I shake him hard enough his teeth clack.

"You're done, Richard." I let him go and he slumps against the wall.

"Bye Dad." Maisy won't look at him again.

Pausing at the door, I turn back. "Don't tell your wife or your bosses about this. When they ask why you resigned, you give them any reason you want but the truth. And if you warn them? We'll make sure this gets out."

Taking Maisy's hand, we leave behind a broken man as we walk out.

THIRTY-SIX

MAISY

The day after Dad steps down as Ridgeview's police chief, I invite Holden out for burgers at our favorite place in town.

Fox lets me take the Charger. Once we sorted things out between us, he told me I could consider it mine. The way he makes sure I feel free ignites a glowing ember of happiness in my chest.

After Dad admitted to loving Fox's mom, my stomach has been in knots. I don't know how to tell my brother what I know. God, all the things I know. It's enough to make my head spin. I meet Holden out front and relax when he ruffles my hair, then pulls me in for a hug.

"Did you hear about Dad?" he asks.

"Yeah."

"The house is so different without you," he says. "It's weird."

It hasn't been a full day, but since we left the station I've been worried Dad wouldn't take Fox's threat to heart. I'm afraid he'll warn Mom and Stalenko Corp anyway about the information we have on the whole operation.

"What's it been like at the house?" I ask as we head into the shop.

Inside it's decorated like a beach bar with bamboo counters and tropical plants. We place our orders and sit at one of the hightop tables with yellow stools. He shrugs and fiddles with a jar of drink umbrellas on the table.

"Well, at first it was fine. But I haven't been home much after they started fighting constantly in the days after you split. I think they want to get a divorce and they've been waiting for us to leave home before doing it. You believe that shit? Like they've made it easier for us by staying together."

I refuse to feel guilty for leaving after arguing with them. It's only the learned response I have that bucks up, so I shove it down. They had no right to treat me like they did.

"Have you been there since yesterday?" I watch him carefully.

"Yeah, I was there for dinner last night before I went out with some friends. Mom was pissed when Dad announced his resignation out of nowhere in the middle of eating. She threw her plate at him and called him a dickless coward."

My eyebrows fly up. Mom's always been the more cutthroat of our parents.

"What did he do?"

"Nothing." Holden swipes a hand over his mouth. "She stormed off and slammed the office door. I was sitting there with salmon halfway to my mouth and he just kept eating even though there were broken pieces of plate all over the floor and her dinner staining his shirt. Top ten most uncomfortable and awkward moments of my life, Maise."

When he doesn't mention how or why, I unclench my fists in my lap and pluck at the frayed threads of my shorts. The plan is going okay then. That makes me feel better. Now we're only waiting for the DEA agent Devlin was in touch with to review what we sent. The wait is killer.

Our food arrives and Holden changes the subject, stealing my milkshake for a sip before I've had any. "You'll never guess what happened. Like, fifteen minutes before I pulled up."

"What?"

"Ohio State reached out. A guy from the admissions office called and said there was some mix up, but if I still wanted to play for them I could transfer from the community college and start next semester there."

"Holden, that's great." I lean across the table and squeeze his wrist. "Will you go?"

One of his shoulders hitch. "I don't know yet. At first I was like what the fuck, you know? I'm hesitant because in the last year I think I'm actually glad I lost the draft."

Holden said that the night I left home. Whether he takes it or not, I feel better knowing it's there if he wants because Fox reversed what he did.

"Do you want to play football still?"

He mulls it over, taking a huge bite from his burger. "I think losing it is what made me realize I don't love the game as much as I thought I did. I've found other stuff I like. Community college really isn't that bad."

The corners of my mouth quirk up. I'm relieved to hear Holden found some peace after a year of moping over this. I wonder how much the girl he brought to Thea's opening day at the bakery had to do with this new leaf he's turned over.

"What about you?" he asks. "Will you go to Northwestern?"

"No." I don't even have to think about it. "I want to know —" *Myself* "—what the world's got to offer before I dive into college. If I do at all."

"That's good. There's no reason you have to decide now. Take a year, two. However long you need."

"I want to go to California."

"Yeah?" He grins. "Yeah, I can totally see that for you. When?"

"Soon." The longing in my voice is clear and I know he hears it when his expression turns soft.

We drift into lighter topics and I get to enjoy hanging out with my brother for the first time in so long. By the time we're finished with our burgers my stomach hurts from laughing so much. I feel lighter. We make plans to grab lunch again.

"Don't even think about starting your road trip without saying bye."

"I won't, promise. See you later." I wave after I steal Holden's last fry.

"Hey!"

Laughter fills my voice. "Should've been faster then, dude! Bye."

He waves me off as I head out. A smile lingers as I pull out my phone and find Fox checked in on my hang out with my brother.

Fox: Having a good time?

Maisy: Yeah. On my way home now.

Fox: Home. I like the sound of that. Come back fast so I can show you how much.

Maisy: Are you in the garage? Maybe I'll spread out on the hood of the Charger for you again.

I'm too busy grinning at the next flirtatious text I'm writing to pay much attention to a guy who leans out of an alleyway when I pass. Hands grab me from behind a beat later and my scream is cut off by his big hand covering my mouth. Panic surges and I try to break free without dropping my phone.

Some part of my brain knows my phone is important, I can't lose it if I'm taken to a second location.

Don't drop it. Don't let go.

My hand hurts from how tightly I grip it. All those times Dad worried about a kidnapping roll through my head. I thought he was paranoid, but I was so wrong.

Pain stings my arm and then my limbs stop obeying, feeling like lead weights. My eyelids weigh a million pounds. *Oh shit, I can't!* The harder I breathe, the more difficult it becomes to fight my attacker off.

Everything goes dark. I'm trapped in my mind screaming.

* * *

When I crack my eyes open they feel dry. I blink a few times, trying to get my sluggish brain to work through the fog. It's like I took too much of the cold medicine that always makes me groggy. I scrunch my face up and move, only to find my wrists are restrained by zip ties.

The fuck—?

"Jesus, about time." Disoriented, my head snaps up at the menacing, slightly accented voice coming from the shadows in the corner. "I only gave you half a dose of sedative."

"Where am I?" My tongue feels stuck to the roof of my mouth.

As soon as I ask, my stomach sinks. On the wall of the box-shaped room in large black stenciled letters is a familiar logo—SynCom. The shell company Russian thugs are using to pull the strings running Nexus Lab.

They brought me to the abandoned warehouse? Shit. I'm in serious trouble. Fox and I never had time to find a way into this place before Ethan interrupted us.

Blinking rapidly, I remember. I was on my way back to Fox after lunch with Holden. Someone grabbed me. My arm twinges with the phantom pain from where the needle stabbed into my skin. I don't feel my phone on me, unsure if I won the fight not to drop it or if this thug took it from me when he kidnapped me.

"You're nowhere special, little girl," my babysitter informs me.

He's a rough looking guy with yellow teeth and a barrel chest. Older than me by at least fifteen years, but not as old as my parents. What's worse, I recognize him. I thought he was Mayor Taylor's bodyguard when I ran into Mom in town. Sweat beads his brow and his hair is buzzed short. He stalks closer from across the room and nudges his heavy boot against the rung of the metal chair I'm tied to.

Against my instinct to keep him in my line of sight, I tear my gaze from him and take in the room we're in. It's dusty from disuse. There's a single door in the corner and a high window that's clouded over with grime letting in a minimal amount of light. The ceiling is low, like this is an office framed out of the larger warehouse.

"Why did you take me?" Some of the aftereffects of whatever he drugged me with lingers, clinging to my head like a stubborn cobweb. "And what the fuck did you give me?"

He barks out a laugh and my nose wrinkles at his sour cigarette-tinged breath wafting down on me. "A benzo. Midazolam. You must be a lightweight, princess, that shit's mild as fuck."

I grit my teeth and lean back when he bends to my level. He clamps a hand on the back of my neck and it feels nothing like it does when Fox holds me like that. A protest leaves me as he keeps me still while he lifts one of my eyelids, squinting at me.

"Probably still have some of it in your system. Be good and I'll give you some water in a bit. Can't have the pretty princess suffering."

I glance around the room. "And where will I pee? I don't see a bathroom."

He snorts and motions to the corner. "Right there." His eyes gleam and my stomach turns. "I like to watch."

The breath I draw in through my nose to calm myself is shaky. I squirm, feeling the bite of the plastic zip ties around my wrists and the scrape of rough rope rubbing my thighs raw. How the hell am I getting out of this?

"Why am I here?" I repeat, unsure if I want the answer.

The thug laughs again, like this is a game. "You're bait to catch your little boyfriend. One of our guys is waiting to catch him when he comes looking for you at that burger joint."

He turns away to grab another folding chair I didn't see before. There's a gun tucked in the back of his jeans. Raking my gaze over him while he's distracted, my heart sinks. I can't tell if he has my phone on him or not. Coming back, he pops the chair open in front of me and kicks back in it as if we're just chilling.

"Besides," he adds after stretching and folding his hands behind his head. "Two birds with one stone and all that." The amusement drops away, stripped back to the cruel nature beneath. "We'll use you to teach your mom a lesson about what happens when orders aren't followed."

My pulse races and my palms tingle with the horrible dread pouring over me. I thought my parents would let me go easily, and maybe they would have if I didn't get involved with plucking apart the threads of their empire, but I didn't stay away. I took charge with Fox, forcing Dad to resign, getting federal investigators to take a closer look.

Stalenko Corp has built up their operation over the last decade and all it took was Fox and I to make it wobble.

They wouldn't have touched me if they didn't think we were a threat.

Licking my lips, I push to see if he'll keep talking. "What sort of lesson?"

"Ransom. See?"

He digs out his phone and I tense when he pulls mine from his pocket, too. He shoves it away and I pray it's still turned on. *Find me, Fox.*

The photo I'm shown makes bile rise in my throat. I'm tied to the same chair as now, unconscious, my head pulled back by this guy while he takes a goddamn selfie angle photo.

It's sent to Mom's number. The read receipts are on. The message is marked as seen. No response.

Mom knows I'm here, in danger, but she hasn't done anything. The last remaining shred of hope she ever cared for me turns to dust. At whatever expression breaks past my mask of indifference, my kidnapper chuckles as if we're playing a game.

"Your mom was told to bring you to heel when you and your little boyfriend started poking around. Our security detail already knew about him, but we saw you on the surveillance feed sneaking around here. Once we realized who you were, we connected you back to your parents." He clicks his tongue in disapproval. "Naughty princess."

"What happens if my mom doesn't agree to pay the ransom?"

The ugly grin he gives me makes me wish I hadn't asked.

"Then," he says, taking a fistful of my hair and wrenching my head back.

I cry out, squeezing my eyes tight. Waiting until they open, his grin widens at the moisture clinging to my lashes. I press my lips together, refusing to let the thousands of protests past my lips like he wants when he forcefully fondles my breast through my tank top. I will not give him more power over me by crying and begging for this to stop, no matter how bad I want him off me. He watches the determination in my gaze and moves his rough touch lower, down my side, plucking teasingly at the waistband of my cutoffs. Disgust bubbles like acid in my stomach at the hunger in his gaze.

"Then you're all mine," he promises.

THIRTY-SEVEN

FOX

The last text response she sends cuts off in a string of unintelligible letters and autocorrected phrases that make no goddamn sense. One minute she's flirting and painting a sexy as fuck picture, the next it's like a switch is flipped. It immediately twists my stomach with a bad feeling that I confirm as soon as I hack into the CCTV feed for where she'd been.

The street in front of the beach-themed burger place where she met Holden is empty, no Maisy in sight. The Charger is still parked. There's no way she disappeared. She was just texting me five minutes ago.

I skim back through the recording a few minutes and my blood runs cold. Maisy has her head bent over her phone, unaware of the big burly guy trailing her. He's good, a professional that knows to keep back far enough that no one would suspect anything. Unless you've learned to see this shit like I have.

He goes for her and my heart jumps into my throat as my knuckles turn white from how tightly my fists ball. I gave her my gun to protect herself, but it's probably stashed in the glove compartment of the car. She gives him hell, kicking out, but his fist rams something in her arm and the fight seeps out of her as he uses his thick muscled arms to trap her against his chest until her body slumps. He pockets her phone and adjusts to distribute her weight.

"*Fuck!*"

Horror grips me by the throat as I watch the man drag Maisy to a blacked out SUV parked nearby. This can't be fucking happening. We've avoided them so many times and the minute I drop my guard, she's taken right off the street.

There's no time to waste. Jumping up, I rush around the apartment, grabbing anything I can that will help. I have to improvise and work with what I have on hand because nothing will keep me from getting her back and keeping her safe.

I send out a prayer to whatever might be listening as I throw my leg over the motorcycle. The gravel kicks up behind me as I tear out onto the road with my phone attached to the mount and a map tracing the location of her phone.

Hold on, Maisy. I'm coming.

* * *

Two blacked out SUVs are parked at Stalenko Corp's shell company warehouse where Maisy and I met Ethan Hannigan. I don't want to tip them off, so I cut the engine and walk the bike along the tree line. I keep low once I find a spot to leave it, calling on everything I've learned from Wren, Colton, and the rest of the Crows in the last few years. My gaze constantly sweeps for any threat. I freeze and crouch low behind a concrete loading slab at one side of the warehouse as a guy comes out of a nearby door, phone pressed to his ear as he slips sunglasses on.

"We'll make sure she understands what's at stake. Either she pays the ransom, or we kill the girl. Yeah. Yeah. Got it."

My heart drums a furious beat in my chest. It takes everything in me to stay hidden as the guy gets in one of the SUVs and pulls out. Hopefully that means they've left Maisy with a light detail inside. I will raze this fucking place to the ground before I let them harm her.

It takes more time than I'd like to case the perimeter to check for where the surveillance cameras are, taking their feeds out one by one with a methodical focus. When I make it to a door at the back, I use a knife from my kitchen to pick the lock.

A set of metal stairs leads up to a catwalk. I take them to get a better vantage to find where they're keeping Maisy. It's bigger inside than we first thought, but we barely had time before. From the catwalk that wraps around the perimeter and cuts across the middle, I can see they have several uses for this place to keep an eye on their operation under everyone's noses.

On the lower level, a man smoking a cigarette crosses to a door where the glow of a monitor spills out from the room. I start there, creeping down silently. Pausing outside the door, I listen.

"Is something up with the feed? What's all over the screen?"

"Dunno. They're all like that. Bird shit?"

Guess again. I sprayed WD-40 on the lenses. Their cameras will be toast and it keeps the feed blurry. Keeping low, I move into the room. A bank of computers shows the exterior security feed and a sports game on mute. Two guys are at the desk, the one with the cigarette leaning over the one seated.

This would be easier if I didn't have to take them out at the same time before they alert anyone else. While they're occupied, I peer around and find a brick propping the door open. Perfect, distraction and a weapon. I heft it and adjust my stance. Taking aim, I fling the brick at the guy with the cigarette and it catches him in the back of the neck.

"What the—"

Before either of them process the attack, I'm moving in. I smash the first guy's head to the desk to finish what the brick started and catch the seated guy around the neck in a stranglehold. The cigarette drops from the other guy's lips as his eyes roll back. He crumples to the floor while I clap my hand over the guy in the chair's mouth, tightening my arm until he goes slack.

Wasting no time, I drag their unconscious bodies to the floor and search them. I take their cell phones and smash them with the brick. On the cigarette guy, I find plastic ties in his pocket and use them to secure their wrists behind their backs, looping them both together. When I step back, I rake a hand through my hair and move to the bank of monitors. Nothing seems out of order. I tap a keyboard shortcut sequence Colt showed me and the monitors cut out, then reboot with blue screens of scrolling computer code.

My insides burn with the need to get to Maisy, but she wasn't on the screens before I cut them. I slip out of the room and head down a dimly lit hall. I freeze, pulse jumping when a grizzly looking guy with a beard exits a room ahead. He doesn't see me, turning away to head further into the hall. His head is bent like he's busy texting.

As quiet as I can be, I rush him from behind and use the momentum to shove him against a doorframe of an open door. At the same time, I sink a fist into his side. The man groans, doubling over where I hit him, instinctively swiping in defense. He lands a hit, catching me in the side with an elbow, throwing my footing off.

While he's still reeling, I grab the back of his shirt and drive my knee into his gut. He grunts, fingers scrabbling. One more blow to the head takes him down. Panting more from adrenaline than exertion, I catch him and lower him to the floor.

The hall has nothing useful, but inside the open door there's a room with pipes running up the exterior wall. I drag the guy over to them and pull his hands behind his back before I secure him to the pipes with the zip ties.

My thirst for destruction isn't over. It won't be until I find Maisy and get her out of here. At the end of the hall, I find I'm at the other end of the warehouse. There's another room built inside the space that looks like an office.

When I silently crack the door, I find Maisy inside and burning hot fury rockets through me. The guy who attacked her on the street is all over her. She's tied to a metal chair with rope around her legs. His hands lift her tank top while she juts her chin, face turned away.

My grip turns deadly on the door handle. It's only because he's within range to hurt Maisy that I don't charge him like my instincts scream at me to do. If I had my gun, I'd empty every single bullet into him. He's a dead man.

"Just want to look at what I get to play with later," he says gleefully, squeezing himself through his jeans. "Gonna bite those perky little tits until you scream, sweet thing."

She grits her teeth and takes measured breaths through her nose, ignoring his unwanted touches. Searing fire races through my veins. I want to rip this fucking asshole's head off with my bare hands for touching her.

Look at me. Look here, baby. I'll make it all better. Just hold on one more minute.

Staying silent, I creep inside. The thug is too busy molesting Maisy to notice me winding a length of electrical wire from my garage around my hands. She notices, though. Tears glisten in her eyes and spill down her cheeks.

It'll be okay, I mouth to her.

My brave girl gives me a fierce look and nods. The guy all over her chuckles and murmurs to her, assuming she's warming up to him exposing her.

"Get the fuck off her," I growl as I loop the wire around his neck and pull hard.

A strangled noise of shock catches in his throat as his spine snaps straight. His fingers scrabble at the wire pressed tight to his neck, but I'm taller and I got the jump on him. I keep my elbows tucked tight as I drag him away from Maisy. His legs kick out and flail.

When he goes slack, I wait a few seconds more, then drop him to the floor. Then I'm on him, using my hands to finish the job. His unconscious face turns purple.

"Fox, don't," Maisy calls. "Please don't kill him." She grunts, struggling against the bindings. "Just get me out of this fucking chair so we can leave."

My nostrils flare and I dig my thumbs harder into his jugular. I barely recognize my voice when words slip free. "He deserves it."

"Don't," she says again in a tight voice.

With a bitten off snarl, I let go and kick the fucker in the side before I hurry to crouch at her side.

"I'm sorry." I frame her face, sweeping my thumbs across her tear-stained cheeks.

"It's not your fault. It's our parents who brought this kind of danger here."

Her expression is grim and though she's doing her best to remain calm, I can tell by the tremor in her limbs as I untie the rope that she's seconds from her breaking point. I don't know how long that sick asshole was tormenting her like that, assaulting her body for his own pleasure. My teeth grind so hard my jaw aches.

Once the rope is loose enough, she curls into my chest with a small, anguished sound that cracks my heart in two. I fold her into my arms and stroke her tangled hair.

"Shh, it's okay. I'm here. I've got you."

Her wrists are pink and raw where the brittle plastic ties kept her restrained the more she fought against them. I carefully slide a pocket knife with a serrated slope in the blade between her wrists and the plastic, cutting the bindings away. She rubs them, cradling them close to her chest.

Cupping the back of her head, I pull her close and kiss her forehead.

"Look out!" Maisy yells, pushing me off balance from my crouch so I sprawl to the floor. "He has a gun!"

The thug lumbers toward us with an outraged bellow. His neck is red and angry from the wire and my hands, his eyes bloodshot where a vessel burst.

"You're dead!" he swears as he comes at me.

"You first," I spit.

Scrambling back, I swing around onto my knees and launch at his lower body with all my might, upsetting his center of balance and tackling him. He crashes to the floor and we both struggle for the gun he tries to aim at me. I slam his wrist down on the dusty concrete and he spits in my face, swinging at me and catching the side of my head with his fist. It knocks me to the side, but the punch isn't hard enough to do real damage.

"Fox!" Maisy's yell sounds to my left.

"Don't! Stay back!" I command.

"Like hell!"

The guy beneath me screams when she stomps on his hand while I grunt and rip the gun from him, using it to whip across his face to knock him out for a second time. I'm panting as I rise to my knees over his prone figure. Blood trickles from his temple from the force of the blow, but it's not enough to sate my need to end him.

"Did you kill him?" Maisy whispers.

"No. He's out cold." I climb to my feet and tuck the gun into the back of my jeans. "Better fucking stay that way this time. You okay?"

"Yeah."

"Come here." When she's close I kiss her, hands fisted in the back of her shirt. She makes a small sound and breaks away to bury her face in my chest. "You're okay now." I don't want to ask, but I force the question past my lips anyway. "Did he...did he touch you anywhere else?"

"No." Maisy pulls back far enough to wipe beneath her eyes and shakes her head. "He tried to scare me, but I don't think he was allowed to get away with too much on the off chance my mom was going to pay the ransom."

A relieved breath gusts out of me. "I subdued the others, but one got away before I snuck in. Eventually Stalenko Corp's higher ups are going to find out when he comes back. Let's tie him up like the rest and get the fuck out of here."

Maisy nods resolutely and picks up the discarded length of auto electrical wire. "I knew you'd find me."

"Always. I knew as soon as your text came through all auto-corrected."

She curls her fingers around the wire, knuckles white. "Thank you."

Something in my chest shifts and expands. "You don't have to thank me, Maisy. I love you and I'll protect you."

She turns those beautiful hazel eyes on me, shining with a fresh bout of tears. "I love you, too."

Together we drag the thug across the room to a pipe running along the floor. She rifles through his pockets, retrieving her phone while I take out the zip ties I picked up and secure him to the pipe. I still want to kill him. More than that, I want to rip his skin off piece by piece and grind his bones to dust, but I need to get Maisy out of here.

THIRTY-EIGHT

MAISY

When we make it to Fox's hidden motorcycle outside, I turn to him with my heart sitting in my throat. "I had everything under control."

He chuckles and scrubs a hand over his face, then tugs me into his arms and speaks against the top of my head. "I love you."

I breathe him in for a moment, letting his strength soothe away the last couple hours of horror. He holds onto me tightly as if he never wants to let me go. A lump forms in my throat. I don't realize how much I'm shaking until he buffs his hands up and down my upper arms.

"Come on. I need to get you back before the adrenaline crash hits and you're not able to hold on." Framing my face, he tilts it up and gives me a smile tinged in darkness. "Before today I would've tied you up to make sure you'd have to hold on, but I think we can save that for another day."

A snort jerks my head. I have to laugh, because if I don't I'm on the brink of breaking down under the weight of it all.

"You think?" My wrists still throb. The skin on my thighs is tender, putting off heat from rope burn. "Let's go."

The drive back is a challenge. Riding a motorcycle after being banged up highlights every ache in my body with each small bump in the road. I press my cheek into Fox's back and seek out the sensation of freedom that I love when we're on the bike to keep my mind off everything else. Thankfully it's not too far to his place.

Once we're at his converted warehouse, he sits me down on the same stool he used when I cleaned up his cuts after we were shot at. Those stormy blue eyes watch my expressions carefully as he checks me over. Physically, I'll be fine. Some minor bruises, skin abrasions, and the rest of the sedative dose will fade with time. The lasting damage is all psychological.

"I want to shower," I say.

No amount of strength of character or confidence in my body spares me from the mental horror I endured today. I can still feel his breath and disgusting hands on my skin, his rough grip lifting my shirt up to expose me, the sadistic way he laughed and got off on the power he held over me as I was tied up and unable to fight back.

My skin feels dirty and I want to scrub at it until I wash it all away. It won't take away the memory, but I won't feel better until I can do something to wipe away the lingering sensations of the violation of my body.

I never should have faced what I did today. Kidnapped. Held for ransom. *Assaulted.*

Dad swore yesterday that everything they did was to protect us. Bullshit. If they wanted to protect us, they wouldn't have welcomed that kind of danger into this town. Mom wouldn't have waited so long to save me from the criminals she works with. For all I know she saw the photo of me unconscious and bound then went about her day, not caring what happened to her daughter. The read receipt is burned into my brain and there's no coming back from that.

"Come on," Fox murmurs, taking my hand and leading me to the bathroom.

He starts the water, testing the temperature on his wrist before turning to me. I strip out of my tank top and fling it on the floor. A fierce rumble makes my gaze dart to him. His attention is on my breast, on the fingerprint shaped red marks. He holds a hand out, but curls his fingers into a tight fist, his skin stretched so the scar on his knuckles stands out.

Breathe, I coach myself, drawing on a meditative headspace to keep myself from shaking apart at the seams. In a hurry, I shuck off my shorts and step under the hot spray of water.

Fox turns to go. He promised he wouldn't leave me alone. A broken, panicked noise escapes me and he's back, jumping into the shower with me, still fully clothed.

"Shh." His arms hold me close while I cling to him, taking ragged breaths that make my chest heave. "I'm not going anywhere. I thought—I was going to give you privacy, but I'm here."

"Don't," I choke out.

"I know," he soothes in a jagged voice as he strokes my hair. "I promise that will never happen to you again."

We stay like that for a moment, his arms around me, keeping my trembling frame tucked against his chest. His clothes are soaked, the t-shirt sticking to his body while I stand there naked, half-wishing for the water to be scalding enough to burn the dirty layer of my skin off.

Straightening my spine, I reach for the bar of soap on the ledge. It smells spicy with a hint of the ocean we both confessed to missing, like a forest meeting the shoreline. It's *Fox*. I press it to my skin and start lathering. In a few movements I find myself scrubbing rough enough to chafe. I don't realize I'm panting until he gently pries the soap from my death grip.

"Let me."

Turning me around, he winds one arm around my middle and pulls me into his chest. I hold onto his arm to keep myself standing as he helps wash me. He doesn't let me go, supporting my weight when I sag against him, keeping his face pressed to the side of mine. I let my eyes close and focus on him.

The water shuts off and I crack my eyes open. He strips out of his wet clothes, the drenched material slapping to the floor. Stepping out, he offers a hand.

Fox dries me off and sits me down on the edge of the bed. The shower helped to make me feel more like myself. After he pulls on a pair of briefs, he rummages beneath the platform he built for the mattress out of found materials and kneels in front of me.

"Let me see your wrists." His voice is low, gentle, but infused with the power of his command. I offer my hands to him. "This will help."

Producing a tube of lotion, he squirts some onto his fingers and rubs it into my wrists with slow circles. My lashes flutter and a soft sigh leaves me. When he finishes with my wrists, he moves on, applying lotion to the irritated red patches of my thighs where the rope keeping me in the chair scraped me raw.

He glances up at the curious noise I make. "What?"

"I didn't think someone all rough and tough like you would bother with skincare," I tease.

Color tinges his cheeks and the corner of his mouth curls wryly. He scrapes his thumb nail over his lip and leers at me through his dark lashes. "It's not for my face." His brows lift and he traps the tip of his tongue between his teeth. "I didn't touch other girls, but a man has needs, Maise."

It takes a minute for his meaning to register to my sluggish mind. "Oh. Ohh, okay. I feel you." Smirking, I lean into him. "You and Righty? Same."

A husky laugh rumbles in his throat and he moves to my other thigh, taking his time to rub the lotion into my inflamed skin. As he cares for me, an intense wave of drowsiness has me swaying.

"Lay down, baby." He brushes damp tendrils of hair from my face and nudges me onto the bed. "I've got you."

I shift back, then freeze. "You won't leave?"

"No. I'm right here. Not going anywhere."

He follows me, opening his arms once he's settled. I burrow into them and breathe him in, nose tucked against the crook of his neck. He rubs my back in comforting circles.

"Are you cold?"

I shake my head. "Just hold me."

His arms cinch snugly around me. In his embrace, I'm safe, I'm loved, I'm protected.

"Thank you," I whisper, letting sleep claim me.

As I doze, I'm vaguely aware of him murmuring to me. I don't know what he says, but he never once leaves my side. He's there for me.

It's dark when I feel lucid again. I don't know if it was a lasting reaction to the sedative, the emotional overload, or a combination of it all, but when I wake up it's like I'm coming out of an intense nightmare. My limbs are heavy and the aches in my body are more prominent. I wish I could just fucking forget it all. Lock it in a damn vault in my mind and never face it again. I release a groan and roll over to find Fox's gaze on me in the dim shadows.

"You're awake," he says.

My cheek drags over his tattooed bicep beneath my head when I nod. He tucks my hair behind my ear, tracing the pads of his fingers down the side of my jaw.

"What happens now?" I ask.

He draws in a slow breath. "I know a guy not too far from here who has an endless supply of explosives. Well, Colt does. Part of his network. It's a day's drive away."

Phantom fingers squeeze my breasts too hard and air hitches in my throat. I picture fire and ash, imagine the man who took me screaming in agony while I watch his skin melt off his bones. For a second, I want it. It scares me I could feel so violently toward someone, but it doesn't make this go away.

"No. That makes us no better than them."

"I'm not a good man, Maisy." The way he grasps my jaw with his entire hand is firm, but not enough to hurt me. His gaze bores into mine. "They hurt you today and they deserve to burn for it."

A shiver runs down my spine. The sinister darkness in his tone calls to a part of myself I've never been aware of before. Maybe it's wrong to love this side of him, to know that he would destroy anything that dared hurt me. Maybe it's not what society deems normal, but it's me and it's him. That's all that matters to me.

"Not everyone working at Nexus Lab is guilty. We can't."

He sighs. "If the investigators don't make a move soon, we're doing this my way."

I concede. Days ago he was ready to walk away from this after he found the answers he was looking for about his parents. It's because of me that we're still seeing this through.

"After it's over, we're putting this town behind us." I shift closer when he buries his fingers in my hair and draws my forehead to his lips. "You and me."

"You and me," he responds.

THIRTY-NINE

FOX

Standing out front of Nexus Lab to watch while law enforcement agency vehicles swarm the place is gratifying. The DEA and FDA special unit agents file in and out of the circus with boxes full of paperwork, computer towers, and panic-stricken employees who are having a hell of a Monday. My arm slides around Maisy's waist to pull her against my side and together we wait behind the barricades for the big finale.

I had Colt's guy with explosives on call, ready to pay him as much as he demanded to clean him out, but they finally came through. Ethan Hannigan tipped us off from wherever his trail took him and we arrived before the rest of the numerous news crews did.

It's been three days since Maisy was taken to the abandoned warehouse. I drove by it while she was with her brother, unwilling to leave her alone still. It was cleared out, as I suspected. Stalenko Corp probably pulled back so their lawyers could do the heavy lifting in connection to Nexus Lab taking the fall. I only hope this will all be enough for them to feel pressure from federal investigators breathing down their necks so they can't do this again.

Maisy tried to call her mom once, but it went to voicemail. She hasn't tried since. They're done, I think. Whatever chance there was that she could have some kind of relationship with her parents died the day her mom allowed her to be kidnapped and did nothing when she was hit up for ransom.

I can't decide whether it's worse to lose both parents in a suspicious accident, spend a decade believing they were innocent, only to find out they were far from it, or be forced to look them in the eye while they spend years controlling every move to maintain the wicked life they hide from their kids.

Both scenarios fucking suck. At least we have each other to lean on when we're bogged down by the misery of our shitty parents. Her friends are there for her. Thea bought her a journal after Maisy told her what happened and decided she didn't want to see a shrink yet. I've caught her scribbling in it after meditating.

"This is more people than I thought there'd be," Maisy says at my side.

"People love drama. They've come to see this madhouse so they can gossip about it when it's on the news."

She hums in agreement.

All around us, news anchors are describing the unfolding scene for the nightly lead in with the breaking story. It's not only local stations, but national coverage reporting the downfall of Nexus Lab. I overhear one of them detailing connections to several prominent businessmen here and satisfaction swirls in my gut.

We did this. We blew the lid off the deceitful underbelly of our corrupt town to expose the truth.

It isn't exactly what I hoped for when I came back to Colorado to seek retribution from the family that destroyed mine, but my hunt for revenge helped me find my way back to Maisy. I came here to ruin her life only to find out I still can't live without her. Everything I endured was worth it to find happiness with her.

For the longest time I thought we could never salvage the special connection we had as kids. I thought it died the same day my parents did. But I was wrong.

Maisy is my kismet, the one I'm supposed to love.

I thread my fingers through her hair, catching it in a loose grip. Using it for leverage, I angle her head back and hover my lips over hers. She gazes at me with passionate fire in her hazel eyes. It's a beautiful sight. She's more than the girl I fell in love with years ago and promised forever to. My wild daisy, the strongest fighter with a big heart and an adventurous spirit waiting to be let loose.

I never want to be apart from her again.

Tired of waiting, she closes the small gap between us to steal the kiss I didn't give her. I hum into it, cupping the back of her head as we kiss languidly. Victory tastes fucking sweet.

A commotion draws our attention to the front doors of the building. They fly open and two agents escort a furious Jacqueline Landry out in handcuffs. Maisy draws in a sharp breath as her mother's icy gaze passes over us. It's subtle, but Jacqueline stiffens. I almost wish she'd struggle and pitch a fit, but that's not who that bitch is. She'll save face until the end.

Dramatic fit or not, she knows we did this to her. It's enough.

Reporters rush to flank the group surrounding Jacqueline on her walk of shame, shouting questions and asking for a statement from the company's public face.

"What made you accept a deal like this?"

"Do you have anything to say about the raid on Nexus Lab?

Were you aware the drugs your company produced were sold on the black market?"

"Is this related to your husband's sudden resignation from his position as police chief?"

"No comment," Jacqueline hisses.

I scoff and Maisy slides her arm around my waist. *Was it worth it?* That's what I want to ask her, Richard Landry, and my parents. If any of them could go back, would they let greed rule them again?

Jacqueline glares at the DEA agent that opens the back door of one of their vehicles near the barricade we're behind. It makes something old and decayed unlock in my chest as we watch her be folded into the back seat.

The Ridgeview, Colorado that anyone knew will never be the same after today. The secrets are spilled into the light.

Maisy turns to me. "I've seen enough. Have you?"

"Yeah."

Tossing one last glance at the car Jacqueline was stuffed into, I turn my back on a dark chapter in my life feeling lighter, walking hand in hand with the girl I love.

A week later, I'm breathing in the midsummer mountain air under the late afternoon sun with Maisy and her friends. The grassy sloping clearing we're lounging in is full of wild-flowers and butterflies floating on the breeze. It's just off the road, our cars and my motorcycle parked in a gravel ditch at the edge of the field. Devlin and Connor kick a soccer ball back and forth shirtless while Lucas cracks open a beer and offers the first cool sip to Gemma sprawled between his legs.

Thea is braiding Maisy's hair in two french braids, Blair's

already done in some intricate looking crown made of shiny dark hair.

She's been more herself this week, her smiles coming easier. I've been waiting for her to wake up from nightmares, but they don't plague her the same way they claimed my mind for years. What happened didn't break her.

The news has daily coverage on Jacqueline and the pharmaceutical company's illicit drug ring scandal. Jacqueline is the public fall guy, but details about the investigation have also come out with information on the mayor's involvement, and about my parents and their own sins that led to their fatal demise. It's strange, after finding out everything I thought I knew about them was a lie, I don't want to shy away from the whispers that continue when my name is mentioned.

It doesn't matter. Maisy knows who I am. That's all I need, a few good people who I consider my family to have my back.

Since the news broke, she's been spending a lot of time with her brother. We leave town today for the road trip she's dreamed of for half her life. She tells me Holden has plans to follow the girl he met at the local community college when she transfers for the fall semester to a different school. They're both done with Ridgeview. The only good thing this town has is her friends. Without them, we'd never come back here again.

"I brought you something." Maisy appears in front of me, shuffling on her knees in the grass. Her hair is braided, a wild-flower tucked behind her ear.

I rake my teeth over my lip, grasping her hips. She holds up a daisy between us with thin purple petals, identical to the one I gave her when she was eight and the ones I picked for her to win her heart back. The corner of my mouth kicks up and I take the flower. She presses her lips to mine and I drag her into my lap, deepening our kiss.

Connor pauses his one-on-one soccer game with Devlin to

howl like a coyote. Laughing, Maisy breaks away and tucks her face into my neck.

"The fuck is that supposed to mean?" I ask him.

He shoots me a mischievous grin. "Watch and learn, Foxy."

"No," I bark, nearly choking when Maisy's tongue darts out against my throat. "Don't pick that up from Colt."

His smirk is unrepentant as he scoops his wife into his arms and plants a kiss on her lips while she giggles. Lucas does the wild howl this time with his hands cupped around his mouth.

"What the fuck," I mutter. "Your friends are crazy."

Devlin chuckles as he drops to the grass nearby with the soccer ball tucked beneath his elbow. Blair wraps her arms around his shoulders from behind and kisses his cheek.

"It's the SLHS coyote call," Devlin explains. "I don't know how far back it goes, but when there's PDA, the mascot is the calling card. A right of passage in a way."

I shake my head. "This fucking town."

"Tell me about it," Blair says with an exasperated roll of her eyes. "High school here was weird as hell."

"You love it," Gemma says slyly, keeping her eyes closed and her face upturned to the sunshine while Lucas slips his hand beneath her shirt to caress her stomach.

"You learn to deal with it," Thea offers after she extricates herself from Connor. Her cheeks are pink and there's a brightness lighting her eyes up. "Who's hungry?"

A round of agreements go around. Maisy and Thea hand out sandwiches from a huge picnic basket. Laughter echoes off the treetops as we eat and enjoy the summer day. Gemma breaks out a camera and captures it all.

When the sun begins to dip lower, Maisy nudges me. "We should hit the road soon. I want to watch the sunset before we get to our first Airbnb."

The plan is to hop from rentals in the towns we pass

through to camping in national parks as we meander our way to the west coast.

"Already?" Thea gives Maisy a sad smile. "I'm going to miss you."

"I'm going to California, I'm not dying, babe, jesus." Maisy wraps her in a bear hug until they tip over into the grass. The other two girls join the dog pile of affection. "I promise to keep up with the group chats. Instagram and text."

"Chase your dreams hard," Thea mumbles from somewhere in the mix of girls tangled together.

"You bet," Maisy says. "There's nothing holding me back from myself now."

"You're going to have the best damn time," Gemma says.

"FaceTime us if you get service in the parks at night?" Blair asks, glancing from Maisy to Devlin. "I'd love to see what the stars look like out there."

He gives her this private smile that puts color in her cheeks.

"All the things," Maisy agrees, getting up and dusting off her cropped leggings.

My heart stutters at the sight of her, with grass sticking to her braids and one of my t-shirts knotted in the front so it shows off a strip of her taut stomach she's stunning. And *mine*.

After another round of goodbyes, we walk hand in hand to the line of cars by the edge of the clearing. The couples trail behind us, each with their arms around their partners. Maisy waves back at her friends and I follow suit, lifting a hand.

Maisy meets my eye and hooks her fingers in the belt loops of my jeans, luring me close for a kiss. I give her what she wants.

As a group, her friends give us a loud coyote howl that devolves into laughter.

"Ready?" I ask.

The curve of her smile is full of excitement. "So ready."

Framing her face between my hands, I kiss her again. "Good."

We climb on the bike and a flutter moves through my chest. This is it. Her arms slip around me and she squeezes my waist, resting her chin on my shoulder.

"Take me on an adventure," she whispers.

Grinning, I rev the rumbling engine and run my fingers over the braided leather bracelet carrying stones I gave her. She used to say the same exact thing when we played on our street as kids.

"Hold on tight, baby."

Her arms tighten and I gun it, taking us onto the road that will cross over the Rockies. The sun shines down in golden rays.

As we cross over the mountain range, Maisy lets out an elated cheer at the top of her lungs.

This is everything I want—the open road, my wild daisy girl wrapped around me, and the wind kissing our cheeks.

EPILOGUE

MAISY
2 Months Later

Summer is drawing to a close, but when we reach the west coast it feels like it will never end, keeping us in a perpetual bubble of sunshine and golden warmth. The beach I picked out on the map is deserted. I relish the sound of waves crashing and the taste of salt air on my tongue. I've missed this.

As soon as we got here an hour ago I snapped a photo and sent it to Holden and my friends. A giddiness swept over me as soon as my toes touched the sand. Tears pricked my eye while I stood at the water's edge brushing my fingers over the bracelet I made from Fox's stones when we came here as kids.

My brother and I are closer than ever since this road trip started, despite both of us no longer living in the same town. We have to hold onto each other because I don't think either of us will reach a place of trust with our parents again. Dad keeps trying to call, but I don't want to talk to him. As far as I'm concerned, Mom can rot behind bars for leaving me at the mercy of the people who attacked me. It's what they both deserve for all their misdeeds.

I have the love of those who actually care about me—my friends, my brother, my boyfriend. They're all important to me. They're more family than my parents have ever been.

Without them, I wouldn't have followed my dream to finally leave town. Now here I am in California at last.

I filled up the first journal Thea gave me and picked up another on our way out here. It's cathartic to reflect. I love pouring my thoughts into it, the good and bad, and documenting the memories we're making.

After we walked up and down the beach looking for new rocks to add to our collection we started on this trip, I sit on the bike in front of Fox, facing him with my legs straddling his powerful thighs. His hands are inside the oversized sides of my loose tank top, thumbs teasing the curves of my tits. I slide my arms around his neck and bite my lip.

"It's just us here. Like our own little world."

A rumble sounds in his chest and one of his hands slips further into my shirt, tracing my spine down to my ass. He hauls me closer so I can feel the hard ridge of him against my core. My breath hitches and I rock against him.

"Do you feel free now, baby?" he murmurs against my parted lips.

The sinful rasp in his voice sends a bolt of heat right to my clit. With a soft moan, I nod. He kisses the corner of my mouth, grip flexing on my ass to grind against me.

Smirking, I peel off my top and let it flutter to the sand, feeling every ounce of freedom I've claimed. I no longer have to regulate myself or do anything I don't want to do. There are no reputations to uphold or expectations to meet. I can live on the wind, with Fox at my side where I'm happiest.

He bends to place a kiss on my throat, then lower to my

sternum, then captures one of my nipples in his mouth. Waves crash against the shore and a pelican swoops overhead. A carefree laugh escapes me. His lips move back up to brush over mine.

I lean back, but his hand comes up to grasp my throat, pulling me back in.

"Not done with you yet," he whispers in a smoky, seductive tone before he kisses me again, deeper this time. "Never will be."

"I'm all yours and you're mine."

He takes me apart with his hands and mouth until we have a new memory of California, the first of many where he makes me feel wild on a beach.

I'm happy, fulfilled by chasing whims and traveling. I'm beginning to discover the parts of myself that have lived deep inside for too long, neglected before now.

The freedom is addictive after I've gone so long without it, hoping and wishing for it. There's a light in my heart every time the wind moves through my hair, with each choice I take for myself. What makes it sweeter is doing it all with the person who has my heart—him.

EPILOGUE

FOX
1 Year Later

Southern California suits us both in ways I never imagined. It's like our hearts knew we needed this to be our home the minute we first stepped foot in the state all those years ago on a combined family vacation, then spent every minute since missing it until we made our way here at the end of our road trip last summer.

Maisy turned her longing for the Pacific ocean into a bracelet with the small stones I found for her to hold onto the memory, while I inked it into my skin and sought out solace in a foggy cove in Maine until I returned to her.

Kismet, as my girl would say. She's got me believing in fate.

We did exactly what we dreamed up back in my converted warehouse in Ridgeview—she opened a yoga studio that opens right to the beach and I have a workshop-garage space where I spend my time making whatever my hands create on instinct. More often than not I think the shapes I twist out of the found materials remind me of Maisy, just like the piece we keep in the bedroom of our bungalow a few blocks from the coastline.

Wiping my greasy hands off on a rag, I step back from the classic '67 Camaro I've been tuning up for a customer while Maisy had her morning sessions at the studio. I want to finish up and beat her back to the house so I can get my surprise ready. My stomach dips at the thought of what I have planned and I toss the dirty rag onto the bench along the wall.

I wash up and close up the shop, strolling out into the alley that connects to the main strip of Venice Beach. As I walk the boulevard, I pull my hair into a small knot with one of the hair ties I stole from Maisy's nightstand tray I hammered out of a piece of copper I found in an antique shop. It's getting long, but Maisy likes it.

The walk back to our bungalow isn't long. The porch is covered in plants, wind chimes, and a couple of stray cats we fed once that have stuck around. I bend to rub the tubby orange one's clipped ear, smiling when he bumps his head against my knuckles.

"Big day today," I tell him as I unlock the door.

A quick glance at the clock lets me know I have just enough time to shower before she heads home from her yoga studio. I race through it, skipping a shirt and heading into the front room in just a low-slung pair of jeans with rips in the knees. After ducking outside to pick one of the wild daisies from our garden, I lay it on the coffee table next to her stack of journals and slip the finishing touch onto the stem.

I searched high and low for a ring, then it hit me. I needed to make it. Maisy has never been a girl that cares about diamonds, more happy to make a bracelet or necklace out of stones she finds meaning in. Jewelry wasn't something I'd tacked in my tinkering before, but Maisy is my muse and I'm damn proud of what I made.

The ring I crafted is her, me, *us*. Gold and silver metal twist together to shape it, twining around two stones, one her favorite crystal, amethyst, and the other a small piece of polished sea glass I picked up for her—both we found while walking on the beach. Around the stones I formed golden petals out of hammered metal.

Her muffled voice cooing to the porch cats has me sitting up straight on the couch. Despite the shower, my palms prickle with sweat. I rub them on my jeans and wait for her to come through the door.

"I'm home," she calls.

"I'm right here."

A warm smile turns on me and I swipe my tongue over my lower lip. I love this beautiful girl. Her light brown hair is up in a topknot and her loose workout crop top reveals her tan skin I'm itching to taste. I can never get enough.

Maisy drops her keys in a bowl I made and joins me on the couch with a content sigh. "How was your morning? Did you finish on the Camaro?"

"Just about." My arm drapes over her shoulder. "Got something for you."

"Yeah?"

I motion with a jerk of my chin to the table, where her daisy is waiting. She makes a happy noise and picks it up. Every day for the last year I've given her a flower I picked.

The ring slips off the stem and she catches it with quick reflexes before it drops to the floor.

"Hey, this is..." Maisy trails off as she gets a good look at the daisy-shaped ring in her palm.

Her gaze darts from the daisy, to the ring I made just for her, to me as I sink to the floor on one knee, pulling her down to sit on my thigh. Her arms automatically loop around my shoulders, absently tracing my tattoos. Those gorgeous hazel eyes widen.

"Oh." It comes out on a surprised sigh.

My gaze bounces between hers. "I promised a long time ago that I'd marry you one day because you're my daisy. What do you say?"

Maisy's breath hitches and she digs her fingers into my muscles. Her mouth curves into a wide grin. "I say yes."

A well of happiness overflows in my chest and I crush her to me, releasing a short laugh against her hair.

"You made this?" she asks when I lean back.

"Do you like it?"

"I love it." Her gaze is warm and fond as she tilts the ring side to side to study the details I put into it. "I recognize the stones. It's perfect."

I swoop in to kiss her, closing my fingers over the ring. With my forehead resting against hers, we both watch as I guide the engagement ring onto her finger.

"You're perfect, little daisy," I murmur. "You make me happy."

A soft, affectionate sound escapes her and I lift up, situating us back on the couch with her in my lap.

"So, locking it down, huh?" Maisy sasses.

I smack her thigh with a low growl. "You've known since you were eight that I wanted to marry you."

"Yeah, before you decided to hate me for ten years."

"Even then, I wanted you, baby. Especially then."

She cups my face with one hand and bumps her nose against mine.

My phone vibrates and I fish it out of my back pocket. "That's probably Lucas or Colt. They knew today was the day I was springing the question on you. They're not going to leave us alone to celebrate until I let them know how it went."

She laughs and tucks her face against my neck while she holds out the ring to admire it.

As soon as I unlock the phone, the screen glitches. An animation of a crow flies across the screen and lands on a skull. *Shit.* My stomach clenches. I promised Colton, and now Wren is calling to collect on the favors I owe to my brothers.

Cinching my arm tighter around Maisy, I tap on the animation and the encrypted message loads.

"Goddamn it," I mutter.

"What is it?" Maisy asks.

"We're going to have to delay our celebrating for a little bit." I tilt the screen toward her to show her the message. "I have to go to Thorne Point. It has to do with Ethan Hannigan."

Her brows draw together. "The journalist we met in Ridgeview?"

"Yeah. Something happened to him. He's missing."

"Oh shit," she murmurs, concern lacing her tone. "Do you think something bad happened?"

Shrugging, I shift her off my lap and get up. Damn, I'll have to get someone to cover the shop. I don't know how long this trip to the east coast will take. But this is what it means to be in with the Crows; when they call in favors, there's no hesitation. They helped me time and again, now I'll do the same for them.

"I'll be back as soon as I can," I promise.

"Fox Michael Wilder." Maisy crosses her arms and plants herself in front of me to stop me in my tracks. "If you think I'm letting you go all the way to Maine to help Colton without me, you're wrong. We're going together."

My heart fucking melts. "Okay. We go together. Me and you."

"Me and you," she repeats with a resolute nod. "No matter what."

Wherever we go, it's always together.

* * *

Thank you so much for reading SAVAGE WILDER! The Sinners and Saints series is complete, but we're traveling to Thorne Point to follow the Crows next in Crowned Crows of Thorne Point. **Coming Soon! Sign up here for pre-order updates!**

Dying to know how Connor blackmailed Thea? Find out what happens when one mistyped number and a risqué photo sent to the blackmail king of Silver Lake High turns the nerdy neighbor's life upside down...

One-click RUTHLESS BISHOP now!

"My favourite Sinners and Saints book yet! I've been so intrigued by Bishop, and to say I was excited to get my hands on his story is an understatement.
Bishop and Thea's story swept me up from beginning to end. There were moments that had my heart racing and biting my nails, and moments that had me fanning myself and swooning."
— *Becca Steele, bestselling author of The Four series*

To see what's next for Fox + Maisy, enjoy a free bonus scene that includes a special series epilogue. **Download a free bonus scene at bit.ly/SWfreebonus**

THANK YOU + WHAT'S NEXT?

Thanks for reading Ruthless Bishop! If you enjoyed it, please leave a review on your favorite retailer or book community! Your support means so much to me!

Need more Sinners and Saints series right now? Have theories about which characters will feature next? Want exclusive previews of the next book? Join other readers in Veronica Eden's Reader Garden on Facebook!

Join: BIT.LY/VERONICAFBGROUP

Are you a newsletter subscriber? By subscribing, you can download a special bonus scene featuring Thea and Bishop from Ruthless Bishop, as well as bonus scenes from Tempting Devil and Wicked Saint.

Sign up to download it here: BIT.LY/RBFREEBONUS

ACKNOWLEDGMENTS

Readers, I'm endlessly grateful for you! Thanks for reading this book. It means the world to me that you supported my work. I wouldn't be here at all without you! The response to this series and these characters has seriously blown me away. I love all of the comments and messages you send! I hope you enjoyed your read! I'm really excited to bring you more characters to love!

Thanks to my husband for being you! He doesn't read these, but he's my biggest supporter. He keeps me fed and watered while I'm in the writer cave, and doesn't complain when I fling myself out of bed at odd hours with an idea to frantically scribble down.

Bre, girl can you believe we're at the end?! Thank you for being here with me from the beginning! I seriously couldn't have written this book, or this entire series without you. I'm so glad to have you to talk to when the brain gremlins misbehave or when the writing process gets tough. You get my characters on a level that blows my mind. You keep me sane and follow my wild babbling when something clicks. Thank you always for your friendship and support, and I'm sorry my muse likes to visit you in the middle of the night! Bring on the Crows!

Thank you to my fellow authors for cheering me on through this one and always being a sounding board or chiming in with a laugh to keep me going, especially Sarah, Becca, Ramzi, Sara, Kat, and Jade for dragging me over the finish line! The indie community amazes me and I love being a part of it with y'all.

Thank you to Ashlee of Ashes & Vellichor for the amazing book trailers for this series! I love the way you can look at something and get it, and I've been in awe of what you've come up with to bring these books to life!

To my beta readers, thank you from the bottom of my heart! I appreciate that y'all read my raw words and offer your time, attention to detail, and consideration of the characters and storyline in my books! Without you, I wouldn't be able to see the forest because I'm too busy staring at one tree. You're a dream team and I'm forever thankful for your help! Your time and hard work are much appreciated!

To my street team and reader group, y'all are the best babes around! To see you guys get as excited as I do seriously makes my day. I'm endlessly grateful you love my characters and words! Thank you for your help in sharing my books and for your support of my work!

To Shauna and Wildfire Marketing Solutions, thank you so much for all your hard work and being so awesome! I appreciate everything that you do!

To the bloggers and bookstagrammers, thank you for being the most wonderful community! Your creativity and beautiful edits are something I come back to visit again and again to brighten my day. Thank you for trying out my books. You guys are incredible and blow me away with your passion for romance!

As always, I want to send a big shout out of love to my writing hags, the best bunch around! I always cherish your support and encouragement of my writing, no matter where my heart eyes and the muse take me. Every book I publish is thanks to you guys.

ABOUT THE AUTHOR
ROMANCE WITH DARING EDGE

Veronica Eden is an international bestselling author of dark new adult romances + reverse harem romances with spitfire heroines and irresistible heroes.

She loves exploring complicated feelings, magical worlds, epic adventures, and the bond of characters that embrace *us against the world*. She has always been drawn to gruff bad boys, clever villains, and the twisty-turns of morally gray decisions. She believes sometimes the villain should get the girl and is a sucker for a deliciously devilish antihero. When not writing, she can be found soaking up sunshine at the beach, snuggling in a pile with her untamed pack of animals (her husband, dog and cats), and surrounding herself with as many plants as she can get her hands on.

* * *

CONTACT + FOLLOW
Email: veronicaedenauthor@gmail.com
Website: http://veronicaedenauthor.com
FB Reader Group: bit.ly/veronicafbgroup
Amazon: amazon.com/author/veronicaeden

facebook.com/veronicaedenauthor

instagram.com/veronicaedenauthor

twitter.com/vedenauthor

pinterest.com/veronicaedenauthor

bookbub.com/profile/veronica-eden

goodreads.com/veronicaedenauthor

Standalone

Jingle Wars

ALSO BY VERONICA EDEN

Sign up for the mailing list to get first access and ARC opportunities! **Follow Veronica on BookBub** for new release alerts!

DARK ROMANCE

Sinners and Saints Series

Wicked Saint

Tempting Devil

Ruthless Bishop

Savage Wilder

Crowned Crows Series

Crowned Crows of Thorne Point (COMING SOON)

Standalone

Unmasked Heart

Hate To Want You (COMING SOON)

REVERSE HAREM ROMANCE

Bound by Bounty Series

(COMING SOON)

Standalone

More Than Bargained

CONTEMPORARY ROMANCE

Made in United States
Orlando, FL
10 August 2022

20796142R00264